DUNGEON CALAMITY

Book Three of
THE DIVINE DUNGEON Series
Written by DAKOTA KROUT

TABLE OF CONTENTS

ACKNOWLEDGMENTS

There are many people who have made this book possible. Firstly, thank you to all of my friends who made their way through the awful early editions of my book in order to give me advice and suggestions on storyline and descriptive writing. A special thanks to Dylan S. and Chandra S. who helped revise this story. Many thanks to both of you for your careful reading and comments!

Some amazing fans stepped up to help cover the hidden costs of writing. So far I owe them for at *least* every cup of coffee that drove this book to completion! Thank you to Steven Willden, David Thompson, Nicholas Schmidt, and Samuel Landrie and all other Patreons for your support!

Next, thank you to my *wonderful* wife, who not only encouraged me to write, but read through and offered detailed suggestions. You are the reason these books exist.

Finally, to someone I haven't met yet. My first child, Grace, will be born shortly after this book comes out. I am looking forward to meeting you very much, my adorable little deadline!

PROLOGUE

"Just ignore it, Rob. Of course you feel like you are being watched. Yer in a dungeon!" the tiny human tried unsuccessfully to comfort his student. He groaned and tossed his hands into the air. "There are monsters going crazy in here, and the place is changing *constantly*. We just need to go through *one* more room, and even with my seventy percent fee, your tuition will be paid for life! We're already on the fourth floor, might as well finish the labyrinth, right?"

"I don't like it." The uncomfortable man shuddered as he felt the alien mind appraising him again. "You *know* I can tell when I'm being watched, and whatever this is, it *is* watching. It wants us dead!"

His teacher sighed. "We *just* went over this. This is a dungeon. Of course, everything here wants us dead, but for the money–"

The teacher's words were cut off as the floor beneath them shifted subtly. A feeling similar to a seesaw dropping made them stumble, and their pulses began to race! The floor dropped only another few inches when a *click* behind them made them whirl around. They were too late to retreat now, thanks to the rising stone that blocked off the five-man group's path of retreat. All light had fled, leaving them in utter darkness and growing despair. Only sharp orders from the leader allowed them to think clearly again.

Regaining their composure after a moment of panic, the men tightened their formation. Their eyes had begun to adjust incrementally when a glimmer of light washed over them, nearly blinding them after their immersion in darkness. Still wary, they edged toward the light. Eyes twinkling with mixed interest and caution, they walked toward the only landmark now visible. Before them lay a tablet of stone on a small, intricately carved pillar. The light fell from above and illuminated words carved deeply into the rock.

"What does it say?"

"Confound it! I can't read. Rob, get over here!"

Rob stepped forward, glancing around as the presence stared at him again. His hackles rose, and he tried to gulp air into his heaving, dehydrated lungs. He stared at the words, easily reading them but failing to understand their meaning.

"Well?" Rob got slapped on his rear, causing goose bumps to spread over his skinny arms. "What does it say, boy?"

"It says, 'You have entered the trials. Trial one: Carry your weight, and the rewards shall be great. Else, one for all.' The punctuation is all funny-like. Whaddya suppose that means?" Rob rubbed his butt; that slap had been way too hard.

"Huh. No idea. What do *you* think that means?" The teacher was trying to act wise, returning the question to his students, but the words came out flat.

"I hate poems. They always mean dangerous things are about to happen. A woman getting them from a nervous love interest, bards making terrible songs, and now traps..."

"Is the light in here getting brighter?"

"The ceiling! Look at the ceiling!" They looked up to see the ceiling—now visible and covered in jagged metal spikes—descending slowly toward them. Rob looked around for an opening, a way out of the trap, anything! As the ceiling fell, a small section of stone lifted. The opening behind it was only spacious enough for one person to crawl through.

"There are spots on the roof that don't have spikes! Five spots, five of us! We need to hold the ceiling up!" the teacher called loudly and calmly. The group rushed to find a spot that they could fit into; the roof was curved specifically to match the average height of adventurers. They raised their hands, and the stone came to rest in each of their palms at the same time. Grunts were elicited from the struggling men as the heavy trap continued to press down until it rested upon their shoulders. Pushing and straining, they heaved and called out encouragement to each other as the minutes passed and their knees began to wobble.

Rob started to panic as he felt a sense of satisfaction from the probing presence. "We're going to die! It's going to kill us no matter what we do!" The feeling of satisfaction wavered as Rob looked at the opening. It wasn't so far away, was it? He could make it in the few seconds it would take the ceiling to fall. His fear-addled mind raced as he thought of the test. One for all, one for all... so everyone would die, or one person could survive? Rob's eyes narrowed. He wasn't dying for these people. He barely knew them! He wouldn't die here, not like this!

"Rob! No! What are you doing?!" Rob heard as he dove under the spikes and crawled as fast as he could for the hole in the wall. The ceiling lowered by a few deadly inches.

"I'm *surviving!*" Rob dragged himself the last little way into the hole and looked around. There! There was a Rune on the floor! He placed his hand on the activation pattern and flooded it with Essence. The cries of his old team were cut off as the wall behind Rob closed off, leaving him in the small space. He waited for an exit to appear. And waited. Rob didn't even realize when he slipped into sleep, the oxygen content too minimal to allow his panicked mind to remain awake.

Outside the tiny room, a joyous scene was playing out.

"It's going up!"

"Rob did it! He must have deactivated the trap!"

"He did nothing but try to save himself! That must have backfired on him." Their leader growled at the jubilant faces. "Think about it. One for all or 'carry your weight'. Rob thought that meant he could trade our lives to save his sorry skin, but it really meant *he* would die to save *us*," he scoffed disparagingly. "While it is sad for him, I hope you all learned something today. This was the worst kind of self-sacrifice. Let's get the *abyss* out of here."

"Look! A chest!"

"Look at all those tokens! They were right about the fourth floor!"

CHAPTER ONE

<What's going on?> I was woozy. My mind felt cluttered and 'off' in an indefinable way. I looked around my dungeon, noting the man dancing near my Core. He was wiggling in an exceedingly creepy way, making awkward noises that would have made a human blush.

"It's mine! You. *Wiggle.* Can't. *Wiggle, wiggle.* Have it! *Awkward hip thrusting.*

<Oh. My. I don't know what 'it' is, but please, take 'it' and go *away.* You are the most disturbing thing I have ever had the misfortune of seeing,> I stammered, knowing that he couldn't possibly hear me. Still, my frazzled nerves weren't because of his social oddity, they were due to his ranking. His presence released a pressure that affected me all the way to my soul. There was no doubt in my mind that this man was in *at least* the Spiritual ranks.

Somehow, it seemed he *had* heard me.

"Damn straight I'll take it! It's mine! It's *all* mine!" The man stopped moving around. "Glad you agreed so early. Mine. I was gonna kill you soon otherwise, and I don't wanna do that! Ha ha! You are a strange, interesting aberration! Also, you make me chuckle."

<I am happier than you could *possibly* know to hear that.> My voice was trembling. What is going on? When did this filthy, overpowered man show up?

"Now you are boring again. Oh well. Don't worry, strange little dungeon. I'll come back when you start doing interesting things again!" The man turned and ran at the wall. Not the door. The wall. He didn't slow down, and as he hit the stone, it shattered from the massive pressure he was exuding. He ran in a straight line, destroying my cursed earth as he went. "Stealing my whispers! Dumbass dungeon!"

I watched him run, creating a tunnel as he went. He eventually broke out of my labyrinth, reaching unaltered stone. He ran through *this* even faster, eventually popping out of the side of the mountain and entering free-fall with an echoing shout of "Wheeeeeee!"

<What. Just. Happened?> I was shaking in reaction, and I looked around myself to see what had changed. What had I been doing? I had some vague recollections of creating new traps and Mobs, collecting materials from Dale and Minya, and researching ways to find Dani... Did that creepy, filthy man just mess with my memories somehow? I haven't been this confused since I became a dungeon Core so very long ago. Just like now, my memories of that time were confusing and fragmented. I remembered a flash of a necromancer's laugh as I was killed, and then remembering how beautiful a day it was... I shook off the confusion and focused myself. What the...? What was wrong with my floor? I had been vandalized!

I looked around and set to fixing the place up. Had that man done all of this? There was a *lot* of damage in the dungeon—walls in rubble, the place littered with filth and remains, Mobs oddly mutated and damaged. Far too *many* Mobs, for that matter. Traps not reset? *What* was going on? I cleaned the place up and quickly set some short-term goals for myself. Clean the place thoroughly, fix everything that was broken, then I needed trackers—things that could live without me and still find Dani. I needed to push myself into the B-ranks. I needed to find a way to communicate outside of myself.

Finally and possibly most importantly, I needed to create powerful weapons that might be able to damage the inconceivably powerful people that might attack me in the future. That twisted old man had scared me badly. I focused inward and began devoting Essence to the tasks at hand. They may seem impossible right now, but each of them needed to be done. I smiled dangerously. My mind was clear, and my will was strong for the first time I could remember. It was time to join—or terrify—the powers in this world.

DALE

The snow crunched under his feet with each step he took, the sub-zero temperatures making the frozen crystals brittle. Dale bowed his head against the wind as it twisted around him, seemingly angry that it had been disturbed from its original flow. With each crunch, he was that much closer to his destination. He looked through frost-laden eyelashes at the changes that had been wrought in the last month. Snorting, he shook his head. Snow that had collected on him blew away as he examined the roads and stone buildings. He reflected on the usefulness of magic. This place had turned from a ragged collection of tents into something approximating a booming village. Soon, they would need to expand to keep up with the influx of people trying to strike it rich.

A light distorted by the achromatic precipitation appeared ahead of him. Dale readjusted his fur-lined cloak and moved slightly faster, looking forward to the warmth of the tavern he was approaching. A bit of melted slush dripped down his neck, and he shivered and frowned; Dale was not looking forward to the impending conversation. He had been avoiding it for too long, though. He sighed. It was now or never. The light became stronger and soon illuminated a beautifully carved, extra thick oak door.

Dale reached forward with snow-laden gloves and found the handle, twisting it and opening the door. His actions allowed a blast of icy wind into the tavern ahead of him. Shouting reached his ears nigh-instantly as people demanded he shut the only barrier between them and the bitter winter wind. The newly appointed Baron stepped in, pulling the door closed behind him. Ice crackled on his fur-lined boots, and enough snow fell off of him to make a decently sized snowball. Dale stepped closer to the roaring bonfire in the center of the room, pulling off his cloak and gently shaking it out. A few people grumbled at him as they were hit by particles of water, but only one voice spoke up.

"About time you showed up, you snail-slow, sandbagging bastard! I thought I was going to have to drink all this ale all by my lonesome... again! Dale looked around and caught sight of his best friend, Hans, cheerfully waving at him from a bench next to the fire.

"Evening, Hans. Or, I guess, good morning?" It was three in the morning, and while most people would be abed, people in the C-ranks—or those with all their meridians open—only needed a few hours, at most, to have a full night's sleep. "What did you want? I want to get *some* sleep before you exploit me for personal gain in the dungeon. If I try to stay awake for too long—happening too often as of late—I'll probably fall apart."

Dale had been undergoing a rigorous training regimen designed by himself and a few experts to maximize his survivability as well as shape him into the best possible leader for the small community that had sprung up around the dungeon. He had just been released by his hand-to-hand combat instructor, a Moon Elf assassin who seemed to hold a grudge against all of humanity. This day's lesson was *supposed* to be about Dale shaping his Essence into usable formations while under attack and emotionally flustered. In *reality,* the training had consisted of Dale standing on a wriggly log and focusing on his Chi formations... while snowballs laced with stones had been thrown at him by *exceedingly* strong and accurate women. While he was naked. Dale was not in the most positive of moods right now.

"Well, Dale, it has been a month since the swarm of infected, and you have not taken any time off from training, sending out messengers, studying *math*," Hans shuddered at that last one, "and I think it is time you explained what is going on." Having spoken, the door opened again, and the rest of Dale's team walked in.

Rose—a Half Elf archer—was followed by Adam—the party's cleric—and Tom the barbarian. Adam was leaning on his staff and was mostly covered by a floor-length, gleaming white robe. Tom naturally drew the eye of the patrons as he entered. He was wearing very little in terms of practical winter gear, mainly just what could be called either a short, fur kilt or a long loincloth. He was trying out a few pieces of armor, so the patchwork set had chunks of plate mail and laminar armor intermixed. The red-haired barbarian wore no helmet but oddly had a massive shield awkwardly strapped to his left side. Where his hand should have been was a grip that tied his shield to his body, but it was obviously uncomfortable. This was most likely due to the fact that his arm, which he had lost in the dungeon, was nearly fully regrown.

The odd collection of people nodded to Dale as they sat. Adam stared at his team leader with glowing yellow eyes, disconcerting not only because of the color but because he seemed to need to blink only a quarter as often as a normal human.

"I don't think that's going to happen." Dale stood, preparing to go to bed.

"Dale," Adam softly voiced, "you *need* to tell us. Things will go... poorly if you refuse at this point. Strange things are happening. The dungeon is changing, as are you, and we need to have trust between us. Refusing now will lead to strife amongst us."

Dale hesitated. Adam had gained the odd ability to see and understand situations at a strange level after being exposed to an inconceivably concentrated influx of celestial Essence. This, more than anything, made him sit back down and reluctantly begin telling them what had happened. Hans stopped him when Dale started to talk about things they didn't know. A strange wind began circling them, cutting off sound from the area around them.

"Burning-wind wall," Hans muttered a quick explanation. "Heats the air to create a distortion that just kinda... stops sound. Feel free to explain now. No one is listening except us."

Dale nodded his thanks and continued his tale. His friends gasped at all the right places, shaking their heads at revealed wonders. The dungeon was alive and intelligent. It relied on a Wisp—a creature of legend—to function properly and remain mentally balanced. The Wisp had been taken, and people were getting worried. Most importantly, their team leader had a Beast Core in him that connected him to all of this insanity and potentially called his judgment into question. Dale stopped talking and looked around at the incredulous faces.

"That is really good to know, but what about *you*, Dale?" Rose took it upon herself to ask the unfortunate questions no one else wanted to. "Are you compromised? Are you a *Beast* now? Will *you* go crazy if the dungeon does? We all know it is getting worse."

"You sound just like Madame Chandra." Dale chuckled softly. "I can totally see the relation." Rose huffed at him and arched a brow. "I'm... okay. Having something to do helps me to not worry, which is why I've been pushing myself so hard. I'm not compromised, and my mental defenses have allowed me to ignore the dungeon in the past."

"That is why you were so twitchy? There was a *thing* whispering in your mind?" Tom interrupted in relief. "Oh good! I had been concerned that you were simply not up to the task of being a battle leader. It is a trait that not many have, after all. I am quite pleased to know that you are mentally sound."

"...Thanks? Twitchy?" Dale replied half questioningly with a confused look around at the nodding heads. "Also, I am *not* a Beast. I do have a Core in me, but no one has been able to tell me what that means. By rights, I should be dead from Essence loss many times over."

"Death arrives for everyone eventually, Dale." Tom gripped Dale's wrist. "No need to invite it."

Dale continued his story, "At this point, I've been doing everything I can to prepare. I want to go after the Wisp, Dani, but I've been infernally busy with rebuilding, repopulating the area, and my own training. Not to mention our dungeon excursions."

"You've been doing well, Dale," Adam said as he looked around the room with his faintly glowing eyes. "About half of the surviving fighters didn't come back after receiving their reward. Their choice is no great loss to us, though. With the dungeon giving out such high amounts of resources on a successful run, dozens more are showing up than those that are leaving. Daily."

"It was also a great idea to build a big tavern right away!" Hans grinned as he took a gulp of his ale. "Plus, since you technically own it, I am loving the discount."

"I'm seeing fewer familiar faces, and morale seems to be getting higher as the survivors' stories are drowned out in the sea of bodies," Dale put forward his thoughts, agreeing with Adam's assessment. "As for the higher rewards, the risks have really gone up as well. I'd be surprised if the Guild doesn't try to rank it as a C-ranked area soon. At *least* that."

Before, there had been clear-cut areas for each type of monster in the dungeon. The big Cats stayed on the fourth floor, there was a clear progression of difficulty, and the rewards had been calculated based on how well a group did overall. Now, the Cats showed up wherever they wanted. If they weren't so lazy, they would have overrun the dungeon by now. Typically, a Cat would now only attack if you invaded 'its' territory. Unfortunately, that territory shifted by the hour. The Goblins stayed on their floor but did nothing to slow the Mobs running rampant in the dungeon.

If the adventurers took a day off for some reason, the dungeon would double its population. It didn't matter if the whole place was full to bursting, more Mobs would spawn. Dale had had to offer extra incentives for groups that went in first in the morning to trim down the overwhelming numbers, just to ensure that they went through level-by-level instead of hopping to their floor of choice. Of course, his team was now the first in every day so they could be one of those that claimed the treasure that piled up overnight. The loot would increase at a constant rate as well, and a chest untouched for a full day might contain anything—from nothing to a child-sized pile of gold coins or an *obscenely* dangerous trap. The traps had been getting more numerous of late. Still, the danger and hardship, coupled with having all of his affinity channels open, had done wonders for Dale. He had flown through the rankings, reaching D-rank four in just a month.

"Look. I know you mean well, and I know it's been a rough few months, but right now, I need to sleep. We will talk later today after finishing our run through the dungeon, okay? I'll make sure to clear my schedule, and we will just chat. Deal?" Dale looked around. The others seemed to agree and responded as such.

"Deal."

CHAPTER TWO

Cleaning up the dungeon had only taken a few hours. The walls were quickly repaired, and Mobs not in pristine condition were culled and replaced. Traps were reset, and rewards were returned to regular yet profitable levels. Looking at my interior like this led me deeper inside myself as well. I looked at the aura representation of my mind and soul, noting that they seemed patched up and tattered. I tried to smooth them further, sinking into my Chi spiral. Introspection is a beautiful event. Staring deeply into myself, I admired the galaxies of interconnected Essence pulsing and shining. This was my mental space, a pocket dimension only accessible via following my Chi spiral to a tiny hole in my soul. It was peaceful. It was healthy and whole. It was beautiful. I began to drift off. *All* I wanted was to stay here forev–

"Cal? Are you listening?" Minya called into an empty room again, the third time this morning. Her voice grated on my nerves as it shattered my tenuous illusion of peace.

My annoyance began to build as my attention slipped from my projects and self-serving repairs. Does Minya not understand how our bond works? It was early enough in the day that there was no one else around, so of course I'm listening! I really have no choice *but* to listen at this point. Stupid bond. Why are sentient beings so annoying?

"Cal, slipping into madness won't help you to..." She took a deep breath, seemingly near tears. "I know that it is getting harder for you to understand me, and your bestial instincts are taking over. I just hope that speaking to you will help bring you back..."

Enough was enough! <Minya. Just because I am *busy* and ignoring you all does not make me *insane*. Stop calling me crazy. I'm *not* crazy! I'm not.>

"Cal! You're here!" she called happily. "I'm so glad you are speaking rationally again. I have so much to discuss with you! Also, I think you are in denial. There are *serious* issues in the dungeon! Just look at the–"

<Have you found Dani?>

"...No, but we have some leads now... someone bought an island recently. We think it was–" She lost my interest as soon as she admitted her failure.

<I'm *really* busy right now, Minya. What do you need?> I disinterestedly asked her as I began focusing on my current reconfigurations. How had I taken so much damage without noticing?

"I want to–"

<No! What do you *need*? Do you have items or knowledge for me? Have you found an opal? Do you need trade goods or money to acquire these things?> Why didn't she understand that I had things to *do*?

"I need to *talk* to you, Cal!" she roared, catching me entirely off guard. I was so startled that my focus slipped, and a small group of Bashers got a wash of Essence, bumping them up a few rankings. Muscular forms lengthened and tapered a bit, and now, they looked similar to long-eared dogs. Maybe that would...? What was I doing?

I sighed at her when I realized she wasn't going to go away. <About *what*, Minya? You have my attention. Go ahead. Speak. Enlighten me.>

"No need to be a jerk, you overpowered rock." She took a breath to calm herself a bit, but I could see that her hands were still shaking. "The council has been debating coming in here to *kill* you. You've been showing signs of severely dangerous behaviors, and every dungeon before you that lost their Wisp has gone insane and caused a continent-scale disaster. Now that they know you are *aware* of any actions they may take, they need assurances that you won't start releasing diseases or something like that."

<Why would I release a disease, Minya?>

"Because you are angry?"

<Minya...> I sighed gently, giving her my full attention again. The entire weight of my mind dropped on to her, and she began to sweat. <I'm not angry.>

"You aren't? What abo–"

<I'm *furious!*> I shrieked far too shrilly, causing my tunnels to rumble a bit. The once blue light that had permeated my dungeon had long since turned into a shifting violet, a patterned red-blue that varied based on my moods. <I did what I could to *save* you all! Now I can't even rely on your people not to *attack* me? Because I'm pissed that one of you *literally* stole a part of my *soul?*> If I had lungs they would have been heaving; my eyes would have been bulging from their sockets.

Minya stayed quiet for a moment as my rage abated. "I know. I'm sorry. What can we do, Cal? How can I help you? I am here for you. You *know* that!"

I paused, thinking. I needed plenty. <What can you do? I need knowledge. I need people out there looking for Dani so I can get her back. *I need revenge!*> The tunnels quaked ominously at my words. If anyone had been near to my Core at that point, they would have felt a small flicker of the madness that had unknowingly dominated me in recent times.

"What can I, *personally*, do for you?" Minya questioned me in a conciliating tone. Calm words on her end drew me back to the issue at hand, and I shook off my near-overwhelming fury. I needed to be practical.

I thought about what I had been working on. Just before I told her everything, I mentally shook my head. She didn't need to know about these projects just yet. My words came out calmly, <Answer a few questions for me?>

"Anything."

<How did that Nick guy—The Collective's leader—use Mana to capture Dani? Dale told me that bastard had bands of Mana holding her in place. I know for a fact that he wasn't a Mage, so things aren't adding up.>

"It is a common magical trap. People who collect rare creatures or easily damaged items can purchase magical containment devices. It is highly likely that he had a net-like version," Minya responded instantly. "What else?"

<And I assume anyone can use them?> She nodded quietly, letting me speak. I was grateful. <I need one. There are multiple variations? One of each type then. Here, use these.> I created a small pile of gold bars at her feet. They clinked and thudded heavily to the ground.

<If you need more than this, tell me. I can always kill off a few adventurers and make more.> I coughed a little, not a physical response but a social conversation tactic. <Being thrifty won't hurt, of course. That pile represents three dead F-ranked men.>

"Thank you. I'll work on finding things that you will find useful. Also, to your earlier question, I *do* have an opal for you." Minya opened her bag, pulling out a shimmering stone that scattered light like oil, allowing colors to play across its surface. "It is the highest grade stone I could get my hands on. You would have had it days ago if you would have talked to me." She couldn't help but throw in an admonition.

<Yeah, yeah, sorry.> I absorbed the stone, examining it and 'tasting' its flavor. It was... spicy. Odd. I created a small replica and fed infernal Essence through it. The lights within brightened considerably, and the Essence flowed into it at an exponentially higher rate than it did even with diamond. <Huh. It does work well for infernal. Good job.>

"So infernal Essence really does move through opal better? That wasn't just a myth? For some reason, I assumed that kingdoms made that story up to catch naive necromancers! This is really something that will help you to become stronger?" Minya's eyes lit up as she realized how helpful she had just been to me. Now I felt bad for yelling at her.

<Apparently, it was not a myth. Where did you get this, by the way? I thought opal was highly guarded? Kind of treated like a controlled substance or dangerous potion?> I was warming up to the conversation. As much as I hated to admit it, I hadn't realized how depressing a month with no social interaction had been. Maybe I should start talking to Bob? My Goblin must be getting bored by now. We could visit each other.

Minya's face flushed. "Erm. Well, after the infection went through the Lion Kingdom..."

<Oh no.> Another thing that was my fault with no real benefit. Did I accidentally topple a kingdom?

"Yeah... the entire country is drawing outcasts and is totally lawless. Huge tracts of land have no guards nor anyone to enforce the law." Her voice became softer, and she trailed off, "On the plus side, the booming black market has all sorts of 'forbidden' things. I can find traps, enchantments, and war Runes that are much more deadly than is typically allowed to the population."

<Good. Do it.> The pile of gold at her feet grew too more than triple its previous size. <Try to find things that are

strange or seem to have no practical use, as well. I'd be particularly appreciative of Runes designed for direct attacks, and... you know what? I'll make you a list.>

Minya was soon outfitted with money and trade goods such as gems. Armed with a list of goods I was interested in, she prepared to leave the dungeon and start her black market shopping spree. At the last moment, she hesitated, seeming to argue with herself for a moment before finally putting voice to her thoughts.

"Cal, do you remember much of the last month?" Minya guardedly questioned me.

I thought. <Hmm. Yeah, but I was so dang busy. It is all kinda... fuzzy.>

"I don't want to upset you Cal, but... you *were* seriously acting insane," Minya started to talk.

<Ugh, not this again. Minya, I'm not–> I rebuked her. At least, I tried to.

"Can you access memories from Cores like this?" Minya held up an empty memory gem.

<Uh. If you smash it in my influence, I get the memories. But... why?> I cautiously replied. I'm not ashamed to admit I was afraid to hear the answer.

"Good enough. Wait a moment." She held the gem to her head and concentrated. After a few seconds, the gem began to glow brightly with swirling light. "Cal, I'm... sorry about this," she preemptively apologized as she smashed the gem.

My thoughts were filled with horror as I watched what she had seen in my dungeon for the last few weeks. Rooms were heavily scarred, statues and walls half-formed and grotesque. Mobs damaged and malformed, out of their minds with pain. Swarms of creatures disproportionate to party size and ranking wiping out dozens of adventurers. Worst of all... unfair traps.

Traps and dangerous things that there was no chance of defeating. Walls that closed and filled the enclosed space with poisons or acids. The only saving grace of these traps was that no one survived to tell about it, or my reputation would have been destroyed. I likely would have been as well.

<Wait. If no one survived, how did you know about it?> I latched on to the hope that she was somehow lying to me. Unfortunately, that was impossible with memory stones.

" *You* told me, Cal. You laughed and raved at their stupidity. You... forced me to watch as you killed them. Somehow, something brought you back from the edge. I don't know what changed today, but for the first time in weeks, you suddenly started talking to me normally," Minya told me sadly. "I bet you don't even remember the majority of our conversations. Truthfully, if I weren't bound to you, and I knew this... I would have killed you myself."

<I would have let you. I don't remember *any* of this...> I softly exhaled.

"Which is why I am telling you now. We need to hurry along with our plans. We need Dani back to even you out." She waited a moment for me to reflect on my actions. "Are you sure you will be okay?"

<I'm sad, Minya. I'm hurting, and I'm going to do what I can to absorb *absolutely* everything. But... I do have my own rules that I play by. If people can prove themselves, if they can find the way out, I won't go too far out of my way to hunt them down,> I graciously allowed, <unless they are part of 'The Collective'. I promise you right now, I'm not going crazy. I also give you permission to kill me if I *ever* get like that again.>

"Not going crazy right now, at least. I suppose that is all I can ask for. Take care, Cal. I'll be back soon." She paused, turning to look around. "One last thing, Cal. Would your Wisp have wanted you to be so angry all the time?" She stepped into the portal after releasing these cutting words and was gone.

<Hey, that was rude and out of nowhere! You... gone? Finally.> Trying not to be hurt by her words, I turned my mind back to the series of impossible tasks I had given myself, trying to ignore how hard her words had struck me. I would make sure to follow through on my plans, I *would* find a way—and to the abyss with the consequences.

I had not been idle this month, I knew that much. Through my, uhm... indiscretions? I had somehow remained focused on the goals I had set for myself. I had been *exceedingly* busy. Now that my mind seemed to be clear, I could finish my tasks much quicker; I could find Dani, I *knew* I could. Unfortunately, undeniably, infuriatingly, I couldn't do it alone. Yet. My plans for the future were slowly coming to fruition, but I had no idea how long Dani could last without me. To further my goals, I had been digging... no, that isn't the right word. I had been *boring* my influence downward. A huge amount of Essence had been devoted to the project. It was only a thin tendril of influence, not even a half inch in diameter, but it was growing deeper by the moment.

<Bob, we have had a bit of a development,> I began talking to my current favorite sentient Mob. Bob was a Goblin Shaman with infernal and wind affinities.

Bob looked up as soon as he heard my voice, then slid to his knees in supplication, almost like prayer. "Great One, we live to serve! What can we do to further your goals? I cannot express my thanks that you have begun speaking to me in intelligible words again!"

I ignored the subtle reminder that I hadn't been myself recently. Looking him over, I was still impressed by how the changes I had wrought in the Goblins had altered their bodies so much. For instance, now there was hardly a *hint* of the speech impediment that had plagued their race for so long. <Research, Bob. For you, always research. The digging is approaching the depth needed. I just wanted to ensure that everyone is ready for any accidental... explosions.>

"As always, we live to die for you." Bob nodded heartily, his happy tone contrasting to the dark words.

<Right, well, I have a new staff for you, if you want it. The staff is the same wood you are using now, aspen? I never actually got a reason for that, by the way.> My curiosity derailed my gift-giving by a bit.

"Ah, yes! Aspen is believed to enhance our abilities to communicate with the spiritual world. It offers greater protection and control over the spirits I must face if I want to direct them," Bob explained instantly. At the start of our relationship, he had been a bit more hesitant to give up the secrets of his race. That had quickly changed. I suppose that seeing a being unendingly resurrect fallen members of your tribe would be a good incentive to open up a little.

<Oh. Alrighty then. This staff looks almost the same as the one you are using, but it has a rod of opal through the center, connecting to a small orb of opal at the very top.> I stopped talking as the staff appeared in front of him. He was nearly dancing with glee as he reverently picked up the staff and channeled a bit of infernal Essence into it. A bolt of purest darkness shot from the orb, impacting a passing Goblin and making it scream and collapse.

Bob looked at the Goblin in shock. "Oops. So... it launches arrows of Essence."

<Yeah, unfocused infernal Essence in this will fire off a bolt of... that.> I looked at the weakly convulsing Goblin on the floor. <Let me fix him really quick...>

I took a moment and restored the Goblin, who scampered off with a sharp look at the sheepish Shaman. <Right, so, I want you to do research with that staff. It should focus your abilities and allow you to complete your Incantations and summoning with much less Essence and far greater control.>

"I... *we* will put it to good use, Great Spirit.> Bob was one of the few Goblins that could work with the alternate versions of himself without getting weirded out. It was always amusing to watch twelve versions of Bob arguing.

<Good luck, Bob. I need to get back to digging.> I focused more Essence into the tendril of influence I was extending downward.

"Wait!" Bob cried out loudly, even for him. What? Bob had *never* stopped me from moving on to other things before.

<Yes, Bob?>

He took a deep breath. "Great one, we are forever in your debt, and we could never hope to repay the lavish gifts you have given us..."

<Go on, Bob, I won't be angry.> I waited for his request to leave. It made sense; they had been fixed, and who wouldn't want to explore the world? I had likely scared them off with my bout of insanity.

"There are a few of us who miss certain aspects of our life outside, and while we are happy to eat the food you provide, we hoped that," here it comes, more people leaving me, "you would be willing to allow other things to live and grow in here."

<What? You just want more *things*?> My voice may have come out a bit strongly, as he cowered a bit. Can't he recognize excitement?

Bob fell to his knees again. "I am so sorry to have bothered you with such a request! I am ashamed and–"

<No, no. What can I do for you, Bob?> I consoled him cheerfully. <You serve me well. I am happy to help make *you* happier.>

He glanced up hopefully. "Ah... we had hoped to make this place more like the outdoors. Plants, flowers, small animals such as birds... maybe some things we can hunt without being hunted in return."

<And? That is completely doable. It might even benefit me somehow. Though, I am sensing a bit more, perhaps? What is it?> I cajoled him. Hearing that you weren't going to be alone forever can really put you into a good mood.

"Well, the thing most missed... and you can say no, really, I don't know the scope of your abilities, and–" Bob babbled away, wringing his hands.

<Spit it out, Bob. I do have things to do.>

"Yes! Sorry! The thing most missed is the feeling of wind. It can get a bit... stuffy down here," Bob finally finished. "The animals are mainly for background noise; we have had a few days where my people can't seem to take the silence. They tend to tear their ears open when it lasts too long."

<You... *want* insects and rodents? I didn't bother because I never saw a use for them. Sure. I'll make bugs and various non-threatening creatures on every floor and instruct the Mobs not to eat them. The breeze might take a while, but I know I can do it. Maybe an updraft generated by heat from my digging...> My mind wandered away as I was considering how to make a breeze, so I didn't hear his thanks. I redoubled my digging efforts and poured more earthen Essence into my deepening depression. To clarify, not the mental state. I mean depression as a 'hole'. Tunnel. No, wait. If it is vertical, it is a shaft. I pumped Essence in an attempt to enlarge my shaft. Um... that still sounds wrong for some reason.

There was a good reason for my apparent waste of Essence. No, not waste—*use*. Brilliant *use* of Essence. Not a waste. I should kill something to clear my mind. To my point, a copy of a Dwarven memory stone I had 'acquired' from Dale recently had come with some very interesting information. The Dwarves had allowed some of their theories to be available to the outside world, thinking that the knowledge could never benefit a race outside of their own.

You see, Dwarves were the only known race that had dug through the earth so deeply that they had found a point where rock ceased to be solid, where the heat and pressure of the world above liquefied everything below. They had never found a way to go beyond this point but noted that this was certainly how volcanoes gained their deadly payload. To me—beyond the obvious benefit of turning my mountain into an active volcano—the fact of the matter was that the Dwarves used the heat and molten metals they found to create wondrous weaponry and formulate deadly traps. I would find a way to do the same.

It was possible that the Dwarves also ignored a huge benefit in the form of cultivation. Maybe they didn't understand the various benefits, but most likely they *did* and simply chose not to share with others. Magma was a massive source of various combinations of earth and fire Essence. At *least* those types, maybe more. They could make a fortune guiding people to the unceasing Essence generation of the deeps. Then again, lava cultivators tended to congregate around active volcanoes, which was very dangerous for obvious reasons. I'm sure this led to an unstable group of people, thrill-seekers, warriors, and such. Maybe the Dwarves just didn't want guests that could turn on them? I could understand that.

I collected my thoughts and focused on the outcome I wanted. If I could tunnel to the depth where the world turned liquid, I need never fear my tunnels being sealed off for I could use the loose Essence of the earth to generate enough power to *surpass* what slowly drifted into here. I also had a river that flowed through my levels. If I could find a way to generate wind, I would have everything I needed to be a self-sufficient elemental dungeon. Bob, with his request for fresh air, may have actually helped me more than he knew. Celestial and infernal Essence were still an issue, but I could work on that. Later. After I finished my current project.

CHAPTER THREE

Looking at my dungeon, I took a deep 'breath' and got back to work. To help keep my mind focused, I had created a plethora of totally sane schemes! I had my Mobs warring every day—not only against adventurers but against each other. The creatures that fought and survived had their memories stored in Delta memory stones and were becoming more confident and powerful by the day. To clarify, not all of them were strong enough to have their own Core yet, but I was able to imbue their memories into them, similar to the Goblins below.

Allowing them to retain their memories and be granted a healthy body upon death pushed my Mobs to remove their various inhibitions. This process quickly forced them to become more vicious and territorial, even when they had started as passive creatures. For example, now even the *Bashers* didn't need my guidance to attack when people came too close! The territorial aspect was something that I had been forcing upon them by keeping creatures bunched together, only sending them after dungeoneers when they got within range. Now, I am happy to report the Mobs did that work themselves! Not needing to dictate every movement left me free to ignore them in favor of working on more important things.

While I was pleased by the progress of my life forms, as my mind returned to my project... I scowled. I hated being interrupted, especially when *Minya* interrupted with her inane attempts to force me into self-reflection! Bah. I refocused on my walls, little by little chipping away the heavy, dense granite and other various minerals and exchanging them for a new type of stone. I had found this material during my downward digging, nearly two miles straight down. It was porous and very light...

pumice! That's the word I was thinking of. Since I was absorbing more dense material, replacing it with pumice had the fringe benefit of giving me a net return of total Essence. That is, I was gaining Essence faster than I was using it while creating my walls.

I could shape the pores in the new stone walls, creating fractals of smaller and smaller Runes. Since it was still a strong-ish material—being rock—I could grow it in Runic formations easily, sacrificing the density of the old material without damaging the structural integrity of the walls. This stone could be integral to the next phase of my plans, but there was plenty to do before I even *thought* about achieving *that* lofty goal!

I paused my efforts, thinking back on my recent conversation with my favorite dungeon born. Though she had gone out of her way to bother me, Minya *had* provided me with a very important piece to my puzzle. Opal. Right now, I was collecting vast quantities of Essence as well as various flavors of corruption and storing it for later use. Whenever I got too bored with the tedium of replacing multiple tons of stone, I turned to a few of my side projects that allowed me to automate the process of Essence collection to a higher degree. Hopefully, this new gemstone would help since I was getting too large to micromanage everything that happened here.

The lining of various minerals through my walls *did* allow a constant flow of Essence and taint to drain into Beast Cores. This had the adventurer-beloved benefit of purifying the Essence in the dungeon without my direct influence. The downside was that the process was slow. Without taking a more active role in the interplay of energy, corruption had begun to build to noticeable levels.

I sighed as I thought about the potentially superb usefulness of this gift... I should really apologize to her. Minya had good timing, even if she had gone out of her way to annoy me at that moment. Infernal Essence had been accruing at a higher rate than I had bothered to keep up with. It moved even slower through the diamond channels in the walls than the other types of Essence did. Because of its low... *viscosity*, for lack of a better word, there was a dense miasma of the corruption in my tunnels. Already over a month had passed since the multiple hundreds of defenders and infected had died in here, and there was no noticeable progress in clearing the taint. Hopefully, supplementing the diamond filaments with an opal version would help me clear the corruption from the air.

I took a deep drink of my collected Essence and, refreshed, began working, threading the opal along every wall over the course of the next hour. A portion of the diamond wires melted back into my aura as I overlaid the original path with that of opal. I connected the shimmering gemstone to the murkily swirling Cores designed to draw in and store the infernal corruption and laughed gleefully. To my immense satisfaction, the effect was both drastic and immediate.

The infernal Essence seemed to shriek with demonic glee as it flowed into the opal, flashing into the Core faster than any of the other Essences bothered to move along their own varied filaments. This confirmed another of my theories... the gems I was using were *not* actually the best type of material for the various Essences! The humanoids above me had it wrong! While the gemstones I was using were *good* at collecting their associated corruption, there would certainly be a better option. I laughed at my good fortune, now all I needed to do was–

A meteorite slammed into the surface, jarring me from my cheerful examination. How long had I been focused on this? A day? The crater left from the impact extended into my influence, so I looked at the remnants of the meteor... a house? That's an odd celestial body... ah. A Mana storm must be forming above. Good, good. I was in a cheerful mood right then; things were going well. I could use some company. I can only talk to myself for so long before I start to go–. Stop that train of thought! Gotta think positive!

DALE

"Mana storm!" a screaming voice woke Dale from his uneasy slumber as an alarm began to howl. A rumble from an impact rocked the ground, making the awakening process much swifter. Dale started to sit up, but his instincts grabbed his attention, and his body shifted into a defensive stance. He blocked the jagged blade tearing through the air, easily returning a double jab. At this moment, Dale was happy that he was always armed, his cursed weapons refusing to vacate their prominent positions on his fists. His pugilistic maneuver paid off. His clenched hand smashing into the robed figure wielding the blade. Surprised when the form didn't go flying through the side of his tent, Dale charged recklessly, doing everything he could think of to avoid the dancing blade.

The robed figure slashed at him, always just *slightly* faster than Dale could manage to perfectly block. Soon he had small, bleeding cuts crisscrossing his arms and chest. The robed figure took a step back at blinding speed, removing his hood.

Pointed ears, ebony skin, and a scowl were revealed. "Enough. Barely passable. Weeks of training and you still allow the blade to touch your flesh. Pathetic, even for a human. You should be ashamed of your weak dedication to the arts."

Dale inclined his head in the smallest of bows, not trusting the other person not to attack. "Sorry, *sir.* I was a bit over-concerned that a *Mana storm* is settling in."

Dale's combat instructor smacked him across the face hard enough to make his nose bleed. "You think your *enemies* are going to care that you are worried about a little *snow*? You think an assassin is going to hold off so you can seek *shelter*? Grow up, child! I should have just ended your miserable existence when we met instead of agreeing to train you. You know what? You need to show greater progress, or it will reflect poorly on *me*. From now on, your instruction is not limited to two hours at *night*," he spat viciously. "I will be training you *constantly*. You should be grateful that I am giving you advanced warning. *Very* grateful."

Breathing heavily as he took in the significance of the Moon Elf's words, Dale managed to grind out a few choice expletives before remembering to respond correctly, "T-thank you, sir. I am... *overjoyed* that you are planning on taking such an *active* role in my daily routine. Does this mean I should be expecting attacks in places like the dungeon? That I'll see you in the latrine and bathhouse?"

The Dark Elf chuckled snidely as he slowly vanished from sight. "Foolish boy. *You* won't see *me*."

Dale switched his vision to an Essence enhanced version but didn't detect so much as a ripple in the ambient energy of the world. "OhmygodIhatethis," he mumble screamed under his breath. A second impact nearby made the ground shake, urging him to head for the dungeon entrance.

The dungeon was the only place nearby that provided enough shelter to weather the storm, and so it tended to become a bit crowded during these dangerous atmospheric events. Dale joined the gathering crowd, trying to wait patiently while the sky was filling with odd effects. Illusions of monsters in the air manifested and dissipated, small portals formed and vanished, sometimes leaving behind creatures or items. One portal stayed open for a few long seconds, blasting a torrent of water out at a forty-five-degree angle. Fish began falling from the stream of liquid.

"Are you bleeding? What? How?" Rose strode up next to Dale, looking at him then at the mesmerizing patterns in the sky. "It is almost beautiful. Not as bad as the last one at least."

"Please stop tempting fate with your poor choices of words." Hans slid up next to her, trying to put an arm around her shoulders.

A blade appeared at his throat, and Rose quirked an eyebrow at him as she played with the small dagger. "I'll stop tempting fate when you do, *Grandpa*."

Hans' face flushed. "I am *not* that old!"

"An early excursion into the dungeon, my friends?" Tom strode up to the gathering, easily parting the crowd with the simple expedient of walking into people who didn't move out of the way in time. The large man had Adam trailing behind him, casually using Tom like a battering ram. "I have a request for mineral samples from the walls of the fourth floor! We can make a pile of gold before breakfast!"

"Looks like we are going in whether we like it or not. Everyone feel up to officially starting the day early?" Dale looked around at his friends, doing his best to clean the drying blood off his face.

"For sure, but let's pop down to the second floor to begin with. The first level is going to be packed. Bleh." Hans shuddered at the thought of a constricting press of people. "Sweaty."

They walked into the dungeon, using their keygems to activate the portal system. With a single step, they were on the second floor. Dale went first, ready for combat. His preparedness was directly beneficial to the group. A Smasher—a stone covered

Basher—was jumping toward the open portal in an attempted ambush. Dale lightly dodged the assault, using his battle gauntlets to 'soft block'. This meant that he didn't directly block the entire attack, but instead angled himself and pushed so that the attack passed him while his actions deflected the soaring bunny into the wall. Trying to block a charge from these overgrown creatures had been the cause of many shattered shields over the last few months, and Dale didn't care for yet another broken bone.

He swiftly moved after the downed Mob, crushing its skull with a heavy stomp. "What a nice way to wake up in the morning." He stretched, chuckling as an Impaler appeared out of a hidden hole in the wall. The infernally-enhanced Basher had flesh-peeling flames covering its jutting horn, so Dale made sure to avoid the sharp bone as he counterattacked. His fist impacted the side of the altered rabbit, and he activated his gauntlet as the blow struck home.

Splat. The entrails and viscera of the animal were blasted out of its body as the fluid repulsion Rune on Dale's knuckles activated. He picked up the corpse as the remainder of his team walked through the portal. "Basher jerky, anyone?" Dale offered the exsanguinated rabbit around with a smile.

Only Tom actually considered it. "Hmm. Perhaps after the fur has been removed...?"

"Don't listen to him, Tom. He is just showing off," Rose grumbled, pulling back the string of her force-enhanced bow. "Must be nice to have permanently activated magical weapons on you all the time. Isn't that right, Dale?"

"Hey, now! Must be nice to use the bathroom without worrying that you are going to blast something back into you, isn't that right, Rose?" Dale rebutted too loudly. He froze in place. "Not at all based off of actual life experiences, of course." He grimaced sourly, realizing he had shared *way* too much.

"Sinking your ship to put out a fire! While I would love to hear the origin of this story," Hans released an uncharacteristically high-pitched giggle, "it does appear that we are going to have to fight. Looks like we walked into a territory war." He gestured ahead of them, where a Coiled Cat was springing back and forth among a group of Bashers that were larger than usual, even for advanced Bashers like the ones Dale had just defeated.

They watched for a moment as the infighting raged on. Rose was the first to notice the oddity. "Shouldn't... shouldn't this be over by now?"

"The Essence patterns in those Bashers are flowing in a different pattern than usual. More highly concentrated Essence is swirling around their skulls, so I would have to assume that they are more intelligent than usual," Adam spoke in a melodious baritone. His body had been subtly undergoing changes since the battle of the infected, dubbed 'The Wailing War' due to the constant crying and howling of the afflicted. His voice was becoming smoother, and other small characteristics were becoming noticeable. His skin was perfectly clear, all signs of scarring vanished, and his hair was slowly turning a silvery-blond. With his pure white cloak and staff, he looked like a Bishop.

"More intelligent?" Hans pondered this revelation for a bare moment. "Gah! They must have started developing Beast Cores! Let's go kill 'em all and find those Cores!"

"Or we could just enjoy the show?" Rose quirked an eyebrow at Hans' exuberance.

"No, cause if we win, we can claim this territory as ours!" Hans started moving toward the Mobs. Actually, if they had

Cores now, they would all be considered Beasts. *Weak* Beasts, but Beasts nonetheless. Hans smiled, now seeing the creatures as walking gold coins.

"I do not think that Mobs would honor an agreement of that nature," Tom responded with confusion evident in his voice.

"He's trying to distract us so he can force us to start fighting," Adam clarified for his large friend, readying his staff.

Hans charged into the fray, laughing as he dodged droplets of blood spraying from his instantly impaled target. The Bashers squeaked indignantly, and a few turned to charge him. The Coiled Cat took advantage of the distraction and pounced on to a Basher, crushing it under his weight. The Cat's claws lashed out, tearing a chunk of flesh—and the Bashers horn—out of its skull. With a *crunch* the Cat bit into the horn, and a flash of Essence entered its body. It shuddered as the muscles along its back rippled with fresh power.

"Argh!" Hans shouted in horror, "He just *ate* a Core! He *ate* it! Dale! Tom! Get in here! It's *eating* our profit!"

Dale complied, charging the Cat while it was distracted. He was able to land a solid blow, but the knuckles of his battle gauntlet glanced off of the metal-reinforced skull of the Beast. There was a bit of an effect from the liquid repulsion Rune, but Dale was used to being able to do serious damage with each attack and failed to use the provided opportunity to follow up with more punches. The Cat shook itself and sprang forward, ramming into Dale with its massive head. Luckily for Dale, there was little momentum to the blow as there were only a few inches between them. His luck was wearing out quickly though as the Cat opened his jaws to take a chunk out of the human it was standing over.

As the metallic jaws came down, teeth punching through Dale's skin with barely any resistance, a golden, cube-shaped barrier appeared in the Cat's mouth. As the metal teeth tried to clamp down, the barrier forced the jaws apart. Adam shouted in a strained tone, "Hurry up, Dale! *Do* something! *Dale!*"

The Cat leaned back, disengaging and rearing to swing its paws at the man scrambling to stand up. An arrow punched into the meaty paw, slicing flesh but failing to penetrate the bone, though the force was enough that the Cat was twirled around one hundred eighty degrees. Tom swung his ingot hammer at the Cat and forced the vertebrae apart, severing the spinal cord as if its metal coating didn't exist. The paralyzed Cat fell and hissed impotently at the group, scrabbling around with its legs dragging behind it, but it was quickly put out of its misery with an accurate arrow to the eye.

"A hand with these Bashers?" Hans called in an oddly desperate tone. Turning to look at him, the group watched incredulously as the Bashers performed complicated maneuvers to dodge the blades Hans was swinging.

"Are you being serious?" Dale stared at the former assassin. "Just kill it!"

"I don't want to go all out against glorified *food!*" Hans huffed as a Basher casually hopped over a low swing.

Tom and Dale looked at each other, shrugged, and waded into the combat. Rose stood next to Adam, carefully aiming at the agile creatures. Tom frowned as his swinging ingot hammer consistently missed every target. "Hold thyself immobile so that I may bring about thine end!" the redhead roared at the whirling balls of fur.

"Tom!" Hans shouted at the lumbering barbarian.

The redhead jumped back, looking for the inclement danger that must be nearby. Seeing nothing, "What?"

"They aren't listening to you." Hans chuckled as he finally slashed one of the Bashers. In a falsetto, he mocked his student, "Hold still so I can kill you! Grahh! You. That's you."

"My voice does not even slightly resemble that," Tom grumbled as he abandoned his hammer, opting instead to slap at the Bashers with his bare hand. He glared at the Bashers as they attempted counterattacks, dodging every swing he attempted. "Dale, you make striking these Beasts look so easy!"

"Helps to have both fists," Dale muttered offhandedly, fully focused on using the nimble Bashers to train his pugilistic accuracy. He threw a few combination punches that stunned the Beast he was focused on, not bothering to use the Runes on his weapons to finish it off. Rose snorted loudly, attempting not to laugh at the unintentional insult. Tom's arm was mostly regrown at this point, but he hadn't had any work done yet to restore anything past his wrist.

Tom lifted his handless arm in what was a poor attempt at a rude gesture. Adam laughed. "You've been spending too much time around Hans, Tom. Why don't you have your shield?"

"You say that like it is a bad thing!" Hans called in mock outrage. The others took a moment to see where his voice was coming from. He was hanging off the ceiling.

Catching a Basher by the scruff of its neck as it jumped at him, Tom sighed and smashed its head on to the floor, splattering blood across his shins. "With my arm mostly regrown, my shield does not fit anymore. Also, I cannot hold it normally since it was forged to be worn as a piece of armor, not be used as a held item. Even if it was, I have no hand in which to carry it."

Dale finished off the last Basher attacking him. "Don't worry about it too much. You should have full use of your hand by the end of the week. At least, that's what the Mage told us."

"Verily, I look forward to it." Tom nodded gravely, swinging the limp Basher into a jumping Smasher, throwing the stone-clad attacker into the wall. He threw his improvised weapon, which released a piteous squeak, hurrying to follow the attack with his ingot hammer. With all his might behind the blow, cracking the heavy stone armor and finishing off the stunned Beast was child's play.

Hans looked around at the carnage. "These all *had* to be Beasts, right? Even if they are low quality, there is a standing order for Cores! The lowest quality Core we can find will still sell for a solid gold, so let's make sure we don't leave any here!"

They got to the grisly task of cutting out the Cores, which were in the horns of the Bashers and seated between the three eyes of the Coiled Cat. The entirety of the Cat then was inserted into a bag since the Guild had found that the bones were interwoven with a type of high-grade steel. The Cat would be skinned, the usable meat removed, then the remainder boiled to leave behind only the gleaming bones. Those were given to the smelters, who reduced them to steel ingots. This was all part of a very efficient operation that used every part of the Beast.

CHAPTER FOUR

<So, Dale, how are things?> When my voice broke his attention, Dale nearly sliced his thumb open with the knife he was using to skin a Cat.

"*It speaks!*" Dale quipped dryly. "*I am not worthy! So feel free to go away.*"

<Of course I speak, and of course, you aren't worthy. You're lookin' good. Healthy. Are you going somewhere? I see you have your suitcase packed. Oh, wait. Those are just the bags under your eyes! You look like rabbit scat.> I kept up a running commentary as he continued working on the carcass.

"*What do you want, Cal? You've never bothered me unless you wanted something,*" Dale mind-groaned in reply. I was instantly angry, a side effect of whatever had kept my thoughts fuzzy for the last month.

Dale shivered as he felt my mood fluctuating. <Dale. Oh, Dale. You know what I want. I want my Wisp back. I want *DANI!*> Dust rose into the air as the dungeon trembled a bit. I tried to calm down, and after a moment, the room returned to a more blue-ish hue as my mood stabilized.

"*I don't know where she is, Cal,*" Dale hurried to think at me—the angry entity—while inspecting the integrity of the walls along with the others.

"That Mana storm must be getting nasty. Let's get further down," Rose muttered to the group, readying herself to continue into my depths.

I finally got control of myself. <I know, Dale. I know. Sorry. Listen, I'm *going* to find her, and I want to know that you will help me get her back when I do.>

"I'll do what I can, Cal, but I am just a D-ranked cultivator. There really isn't much I can do to help bring her back. Even my political power only extends to this mountain," Dale tried to soothe my agitation.

<So do *more*!> I growled in a fury, wishing I could strangle him. <Work harder, cultivate more, throw parties, and make rich friends! Marry a princess! I don't care! I don't care if you think yourself pathetic, you need to be ready!>

"Dale, are you talking to the dungeon right now?" Adam looked at his leader with faintly glowing eyes.

"...Yeah."

I glanced closer at Adam, and his head turned to look directly at me. My perspective. Whatever. <Ugh, that's creepy.>

"He's looking at me right now," Adam calmly stated. Yup, freaky. Hang on though...

<Can I fix him?> I queried Dale, who seemed to be trying to hold back a laugh.

"What? No!" Dale loudly stated, making the others look at him.

"Does it want something?" Hans put a hand on Dale's. "Can you see the dungeon right now, Dale? Is it in the room with us?"

Dale shook off the hand of his patronizing friend. "Knock it off. He isn't an imaginary friend. He wants to 'fix' you, Adam, but I think that usually means he wants to eat you or try out ideas for corrupted growth on you."

Adam stopped and looked downward, considering Dale's words. <You *do* understand me! Also, see? He wants to be fixed! Now, if you just push him on to that spike over there...>

"Avoid that spike, Adam," Dale stated instantly.

I grunted in dissatisfaction. <This is why no one likes you, Dale.>

Dale continued talking to the group, "Yes, the dungeon is talking again."

"Speak out loud, would you?" Rose instructed him crossly.

"What? Why?" Dale was a bit caught off guard by this request. "You will only hear half of the conversation!"

"No, I agree." Surprisingly, it was Hans who interjected. "At least then we will have some idea what is going through your mind."

Dale reluctantly agreed, "Whatever you want, I guess. What is going on, Cal?"

<Well, tiny and tasty human, I have plans, you see.>

"Yes, very mysterious and vaguely threatening of you. I assumed as much. How do I fit into these scary plans?" Dale actually had a good question for once. Oh, wait! Questions!

I chuckled in a slightly sinister manner. <We haven't played our little question game in a while. Do you want to start it up again?>

Dale slowly shook his head. "I'd really rather not. I'd rather be open and honest and have you do so in return."

His words caught me off guard. <Whoa, Dale! What changed? You used to be so adamant against every little interaction! You sound so... *mature* now!>

The human paused, lips quirking as he tried to find a nice way to phrase his next words. "Cal... the difference is that *you're* different now that I know you care. Maybe you don't care about me, my team, or maybe even life in general, but you *do* care about something besides yourself. I now know you have feelings and that loss affects you. Talking to you now... it feels less like talking to a psychopathic individual and more like talking to... I don't know, a living force of nature?"

<That's a decent description of me. A psychopathic force of nature.> My mood soured again with the reminder that Dani had been taken from me. <Well, whatever works for you. Can I count on your help to get her back?>

"Of course, Cal. If there is something I can do, I will. As long as I don't die first." Dale chuckled half-heartedly, fishing for some words of affirmation.

<No promises on that front, but, really, good luck,> I returned bluntly.

Dale stopped laughing. "Right, you are still a dungeon." He grunted uncomfortably. Hans raised an eyebrow at him in consternation. "How are you planning to find her?"

<I'm going to 'bug' people. Places, too. Maybe things as well, just for fun.>

Dale waited a moment. When no more information was forthcoming, he tried to force it a bit, "Care to elaborate?"

<Not particularly! You will find out soon enough anyway.> I had to hold back a laugh as his face turned red. Apparently, I was upsetting him. <Before I go and have fun setting traps in your way, I do have a potential fix for your low ranking. That is, if you are interested...?>

He wavered, deciding between anger and curiosity. He broke down after a moment of deliberation. "Alright, what is it?"

I grinned internally. I knew he couldn't resist the swift way to the top. <Well, Dale, you have a Beast Core in you! I know that cultivating has been difficult for you recently, too many open affinity channels, yeah? Why not take the easy path? You can get stronger the same way Beasts can! Take the Essence right from their Cores.>

CHAPTER FIVE

Dale was unsure of how to respond to my new information. "So, what... eat the Core? Like that Cat just did?"

<Well. If you want? It'd be fun to see you break your teeth. I was more thinking that you would crush the Core in your hand. You know, the one with the Essence-absorption Rune?> I snickered a bit as the pieces started coming together in his mind.

"You planned this?" He looked incredulously at his armored hand.

<Of course I did! You are so unimaginative that if I didn't make interesting things for you, you would just keep on doing the same boring things over and over,> I rebuked him whilst laughing. <Did you think that that Rune would only work if someone attacked you with Essence or something?>

Dale flushed and avoided answering. "Won't crushing a Core make it explode?" He was overly paranoid, in my opinion.

Or he was just a realist. <Maybe? Explode is a strong term. Though maybe chewing it is a bad idea after all.>

He sighed and rubbed his forehead. "At least there is a flesh Mage here if something goes wrong," he muttered darkly. Seriously, where was the trust?

Dale pulled a Core from a Basher out of his bag, holding it tenuously in his hand. His team was looking at him like he was a crazy person, so he quickly explained what he was about to do.

"Dale? Buddy? Maybe you *don't* cause an explosion in an enclosed area? Do it outside if absolutely necessary?" Hans wheedled him. "Maybe you don't want to throw away profit, either? You are basically planning to throw gold–"

"We're right next to a portal." Dale glared at the knife-twirling ex-assassin. "If something goes wrong, please feel free to get me healed. I'll pay you back when I'm able to move." With a deep breath, he forcefully activated the Rune on his battle gauntlet and *squeezed*.

Bamph! The Core shattered, sending out a halo of multi-colored light. Dale screamed as his pinky finger was torn off from the concussive force.

<Hey, it worked! You absorbed most of it!> I cheered for Dale as he howled and gripped his energy-amputated finger stub.

"You son of a– Oww!" Dale gripped his hand as Adam stepped forward and healed the energy burns and lacerations from exploding crystal.

"Well, the finger is gone, but the rest will heal up," Adam pronounced after a few minutes of triage. The cleric wiped his sweating brow as he leaned back. "If we can find the finger, I may be able to reattach it. If it hasn't already vanished."

<Hmm. You should have probably let the material of the gauntlet wrap the Core in its entirety, then there wouldn't have been any Essence loss,> I informed the bleeding human.

"Cal, what the shi–" Dale kept shouting stuff, but now his group was just sitting around being boring, so I had already moved on to other things. Now Dale would have to come up with his own ideas. If he could. Pff. Anyway. What was I doing? Oh, right!

My idea for searching for Dani was ready! That is probably why I was in such a good mood. I'm sure messing with Dale had something to do with my joyful outlook on life too, though. I had been searching for a way to send out creatures that would seek Dani, and an idea had come to me after watching an anthill for a few hours. Bugs! Why did bugs do what they did?

Why did they look for certain things or follow the same paths over and over? They were looking for something. In the case of ants, it was a small chemical trail. Others were looking for food, some for mates. I had no idea what wasps were looking for; as far as I could tell, they were just assholes. I liked wasps.

After some, um, *minor* modification and a few days of altering what they quested after, I learned how to force them to track a specific Essence signature. Now, no matter where they started or how well I hid their target, the bugs *always* found what they were supposed to. There was another advantage to this method—who looks at bugs and gets worried? Even *I* couldn't deal with all of the insects in my dungeon now that I had created them for Bob. Their population grew too fast, it would take way too long to micro-manage them, and they didn't really have great combat potential. But! They could be seekers. I knew it was a long shot, but if I put enough bugs out there, they should eventually converge on a single location. Hopefully, Dani would be there. No... she *will* be there.

To that end, I had been growing all sorts of insects and modifying them with Essence. They were a bit larger than their natural counterparts, and their shape was a bit... *off* from what is found in nature. This was because I had been mixing and matching to make the most versatile creature that I could. All of them could fly, and I had grown them in a low-Essence environment so that they could survive outside of the dungeon. Their survivability was actually surprisingly high in *all* the climates I had tried out.

Now that I was thinking about it, I might as well let the first batch out. It was getting pretty crowded in the incubators, and it sounded like the Mana storm was abating. With fewer people playing defense above, I hoped that more bugs could slip away without accidentally being squished. After opening their pens, the swarm of thousands began buzzing into the dungeon, moving toward the exit. They were only trying to get out, but the adventurers seemed to think that they were a new type of threatening Mob.

"Oh, God! Flying spiders!"

"Look at the size of those claws! Run!"

"Ahhhh! They have stingers!"

Well. I may have made them a little *too* versatile...

"That one is the size of a dog! How is it able to fly?!"

"They aren't attacking! Just get down, and they ignore you!" Finally, someone noticed!

Hmm. Was the size difference really *that* important? I thought that a larger version of something they saw all the time wouldn't be too noticeable. Humans are so strange! They scream like children over a few bugs but go running at the Cat Boss—Snowball, a steam variant Beast—looking for a fight? Bizarre, I tell you.

The last of the swarm was flowing out of the dungeon entrance and was scattering into the air. Hopefully, I would be able to find where they converged in the future. Good luck, love-bugs! I gave them a tearful farewell; it was always difficult to see your creations go off into the world, or so I had heard.

An hour later, after the great excitement of the morning, I was starting to wish I could fall asleep. I was working on mind-numbing tasks. Create a bird. Do it again, slightly different. Again, slightly different. Make a bug. Grow a tree. Grass. I was starting to hate grass. Do you know how annoying it is to grow each individual blade of grass? They aren't even actual blades, just blade shaped! Boo! I started getting antsy when I was planting raspberries and may have accidentally gone off on a tangent and made a new Mob. Making harmless things is just so... bleh!

Bob called my attention to a trap he had come up with. He made me promise not to look at it before it was sprung, but I didn't need to wait long. Some bleary-eyed adventurers were happily approaching a treasure chest, and after thoroughly checking it for traps, they threw the lid open. Boisterously collecting the silver coins and assorted goods inside, they stood straight while chattering amongst themselves.

<I'm a bit underwhelmed.>

Bob rubbed his hands together. "Shh. Here it comes!"

With a scream, a dagger-wielding Goblin was thrown out of the chest; a spring-loaded trap door on the bottom had concealed his hiding place. He impacted the standing human, his weight bringing them both to the ground. The adventurer took a half dozen stabs to the abdomen before the others—who seemed to be in shock—tried to attack the Goblin. Not sticking around to die, the Goblin jumped back into the large chest and slammed the lid shut, slipping into the tunnel underneath and sliding away down an incline. Even if a human found the tunnel under a chest like this, they couldn't follow.

<That... that was amazing!> I started laughing, and so did Bob. The gore covered Goblin entered the room Bob was in a minute later and was awarded a higher quality knife as a reward.

"Glad you liked it!" Bob chortled. "I've been trying to find a way around their trap detection, but any wires or pressure plates are always detected by professionals."

I was smiling now. <Thanks, Bob! That really broke up the tedium!>

CHAPTER SIX

I'm bored again. Digging is boring. That is, it is dull. Not to be confused with boring, the act of digging a hole. Which, I suppose, it also is. I was at a bit of an impasse right now, to be frank. Digging was time consuming, more so since I was starting from near the top of a mountain. It was harder to do the further I moved away from myself and thus slowed down progress and increased energy consumption. Luckily, it didn't take much concentration, or I would have gone as crazy as the council on the surface seemed to think I was.

For the first time in a month, I had decided to take a hard look at what I was doing. Minya—abyss take her—had scored a point in our last conversation. Dani wouldn't have wanted me to ignore my upkeep and get lazy; she has always been a proponent of hard work and judicious rewards. When I looked at a few treasure chests lying around on my second floor, I was shocked to find them stuffed with *gold* of all things!

I didn't give out *gold* on the second level! What had I been *thinking*? ...The short answer was I hadn't been thinking. At least not clearly. High rewards on an entry floor made for fewer people continuing to the *deeper* floors! I deactivated the Runes I had been using to generate treasure in the chests throughout my body and felt a wave of nausea as I noticed how much Essence they had been sucking up. All they were doing was generating coins and bottling health potions. Unendingly. They had been ceaselessly producing gold for a *month*. I recouped some of my losses by reabsorbing the metal and tried to think of a way to fix this situation. I liked the treasure chests because they made for a convenient distraction. People could waste *hours* looking for the hidden boxes, and I didn't have to worry about generating rewards for each individual Mob death.

I didn't want to go back to trying to make rewards for each individual person. I had way too many things to get done. How could I solve this problem? Quickly getting frustrated that I had no one to talk to, I... wait. Bob! <Bob, do you have a moment?> I questioned quietly. He was setting up some kind of dark ritual, and I really didn't want to interrupt him if it would affect what he was doing.

Bob slowed his writing and carefully finished pouring some blood into a long stripe. He stood and stretched before answering, "Sorry for the wait, but if I did this wrong, it would backfire quite terribly. For you, Great Spirit, I will always have—or make—time."

I was touched, and it threw me off a bit. <Thank you, Bob. It has been... hard... for me recently.>

"Understandably so. What can I help with?" I explained my situation and how I was having trouble finding a solution. He scratched at his leathery hide, considering my words. "Well. Too many adventurers to give exact rewards for? That is a good problem to have, I think. Let me ask you this, how many groups have those bags that are larger on the inside?"

His return question caught me off guard. <Oh. I haven't really counted, but it is fairly rare. Maybe one group in ten? Less now that there are fewer experienced groups.>

He nodded. "So then the groups without them can only carry what they can fit in the sacks they carry around or in their hands?"

<That... sounds right? What are you getting at, Bob?>

"I think you need to play on their greed a bit more." He grinned wickedly, and since his mouth was twice as wide as a human's and filled with jagged teeth, it was a truly frightening visage. "How about this?" Bob started talking, and I started getting... *excited.*

DALE

"Stupid dungeon. Stupid me for listening to it," Dale muttered as Adam reattached his finger.

"At least you didn't start with a Core from the Cat." Adam patted his hand. "I'd say you got lucky."

"Question!" Hans raised his arm into the air and waved it around.

Dale rolled his eyes. "Yes, Hans?"

"Did it work, at least?" He looked at Dale's slightly off-color flesh. "The intent was to allow you to gain Essence from crushing the Core, correct?"

"Yes it was, and yes, it did work," Dale grudgingly admitted. "There was a slight side effect of losing a chunk of my hand, though, if you didn't notice."

"I don't think you realize the potential here, Dale." Hans was being serious again, which was always a nerve-wracking experience. "Outside of your *normal* cultivation, you can gain Essence from *Beasts.* Beasts will always have large amounts of Essence in their Cores, and no one has found a way to directly extract and use it before, outside of using it in Rune scripting. I think you should try again, more carefully."

Dale was stunned at the earnestness of his friend. "Is it really going to be as useful as all that?"

Hans shrugged. "It could be, but that depends on if you can make it work or not."

Dale sighed and pulled out another small Core. "I really don't want to do this."

"Please try not to lose another finger," Adam muttered as he looked at the recently reattached digit on Dale's hand.

"I think it's fair for me to say that *I'm* more nervous about losing appendages than you are," Dale grumbled, pulling on the cloth of his cursed battle gauntlet. He wrapped the Core tightly and *squeezed.*

Bamph! The Core shattered with a muffled explosion, but the fragments were stopped by the tough cloth surrounding it. There was a bit of light, showing that there was still Essence escaping the cage of his fingers. However, the vast majority of Essence was sucked into the Runed gauntlet and soon flooded into Dale's Chi spiral.

Dale opened his eyes, which glowed an electric blue as the Essence moved through his meridians. "Oh, *yeah,*" he breathed the words in a husky tone, "it actually worked!" The corruption was separated out, moving into various corruption Cores surrounding his Center.

"This seems like an expensive way to cultivate," Rose mentioned carefully. "While I am glad that it is making you stronger, I hope you also know that every Core you use is going to have to be your share of the loot?"

Dale winced but nodded. "I understand. Luckily, we have a fairly large surplus of gold right now. A month of coin-stuffed chests has really helped with the bills."

They had proceeded deeper into the dungeon only a short way when Adam pulled the group to a stop. "Wait, listen! Listen to all that noise!"

"Sounds like a normal forest." Tom shrugged expansively. "What is the issue?"

Adam locked eyes with his hulking friend. "The issue is that we aren't in a forest. We are in a dungeon."

Hans peeked around the corner. "Uh-oh."

Expecting the worst, the rest of the group tentatively looked inside as well. Still, they were stunned as they stared into the noisy and brightly lit room. It was lush, full of life. Normal, non-mutated flora and fauna abounded in the room, creating a cacophony of sound. Chirping, squeaking, and rustling in the long grass pervaded the entirety of the floor.

Birds flew from nests burrowed into the stone walls, insects moved between various plants, and water burbled down the walls in a small stream. Dale looked around and saw huge Cats rolling in patches of mint, crushing and chewing on it.

"What's happening?" Adam asked, unable to see around his taller teammates. They shuffled a bit, and he looked at the room. Frowning, he questioned the others, "Did we step outside? Are we on the wrong floor? Also, why 'uh-oh', Hans?"

"It looks like the dungeon is building an actual ecosystem." Hans sighed deeply. "This is 'uh-oh' for a few reasons. Firstly, it makes it harder to determine what is a threat to us. If all sorts of animals are moving around, we may get used to the motions and not see the ones that are actually dangerous."

"This could be an issue," Tom agreed stoically. "If our constant vigilance would allow us to be caught unawares, which it will not."

Hans waved a hand at the redhead. "I'm not done! The biggest issue that I see right now is those birds. They are flying all over the place without any kind of pattern."

"So?" Rose glanced at him askance. "Far as I can tell, they are just birds, right?"

"Yes, Mountain Chickadees, to be specific, but what do birds do when they fly over you?" Hans nodded grimly, reaching for throwing knives. "Use you for target practice."

"...This is about bird poop?" Adam made a calculated guess.

"Yes. That type of bird has a nasty habit of staining clothes irreparably."

Rose glared at Hans until he looked her way.

"What?" His eyes were clouded, without a hint of laughter.

"Are you sure you aren't a child in an adult's body? Go fight a Beast. Here, I'll get you started." Rose pulled out an arrow and sent it at the rolling Cats. A deep roar in return caused dust to fall on to them from the ceiling. It *did* also get the birds to hunker down in fright.

The group got ready for the attack as three Cats ran at them, one limping heavily. The limping Cat was a Flesh Cat; the other two were Coiled Cats.

True to their name, the Coiled Cats sprang a great distance, covering the ground in huge, leaping bounds. Tom roared at them in return and took a few steps forward, settling into a good position for hammer swings. Dale bounced on his toes a bit, dancing in place to warm up his legs and arms. Adam stood just off-center behind Tom, while Rose stood to the side firing arrows. Hans leaned on the wall.

"I don't wanna fight," he muttered petulantly. "I like Cats. You know all the different words that have 'meow' in them? Meow, meows, meowed, meowing, homeowner. I don't want to kill Cats right meow."

"You are a total *child*." Rose growled as she released another arrow. The Flesh Cat fell, blood draining from its torn neck.

Tom swung his hammer in an arc, somehow missing the lunging Coiled Cat. It knocked him to the ground and tore a strip of flesh off of him with its razor-sharp claws. Dale was busily engaging the other Cat and didn't notice his friend's predicament.

Adam stepped forward and attacked! His staff came down and... bopped the Cat on the head.

The Cat looked up at Adam and hissed.

Adam looked at the slowly growling Cat. "Tom... now would be a good time..."

Tom couldn't move, pinned by the weight of the metal-laced Cat. The claws lashed out at Adam, striking him squarely on the arm and throwing him to the floor.

"Adam!" Rose shrieked, firing a fat-tipped arrow at the Cat. The projectile impacted its head, bouncing off and stunning the Beast momentarily. Tom used the opportunity to roll out from under the staggered Cat, bringing around his ingot hammer. With a muffled *clang*, the hammer struck the Cat hard enough to knock it unconscious. Rose quickly strode forward, drew an arrow, and pressed the tip against the closed eye, firing point blank. The Cat expired with only a slight spasm.

"Everything okay over there?" Dale had the hand with the Essence-absorption Rune pressed in the space between the eyes of his target Cat, swinging his other hand on to its skull whenever it stirred. The Cat was severely brain-damaged at this point, the blood in its brain being forced around mercilessly.

Rose rushed over to Adam, who was already staggering to his feet. Blood was dripping out of his sleeve. "Adam!"

He stepped back from her. "It is better and worse than you are thinking. The claws didn't cut me; the robe wouldn't let that happen," it was lined with what was essentially Mithril chainmail, "but the hit broke my arm enough that there is a bone sticking through the skin. I can't fix it alone; we will have to leave. Please check on Tom."

She nodded seriously and then moved to Tom, who was holding his side. "How bad is it, Tom?"

He grinned at her as he sweated profusely. "I don't care to look at it..."

Rose moved his hand to the side a bit and was able to see intestines through the gash. "I need a potion over here!"

Dale hurried over and fished a potion out of his pouch. He poured half of it directly into the wound, prompting a howl of pain from the barbarian. The other half was poured into Tom's mouth. His bleeding stopped as a scab formed, and his intestines were pulled into place by writhing muscles. He needed to see a healer quickly, as this was considered a temporary fix at best, and Adam was otherwise occupied.

Hans had walked to the corpses during these ministrations and stuffed them in his bag. He got a dirty look from Rose as he sauntered over. "It isn't my job to kill everything for you. Think of this as... a test. You didn't do well."

"Everyone is on the first floor by now, so the healers should have a station set up. Let's go," Dale ordered, standing near Adam in case he needed help. As they walked, Rose questioned what he had been doing with the Cat. "Oh, the punching? I was trying to drain its Core. That way, I would get the Essence, and we would still be able to sell a quality Core. Win-win. It worked pretty well after it passed out."

"Smart!" Hans enthused. "That way you won't shatter the Core by removing all of its Essence! As long as it is alive, it will pull Essence from its body to maintain the Core. *And* we can still sell it! You've been making good life decisions today!"

His exuberance only increased the glare he was receiving from Rose.

They stepped into the portal, returning to the first floor.

CHAPTER SEVEN

Having all of these people on my first floor was slightly aggravating. Especially since so many of them were sleeping, and I couldn't get any Mobs in to give them a good ol' coup de grâce. Prone target, unconscious... too bad. It was like waving gold coins at a tax collector. I felt like I was going to start drooling. So, like a fart in the breeze, I drifted over to someone else.

<Bob, I finished most of the changes you asked for but haven't been able to fix the airflow yet,> I told my Goblin Shaman. He was scratching at his neck and seemed agitated.

"We thank you, we truly do, but, those trees..." Bob pointed at a new grove near his home half-hex. "Why are they screaming?"

<That's an insect called a cicada. It lives on the tree; it is not the tree itself. Minya brought me some as a present from the dry lands to the east. I was told people found the sound soothing. Not so much for you?> I explained with a chuckle. Of all inanimate objects I'd found, so far I'd only heard rocks scream. Screaming trees. That's a good one.

"The general consensus here is that they are rather terrifying." He gave a weak smile. "Would you mind?" The cicadas stopped singing, to both of our surprise. "Thank you, that was fast."

<That wasn't me. If a predator is nearby, they stop making noise,> I explained as a few humans popped stealthily out of the tree line. <It would seem you have visitors.>

The Goblin paused momentarily, mind whirring. "I've decided we will live with the noisy bugs." Bob nodded once. An arrow whizzed by his head. He dropped behind the wall and shouted, alerting the other Goblins. They hurriedly moved into a defensive position and started releasing projectiles at the group outside.

The tanking unit of the adventurers—a mountain of a man who only carried a spiked shield—charged the wooden gate with a deep bellow. Shield leading, he rammed the barrier, accompanied by a deep crunching of splintering wood. His shout turned into a laugh as he leaped forward again, easily breaking through the wooden egress.

Following the massive man, a few others braved the light rain of desperate yet poorly aimed arrows to charge the open gate. They piled into the open courtyard of the half-hex, setting up a defensive formation so the remainder of their team could easily join them. One of the men was a ranger of some sort and was paying better attention to his surroundings. His eyes lit up as he noticed Bob standing amidst the other Goblin defenders.

"The Wandering Boss is in here!" he shouted to the people behind him with a mixture of fear and excitement in his voice. "Hurry your butts up!"

Ah yes, that was a new thing. There was a Bob for each of the half-hex fortifications, but they all spent most of their time working for me, doing research in a hidden room. Whichever Bob hadn't been out recently would go fight, but they had to go to their own home base so that a particular fortress wasn't associated with him. Also, if he was killed, the freshly respawned Bob could decline to go out the remainder of the day. All of these restrictions added up to Bob being a once-daily unique Mob. As his capabilities for air and infernal incantations—and what he called 'rituals'—made him much more potent than the average Goblin, he had been dubbed the "Wandering Boss" by adventurers.

"Ah, abyss take them! They saw me. Now I have to fight. I hate dying," Bob muttered angrily as he started hopping from foot to foot, gathering ambient Essence for his impending fight.

<So don't die.> I chuckled at his sour glare. <I know what you are thinking, 'easy for you to say', right? Well, I work to not die as well. Unlike you, there's no coming back for me if I were to be destroyed.>

"Humph. Well, at least I can try out my new ritual." Bob nodded at the large series of Runes covering a six-foot area in the courtyard. "It was done anyway, and I needed a sacrifice. Or two. Three?"

I looked at the Rune. It was drawn in blood and seemed very obviously placed to me. <You are sure someone will step into that? It looks dangerous. Faintly evil as well.>

"I don't know for sure that they'll fall for it, but since you always make me carry the nicest prizes, I feel confident that they will come for me," Bob muttered the last bit under his breath as the adventurers piled into the area. "That is a lot of humans... How many people are attacking us?"

I did a quick count. <About fifteen. Three parties. Oh, right. I should have warned you, the whole dungeon is overrun with people right now. There is a Mana storm going on outside. Anyone not sleeping is diving in for early gold. Feel free to go all out on them, I feel like they're cheating.>

"Oh! Really?" Bob perked up significantly at these words, then started gibbering in the Goblin language. Pauses in his speech were accompanied by sharp movements of his now-sinisterly-glowing staff.

"He's starting to summon something! Hurry up, he's distracted!" The humans gave a resounding war cry and charged.

They were met in the open by the most uncontrollable of the Goblins, the Goblin Berserkers. Each of these Goblins had had their mind damaged by repetitive respawning and strangely developed an unusable affinity for fire Essence. Their bloodlust was unmatched in the dungeon, and they threw their lives away for the chance to do any damage *whatsoever* to their opponents. Brutally attacked, the humans were forced to stop and defend. Most of the Berserkers used simple blunt weapons, such as maces or one-handed warhammers. The blows rained down on the humans, heavy weapons whipping through the air as if they were enchanted.

The Berserkers screamed in rage when their first attacks didn't kill their targets, so they redoubled their efforts. They began to fall apart, tearing their bulging muscles with the force used and frothing at the mouth as their bodies unconsciously re-routed Essence to increase their strength. For every attack which damaged them—or an opponent—they seemed to get slightly faster and stronger. They also seemed more feral, less able to deal with changes on the field of battle.

A heavily dented shield blocked one last blow and shattered, opening a human up to a deadly attack. The shield-bearer fell backward, and the Goblin screeched in glee, dropping his weapon and tearing into the now-prone human with his claw-tipped fingers. Chunks of flesh were tossed to the side as the battle raged around them.

The humans seemed to get serious, their formations coming together while they began attacking in waves. They smoothly set their shields, pushing forward as a single unit with an air-shattering shout. My front line was staggered, and the humans followed up with efficient thrusts of their various stabbing weapons. A Berserker took a sword to the neck and fell just in time for a bolt of infernal Essence to smash the offending adventurer in the chest. The rapidly dying man fell to the ground, writhing in agony. His flesh seemed to melt away as a combination of deep rot, fluid, and pus drained on to the floor.

Bob looked at his staff in wonder. "What an excellent weapon! Thank you, Great Spirit!"

<...Might be too good. We'll reevaluate later.> While muttering at Bob, I was looking at the actual effects that the bolt had had on the corpse. For every magical effect I had ever seen, there was a discernable reason for the following reaction. For instance, a sharpening Rune didn't just 'sharpen' a blade. Instead, Essence flowed into the blade and increased the bonds along the edge of it. This had the effect of making the blade thinner and harder to chip, resulting in a 'sharpened' or 'honed' blade.

<So *that* is what infernal Essence does...> I had suspicions before, but this new data would certainly help my research. <No need to reevaluate, you can keep it. We need to know more. Use it as much as possible.>

It seemed that infernal Essence would enter the body and attach itself to impurities in the flesh. After latching on, it would force the Essence of the tissue to deteriorate quickly, generating *more* infernal Essence from the death of the cells around it. To the casual observer, it looked like the body rotted away at high speeds. Since it was targeting impurities, this also explained why infernal Essence had less of an effect on people of higher ranks; their bodies expunged impurities as they reached higher cultivation ranks! Therefore, they were less susceptible to the pure version of this energy.

I really needed to devote some time to the origin of both infernal and celestial Essence. If I could find their source, it would be a great step toward generating them myself. I assumed that death was the origin point of infernal, but I bet there was more to it. In the interim, it looked like Bob was going to die. Too bad!

The Berserkers had been slain, their brutality defeated by the simple expedient of a solid defensive formation. The archers had been counter-sniped by the dungeon-divers, and a group was converging on Bob. I was about to offer him my condolences when I noticed him grinning a disturbing smile. To be fair, with their sharp teeth and extra-wide mouths, most of their grins were a bit frightening.

Bob fired off a bolt of darkness every few seconds, but the shields seemed to block the Essence effectively. I didn't see why he was happy about this until I saw that the pseudo-phalanx was almost to the center of his ritual formation. Their dedication to their shields didn't allow them the option to look where they were walking!

Taking a step forward, Bob openly laughed as the humans warily halted. Poor life choices on their part. The Goblin set the end of his staff down on the stone floor with a resounding *rap*, and the dark glow of the infernal spread from the wood... into the blood underneath it. There was a disturbing organic sound and a small shriek of torturous pain. Each of the humans in the ritual area then slumped to the floor with a hollow clatter.

Hollow clatter...? <Bob, what did that do? And how?> I excitedly asked my minion. <Did you teleport them away?>

"Not done yet," came the short reply. He was still channeling Essence into the ritual, and the glowing lines pulsed one last time and pushed a wispy darkness into the air, which vanished into the armor on the floor. As he finished his work, he collapsed to the floor, breathing and sweating profusely. I looked at his Center, reeling in shock from the huge amount of personal Essence he had used. My guess was that since he hadn't been able to move around, he was not able to use ambient Essence as he usually did.

The armor on the floor clattered and started to move. <Oh, they are still alive in there?> They hadn't moved in a few moments, so I was... oh my. The armor stood up, but it was *just* the armor. There were no bodies inside! The surviving humans—mostly people waiting behind the others, such as archers and healers—cheered as their friends stood back up, calling out to them in relief.

The armor stopped moving, looking at Bob. Totally silent, they did not make a move until he pointed at the remaining adventurers. Then they moved, and they moved *quickly*. At a slightly greater than human walking pace, they marched toward their ex-comrades. Confusion was evident on their faces, which only increased to terror as the blades started to fall upon them. Soon, no humans were alive in the immediate area.

"It... *pant*... worked!" Bob was trying to stand, but even with the support of his staff, it was very difficult for him to do so. The refined Essence from the dead adventurers was making its way to me but was much less than I had been expecting.

<Would you mind telling me what that was? It seemed... taxing.> I hadn't been this excited about *anything* in over a month!

"Yes, Great One. This was a ritual to create walking armor or 'Phantom Armor'. It is the greatest, most dangerous ritual we have been able to recreate," Bob began to explain to me.

<Ritual? You have mentioned that before, but I thought it was just the preparation of a Rune. No? It has to be more than that.> I fired questions faster than the humans had fired arrows, listening carefully to every bit of advice Bob had for me.

"Not quite. A ritual is a series of interlocking Runes that activate one after another in intervals, a set of sequential instructions. It is hard to do because, unlike a Runescript, the Runes do not all activate simultaneously at the end with an even distribution of Essence. These lines," he pointed at the shadow of the lines that remained on the floor, "are called 'symbolic links' and allow you to send various amounts of Essence to each Rune. The trick to this is that all of them must be maintained for the *entire* ritual after activation. The Runes have their own effect, which changes the 'meaning' of the next activated Runes. Then their effect is spread over the entire ritual area. Just like normal Runescript though, the use of catalysts or reagents can aid in this greatly."

<What did this do? In order. What reagents did you use for this?> As ever, I was hungry for knowledge.

"This, as I said, is the most demanding and dangerous ritual that we—the Bobs—know." I chuckled at that. They referred to themselves collectively as 'The Bobs'? Excellent. "To facilitate the effect, we drew the Runes in a tincture of Flesh Cat blood and crushed opal. The first Rune was the Rune to dissolve armor. By using the Flesh blood as a reagent, it dissolved bodily tissue instead!"

I was stunned by this revelation. I knew reagents could alter the effects of Runes, but I had no idea it could be this drastic! Changing the destruction of armor to the destruction of flesh? How did they come up with the idea?

Bob continued his lesson, not noticing my speechlessness, "The next Rune set hardened the armor, fixing imperfections and binding it together tightly. It also inserted tiny speckles of opal across the armor, allowing for easy influx of infernal Essence. The final Rune used the Essence from the body to create a lesser shade, a phantom. The phantom can't hold its shape on its own, so it needs a vessel. The result? Phantom armor!" He proudly waved his hand in a grand gesture.

<Spectacular,> I whispered softly. <How do you control them? What kind of weaknesses do they have?>

Bob started speaking at once, as he had expected these questions. He held up an amulet hanging from his neck. "If this is destroyed, they are banished. They cannot touch it or attempt to take it. Therefore, whoever holds this controls them. They can be banished by simply smashing their armor and waiting, but after they are released, they are beyond furious. They know they only have a few seconds remaining, so they will vindictively attempt to kill anything near them by flooding them with infernal Essence."

<But they move fairly slowly...> I added this comment questioningly.

"Yes, while in armor. *Very* quickly otherwise. Nearly the speed of darkness." Bob grinned then ordered the armors to begin patrolling the floor. The eight creatures marched out and started wandering like normal adventurers. Anyone coming across them would be in for a deadly surprise.

CHAPTER EIGHT

"Try to take it easy for a few hours, will you?" The cleric patted Tom on the washboard abdomen she had just finished fully healing.

Tom nodded at her. "I will do my best, but if needs must, I shall always step into danger to protect my comrades."

Her fingers slipped over his now-smooth skin. "So brave..." she whispered, looking up at him with wide eyes.

Ahem. Adam reminded her of his presence with a clearing of his throat. She flushed and turned away. Adam was the protégé of the most powerful cleric in the area, Father Richard. No one wanted to alienate him, and taking advantage of your patient was a sure way to earn the ire of clerics in general.

Tom looked at his friend with a tinge of anger in his gaze. "Maybe you should get that cough looked at, *Adam?*" the barbarian growled, making 'shoo' motions at him. "If it gets much worse, you could *die.*"

"We have work to do. Spread your wild oats on your own time." Adam turned away, Tom following *very* reluctantly. They walked until they found Dale who was deep in conversation with a trader friend of his.

"I'm glad to hear that your business is going so well, Tyler!" Dale offered his waterskin to the merchant.

"Thank you! So very well, indeed. I was one of the first merchants to return, and I brought enough trade goods with to make a huge profit with the influx of new dungeon divers! I've bought into a few other companies in the area and even started an exotic weapons shop," Tyler boasted happily, taking a long drink from the water skin.

"I am glad! My team is just returning though. I should be off. Good day to you!" Daly nodded and turned to rejoin his team when Tyler paused and caught his wrist.

"About that new store... I hear you are taking requests for materials from the dungeon?" Tyler stammered out, obviously reluctant to ask the question.

"Have a job for us, then?" Dale turned back with a grin, putting Tyler at ease.

"Of a sort," Tyler agreed with the inferral. "The exotic weapon store I have is doing well, but I want to make truly *exotic* weapons. I've hired a smith, tailor, and alchemist to start putting together prototypes. They have various requests for materials that I can't fulfill myself. Interested?"

"Always interested in money." Dale grinned back at the slightly portly man while rubbing his fingers together in the universal language of 'you get what you pay for'. "What are you after?"

"Oh dear, that is a loaded question." Tyler dabbed at his forehead with a sodden handkerchief. "To start with, one of everything."

"Right, well, that doesn't really narrow it down for me, so..." Dale trailed off.

Tyler grimaced. "We don't know what will be useful yet. So we want one of each type of Mob in here with everything attached. If you find Runes used in traps or on weapons, we want that too. Each vegetable, animal, or mineral. As undamaged as possible."

Dale looked at his group, who were as stunned as he was. "That's... a tall order, Tyler. I hate to ask but... can you afford this?"

"Oh yes. As I said, business has been *good*," Tyler looked him in the eye again, the light of greed playing in his pupils. "and when we are done cataloging what is useful to us, we will be able to narrow down future orders."

They worked out a few details, such as the cost of each item, danger pay, and delivery fees. Both walked away smiling, thinking they had gotten the better side of the bargain.

"Well, team," Dale clapped his hands in excitement, "it appears we have steady pay coming our way!"

Rose interrupted his jubilation, "I'm not sure why you bothered. There is no way he can pay us more than we can earn from just emptying the treasure chests on the way."

Dale's smile faded a bit. "I have a feeling that the 'golden month' is over. Remember, the dungeon talked today. We have already seen some changes, and we can't just assume that it won't notice how few people have been bothering to attack lower levels."

Hans winced. "People aren't going to be happy when they notice the decreased rewards."

"Just play it off as the last month being a reward from the dungeon," Adam interrupted the morose thoughts. "You know, as thanks for surviving the 'Wailing War'. Now, people just need to be reminded that they need to *work* for their pay, not just go for a stroll and be entitled to buckets of gold. Prices have been skyrocketing in town; this will be good for the economy."

"You don't know people very well if you think they will be fine with that, Adam," Hans uttered stiffly. "Who doesn't want something for zero effort?" The group tried to think of a good answer for that but instead shrugged and moved to the tunnels. At least they had a paying job to work on. Dale waited until his team was focused on entering the dungeon, then slipped his hand into his pocket and squeezed. A bit of light shone through the fabric, and he shuddered a bit. Smiling, he picked up the pace.

The group started marching through the first floor, attempting to ignore the press of people. After they noticed a dozen people attacking a single Bane—the overgrown mushroom Mob—Hans gave a snort of disgust, and they turned around. They used the portal to jump directly to the second floor, deciding to go back and collect Mobs and items from the first floor when the area was less densely populated.

There were fewer people on the second floor but still enough to make Hans antsy. The rest of the group was fine with continuing and barely paused when collecting plants and Mobs. This high up, the monster population was fairly sparse. Although Cats had been in the area earlier, it seemed none had returned to reclaim the territory.

"The Cats we killed earlier were rolling around over there. Is there anything special about that plant?" Rose pointed at the slightly crushed plants.

Tom plucked the plant in passing and sniffed it. "It is just a mint plant."

Hans grabbed a bit of it as well and inhaled deeply. "Well, yes, it is mint. Specifically, though, this type of mint is known as catnip. Put it in the bag!"

Thus the collection began and soon, not even the normal creatures in the area were able to escape the ruthless group.

"Will they even *want* a pigeon, though?" Rose was holding a weakly flapping bird in her hand, an arrow peeking through the blood-soaked plumage.

"He *did* say one of 'everything'." Dale shrugged, tossing a chunk of broken rock into the bag.

Hans looked affronted. "Dale! Are you just trying to increase the number of items we bring back so that he needs to pay us a higher fee?" Dale nodded with a wide grin, and Hans pretended to tear up. "I'm so proud." Hans sniffled and wiped at his eyes, followed by grabbing a handful of dirt and stuffing it in the bag.

They continued down the tunnels, collecting everything that they could find. Leaves, flowers, bugs, saplings, Bashers, and Cats were unceremoniously dumped into the bag. Even with the bag's ability to reduce the weight carried, it was starting to get heavy. Luckily, they each had their own dimensional bag at this point and were able to spread the weight amongst themselves.

"Everyone, wait a moment," Rose called as they all approached the Boss Room.

"What is on your mind, beautiful?" Hans posed against the wall, attempting to look seductive.

"Eh." Rose looked at him and shuddered. "The golden Bashers? Glitterflits? We need to drag this fight out to the point that they make an appearance. If we are trying to get one of everything, that also means the rare variants."

Dale nodded. "Smart. Let's go for the legs in that case. If we can lower Raile's mobility, we should be able to do damage in small enough increments that the healing Bashers will have a chance to show up. Hans, you have the fastest reflexes—you are on capture duty." Hans gave a mock salute, and they cautiously walked into the Boss room.

The battle was a farce. If they were fighting Raile one-on-one, maybe it would have been difficult. Their frequent excursions to the lowest depths had hardened them and honed their battle reflexes. Sadly, Raile was just an overgrown rabbit without real combat abilities. Without Dani to direct his movements in an unnatural manner, he relied upon jumping or running into his enemies, trusting that his great weight and armor would be enough to finish the job.

Dale took the lead as Raile charged into the room, armor bumping and scraping against the walls and floor. The Mob slowed as he saw them, and his eyes filled with hatred when they landed on Tom.

"You really shouldn't have taunted Raile back then, Tom," Adam informed his frowning friend. "He seems to be holding a grudge."

Tom snorted. "I do not see how. The overgrown rabbit of that time was killed. This animal has always just had an unpleasant temperament."

Taking a strong stance, Dale bent his knees and forced Essence along his earth affinity channels. To those who could see it, his Essence writhed into the ground and twisted into a knotted whip. He stomped his right foot firmly upon the ground, and the whip of accumulated power raced outward. The Essence followed the path of least resistance, flashing through the earth with a lightning-like pattern. "*Huh!*" He exhaled sharply as his hands shot forward and *pulled*, rerouting the Essence in the attack. When he did this, all his Essence in the ground—and even some energy in the stone the ability had passed through—was dragged back toward Dale with a powerful *crack!*

At the point where the Essence changed direction, a powerful shearing force was exerted. The granite making up Raile's armor began shattering along his flank. At a smaller level, the technique acted on the stone armor at a direction perpendicular to the grain of the rock. This force caused stress fractures to appear in a localized area but did not actually do any damage. Contrary to expectation, pulling the stabilizing presence of Essence back to himself was what caused the stone in Raile's armor to uncontrollably crumble. With a deep breath, the

Essence remaining in the technique—albeit greatly reduced—finished returning to Dale's body as the stone scattered along the floor.

"Nice work, Dale!" Hans chuckled enthusiastically, clapping his leader on the back. "Is that the mountain-destroying technique you got from the Elves?"

"Yeah." Dale was breathing heavily; he clenched his fists to hide how much they were shaking. He shook his head to clear his thoughts, grimacing. "It failed. If I had used it correctly, all of his armor would have shattered, and he would have been seriously wounded from the impact."

Raile took a step toward them and fell, his balance completely thrown off. It was a comical sight, but the screams of rage he was releasing sobered the team quickly. A normal rabbit screaming can be heard from five miles away, and this animal was a hundred times larger.

"Still!" Hans shouted right next to Dale's ear, "a month ago, you couldn't use it for crap! Is it the Moon Elf trainer who is helping so much? Are you still owed more techniques from the Elves?"

"Partly!" Dale yelled back, not catching the second question. He was barely able to hear his *own* words over the screaming rabbit. Dale watched as arrow after arrow flew from Rose into the hole in Raile's side. "He has really been teaching me to focus and how to twist my Essence inside my body, but he is *garbage* at teaching me to use earth Essence. Luckily, Craig didn't hold it against me that I didn't train with him for so long. He's been able to squeeze in extra training with me."

Hans held up his hand. "Hold that thought." He flashed away, returning with a squealing, golden Basher. He ended its cries with a swift twist of its head then put the corpse in the bag.

"Abyss, Hans!" Dale yelped at the brutal sight. "If you had caught it, why didn't we return it alive?"

Raile's screams of pain turned to fury, and he sloughed off his remaining armor as he activated his inborn ability known as 'Avenger'. Hans tried to think up a proper response to Dale's words as Tom began swinging his ingot hammer into Raile's side, eliciting loud crunching sounds. Raile's screams turned wetter before trailing off into silence. "I guess I didn't want to go back just yet?"

Dale went silent. "That's fair, I suppose," he muttered softly. "Not like we are short of space in our bags." He looked over to see Tom digging a Core out of Raile.

"We have a problem!" Rose called to the group. Since she was standing over the Boss Room treasure chest. Everyone gave her their full attention instantly.

"There's *no* money?" Hans clutched at his chest and looked faint as she explained the issue. "I understand that 'the month of gold' is over, but... *seriously?*"

"Nothing but consumables," Rose informed them, referring to items that could be eaten, applied, or swallowed. In this case, there were a few healing potions and a vial of potent poison. "Wait, there are also wood coins." She held up a coin with an imprint of a sword on it as well as one that looked like a bar outlined in silver.

"Sadly, it is difficult to spend *wooden* coins," Tom grumbled, shuffling his feet in agitation. He had been hoping to have a more exhilarating fight, and he was sweating in anticipation of battle. "Take them with us anyway."

They stepped into the next room and yelped as sudden light burst into being. As they blinked spots from their eyes, they noticed an empty chest connected to the wall. Hanging over it were large globes containing light potion, which had been uncovered as they entered the room. Next to the chest was a pedestal with a slot in it and elegantly carved pictures above it.

They looked at this odd setup, trying to puzzle out the meaning. There was a person holding a tiny coin, followed by the same person putting said coin into a pedestal like the one standing before the group. The next picture showed the individual holding a sword above their head, which they had apparently gotten from the chest. As Dale's group looked over all of the images, the person in the picture seemed to decline using the pedestal, deciding instead to go deeper into the dungeon. After finding another pedestal further down in the dungeon and attempting to use the coin, this time, the sword seemed to shine.

As the images progressed, there was a similar scene where the person in the depiction had arrived at the deepest level. The sword they drew from the chest this time seemed to sparkle and blaze with light. Rose pointed out a tiny picture beside each place a token was used; it was so small that it was nearly hidden by the mural. Adam was the first to discern the meaning behind the artistry, and his eyes widened comically as he found the *deeper* meaning.

"So many people are going to die soon," Adam whispered into the confused silence.

Tom glanced at him. "What do you mean? Is this drawing a trap of some kind?" He took a step away and raised his hammer.

Shaking his head, Adam explained, "No, nothing like that. If I am reading this correctly, the wooden coins are tokens. We can hold on to them and place them in that slot and receive the reward shown on the coin."

Hans gleefully reached into his bag and pulled out a wooden coin. This one had an image of a silver bar on it. He pushed it into the slot as Adam continued speaking.

"The rest of it seems to suggest that if we keep the tokens and go deeper, we can exchange the tokens for a higher reward. For instance, a sword token on the first level may give you a solid weapon, but the same token taken to the lowest floor seems to suggest an inscribed weapon will be given."

"Wait," Hans spoke suddenly as they heard a *thunk* from the previously empty chest. "You mean to tell me that the coin I just used could have been turned into gold or platinum if I had just taken it a few levels lower?!"

Tom opened the chest and pulled out a large ingot of silver. "Looks like it worked!" he exclaimed joyously. He looked closer at the chest, then told the group that there was an opening in the back of it that went up into the wall.

"Drat," Hans groaned.

Rose slapped him lightly on the arm. "Just be glad it wasn't an item token! Imagine getting a dagger here that is worth a few copper versus the same token giving you a dagger with a sharpening Inscription on it on the fourth floor! We would have lost hundreds of gold." Hans looked relieved at her explanation, but he shivered at how close he had come to wasting a fortune. "Then there is the tiny picture. If we are understanding the meaning correctly, there is a small chance that each token will give out a 'jackpot' when used. I have no idea why the dungeon would offer more than we've earned though."

"The issue I see here," Adam spoke louder as conversations started, "is that greedy people will try to reach beyond their means in order to turn in the token at the deepest level they can reach. Not just that, but unscrupulous parties may wait in a room like this to catch weakened groups off guard.

There is nothing on the token that says only the group that earned it has to be the one to cash it in," he finished ominously.

The group went silent as they caught up with what he was saying.

"Yup. A lot of people are going to start dying in here soon." Rose sighed discontentedly.

CHAPTER NINE

I was enjoying the Phantom Armor's clanking. The metallic stomps created a pleasing counterpoint to the shrieks of surprise and pain coming from the group that had just been ambushed. The party of five had hailed someone they thought they recognized and were asking after his usual companions while expecting the worst. At least, what they had *thought* was the worst. Heh. While at first, they seemed a bit leery when the armored man didn't respond, none of them had been prepared for the brutal assault. In opposition to the ponderous way the armor moved while walking, it was even more agile than the person who had previously inhabited the armor whilst in combat.

Clank. Clank. Clank. The hollow armored boots kicked up sparks as they marched away from the scene of a massacre. I began absorbing the remains, and within a minute, no signs of battle could be found. <Bob, would you look over the ritual again? I added a few more Runes,> I called out to my favorite overworked Shaman.

"My pleasure, Great Spirit." Bob rubbed his tired eyes as he moved to comply with my request. He pulled a half-globe of glass from his pocket and placed it on my ritual diagram. The Runes and various symbolic links seemed to double in size and jump into focus within the glass, allowing him to see the intricate patterns and cuts I had made. He studied the work for another hour before sighing and nodding.

"As well as I can tell," his exhausted voice rang out, "the ritual is correct. I would not let any living creature near it when you activate it, just in case it violently fails... but I don't think it will."

<Thanks, Bob,> I muttered hurriedly. <You might want to exit, then, if you don't want to be around it.>

"I am happy to help, but I need to know..." Bob trailed off as he realized that he was questioning me. I had never punished him for doing so, but he had been a slave and old habits are hard to be rid of.

<Feel free to ask, Bob. I could certainly use the conversation. I'm still getting my bearings and trying to make up for lost time,> I prodded him impatiently. The faster he asked, the faster I could get back to activating the ritual.

"I need to know, why such a *small* ritual?" The words tumbled from his mouth faster than he possibly could have spoken as an unenhanced Goblin. "The power of a ritual is *directly* tied to the size of it! Also, it is so *simple* for a ritual. It only has a single function!" He seemed more flustered than the situation called for, in my opinion.

<That's easy to explain!> The ritual diagram was only the size of his hand in diameter, so I suppose its usefulness could be questionable. <The size is linked to power, yes, but in more ways than one. This isn't a simple Runescript where I can activate it and have a single use effect. A larger ritual will cost more Essence to maintain, and this will be active for the foreseeable future. A small version is all I need for now.>

"And the function?" Bob smirked, thinking I had forgotten. As if I forget things! *Cough.*

<I was getting to it!> I pouted at him, making him snort. <I have been digging for a week straight, and I am bored out of my gem! This ritual will dig in a straight line, no mental assistance needed from me. I just need to make sure it is getting enough Essence and make sure I stay out of the way.>

"Ah, so you will be linking it to a Core? I've been wondering how to do that." Bob's eyes gleamed. "I would love to watch this process. Are you using corruption? Why not simply pour acid in the hole and let it dig for you?"

<Ah, the acid. I tried something like that, but acid is still a fluid. It doesn't dig straight down—it tries to fill whatever container it is in. While this makes a *large* hole, it won't make a deep one, and frankly, I need a deep one. As to using corruption, I had planned on it!> I was overjoyed that he was so interested in my work. <That way the earth will accept moving easier. You could get a good look at how to do this in the future, as I will actually be linking *two* Cores to the ritual—one Essence and one corruption.>

He thought for a moment. "I have changed my mind. I would like to stay and observe this activation and linking process."

I was a bit taken aback, though I *had* pushed him into it a little. <You recall that this has a chance to go poorly? By poorly, I mean go *boom*?>

Bob waved his hand in a dismissive gesture. "Eh, if I die, you'll just bring me back anyway."

I paused for the rest of the joke, but looking at his serious demeanor, I wasn't finding one. <I think you are starting to take death a bit too nonchalantly,> I muttered, a bit upset with myself. Bob died repeatedly in my area after all. To fight *my* battles. I thought about it for a second, but eventually, I mentally shrugged. It was his decision to stay if he wanted to.

I tried to recall details of the portal system I had set up, which was the closest thing to ritual work that I had completed in the past. I was hoping that experience might give me some insight into this matter. As far as I could tell, the main difference between the portal and my boring ritual was how they were activated. The portals were charged. Then all of the Runes were simultaneously flooded with Essence. This allowed the

Runescript to have a single, unified purpose. The ritual, on the other hand, allowed for a Rune to have its own effect, then be impacted by the activation of each Rune in sequence.

This boring—that is, digging—ritual had a few stages of Runic activation. The first determined the size of the affected area. The second set, the Essence type used, followed by a Rune that made this defined area spin. The next determined the speed of the spin, then added a direction, in this case straight down. The final Rune I added determined what to do with the displaced dirt.

<Ready, Bob?> I gleefully and rhetorically bellowed. <'Cause here. We. Go!> I began pulling Essence through a Core I had filled for this purpose as well as earthen corruption through another. The energies intermingled and snapped together, returning to an unrefined state. I hadn't actually expected that, and it nearly cost me my concentration. Only the stray thought that doing so would likely kill Bob kept me on task.

I drew the strand of Essence into the first Rune. It filled slowly but was then activated with a dull flash of escaping light. The area was defined! I focused, and the pathway between the Runes began to accept the still-flowing power. The second Rune flashed, and an emerald-brown disk of energy took shape just above the ground in the center of the ritual area. Power weaved into it, and the disk began to spin. This was so fun to watch!

As the next Rune activated, the spinning increased in speed to the point that a high-pitched whine began to resound in the area. Another flash and the convex disk began dropping, biting into the solid stone beneath. The noise was incredible, and strips of rock began flying around. At least until the final Rune activated. Then the shards of stone began smoothly stacking as a pile, which I quickly and easily absorbed.

I was watching the boring continue, which wasn't boring in the slightest! <Oh, drat. I made the area too large. It doesn't fit into the current hole.> I observed the digging ritual tear up the edges of the current hole, enlarging it a bit. <Still, it is descending faster than it would have otherwise...>

"At least it is taking care of itself now, right?" Bob looked down the hollow shaft, peering into the murky darkness below.

I was free of digging for the moment! <Right. On to more exciting things!>

DANI

"This place stinks," Dani announced contemptuously to the dark-robed man controlling her. She was held with a tether of Mana, like a dog on a leash. "You stink too. Mainly as a person."

A sonorous voice that could make the inanimate tremble with induced fear responded to her, "Little Wisp, you were *so* pretty when you were quiet—like the aurora borealis all bundled up just for me. Maybe we go back to that, hmm?"

"My *name* is Dani, you overpowered necrophiliac," Dani scathingly spat at him.

"That's a disgusting accusation. A slur against my people. Don't repeat this mistake," came the spine-shivering reply. "Besides, this place will not stink for too much longer. I do apologize for the smell, but *I* didn't make it. That would be all the humans who have been dumping their filth into these tunnels for decades."

"We are in a *sewer*?" Dani yelped in disgust. "What is *wrong* with you?"

"Now, now. Don't judge me harshly. From what I hear, *your* precious dungeon was being used as a sewer as well." A cold smile was on the man's pale face as he threw her origins at her. "Also, if you address me again, do so properly. Can't be having the troops hearing about your insolence. They may think that they can... participate."

"Let me guess, that wouldn't end well for them?" Dani's voice dripped sarcasm.

The man's glare made her shiver. "You *will* address me correctly. I am 'The Master', and you will address me as such. Either that or just 'Master'. I have earned these titles, and I will–"

"So, 'The Master' or 'Master'? Why not a shorter version? How about just 'The'? That's part of your name too, right? Or we could get on good terms, and you could go by 'T.M.'," Dani blatantly interrupted The Master again.

"I had hoped to put this off, but I suppose now is as good a time to learn as any. Lesson number one: disobedience is pain," The Master calmly stated. A tiny flutter of air rippled between the two, and Dani began to scream.

DALE

"So, how long do you think it will be until these tokens become common knowledge?" Rose asked Dale as they made their way down the stairs to the third floor.

"Not long enough," Dale voiced his thoughts with brutal honesty. "Though for the time being, I'm more concerned about how people will react to the *much* lower rewards. The gold is gone, powerful items are gone, and wooden *tokens* have replaced them. I'm betting people will be angry. Some people won't believe that there will be any rewards whatsoever anymore. Will our population drop again? Is the economy going to fall apart? Will I be blamed for it?"

"Most likely. You are in charge, so you are to blame for any negatives in their lives. People stink. On that note..." Hans chuckled as he looked at the crestfallen lordling. "Are you still trying to buy the bathhouse?"

Dale's face became tinted with a light shade of red. "I just *really* like not smelling people. If everyone had free access, I wouldn't have to worry about someone brushing past me and staining my clothes with the accumulated grease of a work-week. Everything that isn't *super* nice is already bloodstained from fighting in the dungeon. I thought you," Dale thrust a finger at Hans, "of all people, would want this to happen."

"I just don't think it'll work out like you think it will." Hans scratched his butt and grinned knowingly. "People like him," Hans jerked a finger at Tom, "think that a layer of dirt keeps you from becoming ill and makes you warmer."

"Any insulation *is* insulation," Tom agreed with a nod. "Why is dirt so different? Plus, the animal fat I spread on my skin keeps it warm, smooth, and un-chapped in the wind."

"Maybe, but it *rots* if you don't clean it off!" Hans and Tom devolved into a snarling conversation they had slogged through many times before.

Adam joined Dale's conversation, "Some people will leave, but others will see opportunity. I would be very surprised if these tokens didn't become uncommonly popular at shops in the future."

"Why is that?" Dale would have latched on to any hope offered. Adam's words made his heart pound with anticipation.

"Think about it." Adam twisted his lips coyly. "The token is lightweight, gives you what is shown on it, and even has a number on it to represent the floor on which you earned it.

While they don't have any value by themselves, they are an easy way to trade or exchange goods. Like money, almost. They only have the value we assign them"

Dale pulled out a token and looked at it. He hadn't noticed the number on it before now. What else was he missing when he glanced at things? How much more did other people see?

Hans looked at the token as well. "How do you know that number doesn't mean you will get two of the thing?"

"Because you only got a single bar of silver," Adam rejoined easily. "There is the third-floor entrance. Let us discuss this further when we have made it to the end?" The group agreed and fell silent, listening for any Mobs that might be creeping towards them.

This floor seemed to be the most affected by recent changes. The blue light that permeated the dungeon was brighter here, allowing for a greater range of vision. The Goblins they saw off in the distance seemed to be industriously moving about, and the drone of insects filled the fairly humid air. Adam flinched when a finch flew past him, barely an inch worth of space between him and its suddenly flapping wings.

The others chortled at Adam when he was alarmed but increased their vigilance accordingly. If that bird had been a hostile Mob, Adam could be dead right now. They walked across lush grass, a nice change from the hard stone floors. There seemed to be paths to follow, but only a moron would happily walk an unknown trail that seemed 'safe' in a dungeon. Being so wary was tiring, and the group was also getting hungry. Still moving cautiously, they stopped at a raspberry bush, and Hans checked the conglomerate fruit for poison.

"The fruit is fine," Hans declared after a moment of inspection, "but the thorns have a nasty, subtle poison. It is a contact poison that seems to mimic a potent sleep potion. One touch and you will not be able to keep your eyes open. You don't even need to get stabbed, just brushing past it will knock you out."

"Can you safely cut off a sprig of it and put it in the bag?" Dale anxiously requested, staring at the juicy-looking raspberries. "I should have eaten more this morning."

"I have a lifetime's experience handling poisons. A little plant like this isn't going to be enough to–" Hans yelped as the vines of the plant swung at him. He easily dodged the fibrous assault and glared at the offending, innocent-looking plant. Hans drew and threw a knife, easily cutting down the entire bush with a single attack. The sap that poured out was similar to blood in its consistency, making them question whether this was actually a plant, an animal, or a hybrid of some kind.

"Oh, take two of these things! We can turn this in as an uncategorized Mob to the Guild for a reward!" Rose brightly reminded them.

"Nice!"

Feeling a bit better about their assured payday, they formed into their usual formation and began cautiously picking their way through the area.

"We need to collect some Goblins as well," Tom reminded them as they passed another half-hexagon fortification. He lifted his warhammer. "Anyone opposed to the... direct option?"

"We may as well call it the 'Tom option' at this point." Rose grinned and limbered her bow.

"One moment," Dale called as he pulled a Core out of his pocket. He wrapped it in the cursed cloth of his gauntlet and shattered it. *Bamph!* As Essence raged into him, he took a sharp breath through his nose and shuddered. Dale groaned as he shook the broken shards from his palm. "Oh-h-h, that feels amazing." He opened his now-glowing eyes and grinned at the people staring at him.

Hans cleared his throat. "You know, I've met a lot of drug addicts..."

"You can't get addicted to cultivating!" Dale exclaimed indignantly, looking around for support as the others pointedly looked away.

"I'm not so sure. Feels good, gives you a rush, costs a *lot* of money, and makes you want more?" Hans' eyebrow bounced a few times. "Any of these sounding familiar?"

"Maybe I don't do this so often. Fine," Dale grumbled with a blush.

"What are you doing with all the stored corruption, anyway?" Rose prodded him, hoping for an answer to issues she was having.

Dale's mouth opened and closed a few times as he tried to think of a good lie. The silence stretched long enough that he was forced to tell the truth. "It gets separated into... other Cores?" He grinned weakly, preparing himself for the ramifications of explaining his good fortune.

"...Cheater!" Hans choked on his own words. "You mean to tell me you don't need to refine your Essence? You just *gulp* it down like a Dwarf at an open bar and go on your merry way?"

Dale looked at the incredulous, glaring faces around him. "Well, I mean... I still refine it! I still have to hold the cultivation pattern and..."

"Hey, dungeon! Can I get one of those?!" Hans started shouting at the ceiling. "Don't ignore me, you giant hunk of rock! I'll say nice things about you to other people!"

<Oh abyss yeah, he can!> I spoke into Dale's mind. <All he needs to do is be *ju-u-st* about dead and start to dissolve his aura or swear a binding oath to me!>

Dale coughed. "Sorry, Hans, it isn't possible. There were extenuating circumstances for me."

<Oh, you rat bastard.>

"Ah, it was worth a shot." Hans clutched at his chest in fake distress. "Well, let's go take out our sorrows on those unsuspecting Goblins."

CHAPTER TEN

"So what happens now, Great One?" Bob needled as he dropped a light-potion-covered stone into the deepening hole. It dropped for a long while, then was torn apart as it finally found the whirling disk that the ritual had created.

<That's a good question, Bob.> I 'inhaled' deeply as I thought about how to answer. <I have a series of priorities that I feel are my best option for completing the long-term goals I'm after, but I am unsure which way I should tackle them.>

"Perhaps talking about it is the best way to decide?" Bob gently offered an ear.

I mentally nodded and verbally acquiesced, <You are probably right.> I gathered my thoughts and began speaking, <Well, rescuing Dani is, of course, my only *real* priority, but I feel there are other things that I need to do in order to make this happen. I need to find her. In just as difficult of a proposition, I then need to *get* to her or have someone else do so. I know she is still alive because I can feel a trickle of Essence flowing to her from my aura. I don't know if it is *reaching* her or just draining into the world, and I can't follow the trail of it because my aura is too diffuse outside of my dungeon.>

"That is what the... bugs... were for though, correct?" Bob chipped away at my mounting frustration with this comment.

I took a deep, calming, mental breath. <Yes, hopefully, the bugs can follow that trail to her. I heard a story about a fish that can follow a single drop of blood in miles of water; I hope I made my bugs to at least that equivalent.> I paused a moment, wistfully reminiscing about my Wisp.

<Hopefully, finding her is being taken care of as we speak. Next, getting to her or getting *someone* to her. I have plans for both of these possibilities. There are only two people I trust to get to her besides myself. Dale or Minya. Dale is too weak; he wouldn't survive even a moment against truly powerful people, and they *must* be powerful, or Dani would have returned to me by now. I will send Minya as soon as I have a location, but I really don't know what she is capable of.>

Bob had gotten quiet. "You do not trust anyone else? Perhaps... a Goblin you may know?"

<Don't belittle yourself, Bob.> I snorted as I realized he was now thinking I didn't trust him. <The changes I made to your bodies... they were more extreme than you seem to realize. You now need a fairly dense amount of Essence just to survive for any length of time, and I don't know how we could make that happen for you. You can leave the dungeon, but you will need to make fairly frequent trips back here to live.>

"I see." Bob dipped his head in thought. "Thank you for telling me."

<I *do* trust you,> I assured him, just to be clear about it. He smiled faintly in reply, not saying anything aloud. <Bob, if they can't get to Dani, or they dither and take too much time, *I* am going to go.>

Bob had a nonplussed look on his face. "But... if you leave, the dungeon will die. You will need to refill it with your influence again, and you will be much weakened!"

<That is why I plan to take the dungeon with me,> I settled the conversation grimly. His face was even more bewildered at this information. <Bob, what would you say if I told you that I am making all these changes to the dungeon in order to make myself lighter? What if I told you that I am planning to fly?>

Bob had a look on his face that I *assumed* meant he doubted my ability to make myself fly. That or a disparaging comment about my sanity. He opened his mouth to say something, but luckily, a phrase on the peripherals of my thoughts caught my attention.

<One second, Bob. An interesting business opportunity has come up,> I told my favorite Goblin. I focused on Dale and *pushed* my thoughts at him. Ever since he had set up mental defenses—and actually gotten good at them—I had needed to work to project my thoughts at him. I was careful to never tell him this. If he knew I was using his defenses against him, he may lower those defenses a bit. Then I couldn't have private conversations while he was around anymore!

<Oh abyss yeah, he can!> I spoke into Dale's mind. <All he needs to do is be *ju-u-st* about dead or swear a binding oath to me!>

Dale then blatantly lied to his teammate about what I told him.

<Oh, you rat bastard,> I called at him, pretending to go silent again. <Dale! Dale. Can you hear me? Hellooo. Okay, back to you, Bob.>

Bob was still looking stunned. "You are going to learn how to *fly?*"

<No, no, I already know *how* to fly. It is just falling with style, after all. What I really need to figure out is how to make the dungeon float and move around while under my control,> I cautiously explained, not wanting to ruin the surprise. <I don't want my movements to be dictated by whichever breeze is strongest that day.>

Bob seemed a bit out of it this morning. He blinked blearily before responding. "That seems... difficult."

<You are correct; it *will* be difficult. I'm not going to lie, the other options seem more feasible. Letting someone else do the traveling feels like the dungeony thing to do, in all reality. But this comes with a fringe benefit. I've always wanted to travel,> I admitted bitterly. The full truth was that I had wanted to travel with *Dani*.

Bob smiled. "Ah, yes. Travel the world, see the sights..."

<Absorb objects from faraway lands...> I agreed dreamily. I shook myself, knocking a few unprepared people off their feet. <I am on the cusp of reaching the B-ranks, but I have been putting it off. I want to build the next level of the dungeon as a defensive layer while I work on breaking through to the Mage ranks, but I just have no idea how much time remains before something bad happens. What if something terrible is done to Dani. What if I am too late to save her?>

"Well, Great One... may I speak freely?" Bob seemed to be psyching himself up. That or hyperventilating. "I must warn you, you won't like what I have to say."

<Uh. Yes. Of course, Bob. Go ahead.>

"You are kind of being a... whiny little toad," Bob announced as soon as he got permission. I released a sharp gasp of bewilderment. "You hold the power of creation, life, and death! You can create stone from air and fire from water! You plan to make a mountain *fly*, for abyss sake! Now you are allowing yourself to be held up by '*what ifs*'? No! You enter the Mage ranks! You *become* powerful enough to shake the heavens! And, blast it, you go rescue your Wisp!"

Bob was glaring around him, looking for a focal point. Deciding that I was the wall, he jabbed a finger at the granite. "Do you understand me?"

<I do!> I yelped in consternation. Then I went silent. <Thanks, Bob. I may have needed that,> I admitted ruefully.

"Everyone needs tough love sometimes." He smirked as he leaned on his staff. "Even overpowered rocks, apparently."

<Hey, maybe I was just a whiny brat in my past life.> We both chuckled at that as I began coalescing my power. Bob hurriedly walked back to his fort. <There is no rush. It will take a week for me to even begin to ascend.>

Bob slowed down. "You will need to teach me how to reach the Mage ranks someday."

<I look forward to it!> I let him leave as I started rearranging my short and long-term goals. I felt like I had my purpose back, a direction in life! Reaching for the Mage rankings would leave me potentially defenseless while my mind expanded, so I needed to set up the dungeon to survive without my guidance for a few weeks.

Sealing off my doors would still work, potentially, but I felt like it would be a bad idea now. The last time I had done so, it had only been for a few days. A few weeks? Ha! Being the impatient creatures that they were, I was sure that some annoying human would decide that they 'needed' to get some money. There were ways to get in if they *really* felt the need to do so. Most of those ways involved direct damage to me, so no thank you.

My guardians needed to stay strong and plentiful. To this end, I needed to create a template for their pattern that didn't rely on my influence. Currently, I had my aura mimicking their pattern and absorbing ambient Essence to create young versions. That would soon be impossible because I was fully removing my aura from the area, albeit temporarily.

I pondered this issue for a while but finally decided on a course of action. If Cores could be modified to hold memories, why couldn't I use them for other things? I created the pattern needed to generate a Basher and pushed it into a Core. Happily, it seemed to successfully etch itself into the interior of the gem! Good, all is well... I poured Essence into the template. The Core stored the power for a moment, filled with blood, and exploded!

<Oh, for... ugh. Why didn't that work?> I retried, forming the pattern again. I watched from the interior of the Core as Essence flooded into it. Ah, there is the issue! The Core exploded again, making me yelp from the unexpected demolition. I chuckled apprehensively; I had forgotten to cut off the flow of Essence.

When I was using my aura to create items or creatures, they were created on the spot, right in the center of the template. Putting the pattern in a Core was essentially an attempt to do the same thing. Unfortunately, generating something *inside* another thing didn't really work. There were space requirements after all, and two things cannot occupy the same area at the same time. The Essence was flowing in, activating the pattern, and creating something simultaneously. I needed to find a way to change that.

Would it be as easy as adding an Essence output Rune? *Paff!* Nope, it exploded again. What if I added more Essence at once? *P-PAFF!* Drat, just a larger explosion. What if I tried... Hold on a moment, I have an idea! There was a type of technique that Dwarves had created, an illusionary projection they used to design models before building them. They used this for many things: buildings, weapons, armor. What if I did something similar?

It took the better part of the day, and the only thing that caught my attention in this time was Dale's group fighting Snowball to a standstill. My massive fourth-floor Boss was hesitant about dying, and if it took too much damage, it would retreat into the deep steamy areas of its territory to heal. Hans was complaining about the lost profit potential. Heh. If you really wanted a trophy, you should have killed faster! Smelly humans. I made a rock fall on them, and Tom got a nasty cut on his head.

My experiments came to fruition, and I looked at the ungainly system I had put in place. A sprawling ritual covered a ten-foot span, and a dozen utility Runes were spaced equidistantly around the ritual diagram. Sympathetic links connected all of them, some of the Runes connecting to up to eight points at a time. Even though it was a giant mess, it worked in a fairly straightforward manner. The Mob I wanted to spawn would have its pattern recorded in the Core. This Core was then placed in a socket in the exact center of the diagram.

When the first Rune was activated, it would make a replica of the Core suspended in the air. This replica would slowly spin, helping to maintain the illusion. For some reason, if it didn't move, the image would begin to distort and warp. This Rune was followed by another that was a... well, the best way to describe it would be a representation of time. It was a constant switchback of Essence—a maze of sorts—that slowed down the flow of power and would allow an interval between Mob spawns. Roughly ten minutes after the ritual completed, it would begin again. This meant that a Basher was made almost every ten minutes exactly. Cats were made every twenty-five, and Goblins could be done in about forty. My only explanation for the discrepancy was that perhaps sentient creatures were harder to make than animals.

The next Rune limited the Essence that would go into the process, or else a single Mob could be continuously pumped full of power. Usually, this would create... erm... really *fun* to see fatalities? The kind that used to make Dani leave the experiment room gagging. Was it common knowledge that a drop of blood caught in an Essence stream would make an erythrocyte swell to the size of a watermelon? This is what I imagine blood cells in continent-sized monsters would look like. Very squishy. Hmm... I might have to drop one of these on Hans, just to see his reaction.

After a quick chuckle at my evil thoughts, I inspected the next Runes. A stabilizing Rune to keep the pattern intact, a containment one to force it to follow the pattern, then size, shape, and control Runes. Looks correct now... All that was left was to activate it! Here we go! Essence flowed in, following the symbolic links. Good, good, the image is taking the Essence, the shape Rune is activ–

EEeeeiiieeEEEiiiEEE!

I blinked, trying to see through the haze and distortion of frantically twisting Essence. Rock dust was thick in the air, and my sense of hearing seemed to be damaged. All I could hear was a high-pitched noise. I moved the main part of my consciousness out of the twisted distortions of Essence, and all of my senses were instantly restored. I didn't use the same type of easily damaged sensory organs that humans did, after all. Mine were attuned to the flows of my aura. I looked at the twisting confluence of Essence and corruption, and the damage to the rest of the area.

The stone for forty feet in all directions had been fragmentized, a blast comparable to B-rank zero cultivators intentionally shattering their Center. There were a few screams that drifted into the open air above the room; the weakened ceiling had collapsed, dropping a few unsuspecting humans through the unexpected hole. Heh, that'd be a good trap name. Pitfall? Nah, 'unexpected hole'! It seemed that the falling humans had been non-cultivators, as none of them survived the measly fortyish foot drop.

I quickly extended my influence upward, gaining control over an area that reached all the way to the surface! Who said good things can't come from failure? I patched the open area, quickly weaving it shut so that more humans couldn't gain easy access where they weren't allowed. Crisis averted. I worked my mind into the tumultuous energy in the room and brought it under my control. It took a minute, but the Essence was quickly re-integrated into my aura. A few minutes later, I had recreated walls and a ceiling, filling in the spherical emptiness that had resulted from my failed ritual.

<Ugh, it's like I'm violating the laws of nature or something,> I grumbled to myself. <Ah well. Who's gonna stop me?> I quietly snickered at the joke no one else would understand.

It took me an hour to reset and redraw the ritual, and I griped at the lost time as I inspected the diagram. I think I found the issue, though. The 'control' Rune needed to be activated before a few of the others. The segment that contained that portion would generate a fault in the links if it was referenced last, so I placed it before the 'follow pattern' portion. Hopefully, this would allow me to avoid a segmentation fault, but I didn't know for sure. I really wasn't able to gain any useful information from the last one; the diagram had just blown up without any warning.

Ritual adjusted, I began the process again. I winced as Essence entered the 'shape' Rune, but the ritual stayed stable this time! There was a charge building in the air, enough to make a human's hair stand on end. With a *pop*, the Essence compressed like an imploding bubble, and a Basher fell to the floor! Sure it broke a leg, but it worked! You would think a second-old Mob would have better instincts for landing while falling, but I guess not everyone was perfect.

I exchanged the Basher pattern Core with an Impaler pattern and repeated the process. Sure enough, it worked as well! It failed for a Cat, but after a few minutes of dumbfounded rage, I found that the Essence provided wasn't enough to create this type of Mob. I allowed more to flow, and a mewling kitten appeared.

<Works for me!> I happily created side rooms on each level that were well hidden and set up the rituals in them. To avoid having to personally power them, I assigned a version of Bob to each room. He would exchange the Cores powering the ritual whenever they ran out of Essence as well as the corruption that was needed for more specialized Mobs. The whole process took two days, but I think it was worth the investment. Seeing as there were other regular tasks that required a sizeable portion of my attention, in the future, I would only have to momentarily check in to ensure all was running smoothly!

I set up a ritual above each treasure chest which allowed for an exchange of tokens and created a large variation of the wooden coins. The ritual would stay one step from completion, and the token would focus the Essence into the configuration of the reward like Cores were currently doing for Mobs.

This led to the problem of how to distribute rewards, the part that I was the most excited about. The Mobs that were killed in an area now had a certain... *weight* to them. When they were killed, their Essence would have a numerical value associated with it, which would, in turn, affect the nearest non-hidden chest. The longer the chest went without being opened, the more valuable the tokens inside would become. As long as Mobs died nearby, that is.

If the group opening the chest had gone past a certain threshold of 'weight' to their kills in the area, there would be more tokens. This was a complicated process to automate, but I couldn't expect a Goblin to go around putting presents in boxes. Even if they stocked them from below, some cultivators were *fast.* I would become a laughingstock if someone noticed a

Goblin's hand dropping tokens through a hole in the back of a chest. Hopefully, no one would catch on to the system and find a way to abuse it. I couldn't think of everything so I would need to make adjustments on the fly!

The reward system took another day to perfect, leaving me just four days before I would attempt to ascend. A stray thought crossed my mind—what has Dale been up to for the last few days?

CHAPTER ELEVEN

"Ugh. Stupid Cat. Why did it have to run off?" Hans grumbled impatiently. "Now I have to stand guard while these munchkins cultivate on the off chance that a giant Cat is sneaking up on us." He let out a long-suffering sigh.

"Oh, woe is you-u-u," Rose sang softly, making the others snort. They were all sitting with their eyes closed, greedily absorbing the Essence of the heavens and the earth. This area next to the Silverwood tree was filled with enough Essence that it physically affected them when they walked in. Like strolling through a warm mist in the early morning with a lover, they felt both cleansed and joyful.

They were the only people in the area as far as they knew. Now, there were a few Dark Elves guarding the tree that they *didn't* know about. So long as they didn't try to damage the tree, Dale's group wouldn't ever know about the guards. The party sat quite a distance from each other so they could cultivate without disturbing the Essence around the other members of their team.

Anywhere else in the dungeon, Dale and Rose's cultivation would draw complaints from other people. Simply put, they took in so much Essence that they were able to deplete the area temporarily. Here, they both had their affinity channels opened to the maximum, and there was barely a tremor in the air around them. With every breath, they pulled in purified Essence along with oxygen, allowing Essence to travel unaided through their systems.

Dale began grimacing as he tried to wrangle the new mass of Essence that was flowing into his Core. It was unruly, and he was having trouble making the spinning Essence into Chi threads thin enough to not disrupt his Chi spiral. To his great annoyance, he had to cultivate in short spurts, stopping and starting constantly as he pulled at the strings.

Rose was drinking in huge amounts of Essence as well, but her body was trying to pull it away from her Center to use for its own purposes. Twenty years of being unable to cultivate had made her body damaged, and the repairs were taking far longer than she wanted. Her cells—like everyone else's—pulled Essence specifically into the powerhouse—the mitochondria—which allowed her to become stronger at a cellular level. Being starved for Essence for so long, they tried to take more than they needed. If she didn't carefully regulate her cultivation, her body would literally fight itself for greater access to the life-giving power.

For differing reasons, the two of them both muttered the same phrase, "This is so annoying!" causing them to look up in surprise and guffaw at the coincidence.

Hans rolled his eyes and took a few moments to inspect the others. His student, Tom, was sweating profusely as he struggled to surpass his previous limits. The amount of fire corruption in his Center was already making it difficult for him to progress, so Hans made a mental note to be stricter with his training regimen in the near future.

Adam was cultivating with a serene expression on his face, and the light in the room coupled with his pure white robe made a halo of brilliance radiate near his head. The celestial corruption in Adam was at a point where it should have been lethal, yet it didn't seem to be having an overly detrimental effect on him. Hans shrugged. Only time would tell for sure.

Eventually, Tom stood up, looking nauseous. He waved to Hans, who correctly took the gesture to mean that Tom had absorbed as much Essence as his body could handle and would be taking over the guard duty.

"Thanks!" Hans collapsed to the floor and began greedily absorbing the abundant Essence in the air while writhing around. Unlike the others, he was an intentionally *loud* cultivator. "*Uhhhhhgh.* This feels *so* good. Oh, yeah, fill my affinity channels." His antics always made Rose scowl and the others laugh.

It took about an hour for the entire group to finally admit defeat. There were legends of people that could continuously cultivate for years at a time, but the reality was that too much Essence for long periods could permanently damage the meridians—damage similar to having lightning traveling through your body. Literally, for some cultivators. Short bursts were possible, but there is only so much of a foreign substance that the body could quickly turn to its own use. This is why cultivation techniques that allowed for large amounts of Essence to be held were so sought after; if you had as much as you could handle, you could 'store' the Essence in a holding pattern, slowly adding it to your Chi spiral. Dale would have had one if he hadn't lost it to his gauntlet. A frown crossed his face at the memory.

The intrepid adventurers stood, stretching and limbering up happily. Each of them felt that they had made good progress for the day and was excited to enjoy a night of relaxation. As they were leaving, they used their tokens at the exchange chest. Their earlier suppositions seemed to hold true, as silver tokens from the third floor turned into gold bars, and average-looking weapon tokens released minor Inscribed weapons. Each of them was using a weapon more suited to them than what they found, so they happily made plans to split the profit that selling them would bring.

"Do we even *know* anyone that uses a halberd?" Hans scoffed after he pulled a large polearm from the chest. "These things are basically useless in a dungeon! Half the time the tunnels are so narrow..."

Tom looked at the long weapon. "I think that would be an acceptable weapon in here. Why is it such a disagreeable armament?"

"Pff! This dungeon is an outlier!" Hans jeered, twirling the shaft of the halberd in his palm. "Most dungeons really make you work to even stand up straight. None of you believe me, I can tell. There is definitely something different about this place though. Smart Mobs, *fortifications*," he spat the word in disgust, "and now an ecosystem? You don't normally see things like this in a dungeon below the A-rankings."

"Is it really that different than the norm?" Dale inquired as he walked.

Hans bobbed his head. "Yeah, it's special all right. Prolly why Frank has been so shitty toward you in the last few months."

"What do you mean?" Dale asked as they started moving toward the exit portal.

Hans glanced at him with a smirk, which died as he saw that Dale was serious. "Really? The backstabbing in council meetings, the constant attempts to get more control, the plans to eke every last copper he can get out of you?"

Dale shrugged. "Seemed like just a Mage thing. You know, loss of touch with non-Mages, general snobbery, and sense of entitlement?"

Hans nodded. "All true, yes. Frank, though, he's a good egg. Just been under a lot of pressure recently, and you know what happens when eggs are under too much pressure, right?"

"Ahm." Dale paused, thinking it was a rhetorical question. "They crack?"

"They crack!" Hans shouted in agreement. "Yeah. Frank is just the leader of *this* branch of the Adventurers' Guild. The main headquarters has been getting numerous requests from other Guild Leaders to replace Frank as the main leader for the area. So, Frank had to show that he was making strong inroads into cash flow, influencing the area, and creating strong connections overall."

"How do you know all of this?" Dale prodded his friend with a stiff finger. "I know you are on good terms with him, but it is surprising that he'd tell you all of this."

"Huh? He doesn't *tell* me these things!" Hans looked affronted. "The walls of a tent are just really thin, and his voice tends to carry if the wind is *ju-u-ust* right." Hans grinned and made a gesture and was lifted off his feet by a burst of swirling air.

Dale laughed at Hans' antics "You are so–" *Wham!* Dale was thrown into the air as a staff came out of seemingly nowhere and hit his lower legs from the side. The staff whipped around and slammed him into the ground hard enough to make him bounce.

"Situational awareness, you stupid *twit.*" his Moon Elf instructor screamed down at Dale's groaning figure before vanishing into thin air.

Dead silence reigned for a moment as Dale slowly got to his feet. He coughed into his hand, a bit of blood flecked the spittle. He had bitten into his tongue as he hit the ground. "Oh, right. Hey guys, my combat instructor will be testing me constantly now. So. Ya-a-ay," he finished weakly. Luckily, he had progressed in his cultivation to the degree he had. A year ago, that strike would have broken his ribs at the *least.*

"*That's* how you've been training?!" Rose gasped into the quiet. "With *him?* But! But! He *hates* humans!"

"It shows." Tom crossed his arms and nodded as if he had spoken a great truth.

"He's still here. Don't say anything you will regret." Adam gestured at a corner they were approaching. The Elf reappeared, pointing a dagger-like finger at the cleric.

"You will *not* give away my position in the future, or I will consider you a hindrance to my training methods." The Elf glowered at Adam before vanishing. "This training is not for *you*, but I could *include* you."

"Sorry, Dale. You're on your own." Adam grimaced as a chill went down his spine. "It's too bad. I really liked you."

"Don't talk about me like I'm already dead. Just get me through the portal," Dale whispered nervously, eyes darting around. He didn't know it, but this type of encroaching paranoia was exactly what the Elf wanted to see. The group stepped through the portal into a cluster of people waiting expectantly on the other side.

"Dale! About time! We were just going to send a party in to seek you out," Frank spoke in a frazzled, angry voice.

Dale looked at him with slightly unfocused eyes. "Oh. Hey, Frank. What's the matter?"

High Magous Amber strode forward. "It seems that a delegation from multiple Kingdoms and races arrived all at the same time today. This wasn't planned, and tensions are high as we try to find suitable accommodations for all of them."

Dale's gaze sharpened, and a dark look passed over his face. "Are they causing issues?"

Frank shook his head wearily. "Not as such; it is more that their presence is *going* to cause issues. We have a group of High Elves, a Dwarven delegation from the Stoneheart Mountain Kingdom, and Amazons from the Tigress Queendom."

"I'm guessing they all want something from us?" Dale looked at the sunken eyes of the Guild Leader. "Hey, Frank? You know that I won't accept a replacement for you from the Guild, right? I trust you to do the right thing, and I wouldn't know the motivations of a different person. Take it easy."

Frank was so surprised that he couldn't find any words to say. He tried a few times, then simply nodded and seemed to relax a bit. "Thanks. Means a lot," he finally voiced gruffly.

"We still have an issue, people," Amber prodded them tersely. "What is your play on this? Should we make them wait? Make them find their own accommodations? Or act the part of the generous host and entertain them?"

Dale's brow furrowed as he tried to precisely recall what the correct protocol for this type of situation would be. Luckily, the court etiquette memory stone he had received from the Dark Elves covered this sort of thing. Well, for all races other than the High Elves. Somehow, he didn't think kicking them out without a word would be a good move politically, so he ignored that advice.

"Give them two hours to make ready. Have a human guard show them to the bathhouse and pay the tab if they choose to use it. Show them to the Pleasure House and do the same. We need to treat them as foreign dignitaries, at least until they show a direct threat to us or tell us what they want. *Then* we can gracefully boot them out if they become an issue," Dale finally issued the orders. He turned to Tyler, the only non-cultivator on the council. "I'll get cleaned up and put on those clothes you forced me to buy."

Tyler smirked. "Aren't you glad you listened?"

"Yeah, yeah," Dale grouched. He looked at his team. "Sorry, all. Duty calls and all that."

Rose's eyebrow twitched. "You'd better not forget about that 'talk' you promised us."

Tom had been uncharacteristically quiet but seemed to find his voice, "Dale, I think I may join you for this."

Most of the people were surprised by this statement. Tom was well known for his hatred of meetings. Dale simply looked at him, and Tom shrugged. "I have my reasons."

"Go get cleaned up then," Dale conceded, cracking a smile. "Can't have you smelling like rotting animal in an enclosed area like the council room!"

They all parted ways, and Dale hurried off to bathe and prepare himself. The wind had picked up, and the driving snow was impeding his mobility a bit. Only slipping once, he got to the bathhouse and quickly paid a full silver for the privilege of skipping the line and getting a hot bath. As he disrobed and sank into the heated, scented water, he sighed in contentment when his bruises and sore muscles began to be soothed.

He didn't have *too* long, but he figured that he could spend a good quarter of an hour here. Thoughts of the day were spinning in his mind. He replayed his use of the earth shattering technique, trying to figure out what he had done wrong in his battle with Raile. Dale closed his eyes and extended a string of Essence into his surroundings, working with it in an attempt to get better at controlling Essence outside of his body.

Surprisingly, his Essence moved through the water easily. Dale looped the string a few times, and in a moment, there were small waves flowing away from him. He felt like he was swinging a rope lasso, and the pattern of waves seemed to reflect that. He chuckled and watched the moving water, only to see the waves break against seemingly nothing a few feet from him.

Confused for only a moment, his eyes widened, and he gulped. "Uhm. Teacher?" His eyes remained locked on the empty space. His Moon Elf teacher appeared in the large pool of water, a bitter smile on his face.

"Pure luck. You brat." He vanished again, and Dale watched as ripples of water followed an unseen form to the edge of the pool. The door opened and closed by itself. Dale held his bare knees and rocked back and forth while taking deep breaths.

He slowly stopped panicking and continued experimenting with his Essence. Dale was surprised at how easily the water seemed to react to his extended Chi thread as he was used to having to force earth and stone to do what he wanted. Curiosity overcoming common sense, he stood up and looped his Essence in the pattern needed for the earth shattering technique. Instead of passing the thread of power through his earth affinity channels, he went through his water channels. Unbeknownst to him, doing this caused the thread to pass through the Core in his body that accumulated water corruption. He completed the technique, and as Dale forced the Essence back to himself, a detonation of water shot as a geyser to the ceiling!

Shocked, Dale almost didn't re-absorb the partially used Essence. He barely remembered to control it as it slammed into him, his mind enthralled at the water pouring like rain from the wood above him. The door to the room slammed open as a guard rushed in.

"My Lord!" the guard called frantically. "Are you safe..." he trailed off as he noticed Dale standing in an odd position in the bath, nude but for the gauntlets on his hands. A drop of water landed on the guard's nose, causing him to sputter and take in the whole scene.

"I was... um. I was testing something," Dale managed to say as he quickly turned red from embarrassment. Nearly half the pool of water had been emptied. "It. Ahhh. It worked."

"I... I see." The guard backed out of the room. "There is a Mage impatiently waiting for you in the entrance room. I'll let the attendants know that they may need to... draw some water for this bath." He gently closed the door.

CHAPTER TWELVE

Smashing a Core in his hand and instantly feeling more alert, Dale strolled into the church. The amphitheater had become the standard gathering place, as it was currently the only place large enough to allow for the residents of the area to listen and participate in council meetings. Several tables had been set together to form a single large table, specially placed for this occasion. There were many people that had arrived today, and the meeting had a far higher attendance than usual. The raised seating of the amphitheater was filled with various groups of scribes who sat with quills poised, eagerly awaiting the discussions and negotiations that would be taking place.

The angry muttering that had filled the area quieted a bit when the City Lord entered, but the noise was not fully silenced. Appraising looks were turned on the outwardly calm human striding toward the head of the table. A few, looking at his contained Essence density and therefore his ranking, snorted and crossed their arms. Others wore stiff smiles, while a few looked outright hostile. When he sat down at the head of the table, a golden-haired human huffed and sat forward.

"Where is the woman in charge?" she demanded aggressively. Dale looked at her calmly, his eyes flashing an electric silver-blue as he assessed her ranking. A high C-rank, either eight or nine. He was still getting used to this process and hadn't perfected his abilities.

"No woman is in charge. We do have several on the council, but the final decision on all legal matters is mine," Dale calmly stated with an attempt at a professional smile in the face of her scowl. "There isn't even anyone in the shadows pulling the strings either. I'm not married."

"How do you *ever* get things done?" She snorted rudely, looking at the others in her delegation with mirth. "This is ridiculous. A man can't be in charge. We should go."

Madame Chandra, who had been silent to this point, cleared her throat. "I assure you, it is no joke. Baron Dale has taken great strides forward in his ability to be a good leader. He works harder than anyone I know, he trains in the harshest but most rewarding ways, and his efforts to rebuild after the recent 'Wailing War' have been immensely successful. Notice how our little town has buildings? Walls? All but the church were a pile of rubble or scorched leavings a month ago, and even the church needed significant repairs."

The Amazonian tensed as she looked closely at Chandra. "Ah, the betrayer of womankind, the herald of necromantic war, Madame Chandra the Dark Valkyrie. Taught any necromancers to hate women recently? Shown them how to cultivate? Kill off a city of defenseless children?"

"Pah, the only impressive thing I've seen here is this quartz we are standing on!" a Dwarf spoke into the outraged silence. "I've never seen quartz this clear and colorless before, and if I'm not mistaken, the whole thing is Inscribed!"

"You should have seen it a little over a month ago." Dale wryly chuckled, more than happy to change the subject. "This used to be *celestial* quartz. It was shattered in the attack, though."

"Got any left?" The Dwarf grinned, rubbing his hands together in an obviously joking manner.

"Is this what you all came here to discuss? Merchant business? Not so much? Did you come to deliver insults as *representatives* of your people?" Frank spoke over the sudden increase in noise. "No? Then we will speak in order of when you arrived. High Elves, you will go first, then the delegation from the Tigress Kingdom, then the Dwarves."

"The Tigress *Queendom,* you ignorant, inbred oaf!" the golden-haired beauty sneered.

Chandra barked a laugh at her, "Ha! That's funny, an *Amazon* calling someone *else* inbred! If your people were any *more* inbred, you'd all be sandwiches!"

"Enough!" Frank bellowed, slamming his hand on to the table. "Elves! You got here first! State your reasons for attending this meeting. Please!"

"If I knew we would be allowed to speak based on travel time... ah, drat these short legs." The Dwarf sighed with a long-suffering look on his face and winked at Dale.

Dale leaned forward before the Elves could speak. His tone remained mild as he addressed the Amazons, "That will be enough of that, Miss. Another insult and you will be escorted off my land. I am building a meritorious society here. Anyone who has the skills needed to perform a task better than others will rise. Male or female. Human or otherwise. Elder or child. Cultivator or not. Please try to respect that." He sat back, ignoring the glare she was sending his way. "High Elves, thank you for coming here. How can we work together to reach a mutually beneficial friendship?"

"What a *lovely* way to start the conversation!" A male Elf leaned forward, flashing a beautiful smile. "As a matter of fact, we have arrived because we heard about a heavily propagated rumor that a Silverwood tree was in the area?" His eyes held no hint of anything but happiness as he was speaking.

Dale nodded, having assumed that was the reason they were there. "A Silverwood tree is indeed growing within the dungeon below." His bold claim made the Elves nearly dance with glee as they broke into excited chatter. The main Elf smiled beneficently and asked, "What would we need to do for you in order to have access to this lovely specimen?"

"Unfortunately, that small detail is not within my purview." A deep breath escaped Dale's lips. He wasn't looking forward to this next part. "I have an exclusive agreement with the Dark Elves. If you want access to the tree itself, you will need to talk to them."

"*What?!*" The joyful face twisted into a hateful mask. "The Darkies? You went to *them*?"

"*They* came to *me*," Dale calmly replied as the High Elf seemed to be having a breakdown.

"Y-you can't trust *Darkies!*" the Elf sputtered caustically. "They are little better than mercenaries! They will break an agreement as soon as it is more beneficial for them to do so! As a matter of fact, they completely stopped all contracts with us in the last few..." His voice trailed off as a look of realization appeared on his face. He continued weakly, head held in his hands, "Of course they did. They have no need for access to our trees anymore... You have no idea what you've done. Idiot human!"

Having obviously waited until this announcement, the Dark Elf princess, Brianna, strode into the room smugly. "He basically freed us from the position of little better than barely-tolerated slaves?" She sat in the only empty council chair. "Dale doesn't need to worry about betrayal. *I* was the one to sign the Mana contract we agreed upon."

The High Elves stood. "Well," the speaker spoke pseudo-sadly, "I do hope the next person in charge of this area will be more inclined toward intelligent contract agreements." With that thinly veiled threat delivered, the group started to leave the room.

"Ah. Planning to have me killed off?" Dale plainly and boldly questioned.

"Unfortunate accidents happen to humans all the time." The Elf shrugged carelessly. "Best of luck in the coming days... hours... whatever you have remaining."

"You would do well to realize *exactly* who you are threatening," Brianna stated in a bored tone. "Dale here is a landed Baron in *both* the Lion and the Phoenix Kingdoms, and a *Duke* of the Huine nation. Attacking him would start a *very* large scale war against the High Elves."

The group leaving slowed, looking at each other. They grudgingly walked back to their seats and sat down. The main Elf—frowning—opened his mouth, but Dale cut him off with a slice of his hand, "Nope, your turn is over for now. Amazons?"

"We heard that there was clean Essence and powerful weapons in the dungeon. We want access." The spokeswoman jumped directly into conversation, ignoring the annoyed squawk from the Elf.

Frank coughed into his hand, eyes lighting up. "Are you registered with the Guild?"

She shook her head sharply. "Sign on to a Guild run by *men*? Please. What would be the point? Get drooled on by cattle as we walk around in tight leather armor?"

Tyler took over, as business and taxes was his area of expertise. "For non-Guild affiliated parties, the tax rate is currently twenty percent. For a foreign group such as yourselves, there is a ten percent rate that you must pay directly to Lord Dale's personal account. There is also an export tax of fifteen percent for *both* the Lion and Phoenix Kingdoms. Though Dale is a Duke of the Dark elves, they have no authority to claim taxes, else it may be higher." Dale was startled at the amounts stated; he had no idea it would cost them that much to go into the dungeon.

Apparently, neither had the Amazon. "Y-you want us to pay a *sixty percent tribute* of the goods we collect in the dungeon?"

"And I will require a *binding* Mana contract to that effect," Tyler finished cheerfully. His eyes were alight, and he was happily thinking of ways to invest the money they would bring to the city. Maybe Dale could finally get his city-run bathhouse. The lady tried to argue, but her attempts at negotiation met only stony yet merry resistance.

Having failed completely to get concessions, the Amazonian ground her teeth, leaned back, and nodded. "Fine. Expect trainees to arrive at the start of the week. We'll get your contract signed, even if it is an abyssal deal."

"To the Dwarves!" Dale spoke with gusto, pointing at the stout people and moving the meeting along before tempers could flare higher.

The Dwarf gave a friendly wave. "Hey there. We tracked a recent purchase of Mithril to this Dungeon. We also want access."

The council looked amongst themselves; they knew this information would leak out, but it was faster than they had expected. Tyler sighed as he uncomfortably broke the silence, "It is true; the Mithril came from this location."

A mad rush of noise followed this statement as the other delegations suddenly started speaking over each other. Tyler waved his arms. "Hey!" he shouted sharply, calming the groups down. "It has only appeared *once* in a way someone could claim. Once in over a cumulative *five thousand* different dives into the dungeon!"

"And who got it?" The Dwarves were eyeing the merchant with undisguised greed.

"Th-that isn't for me to say." Tyler swallowed at the glares that were being directed his way. First the Amazons, now the Dwarves!

Dale interceded on his friend's behalf, "We have a policy of discretion, which I am sure you can appreciate. If they want you to know, they will come forward with that information themselves. We've had issues in the past with people attacking someone for a large sum of money or a powerful, Inscribed item." Tyler nodded sadly at this, remembering the time when he nearly lost an expensive pickaxe to thieves.

"You aren't making many friends today, lad." The Dwarf sat back and steepled his sausage-like fingers.

Dale sighed and wryly smiled. "Truly, I *am* trying to make friends, but none of you are giving me good incentive to help you out. They threatened us," he waved in the general direction of the Elves, "they have been needlessly rude," he waved at the Amazons, "and you hit against a city regulation. To your credit, at least you've been polite about it and haven't threatened me. Is that about to change?"

The Dwarves gained a considering look, and the spokesdwarf slowly nodded. "Alright, you make a good point. What would you say if I told you I'm authorized by Thane Moonshadow to open trade routes between our cities? Could that grease the wheels of our discussions?"

There was silence for a few moments. Most of the gathered people were quiet due to shock, but Dale kept his mouth closed out of confusion. "I'm sorry to say, I don't–"

"Dale, hush!" Tyler gave a small panicked laugh as he squeezed Dale's arm hard enough to bruise a non-cultivator. "This needs to be a private negotiation."

"... I see." Dale nodded at the Dwarf. "If you would be so kind, can we resume this discussion after this meeting?"

"Certainly," the Dwarf magnanimously agreed, giving a self-satisfied smirk at the Elves. "Let's have a drink later?"

Dale turned to the High Elves. "Access to the Silverwood tree will have to be granted by the Dark Elves. I'm sorry. There is nothing I can do. We made a deal. Now, access to the dungeon is a different matter. That *is* under my control and mine alone." His eyes darkened. "As of this moment, you will not have access to the dungeon."

"*What?*" the Elf roared for the second time today. "Then what in the *abyss* is the point of talking to you! Even if we successfully bargained with these trumped-up marauders, we couldn't do anything about it!"

"You are going to have to *earn* access," Dale asserted powerfully. "It will *not* be easy. It will *not* be cheap. You think the *Amazons* have a high rate?" His voice was rising in volume as he whipped himself into a fury.

"They, *at least*, didn't waltz in here and threaten to kill me! I'll agree to whatever terms the Dark Elves negotiate on my behalf. Have fun with that! Good day to you!" With this declaration, Dale ended the meeting and walked out with the Dwarves, leaving behind the fuming Elves as well as the Amazonians, who were now feeling much happier with the bargain they had made. The Dark Elves also looked pleasantly surprised at the gift Dale had just handed them.

Dale, the council, and the Dwarves were taking a tour of the area to cool their tempers. By the time they found the tavern, the snow was turning to sleet and running down their cloaks. They stepped indoors to a groan from the general populace as the heat was instantly leached out of the building.

"We need to find a way to block that," Tyler muttered as they got jokingly dirty looks from the people drinking inside.

"Can I buy you a drink?" Dale offered the group of Dwarves.

"Oh-ho! You sure do know how to open talks correctly!" came the jovial reply. Dale grinned; he really liked Dwarves.

"Thaddius?" a confused voice came from the bar, catching the attention of the entire negotiating group.

"*Beor?*" the spokesdwarf roared in surprise. Dale looked over and saw the Dwarves that had raised the city's defensive wall drinking at the bar.

"Y-you! Why are you here?" Beor was pointing a shaking finger at them and looked like he had been hit by a curse of confusion.

The Dwarven delegate's face turned red. "Why are *you* here? Did you know that your father put out a *bounty* for your safe return? Did you know he's been worried *sick?*"

Dale suddenly realized a very important fact. The monarch they had been discussing was 'King Moonshadow'. Beor... *Moonshadow* and his brother had been exiled... oh, boy.

"We knew about the bounty! He's a twisted 'father' isn't he, Stonewall?" Beor nudged his brother, who only nodded.

Thaddius stomped his foot on the floor and bellowed, "You *nitwits!* He's been sending delegations to *every* kingdom in an attempt to pull you back to his side! He's dying!"

Beor fell silent for a moment, but when he looked up, his eyes were blazing. "I'm sorry... for the *kingdom,*" he uttered mercilessly as he crossed his arms and arched an eyebrow.

Thaddius' voice became meek. "He rescinded the exile. He built an orphanage, just like you wanted. He even sent me to open *trade routes* when he heard of the Mithril coming from here."

Beor was completely flabbergasted at this piece of news. Speechless, he and his brother looked at each other in silence. Dale—in a flash of brilliance—decided to capitalize on this moment.

"Beor, would you like to join us for a drink? On me, of course. We were just about to open negotiations for those trade routes." Dale smiled as Beor realized what he was doing.

Beor's face cracked into a smile for the first time this evening. "You've treated us good, Dale. Real good. Let's see what kind of bonus we can get you in your trade talks. No one negotiates like a Dwarf, and none better than the Princes."

Thaddius seemed like he wanted to say something about this until Beor continued, "After all, *if* the exile was rescinded, that means I was reinstated as Crown Prince. Following this logic, I have full power to set up trade agreements and treaties."

"How about snackies?" Stonewall giggled drunkenly, smacking his lips loudly after finishing his pint.

Looking surprised at first, Thaddius then turned crafty. "Of course, my Prince. So long as you return with me to present the signed documents to your father." Beor looked a bit put off by this but nodded in agreement. Motioning to Stonewall, Thaddius smiled. "On a more important note, how many has he had tonight?"

Beor looked at his swaying brother, "I think that's his second."

"Second? Second *pint*?" Thaddius seemed very interested. "Is it good or just powerful?"

"Oh, yes. Very good. The 'dungeon special' is brewed exclusively with materials from the dungeon below us. From the hops to the water. Even the barrels are made from a tree that grows down there. The stuff is *packed* with Essence, and even the high rankers can get pretty loopy. They have normal beer too, if you... aren't up to it." Beor chuckled at the excited faces of the Dwarven delegation. "Not your brightest moment Dale, offering to buy the drinks tonight."

Dale looked at all the happy faces and smiled. "I think I can manage for *one* evening."

An hour later, Dale was wobbling in his seat as he tried to finish his second drink from the special 'Dwarfhunter' keg. Surprisingly, the Dwarves had thought the name of the brew was hilarious. "Nuh... no, guys! I don't *want* to be ahn askhole," he drunkenly explained to Hans and Tom, who had joined him in the tavern. The Dwarves were across the room, making frantic arm motions as they tried to make their reinstated Prince get better deals for the Dwarven nation. "Ikt's jush tha, if I come off as too nish, they try and take advantage! I haveta, ya know, seem like a–*buuuurp*–Noble. Haughty, unbending, stuck up. They wanted to *kill* me becaush I wouldn't let 'em have the tree–*urrp*! How messed up is *tha*? How'm *I* the askhole?"

"You *aren't* an asshole, Dale. Every politician gets into situations like this eventually. You can't please everyone." Hans patted him on the arm, ready to dodge away if Dale looked like he would hurl. "I get it, I do! That's why you're pushing yourself so hard, yeah?"

Dale grandly nodded. "Yesh. Any advantage I can geht, I gotta take. *You* taught me that! They... why do so many people wanna kill me, Hansel bread? Khee-*hee*, Hansel Bread. Like gingerbread. Thatsh your new nickname."

"No, it isn't," Hans gently yet firmly disagreed, seeing the mirth in Tom's eyes. "You just keep doing your best, buddy. There's a reason you have guards all the time now."

"Cause someone tried to kill me and dump me in the dungeon," Dale helpfully explained. "I bet the Elves wouldn't evhen put me in the Dungeon. Just lemme rot in the open," he grumbled, swaying heavily.

"Let's get you to bed." Hans gingerly swung Dale's arm over his, half lifting the young man. They stumbled out of the area, moving into the blowing snow in search of shelter. Tom watched them go, quietly fidgeting with his mug... and thinking.

CHAPTER THIRTEEN

"Ow! Ahh! God!" Dale awoke to a simultaneous series of slaps, buckets of frigid water, and strong blows from a flat piece of wood. "*What is happening?*" he roared, leaping from his bed and swinging at the invisible assailants.

"What's happening is that you got drunk, fell asleep, and decided not to come to your training session!" Though not a fire cultivator, his Moon Elf instructor's eyes seemed to be blazing with an abyssal fury. "We need to catch up, so I will be beating you until you get to the training ground. Feel *free* to take your time." The cantankerous Elf vanished, but the slaps and heavy blows had not abated. Dale was knocked to the ground from a particularly vicious strike.

"Celestial feces! I'm going!" Dale leaped to his feet only to be knocked forward again. He dove through the entryway to his tent, having lost his room in the church to the wounded that were still in recovery. He took off sprinting, but somehow, the invisible blows kept pace with him. By the time he got to the training area, he was bleeding from a split lip and had bruises forming across his body. His instructor was waiting there impatiently, obviously faster than Dale could dream of being.

"That'll do," the Elf muttered, allowing the torrent of strikes to finally abate. "You've been getting *complacent*, Dale."

Dale thought he knew better than to argue, but his mouth raced ahead of him. "Things are going well! I'm not getting complacent, I'm just feeling confident about my progress..." He trailed off as the stare turned to a glare.

"*What* progress?" the Elf demanded spitefully. "You are like a child that plays at fighting, and you've outgrown your old toys so you are getting bored! I see you in the dungeon, being careless, taking risks, *missing* an attack upon a monster entirely and letting it close on your cleric. You almost lost a member of your group today because you decided that you wanted a one-on-one duel with an overgrown Cat! You've never landed a blow on me, *and* you still have trouble controlling your Essence! So tell me, brat, *where is your progress?*"

Dale clamped his mouth shut tightly. He knew the Elf was right but was shocked at how long he must have been following him to know all of this information. Dale seemed to deflate, nodded, and smoothly moved into the 'ready' position, showing he was prepared to begin training.

The Elf scoffed. "Ready, hmm? Well, not *everything* you do is the worst I've ever seen. I saw you take a technique designed for earth and use it as one for water. Somehow, you were able to instinctively grasp the changes that needed to be made for the element. You could be an overwhelmingly powerful Essence user someday; it seems you are a natural!"

Dale brightened a bit, but the Elf heartlessly continued, "Too bad you suck at everything else. Today, you are on protection duty. That scarecrow," he pointed to an effigy awkwardly dressed in ladies clothing, "is a princess. Keep her safe."

A howl resounded through the air, and the area seemed to brighten as eyes opened all around them, reflecting the moonlight. A massive wolf—easily as large as the Boss Mob Snowball—stepped into the light. With a snarl, it charged the scarecrow. Dale ran at it, pumping his legs and jumping. He knocked the shadowy beast aside, and it rolled to a halt with a yelp. Dale jumped on it, pounding away until it was still. His final blow was interrupted as he was suddenly impacted from the side, his ribs groaning in protest from the abrupt shift.

"Your mission was a failure!" the Elf ranted over the sounds of tearing cloth. He pointed at the destroyed mannequin that was being torn apart. "Was your job to kill the wolf, or was your job to protect the *princess*?"

Dale looked up to see two wolves fading away, chunks of scarecrow dropping from their vanishing maws. "I was trying to stop th–"

He was interrupted. "Do you want to be a duelist or a cultivator? If you can only handle one thing at a time, being a warrior of cultivation is not for you. *Situational awareness*, Dale! You focus too hard on only *one* thing, and people will die! Namely you. Again!"

Dale rushed at the wolves nearing the scarecrow, landing a heavy blow and then moving to the next animal. He stopped six wolves this time before the sound of cloth tearing announced his failure. Then an unstoppable force smacked him to the ground.

"Again! Save her! She is going to die, and it will be your fault!"

Dale's mind was buzzing; there had to be more to the lesson! This time, instead of fighting the wolves, he grabbed the scarecrow and ran. The chuckles of his master made him grin until he felt a sharp object tear into his side. He screamed and dropped the 'princess' who was subsequently torn apart.

"Better, smarter." The Elf nodded at him as Dale looked for what had stabbed him. He finally noticed that the scarecrow had a knife. "Sadly for you, looks like the princess didn't want to be saved. Today's lesson, Dale. I'm sure you've heard it before, but let me reiterate. Trust no one and nothing. An attack can come from anywhere, at any time. Also, never again get drunk to the point that you are unaware of your surroundings!"

The training progressed. Wolves became warriors, then assassins. Spells were introduced, and Dale soon had second-degree burns and minor frostbite. Every simulation was different, but they all had at least two things in common: Dale was subjected to extreme pain each round he failed, and he failed all of them eventually.

As dawn approached, Dale was allowed to stumble back to his tent. He unstoppered and drank a large health potion, passing out immediately after. Hopefully, that would boost his regenerative capabilities to the point that he wouldn't need a cleric when he woke up. There was no energy left in his body.

A few hours later, he was shaken awake by a concussive *boom* followed by a flash of light and a few screams. He groggily got up, crushed and absorbed a Core with a shudder of pleasure, then raced toward the thunder, hoping to help whoever was under attack. Dale got to the point he was sure had been the origin of the noise, but there didn't seem to be any issue. There was a large area without snow but no signs of combat or destruction.

He glanced around and noticed a few shell-shocked witnesses, right away marching over to them. "What happened?"

He received a blank look in return from the cowering man. Dale slapped him, and the man finally mumbled, "Cindy... Cindy. She... she's so good to me."

Dale gripped the man, and spat out through gritted teeth, "What. Happened."

Unfocused eyes looked up at him. "So thin. Ow. So strong. Very wow." Dale shook him again. "Jeez, stop! A column of light came out of the ground and ate her. The ground *ate* her!"

"Dale, what's happening? Let him go. You are hurting him!" Rose strode over, looking at the gathering crowd. Dale let go of the man, who already had a bruise in the shape of a hand forming on each arm. The man sunk to the ground sobbing.

"Sorry, buddy." Dale handed the man a healing potion from his pocket. He always had spares in his pockets these days. "Rose, it looks like the dungeon somehow opened a pit or something. I think a few people fell in, and it closed on them."

"It got to the surface? That isn't supposed to be possible." Rose gasped at the revelation.

"I... I don't know what to do about this," Dale admitted ruefully. "I'll let the council know; they can come up with a plan."

"Sounds good. Um. When you are done, come to the dungeon. I assume you'll miss breakfast, so I'll grab you something." Rose turned and went to find the rest of their team. She looked back at him with a grin. "By the way, we have some new toys to try out."

Dale had no idea what that meant, so he nodded and went to tell the council of his findings. Running into Frank, he quickly gave him a synopsis of the situation and went to find Rose. As she had told him, the rest of the team was already there, sly grins on their faces as Dale walked up.

"Hi, all, what's going on?" Dale looked around at the nearly dancing members of his team.

"Can I tell him?" Hans begged the others, nearly jumping up and down. Normal for him, but the others were just as excited.

"No!" Rose exclaimed, glaring at him. "Tyler will be here any second. Just let him have his moment."

Tyler came up to them just then, huffing and puffing as he carried a large case. A few people were carrying boxes for him, and he thanked them and gave them a coin for their trouble. "Dale! You are going to love this!" Tyler started opening boxes. "We were up all night testing various methods to use the materials you all brought us and came up with some interesting innovations!" He pulled out a quiver of arrows and handed them to Rose.

"I call these 'Oppressive Arrows'. As the name suggests, we use material from the 'Oppressor' type Basher. What it *should* do is generate a spiral of wind around it when it gets to a certain speed. This will make the arrow spin in place ten times faster than feathers allow for, greatly increasing accuracy and penetrating power!" Tyler explained gleefully. "Not exactly an Enchantment but far more cost-effective!"

Next, he pulled out a small net that was sewn to be a bag filled with a plant. He looked a little nervous about this one. "Alright now, let me explain something. We have tested the weapons, and they work in a controlled environment... but most of this gear is untested in reality. The reason we are *giving* all of this to you is that we were hoping you would test it for us in the dungeon. But... well, just keep your weapons handy."

Some of the excitement left the faces around Dale. Tyler blithely continued, "This handy little satchel is filled with crushed and invigorated dungeon catnip. It can be used for two different purposes. If you aren't currently fighting them, tossing this satchel at a Cat should be sufficient to make it ignore you. Otherwise, you can use it as a lure to draw more Cats in. If you burn it, the smoke will make them come running. Careful with this." Tyler handed a few to Hans, much to the horror of his comrades.

"You say be careful with it, then hand it to *Hans?*" Adam spoke in a hushed tone.

Hans' jaw dropped. "I'm careful!"

Tyler looked around to see if they were serious. He shrugged expansively. "I'm just gonna keep going. Essentially, we were able to make weapons or armor out of most of the Beasts. From Raile, we were able to make a disposable shield. If you touch it to the ground, it'll stick there and basically become an immovable barrier. It is stone though, so it will shatter given enough force. We made something similar out of the Smashers, but we're marketing it as instant handholds. Touch it to a wall, and *bam*, you have a hand or foothold. Slightly larger ones can be used as platforms."

"You did this in a *night?*" Dale wondered incredulously, awed at the variation between the items.

Tyler cracked his knuckles. "It pays to have people from such differing backgrounds to work on these. We even have..." He looked around. "Don't laugh, but we have a scientist."

Hans chortled against instructions, getting a glare for his trouble.

"What is a scientist?" Adam asked the question everyone was thinking.

Tyler started to reply, but Hans interrupted and took over the explanation, "A scientist is a person who tries to measure the world, saying that there are 'immutable' laws that affect everyone equally. Laws that can't be broken. They try to explain things in terms of the effect they have, how 'dense' they are, or *anything* rather than by the Essences they are composed of."

Tyler rubbed his head. "He has some great ideas though. His work on gravity alone could–"

"I've heard of that!" Hans interjected. "Yeah, gravity is real, but it isn't a universal constant!" He picked up a rock, dropping it. It landed on the ground. "Dale, lift that rock with Essence!"

Apologetically looking at Tyler, Dale lifted the small stone with a speck of Essence, and it hovered in the air. Hans looked smug. "Oh, look. Something gravity isn't affecting. Theory *disproven.*"

Tyler wryly retaliated, "Dale, stop using Essence, but don't drop the rock." Dale cut off the flow of Essence, and the rock thudded to the ground. "Oh, look. Now that the rock isn't being acted upon by an outside force, *gravity* reasserts its dominance."

"It doesn't affect everything! It can be disproven by, uh, Dale, lift that rock and–" Hans started saying.

"No!" Dale barked. He grinned at the looks he got from the arguing men. "We have things to do. Argue with each other *later.*"

"Fine!" the two men spoke in unison, then glared at each other.

Tyler coughed, trying to recapture the moment. "Uh. The other items are still being worked on, but if you would test these, I would appreciate it."

"Sure thing, Ty." Dale waved and joined his group as they walked toward the dungeon portal.

Dani

The cloth that was covering the cage Dani was being held in was yanked away, and her light revealed a strange stone formation. "Where are we?" she demanded of the man suspending her in front of himself.

Dark eyes landed on her. "Where are we...?"

Dani sighed in frustration. "Where are we, 'The Master'?

"Still in the sewer, little Wisp." He motioned, and a few people stepped forward. The Master set Dani's cage on a stone outcropping and spoke over his shoulder at her, "You are about to witness a great miracle."

Dani had no choice but to watch as one of the people stepped forward from the group, a fanatical look in his eyes. "I beg of you Master, use me for this task! I have been your most loyal follower and will continue to be, forever!"

The Master looked at him with a cold smile. "It *will* be forever if you do this. I will confer immortality upon you, allowing you to avoid the trials of human cultivation and weakness. Are you prepared for *this* to be your afterlife?" He waved to indicate the world.

"We have all seen what awaits *us* in the afterlife, Master," the man spoke sincerely, shuddering a bit. "If you allow me this honor, I will prove my faithfulness every day!"

The Master was quiet for a long moment. "So be it," his voice thundered out, and around them, a cheer rose into the air from the assembled forces. He looked out into the crowd and began to speak, "Ten years I have been working on this, ten long years of my attention on a single object. This and the sacrifice of our brother will open the path... to our ascension!" The cheers were deafening.

"I have never led you astray; I have never lied to you," The Master spoke again as the cheering quieted. "Do you trust me to lead you into the future?"

"*Yes, Master, YES!*" the crowd bayed.

The volunteer was being stripped by the two attendants standing with him, and he joyfully lay on a stone altar, tears of happiness rolling down his face.

"What in the abyss is going on?" Dani muttered, looking at all of these psychopaths.

Infernal energies began to flood from The Master, a miasmic aura that seemed to howl in rage. Dani was far more terrified when she realized that this must be spiritual energy. It was far too powerful to be Essence or even Mana. The world seemed to shudder in its presence, colors fading to gray. The monotone hue spread throughout the open cavern, allowing vision to what had been the darkest corners, but there was now no light nor darkness.

"Behold the monotony of the void, Brother." The Master rested his hand on the man lying on the altar. "There is no escape for your soul here, no way for you to be yanked away by the piddling *God* that demands a natural death for all things. Are you prepared to save us all?"

"Yes!" The man howled in excitement. "To immortality! For the will of The Master!"

The Master nodded and turned to the crowd, raising his arms. "Now, shall we begin!" he roared, not as a question but as a way to rile up the awaiting fiends.

The crowd was loud enough to shake dust from the low ceiling. "*Sacrifice him! Sacrifice him!*"

In his hand, The Master held aloft a chunk of purest opal. "In this artifact, there is one item that will save us all, nay, it shall push us into power the world over!" He turned to the altar. "To victory!"

"*To victory!*" the man lying down echoed along with the waiting masses.

The Master raised his hand... and slammed the opal deep into the eagerly awaiting heart of the man before him. A concussion of power flowed from The Master into the glittering stone, trapping the soul of the man before him. In a moment, the twisted ritual was complete.

Covered in gore, the dark cloaked man stepped toward the strange rock formation. A pitch-black stalagmite and stalactite were nearly touching. The Master pulled the opal out of the fresh corpse with a wet *slurp*. He placed the stone between the unnatural rock formations just as the opal crumbled away. "It begins!" he intoned solemnly. "Bring forward the offerings!"

Dani watched in horror as the newly born infernal dungeon Core began to glow with a dark maroon light.

CHAPTER FOURTEEN

"Haven't seen Evan in a while," Dale commented as they arrived on the third floor. He missed the Dwarf Orc hybrid. "I bet this floor is dripping with gold at this point. He'd like that."

Adam grunted, an odd sound coming from such a lustrous face. "I am told that he is on vacation."

"Oh? Who told you that?" Hans questioned the cleric. "Who's your source?"

Adam's eyebrow twitched. "People will answer questions if you *ask* them for information."

"Eavesdropping is more fun." Hans strolled through what—for all intents and purposes—seemed to be a meadow. "I could just take a nap in here, ya know?"

<Please. Please do it. Nap.> Dale shook his head as if an annoying fly was buzzing around him.

"Look, another person alone in here," Rose commented, pointing to the east. The person she was referencing was hidden behind a grove of trees by the time the others turned to look. "Strange, I saw someone like that the other day, too."

Tom shrugged and changed the subject, "Why are we on this floor? Cultivation is best done near the Silverwood tree."

"We have a job request," Adam informed him. "Someone saw the Wandering Boss with a staff that he was using to blast infernal Essence as bolts of darkness. We were asked to acquire the staff and trim down the Goblin population."

"It does look pretty crowded over there." Rose was staring at a fortification in the distance.

"Apparently, a couple parties were wiped out recently, so people got too nervous to fight regularly on this floor. Not enough adventurers are hunting down the Goblins, so if something isn't done soon, they are worried a breakout will occur," Dale quickly explained. Looks like the council meetings were good for something after all.

"Rose, wanna soften them up?" Hans offered quietly. They were getting close enough that speaking too loudly would draw *very* unwanted attention.

Rose shook her head. "Sorry, they are still out of range."

"Try out the new arrows," Hans suggested, pulling out an Oppressive Arrow. Rose glared at him.

"Hans, I said that I am out of range." Her frustration was boiling over with this maddening man!

He waved a hand frantically to remind her to keep it down. "Tyler said these would be more accurate, right? More penetrating power, too. All this adds up to longer range on your shots. Try it. I believe in you."

Rose was quiet at that point. She grudgingly set an arrow to her string, drew back, and fired. The arrow *screamed* through the air, hitting a Goblin in the chest and punching through the fresh corpse to hit the stone wall behind it. She stared down at her bow, happily surprised by this development.

Tom raised an eyebrow at her. "Did you forget that your bow has a force enhancement enchantment? You should have been able to hit him even if using a regular arrow."

"It hasn't activated before this," she muttered, looking at her faintly glowing bow. The light vanished almost instantly.

Adam chimed in, "Maybe you need to aim at things beyond your normal range?"

She slowly nodded as the Goblins began to howl a warning. "That would explain it. I haven't practiced at this range before, ever. I've been practicing other things."

"Well, don't stop now!" Hans called as a few Mobs started running in their direction. "Berserkers incoming!"

The Berserker Goblins charged at them, howling their fury. They wore no armor but were agile enough to dodge normal arrows at close range. Tom and Dale started to move forward to intercept them, but Dale stopped himself.

"Wait, Tom!" Dale shook himself from his battle-lust. "We need to stay in formation!"

Tom looked over with a face full of disgust. "Why the change? Our combat to this point has been effective, to say the least."

"Get in formation, Tom," Dale barked as the Goblins reached them. Goblin archers were also running toward them, hoping to get in range before the Berserkers fought. Tom reluctantly yet swiftly rejoined the formation. He swung his ingot hammer in an upward arc, cracking the chin of a Goblin which had lost its footing. With Dale and Tom holding the Goblins back, Hans worked to move between the small battles. He appeared to vanish, popping up next to a Goblin and delivering a swift strike then moving to where he was needed next. The teamwork began to pay off as more melee fighters joined. Without the team working together, they would have been trampled by the sheer numbers of furious Goblins.

Rose focused on sniping the Goblins that were preparing to launch a volley of arrows, her shots devastating now that she had figured out how to activate the enchantment on her bow. She accidentally used a normal arrow, and it detonated into splinters as the bowstring tried to send it off. Rose shrieked as the splinters dug into her, slicing through her left eyelid. Adam grabbed her face to stabilize her, coating his fingers in luminescent golden light. A quick pull removed the shard from her eye without doing more damage, and a muttered Incantation healed her eye to its normal state.

Tears were flowing down her face as she angrily jumped to her feet and started firing arrows again, being far more careful in her selection of ammo. "Thank you!" she called to Adam as he moved to address a deep cut Dale had taken on his bicep.

"It's what I do!" Adam called back with a grin, already working on holding Dale's skin together as the flesh mended. As soon as Dale could use his arm again, he launched forward and delivered a devastating punch to a Goblin that was running at him. Dale twisted his fist as he activated the Runes on his knuckles, and a wet splatter of demolished organs hit the ground just moments before the Goblin did.

"Where are they all coming from?" Dale shouted over the *clang* of Tom's weapon hitting a shield.

"That fortification!" Tom called back, continuing to put dents in the shield in front of him. With a *snap*, the arm holding the barrier in place broke, and the Goblin howled. Tom swung at the open target, and the howl cut off abruptly.

"Thank you, Tom, master of the obvious." Hans thrust his dagger into an unprotected Goblin's artery. "They must have been gathering for a reason, don't ya think?"

The Goblins stopped leaving the fort, and the adventurers quickly finished off the last few that engaged with them. Adam looked at the closed gate, and the Goblins hatefully glaring out at them. "Why did they stop?"

"I have no idea." Dale shook his head as the clangs of armored feet running toward them alerted the group. They turned to meet this challenge, only to see a human running toward them, completely covered in plate armor. "Who is that?"

"No idea," Hans replied carelessly, "but if he doesn't stop running at us in about three seconds, I'm goin' to put a knife in him."

"Hey!" Rose shouted at the still-running man. "What do you want?"

Adam's face had turned as white as his robe. "That's not a man! It's a Mob! Take it down!"

"Don't have to tell me more than once!" Tom happily spouted, running forward and delivering a powerful blow with his hammer. The armor ducked, dodging under the strike. It twisted at the waist in a way that a human never could, shooting a powerful punch straight upward. Catching Tom just above the elbow, the metal fist fully dislocated his arm with that single attack.

Tom fell over, his balance completely destroyed. He tried to roll to his feet, but in his haste, he forgot that he had no leverage and fell again. The armor drew back its sword, preparing to decapitate the half-risen man.

"Oh, *abyss*, no," Rose growled as she launched a fat-tipped arrow. With the force enchantment active, the arrow flashed across the distance faster than the arm could swing down. The arrow impacted with a harsh gong sound, and the empty armor was knocked back several feet. Impossibly, it twisted again, landing on its feet and seeming to glare at Rose.

Tom hurried to his feet, glad the sword had only grazed him. He was bleeding freely from the head wound but still held a battle stance. "Can someone shove my arm back in its socket? I cannot grip nor swing a weapon as it stands."

"Fall back, I'll get it," Adam called as Dale and Hans converged on the armor. Hans lashed out, scoring a shrieking line on the armor but failing to penetrate the metal. Dale began throwing heavy punches but may as well have been hitting a wall. He thought that the force enhancement Rune on one of his hands would be more effective, but the armor would pivot to absorb the force of every solid hit, its knee armor allowing it to fall to a ninety-degree angle before springing upright.

All the while, the armor was swinging its sword. This too was moving in a bizarre way, the arm holding the weapon rotating freely at the shoulder, elbow, and wrist. This allowed for a dizzying array of potential movement, and the two fighters had to be very careful to watch the weapon as it was swung.

"Dale, duck!" Dale heard, dropping to the ground as an arrow passed where his head had been a moment before. The arrow whined as it impacted and bored through the visor of the armor, which subsequently clattered to the ground.

"You really felt strongly that I would listen, huh?" Dale took a deep breath as he stood up. "That arrow was... wow. Nice shot."

Hans patted Dale. "You have good listening skills. Good boy!" Dale shoved the offending hand away with a chuckle.

Adam looked over, eyes widening. "*Look out!*"

Dale and Hans launched forward in a synchronized roll, barely avoiding the writhing darkness that had swung at them. Seeing what had attacked, they started sprinting toward Adam, who sputtered as he tried to cast a banishing Incantation.

The man-shaped cloud of evil was barreling at them, claws of hellfire reaching outward, when it just... stopped. Tom was panting, the only sound the men could hear. Dale moved carefully away from the extended claws, which had been inches from his eyes. He looked at the crawling darkness, noticing chains of violent, shifting light encircling it.

"Guys! Adam!" Rose shrieked as they just stood still. "Banish it! I have no idea how long that will last!"

All of them came to their senses, yet as expected, Hans was still the first to react. His hand dipped into his satchel, and a dart-like knife flashed between him and the consuming darkness. The dagger stopped inside the still body and began glowing quickly. With a paradoxical flash of darkness, the being and knife vanished.

"I knew those demon busters would come in handy." Hans shuddered in disgust.

"What was that?" Dale looked at Rose. "How did you stop it?"

Rose sank to the floor, trying to catch her breath. Her hands were shaking from the adrenaline, but a wide smile stretched across her face. "You aren't the only one in training, Dale. That's a technique unique to people who can combine celestial and infernal Essence. It is called 'bindings of chaos' and is a last resort of sorts."

"What do you mean?" Dale pestered her. "Does it take a huge amount of Essence to use or something?"

"Not so much," she admitted. "It is just that... the uh, bindings? They will ensnare whatever they catch, holding it perfectly, flawlessly, for an... indeterminate amount of time."

"What does that even mean?" Tom joined in, rotating his arm to try and reduce the pain of having it pushed back into its socket.

Rose flushed the color of her namesake. "It means that it will be held anywhere from forever to less than a second. There is no way to know for sure. Whatever is caught won't be able to move, but the captive can still cultivate and think. It just cannot activate abilities or move on its own."

"So it could be really useful or totally useless," Hans clarified in a slightly freaked-out tone. "Next time we see one of those, we have demon busters handy, yeah?"

"Agreed!" Tom nodded fervently. "In the meantime, we should have this armor inspected. It has a repulsive feel to it, like bathing yourself in a latrine during midsummer." He held up the breastplate of the fallen Mob like a person holding a dirty loincloth.

CHAPTER FIFTEEN

My aura was condensing down nicely. While I didn't think the ambient Essence was being reduced, it was strange to have my senses diminished to this level. Right now, I was retracting my aura from the third floor, and a large group of Goblins had gathered to wish me luck with my ascension.

Bob stood forward as the last tendrils of my mind were flowing out of the floor, slinking down the stairwell. "Safe travels, Great Spirit!"

I sighed. <Bob, I keep telling you to call me 'Cal'. That's my name. How many times do I have to say it?>

He bowed, a grin on his wide mouth. "At least once more, Great Spirit."

<I could pop you like a cleric's zit,> I jokingly threatened him.

"Yes, yes, now we get to the whining portion of today's talking." He laughed as I started drawing Runes on the ground. "I'll be good. I'll be good!"

<Yeah, yeah. You are lucky I'm in a pleasant mood.> My aura was retracted from the area, and I could no longer sense the third floor. My mood spiraled into a grim outlook as I condensed myself further. I had to do this. I had to become strong enough to find Dani and make sure nothing—and no one—could threaten us again.

I was also a bit nervous. Until I extended my aura—my influence—again, anything that died in the dungeon would just... go to waste. Bodies would pile up, and the Essence from dying creatures and adventurers would just be released into the air. I really expected to have to give myself a thorough, deep cleaning when I came back. Conversely, I was very intrigued about the heady power I was gaining as I brought myself to my Core. My aura was normally too diffuse to affect things directly around non-dungeon-affiliated creatures, but as I condensed, my aura started to become threatening.

I would bet that if I had gathered all of my aura into a single room, I could snuff out a D-ranked adventurer as easily as eating moss. Sadly, there was no way to test this, as people that weak didn't bother to venture down this far anymore. Well. Almost no one, but Tom wouldn't get here in time. My aura retracted along the walls of my labyrinth, leaving behind a sense of emptiness. Ick. I *really* didn't like not knowing what was going on around me.

I caressed Snowball with my mind as I passed him, getting a sleepy look in reply. Eventually, I was in my Core room, alone but for the Silverwood tree. Soon, I passed even that. My Core was glowing with an intense light, brighter than I had ever made it. I looked like a blue star and would have blinded non-cultivators if they looked at me for too long. Sinking into meditation, I focused on my cultivation technique. This next part made me nervous.

I opened the hole beneath me to a far wider degree, and instead of a stream of evaporated Essence, liquid Essence poured out of the reservoir and started replacing the water in my puddle. It didn't take long—the water boiled away in a few seconds—but I didn't notice through the agony I was experiencing. The liquid Essence was dangerous; it attempted to force its way into me, not wanting to follow the paths of my cultivation technique. I fought, *hard,* to force it along the pathways. Allowing it to win would mean my destruction as it ruined my Chi Spiral, entering my Core as a mass instead of a neatly ordered Chi thread. If I could sweat, I would have been soaked.

With constant force of will, I held the power back, only allowing it to go where I wanted it to, even as it started to surround me fully. Soon, the hollow formed in my stalagmite was overflowing with liquid Essence. At least it would have been, but it was vanishing into the air as it left the confines of my rocky depths. It would be pulled back to my reservoir by the Runescript surrounding me, so I wasn't overly worried about the loss.

As I worked to control this power—which I was only able to do thanks to long hours of practice and controlled breakthroughs of my Essence to this point—I sank deeper and deeper into my cultivation technique. Hours passed. I needed to meditate and retain control, which was harder than it sounds. I finally reached the center of my Chi spiral and the hole in my soul that it hid. I passed through the hole, pulling a wash of dense Essence in with me. The hole widened, agony for me as my soul was stretched. I looked around, and even in this time of tribulation, I was reassured by the beautiful galaxy of hypnotic Essence this place was made of. In each point of light, I saw Dani and what she had done to help me, push me, and guide me to this point. For this moment. I steeled my will and pressed forward against the mental barriers holding me in the C-rankings.

My Core, the physical shell that held me in this world... vaporized. I was awash in Essence, my soul bared to the ravages of the elements. Essence no longer had a physical medium to pass through and slammed into my cultivation technique from all sides, doing all it could to destroy my mind, my connections to everything I had created. The world seemed to darken as I was compressed, driven deeper and deeper into the pocket dimension of my soul.

I screamed in mind-shattering agony, an unprotected soul being torn asunder. As I was flayed, the realization of my fate if I was to let this continue entered my thoughts. I steeled myself and fought back! *No!* I would *not* be torn apart! I would not cease to be! I. Would. *Ascend!*

The world was instantly dark, and mercifully, the pain was gone. Oddly, as if through a veil, I could see myself still being slowly destroyed by the corroding forces of untempered power. It was oh so very slow though. I looked down and saw a beautiful mosaic of interconnected power. I looked up and saw a tower that was higher than the tallest point of my mountain. I tried to move, and around me, six paths of various colors appeared. I looked at the paths, and they seemed to be angled toward a floor above this one. There was no other floor in range of my sight, so I was confused.

I looked again at the paths, noting their color and feeling the impressions they exuded. The light that created the chroma for each differing option flared, and at their endpoints, they combined to create a globe of accumulated power. As I watched, that globe released a beam of light, creating a spiral that led higher. That light connected to the light from another, forming a new globe, in reality, a 'node' of various combinations of Essence. Mana? Something else? Those pathways branched again, connecting, connecting, and connecting. The light reached higher and higher, coming to rest against the ceiling of the immense tower.

Each place the paths connected had created a node, and each node level with me was whispering into my mind. Luckily, they were arranged in tiers, and the higher tiers were silent, else the whispers would have been overwhelming. I looked upward, trying to get my bearings, and the combinations appeared limitless. I looked deeper into the lights and smiled. The paths were *not* limitless. There was a finite amount of possible combinations. If my calculating mind was reading the combinations correctly, there were six factorial tiers, meaning seven hundred and twenty different levels of unique combinations. Each tier except the first—where I was—had exactly twelve options, meaning I had the affinities and control to choose one specialization out of... eight thousand six hundred forty possibilities. Plus, of course, the six on this level.

For some reason, I was not able to stand at the highest tier from the start. I had to climb. Somehow. This proposition was troublesome for many reasons, but the most compelling was that the nodes made offers that were hard to ignore.

'*Come to me! I am healing and light. Your pain is over; ascend to the heavens, and you will know righteousness.*' This promise came from the pathway leading to the node made purely of celestial energies.

I scoffed and immediately ignored all the murmurs coming from the singular paths, and they went silent. They were the weakest laws of the universe, if the most individually pure. I wasn't ascending to only reach for the basics! As I made this decision, I started floating. Oh? This is how I climb? I ignore the offers of the nodes? Seems easy enough. I'll be out of here in twenty minutes. Tops. Twenty-minute adventure!

'*Come! Grow with me! Alter reality with the plants! I bring patience and encourage life!*' Another weak node on a short path piteously begged. I wouldn't become a plant Mage! I ignored this tier of paths, climbing ever higher toward where true power lay waiting. Moving to the next tier drained a small portion of my Essence, and it continued to slip away as I was forced to interact with this next level.

'*Burn! Consume it all! Reduce the world to ash!*' The third tier, and already, hellfire was screaming to me. I reluctantly swallowed, turning from this path of all-consuming anger. After hearing all the other descriptions from the nodes, I was allowed to move higher.

Each tier took more Essence to reach, and each node called out with more compelling offers; the laws of the universe dangling hidden knowledge, secrets that hadn't been seen in the age of mankind. But... I wanted more than these low levels could offer. If only I weren't forced to listen to all of the offers before moving on! My progress began to slow. At the halfway point, I was nearly trapped by my strong connection to the universal law of disease.

'Rot the flesh from your enemies... let the world be born anew in the fertile soil they will provide.' A dark grin was in my mind, and I almost, *almost,* gave in. Then I remembered the standards I held myself to. There was no way to outsmart a disease, no way to grow as a person from the loss that it brought to others far away. I steadied myself and once again moved upward.

I climbed higher and higher, striving against the oppressive, universe shattering offers. Some of the ideas volunteered left me sobbing. They professed peace and wholeness of soul once again. I reached out... no! I would only take the best, for celestial sake! I turned away. I was weakening though and using Essence at a prodigious rate. I tried to hurry.

After months of so, so *slowly* climbing the tiers, I was nearing my breaking point, listening a little too intently to the offers. When I had arrived, I had assumed that the nodes were just accumulated power. I was wrong. They were the embodiment of universal laws. Complex, immutable. They were also... alive, after a fashion. They had goals and personalities. I was only one tier from the top, but the laws of space and movement were tickling my mind, invoking my long-held fantasies of freedom and flight.

'*Flight? Why be satisfied with mere flight? I will teach you how to remove your bonds, how to move in a straight line, or not at all. Do you know what happens to a planet that hits an object that is not moving at all? The* planet *is obliterated. Why settle for such a lowly goal as* flight?' This law almost had me. I had taken a step on the path and was ready to take a second. A mental step. I still didn't have feet.

Luckily for me, the whisper had made a fatal flaw in its attempt to ensnare me. I stopped, finally silencing this tier after a month of being here. <I promised Dani that we would one day fly together. I promised her... that I would be the best. Do the best. I would be unique and bring her fame. I would unravel the mysteries of her race and how I came to be. I won't fail her!> I pulled myself up to the highest tier, the most complex laws that I would eventually bind my very soul to. My mind was on the verge of breaking; the intensive exhaustion I was feeling was trying to get me to pass on to eternal slumber.

I stood on the top tier and looked at the twelve highest laws I could attain. They searched me as well, and a few willingly went silent. These were the oldest laws of the universe, and everything below them was simply a dumbing-down of their intricacy, a single facet of their being. Only three still whispered, but each syllable was a planet's population screaming for my attention. The words beat against my battered form, and I nearly faded then and there.

'*I am creation! I am the brush that forms a line, the hammer that beats the iron, the chisel that shapes the stone. I am creativity, and insight, and thoughtfulness. To bring into the world, to make something new, is my purpose. Step on my path, join to me, and it will be your purpose as well.*' My mind was elated at this offer, and I went to joyously throw myself along the path. I was stopped mid-lunge by the next, a breathy voice.

'*I am love.*' I turned, waiting for more. That whisper had brought me to tears, and I didn't even have eyes. '*I am boundless, endless. I am what brings together others. I am the end to loneliness. Join me, and you will never be alone again.*' Laughing with happiness, I turned toward this voice.

An organic, disturbing mutter brought me to my senses. It seemed to be speaking to itself. '*Loneliness?*' A sound followed, a laugh like feces hitting water. *Bloop.* '*Loneliness is success. It means everything has fallen to you already, that you have killed them all. Bring all things to their end. Give yourself to me. Through you, I will reduce the world to nothing.*'

I turned slowly to this voice, a voice I knew well but somehow had forgotten. <Hello, Madness.>

'*I am so much more. Madness is only the least of my names. I am the end of all things, the final destination of the long-lived. I am Kings and Queens. I am all things forbidden. Release me into the world once again, young one.*'

I slowly shook my head. <No. Not you. I would rather go to a lower tier than become what others expect me to be. I won't go insane. I won't destroy everything. Just *mostly* everything. Be quiet.>

'*No.*'

I was startled enough that I nearly toppled over. Before now, I had been able to silence every susurration. I looked over the other two, but Madness continued to breathe into my ear like a lover. I did my best to ignore the disturbing feeling.

'*Feel free to choose another. Unlike them, I won't be angry. I won't refuse you when you come back to me. I'll be here. I will always be waiting. Willing.*' Madness tickled my ear, causing me to shudder. '*If you live long enough, you* will *be mine. You almost were... so recently.*'

I looked at the other two laws wide-eyed, trying to see the secrets they held without committing to them. The entire time, they were an undertone to all noise. They enticed me. Offered glimpses into their power, always tantalizing, never committing to me. I sighed and thought. I meditated, trying to decide, all the while, they slowly got louder. Suddenly, I came to a realization. My head snapped up, and the laws went silent, even Madness, though begrudgingly.

<There's more.> I was sure of it. I looked around the tower of ascension. I looked down at all the tiers I had passed. The tier I was on was still a circle, still a separation of paths! I was here for Quintessence. The source. I was *not* here for a pale shadow! I *forced* myself higher, pushing into the murky barrier of nothingness that formed the ceiling above me. I strained, putting everything I had into this action. The barrier pressed down, the pressure building to unbearable levels. <I know you are there! This ceiling is a *lie*!>

I began to break. All of me, everything that I am, was beginning to fracture. My Essence began to vanish at a horrendous rate. Unbeknownst to me, at that point in time, my Silverwood roots surrounded my body and somehow entered the trial with me. The roots punched through my consciousness, penetrating the darkness above. The roots writhed, pulling open holes in the barrier. I strained as my thoughts began to fade, but I began to pass through! Every inch was a battle, but I was going higher! Higher! Yes!

I stood on a platform of slowly swirling darkness, looking up at a shining, iridescent, *flawless* node. The paths from below all stemmed from this, and it was the only law on this tier. Unlike all the others before it, this one was silent.

<Please. I want to know you. I want to bond with you, to become a Mage with you as my law,> I gasped out, the strain of this level a constant pain on my mind.

It uttered a single word to me. '*No.*'

The force of this word sent me flying, crashing into the floor miles away, yet not having moved at all in relative position. The node was still directly above me. I tried again. <Please! I want to be the best, the strongest, the most versatile! I want to unravel the mysteries of the world, and I want to find Dani! Let me bond with you, please!>

'*No. Go away.*' I was sent away again, this time with far more force. I landed in a piteous heap, a jumble of soul and thought. I rose again. I would always rise again.

I screamed up at the pulsing node, <Got you to use three words that time! Soon you will be telling me your Name, and we will be the best of friends!>

'*We won't.*' I'm flying again but not really in the way I've dreamed about for so long.

DANI

Dani watched in horror as the infernal Core was force-fed sacrifices. There seemed to be an endless trail of creatures: Beasts, people, Runes, weapons, and other various artifacts. The wealth of a kingdom could not have purchased all of these goods. The influence of the dungeon was exploding outward. All the while it had reaffirmed its loyalty to The Master and was beginning to reproduce the artifacts that had been brought to it. A huge pile of weapons, armor, and accessories sat off to the side. Runes covered them, and most were inset with at least one chunk of flawless opal.

"What a good pet," The Master spoke, smiling as he watched the pile of weapons grow. His gaze turned and landed on Dani, his smile falling away. "You are bound to this place. We feed you. Why are you refusing to cooperate? If you don't start soon, you will become just another sacrifice."

"What you are asking is *impossible*!" Dani yelled at him, having held her thoughts back too long. "I'm bound to *my* dungeon, Cal! And I will stay that way until we die!"

The gaze turned thoughtful. "Oh? Or will you stay that way until... *he* dies, I wonder?" The Master began thundering orders as Dani became speechless.

"*Cal*," Dani released a horrified whisper.

Chapter Sixteen

<*Dani?!*> I had heard a whisper, a far-off part of me hearing my name being called. I forced myself up from the inky darkness of the floor, looking up again. The node hung there, suspended in the air like the sun. I began to scream at it, <Why won't you let me...>

'*You are flawed. You are imperfect. You are broken. Joining with you would be a waste, as my power would likely only shatter what is left of your wasted soul.*' The voice was still as potent as before and still without anger or malice. I didn't get blasted into the distance at least. That was a plus. At least we were on speaking terms now.

<Everyone and everything is imperfect!> I shouted at the haughty globe.

'*Untrue. For I am not.*'

<I would argue that you are!> I screamed in frustration. <You are an arrogant mass of energy!>

'*Yes. I am all laws perfected, and all laws stem from me. Arrogance was a third-tier. Which you silenced, if you recall.*'

I smiled. I had it now. <If you are all things, then you *are* imperfect! Refusing me because I am imperfect is denying yourself!>

'*Even your logic is flawed.*'

<Your face is flawed!> I instantly retorted.

'*I don't...*' I waited a while, but no further response seemed to be forthcoming. An hour passed, and right as I was about to try again, the law finally began to speak, '*You are not going to go away, are you?*'

<I will literally die first,> I agreed, settling in for the long haul.

'*I think that would be sooner than you seem to think. But...*' the law hesitated, '*it may be interesting to be used in the world. My descendants seem to enjoy it. Madness even more so than others. Plus... you* have *fulfilled the requirements.*'

<Requirements?> I opened my 'mouth' without thinking.

The law was silent for long enough that I thought it had changed its mind. It did speak eventually, to my great relief, '*You pushed higher than anyone before you in the tower of ascension. You work to purify your Essence to the best grade possible. You refuse to settle for less or an easier path. There are other reasons, but those are not for you to know. Are you sure you want me? Your path will be harder, slower to grow than other, easier paths. With your knowledge and understanding and a lesser law, you could enter the Spiritual realm in only a few years.*'

<Yes,> I replied without hesitation. <I want you.>

'*It is decided. Allow me to explain what happens now. The cultivation of laws is not as simplistic as the cultivation of Essence. To advance, to grow stronger, you must form deeper ties to me. You must deepen your understanding of me and become closer to our shared purpose. Still, you must draw in Essence and use it to feed the portion of myself that resides within you.*'

<And this lets me use Mana somehow?> I queried, trying to memorize every word spoken.

'*Pah. Mana. Yes. Until you have formed a connection with me that has fused your spirit with my concepts, you will only be able to use the byproduct of that joining. Or Mana, as you so eagerly call the leavings.*'

I thought of more questions. <Will larger amounts of Essence help me join faster?>

'*Not in the way you ephemerals seem to think, but, yes, it will. Giving me offerings of Mana or Essence will allow me to generate more Mana within your soul and its container. The more dense the Mana, the higher the chances of you finding a new facet of me, deepening your connection and making you closer to me. Study everything, and look for my truth within it.*'

<Will I be able to ask you questions once I leave this place?> I quickly begged, sensing growing impatience.

'*No. It is time. Do you accept me as the law you will live by, my goals as your own, in an attempt to grow as the other does?*'

<I... yes?> I had been caught off guard by the abrupt turn in conversation.

'*Then I accept you. Come to know me, and I will, in turn, grant you my power.*' There was light streaming down, forming a path to step on to. I did, racing along it as fast as I could. At the lowest tiers, I felt that I could have dove in and soaked in the knowledge offered. Here I was barely able to brush the surface of the node before flattening myself against it like an unbreakable barrier.

'*I offer you this knowledge, as much as you can take without outright dying at this time. I hope that you will be the first to progress on my path and hope you get past the least and lowest of my names. For now, this will have to do. I am all that is. I am Quintessence. I am Acme.*'

I screamed as my mind was flooded with thousands of images and concepts. My consciousness fluttered, darkness taking hold for a bare moment. When light returned, I was in my body again, looking out into my final room and up at the Silverwood tree. My mind shook as I worked through the meaning of the law I had attained. Acme. The definition of the word was hard enough: 'The highest level or degree attainable,

the peak of perfection.' How amazing. How wonderful. How...
the *crap* was I supposed to progress in *that*? Most of the flashes
of inspiration had faded from my mind, and I was nervous about
pushing too much right now. I felt *so* weak.

Too weak. Way too weak. I looked at myself and felt
very confused. I was no longer a diamond. I was a hexagon, and
I was *huge*. Well, comparatively. I was the size of a human fist
with six *perfectly* symmetrical sides. My concern at this moment
was that I was empty. I could see my Chi spiral as only a pale,
weakly spinning ghost of Essence, and not a hint of Mana to be
seen. I looked outside myself and saw a raging torrent of Essence
bubbling around me. Odd. Normally, that Essence would be
trying to force itself into me, why is it...? I looked at the shell of
what I assumed to be Core material around me and finally
noticed the truth.

<My outer shell is Mana?> I was pretty happy about
that, as Mana is basically indestructible but also worried as it
seemed that Essence also couldn't permeate it. There were no
openings, no imperfections, no ways for the Essence to flow into
me. The shell was too... perfect. Oh. Oh feces.

I sat in the cistern of burbling food, quickly starving to
death. What was the difference between what was out there and
what was in here? I tried to think, but dying is *really* distracting.
Maybe that is why Dale was so twitchy all the time. Heh. Maybe
I should... no, focus! My Mana is based off of the 'peak of
perfection, the highest grade available'. Maybe that is why this
Essence cannot get through? My Runes created a huge suction
force for Essence, condensing it to this level and purifying it.
Why would this *not* be the best available? Did I have the process
wrong? ...No. It is the Essence that is wrong. I looked at it
closely, and with my discerning vision saw tiny flickers of

corruption. Sitting here waiting to be used must have allowed it to interact with other types of corruption again.

I reached *out* with my Essence—luckily, I could still do so—and with nearly the last dregs of my strength, I willed Cores into being. They sat at the center of each face of my facets, one for each type of corruption. Then I *pulled* Essence through those Cores and shouted in relief as Essence flooded into me from six angles. For a day, all I did was pull in all of the Essence around me until, finally, all but the most recent drops were inside my Core. It was interesting to see because while my outer shell was Mana, everything inside was either my soul or Chi spiral, surrounded by liquid Essence. I looked like a three-dimensional hurricane to the untrained eye. Dang-nab, I'm sexy.

All of my newly refined Essence was being filtered into the hole in my soul, the pocket dimension inside of me. From there I could 'donate' it to the law in exchange for Mana. I could do as much or as little as I wanted at a time, so long as there was a constant trickle going in. From this point forward, there was never a time that I could simply *not* have Essence. I would be forced to make a continuous effort to improve and provide Essence. Otherwise, I instinctively knew I would die.

The reward though... the sweet reward of Mana was worth every moment of agony I had been subjected to during my ascension. I mean that in every way possible. I would go through that torture again and again if that was what it took to keep this power. I had just donated over half of all my remaining Essence, and now, the new energy was flowing through me. It began to take the place of all connections in my body. First, the pocket dimension of my soul was swept clean. Then the swirling galaxies of Essence were replaced by the icy perfection of Acme. The swirls became more pronounced, my soul being gently pushed toward the best configuration possible. I didn't resist the change, knowing that every step closer to my law would help me move through the rankings.

The Mana flowed up and out of the hidden hole, bubbling out like water from a new well. It flowed over my Chi spiral, transforming the Chi threads to thin bands of Mana. The new threads set like stones dropped into the earth from a great height. They seemed immovable, yet followed my commands readily. Just like that, cultivation was changed for me. I no longer needed to do anything and I would still be drawing in the Essence around me like I had at C-rank nine. The Cores would collect the taint, and the Chi threads would take the Essence from my environment by force.

My body finished with its alterations for the moment, and I began to extend my influence back into my dungeon. Aura expanding like a forest of vines in explosive growth, I swiftly reached my greatest range and filled the room. I then flowed into the next room and allowed my aura to unfurl across the entire floor. There was a *slight* problem though.

Before my ascension, my aura was disparate, thin, easily ignored. Now as a B-rank-zero being... when I extended myself, every Mob in the area died of sudden and massive blood loss. Their veins burst as I came in contact with them, so I quickly stopped my reaching. They looked like they had been crushed by a giant stone! What in the...? There was no help for it, I was simply too strong for these creatures. The pressure of my condensed aura in such close proximity was apparently lethal. Before I reconnected to my dungeon, I would need to add a new floor.

CHAPTER SEVENTEEN

"What an odd day," Rose commented as they entered the second floor of the dungeon. "Is it just me, or does this place feel kind of... empty?"

Tom nodded sagely. "I agree. The creatures of this floor are not attacking with their usual gusto! Come fight me, rabbits!"

"Maybe something happened after we left yesterday?" Dale offered his input, receiving shrugs in return. "I still think it was the right thing to do. We had to get that armor to the Spotters and warn people about the new Mobs we came across."

"Eh, we figured it out. Why can't they?" Hans complained darkly. "Take the warnings off of things, and let nature solve the problem that is annoying brats." He got some shocked looks from the others.

"Are you feeling alright?" Adam gently placed a hand on Hans. "You look ill."

"I'm fine, I've just had enough of this *snow*!" Hans kicked at the powder they were walking across. "Look at this, we are two levels down, and *still*, the wind blew snow this far! I'm sick of this constant white bullcrap!"

"You should have been in the mountains two years ago when there weren't walls up." Dale laughed at the shivering assassin. "I think only Tom and I are hardy enough to make it through *that* kind of winter."

"Well, you can have it!" Hans grumped, pulling his cloak tighter. "Let's go somewhere warm! Not even a whole vacation. A day trip! We need a break."

"*Thou* doth need a break." Tom released a booming laugh, getting Hans to stick out his tongue at the small giant.

"This weather is already a vacation for the Northmen like Dale and myself!"

Rose decided to join the conversation, "Dale lived here, *way* south of the northern kingdom. How is he a Northman? Also, while I hate to agree with Hans, a vacation to somewhere warm sounds nice."

"I can already hear the wedding bells!" Hans exclaimed while dancing in place.

Rose closed her eyes. "And *that's* why I hate to agree with you."

"Well, maybe the dungeon will add some flame traps. Just for you." Tom smirked at them.

"Puh-*lease* don't give it ideas," Dale exasperatedly begged, waiting to hear a snarky comment in his head. He started to get a bit nervous when he heard nothing. "Something is strange."

They completed their time in the dungeon with no incidents, getting lost in the labyrinth for only an hour today. Almost as though nothing were working against them. As they sat by the Silverwood tree and cultivated, Dale kept his eye on the area where he assumed the dungeon Core was. "Hans, you see anything *different* in here?"

Hearing the seriousness in Dale's voice, Hans looked around the area thoroughly. "No, everything looks about the same. A little brighter, perhaps? Why, you think Snowball is trying to creep up on us? *I'll skin you, you giant ball of fluff!*"

Snowball had gotten quite good at running away when it was seriously injured, and no one was foolish enough to chase it into the deep steams in its territory. Since they had been unable to bring him down today, they once again had to watch out for potential sneak attacks while cultivating.

"No, I just have a strange feeling," Dale explained away his nerves.

"Maybe it is the fact that the dungeon hasn't even bothered to look at us today?" Adam presented this idea quietly. His words made the others look at him, then at Dale for confirmation.

Dale nodded slowly. "Yes. No contact at all today either. Even when it was not exactly *talking* for a month, it would at least give us a cursory glare and mumble a few nasty slurs about our parentage." He shuddered as he remembered the last month and a half. The people who knew about the dungeon being alive all found it odd that the being seemed to think it was perfectly sane when it was obvious to most that its mind was slipping.

Normal details of the dungeon had been sloppy. Walls and floors that were damaged from attacks or traps remained scarred for days or, in some cases, indefinitely. Half-formed devices that failed to do anything, sickly mutant Mobs ran rampant. Most often, killing the Mob was a mercy to the pathetic creature. Still, the denial the dungeon was hiding in had not fooled anyone but itself.

"It seems that its mind has stabilized, at least for now, Dale," Adam told him quietly, guessing at his thoughts. "Things have been getting better in here. I think it found motivation somehow."

Hans had a crooked smile on his face. "Sure, but is that a good or a very bad thing?" he wondered aloud.

"I think... good," Dale slowly decided, nodding to himself. "I am also thinking that it is going to get very dangerous in here soon, and we need to train harder. Sorry, Hans. I don't think a vacation would be good right now."

"Workaholic," Hans muttered with a huff of breath that stayed visible in the freezing air. "Can we get going, then? I'm going to be training my liver in the tavern if any of you need me."

They all agreed on a time to meet the next day. Moving into the portal and stepping out into the church, they found a dangerous political argument raging.

"This will not stand, I tell you!"

Apparently, they had walked out into a heated debate among the visiting royal delegations. Dale looked around and was surprised to see people that hadn't been in the prior day's meeting. At a glance, he was able to see Crown Prince Henry of the Lion Kingdom as well as Crown Princess Marie of the Phoenix Kingdom. They must have rushed here to be a part of the current negotiations.

"These restrictions are *stifling*! There is no point in participating in *any* event from this place! No weapons, treasure, or access to the Silverwood tree? Why would we bother?!" the High Elf ambassador was shouting, cheeks tinged red, hair askew.

Princess Brianna of the Dark Elves calmly explained herself, for what must have been the sixth time, "The point is to build up goodwill so that you eventually *might* have access. You think *these* restrictions are stifling? Try to get access to Silverwood pollen from the High Elves as a Dark Elf! We've been reduced to *begging* in order to barely sustain our population!"

"You brought it on yourselves," the High Elf retorted coldly.

Brianna smirked, a dangerous glint in her eye. "As. Have. You." The area settled into an uneasy silence as Dale stepped forward to take a seat at the table. He snorted as he saw Hans sprint toward the room's exit.

Remembering his etiquette training at the last second, Dale gave a deep bow to both the Prince and Princess before sitting. "So. How are things?"

His words brought forth an explosion of noise as tempers flared. Henry gave him a *look* before chuckling and shaking his head. "Baron Dale!"

"I think the town is going by 'Mountaindale', actually. Not Barondale," Dale responded jokingly, not bothering to keep the smirk from his face.

"Subtle. Humility suits you." Henry gave him a real smile this time. "It is good to see you looking so well! Healthy. *Alive.*"

"I am surprised every day that I awaken, Your Majesty," Dale spoke formally. The High Elf snorted something that sounded suspiciously like 'me too'.

"I just don't see what *worth* there is in becoming allied with this... work camp," the Elf's voice sliced through the air, drawing attention back to himself.

Brianna cut off any further words from him, "Oh, yeah. Me neither. After all, there are neutral-affinity dungeons that create artifacts, have portal systems built-in, and are growing Silverwood trees all *over* the place. This particular dungeon *definitely* won't be an important place in the future. You're right. You should go."

"Nay, Princess, he does have a point," the Amazonian delegate spoke with more deference than Dale had ever heard from her. "This is a work camp and mining facility with a sprinkling of herbalists and deranged alchemists. While a potentially excellent place to cultivate, the cost-effectiveness of the action does not make it viable—at least on a scale large enough to make it profitable."

"It all comes back to one thing!" the Elf jumped into the conversation feet first. "This place is desolate, remote, and useless but for the dungeon. What do you export? How do you get food? Is it all just weapons and money? That is nice but achievable elsewhere. The price of food is so high that we would be hemorrhaging money if we tried to stay here for any length of time."

Dale was aghast at the ideas being bandied about. He hadn't even thought about it. If the portal was to close, this place would likely starve. Wait, no! They could eat the Mob meat from the dungeon, and they had a source of clean water. There were more logistics involved, but... it was true that the town had no greater purpose beyond cultivation and the other reasons they had listed. What could he do to draw others here? Make this a proper city? He was so deep in thought that he almost missed the answer when it was given.

"Excuse me!" An awkward man stepped forward, nervous energy making him cough and smooth his shirt repeatedly.

"Who are you, and what do you want?" a guard asked, weapon already in hand and leveled at the intruder's heart.

"My name is Mason Masonson," Mason proudly announced. His name drew a few chuckles from the assorted royalty. "I am the official city planner for the city of Mountaindale, and I think that my plans and notes will be able to solve at least some of the issues we are facing here."

A few people snorted at the non-cultivator and started to argue again, but Dale motioned him forward. Mason nodded at him and continued, "It is true, Mountaindale has little in the way of food or city splendor, no wonders of the world, nor easy access. But! It has one thing that most other places do not."

The High Elf sighed, happy that his point was being made for him. "Yes, yes, the dungeon is impressive, but–"

Mason cut him off, "No! That isn't the point I am trying to make! Also, could you move your seat a bit to the right? You are making the whole pattern of chairs asymmetrical. No? *Ahem.* As I was saying, this town is a bastion of cooperation and political equivalency between multiple races and kingdoms."

Taking a breath, he charged forward with his explanation, "My suggestion is this: form an academy on this spot to house and train cultivators. The political neutrality will allow Nobles from most known lands to interact without great bias or territorial urges. This may well allow connections to form between them. Furthermore, neutral Essence will allow for a student body impossible in other locations. Clans, families, and cultivators will be able to remain in a singular location! This combination will bring trade, revenue, and greater bonds between the kingdoms!" He looked at the glowering Amazons and hastily added, "And queendoms."

The suggestion was met with an interesting mix of reactions. Most people seemed troubled, but it seemed that the overall consensus was a moderate to positive acceptance. The High Elf spoke up, "That is all well and good for all of you but does not particularly help *my* cause."

"I'm sure," Henry's baritone voice stopped the argument that threatened to return in full force, "that we could find exceptions to the trade embargos for students as well as people that come here to teach. An academy fits very well into my hopes for my people. Marie? Would you agree?" He looked at the Princess sitting near him.

"I do agree. Although competition for teaching positions may quickly become fierce. Especially if we reduce restrictions on teachers to a greater degree than even the students," Marie stated blandly, as if there wasn't a room full of people hanging on every word she spoke. "Of course, the teachers would need to actually be *good* teachers. Not just figureheads that ignore their students. I can also see benefits for the Guild; having access to a center of learning could streamline Guild admission. Imagine not having to spend *years* on each new recruit. Kingdoms could use it to train their own talented youngsters as well." Her speech was met by almost unanimous glee.

The High Elves furiously discussed amongst themselves, shooting glances at the nearby Dark Elves. They eventually turned back to the meeting. "We will need to know exact details, but we will... tentatively agree to this. For the time being."

Thaddius, the Dwarven ambassador, smiled broadly as well. "I would love to offer the services of my people as well! We can have the campus built in no time! For a long-term modest reduction in the taxes and tariffs, of course..."

"I will leave the details to my trusted councilors." Dale nodded at the council members and excused himself. He had a few questioning glances thrown his way. Dale simply nodded at the people vying for his attention and quietly reminded them that this was council business, and he trusted them to make the best deal for the area. Father Richard smiled at this indirect praise, and Frank bobbed his head seriously at the young lord, determined to prove his worth and live up to the trust that had been given to him.

Dale kept smiling until he was out of the building. Then looking around to ensure he was alone, dipped his hand into a pocket and crushed a Core. Essence flowed into him, and he started to sweat as he brushed against the barrier to the next ranking. His fully open affinity channels and daily cultivation— coupled with shattering Cores—had pushed him to the brink of D-rank-six. He was having trouble progressing at this point and so kept trying to force a leap in ranks. Breaking Core after Core, he did his best to force a breakthrough. He was close, he was...! Dale suddenly stiffened and bent over. After violently vomiting on the ground—an unwelcome reminder that his body currently couldn't handle the amount of Essence contained in it—Dale stood and hurriedly wobbled off to find Craig.

Craig was currently giving a lecture to a few new members of the Guild, sharing a few pointers on their combat styles. Dale tried to be patient but ended up puking again. After glancing over at him, Craig nodded at the men, dismissed the people trying to learn from him, and hurried over.

"Dale is everything alright?" Craig's eyes widened. "Ah. You are already at this point? Why do I keep being surprised by you? Come with me." He turned and led Dale to a secluded area.

He shook his head at the trembling Dale. "You went beyond your limits without comprehension of the consequences. You aren't too far over though... Why didn't you use a technique and remove some of the Essence before coming to me?"

Dale opened his mouth to reply and then snapped it shut. "I..."

"Didn't think of it?" Craig put a hand on Dale to guide him to a large rock. "Well, at this point, you should just use it to fuel your advancement. To get into the sixth of the D-rankings, you need to learn how to store excess Essence in your aura. Currently, your cells are saturated, meaning they cannot hold more in them. Your Center... my pardon, your *Core* is able to hold the Essence, but locking it all away is detrimental to your growth. I believe you are already familiar with the act of tightening your aura? Preventing empaths and weak mind readers from gaining access?"

Dale nodded, too sick to respond properly.

"Good, that will make this easier." Craig motioned for Dale to sit. "Now, similar to using a technique, release Essence into your aura, where you normally work to keep it compact. It will be a strange feeling, like bleeding heavily. Worry not, you aren't losing your Essence, just moving it to an unused storage area."

Dale did as instructed and would have panicked if Craig hadn't given him the warning he had. He kept releasing Essence into the aura around him, until finally, Craig told him to stop. Dale opened his eyes to see Hans sitting right in front of him, their noses almost touching.

"Boo!" Hans barked, almost making Dale wet himself. "Ha ha! Always fun. D-rank six, huh? First time boosting your aura? Feels a lot like letting out a fart after holding it in for a long time, yeah?"

Craig slapped Hans to the ground. "Must you always be so crass?"

"Uh-huh," Hans affirmed, hopping to his feet and offering a hand to Dale.

"Work to keep your aura as close to your body as possible, as tight as possible," Craig demanded as Dale rose. "As you approach the C-ranks, your aura will become dense enough to slow down many normal attacks. It isn't a shield, but a few tenths of a second can mean victory or death." It was already dark, so Dale thanked his teacher and hurried off to find his combat instructor—before *he* came looking for Dale again.

Craig watched the young Lord go, turning to Hans after Dale was finally out of earshot. "He is going to tear his body apart if he keeps cultivating at that rate. Did you try to get him to take a break?"

"I suggested a vacation. He was adamantly against it." Hans grimly watched the silhouette of Dale disappear. "Poor kid thinks things are going to start getting dangerous below, and I agree. At least the way he is training, his body should mitigate the effects of Essence poisoning. His work ethic would put a *royal* to shame."

"Too bad his cultivation technique isn't at their standard," Craig agreed begrudgingly. "His current formation is having a hard time processing what he is taking in. If he gets even a *little* corruption in his Core, I highly doubt he will ever be able to even enter the C-rankings. I have no idea how he is able to refine so much corruption out in so short a time with such a sub-par cultivation technique."

"Well, actually, let me tell you about that..." Hans threw an arm around Craig and started walking away, explaining a few things he had learned recently.

Craig stopped moving after a short discussion, turning and trying to chase after Dale. Hans grabbed his robe and held him back. "Let me go! I want him to talk to the dungeon for me!"

"Ha! I already tried that!" Hans' body began shaking from laughing at the struggling monk.

CHAPTER EIGHTEEN

I was really having trouble getting more Essence into myself. I wasn't starving, per se, but I needed to find a way to create greater throughput or I may have trouble in the future. I think a part of it had to do with my current restriction to this room; without my aura spread throughout the dungeon, anything that died did not have its Essence rushed to my Core. Right then, I was relying on the Runes around me to pull in ambient energy. Hopefully, the Runes would overpower other flora or fauna that are trying to draw it in, but the current, *diminutive* trickle of power was making me doubt their efficacy.

My 'eyes' rolled as I chastised myself. Realistically, my plans wouldn't change because of the lack of energy. If anything, I needed to accelerate them. So. Creating a new floor. Because I did not have a great glut of time, I knew I needed to do something drastically different than the floors above. Having decided on a minuscule floor only measuring a few hundred meters in diameter, I began sinking the entire area I was occupying including the Silverwood tree. Similar to the fourth floor, my Core area was attached to the main room of this floor by way of a short corridor. The space I had previously occupied was covered over by a reinforced clear Quartz 'window' to allow light to filter down. When I found better materials to hold corruption, I would replace this as well as all of the material in the 'windows' above.

I released my aura, and my mind fully engulfed this new floor. Ahhh, much better. I had been feeling a bit claustrophobic. What to do with the area though...? It was too small for a maze, really had no room for tunnels either. Oh! Why not a floor devoted entirely to a Boss? My floor Bosses to this point were... decent but still fairly easy to circumvent or defeat with enough tactics and knowledge. On top of that, Snowball had taken to running away! *Running. Away.* What was even the point? Stupid Cat, doing whatever it wanted. I wanted something... more. More deadly, more vicious. Harder to avoid. No more sneaking around to get past it and move on to a deeper floor after emptying the chest it was guarding. From this point forward, I was going to place restrictions on movement. Something along the lines of—you want to get past this room? You need the key in the chest. Where is the chest? The Boss *ate it!* Good luck getting to it without taking down the Boss. Viable option? We'll see. I believe in myself.

Still, I wasn't sure what to actually *make*. I struggled with my thoughts before nearly slapping myself in the face. Creating a Boss was not the point of this floor right now! I dug deeper to give myself a way to dampen my aura enough for the creatures above to survive. Now that I was fully entrenched in my new home, I released my aura and started expanding. I flowed up to the next floor like an unstoppable tsunami, needing to reassert my influence in the area. Snowball roared happily as I reestablished a connection with him, scaring a group on this floor enough to make them decide to leave.

My bond with the great Cat seemed odd, and I thought about it as I moved on. Oh! I see, since I had reached the B-ranks my bonds were now made of Mana instead of Essence. I paused, reached out, and stirred the ambient Essence, just to make sure I could still use it. I could, very easily in fact. It made me wonder why Mages only ever seemed to use Mana. Ignoring a resource like this was just... wasteful!

I pressed on, flowing to the third floor. The Goblins began to rejoice as they felt their connection to me reform, stronger than ever. The group of people fleeing the third floor hesitated and ran to use the portals instead of retracing their steps. I laughed at their fear. They were running from *noise*, not even a real threat! Interestingly, there were several creatures that had been born while outside of my influence. While their parents were indeed made by me, it seemed that the standard rules were lifted for the few births over the last... um.

<Bob, how long have I been gone?> It had seemed to be months, possibly years, so I was prepared for some weird stuff to happen.

"Roughly a week, Great Spirit," Bob happily informed me while assessing my increase in power.

<That's it? Huh. I guess torture of the soul is far faster than for the body,> I wondered aloud.

"Torture?" Bob gasped in righteous fury. "Who would *dare*—"

<The ascension process, Bob. It was very... harsh,> I told him solemnly. <You'll get there someday, and I hope that I can be there to help guide you through it.>

"You would do that for me?" Bob seemed surprised for some reason. "What tier of Mage are you? If that question makes sense. In the past, I've heard Mages boasting about their 'tier'. Oh! Also, congratulations! The world has another Mage, and we are all the greater for it!"

<Hey, thanks, Bob! As to tier... top, I guess? The highest possible? Does that mean anything to you?> I warmly kept a bit of attention on him as I refilled the dungeon with my aura. It seemed smaller than I remembered. <Just for your edification, I also completed a new floor, but am uncertain of how to populate it. I have a few ideas, but I think I will let you hear about it through the mutterings of terrified adventurers. More fun that way.>

Bob chuckled at my vehemence. "I look forward to it! I am unsure what the differences between the tiers are, and I don't know why it matters. All are still ranked in the normal way. Also, on an unrelated note, you should keep an eye on the walking armor. They have gathered quite a kill count, though a few of them have stopped functioning."

<Oh? Are they that strong?> I looked around in interest. Bob had good taste; his recommendations were usually correct.

"More that they have a... unique way of moving during combat. I think that it will pique your interest." Bob allowed a frightening smile to cross his face.

<I look forward to watching them! Until then, any news from above? Has Minya contacted you, by chance?>

"Not yet, though your ritual for digging has been throwing odd things into the room that you have not been able to absorb. I'd suggest you clean that out soon. It is going to start overflowing otherwise," Bob informed me with a grimace. "It also smells terrible."

<I'll look at it.> I turned my attention to the room and would have winced if I were a human. Bob had *not* been joking when he said it was about to overflow. Beyond the dirt and rock, there was a variety of... stuff. There were gemstones, metals, and shards of bone. The most concerning though was a fountain of black fluid that was spewing into the room. It had apparently been a pocket of pressurized fluid because now it was splashing against the ceiling. I began absorbing all of the refuse in the room, collecting a few things I had never seen before. The black sludge coming up was an oddity. It stank, but it contained *celestial* corruption of all things!

I looked into the makeup of this crude oil—for that is what it was—and was amazed by what I found. Every bit of it was slightly different than the rest! It was an amalgamation of concentrated life! There were plants, animal tissue, and various minerals. I poured a small amount of celestial Essence into the room to see what happened, and it was instantly sucked into the fluid! Had I found the best absorber of celestial corruption? I think so! I played with it for a bit, trying to find a way to turn it into a solid form. I was startled when I noticed something. I was wrong. Rare, I know, but it *does* happen. Ask my wife—I mean, my Wisp.

The oil was full of celestial Essence, yes. It absorbed more when offered Essence, correct. But, oddly, there was an issue with my earlier supposition that it was a celestial Essence gathering device. Lurking under the celestial Essence was something that should have been impossible and had been impossible for all of known history—infernal Essence. I was looking at a source of *chaos* Essence! While these two were the main types of corruption present, *every* type of Essence was contained in this amazing solution! I tried a few experiments with it. I solidified it by adding earth corruption, creating a sticky tar. I poisoned water with it, creating a dangerous liquid that could likely kill via prolonged skin contact. For fun, I burned it. This released actual chaos Essence into the *air*! What could this gas do to a person? Was it poison? Would it affect their mental state? I needed to know! I needed more.

I followed the hole in the floor downward, extending my influence swiftly. I kept going and going. I was amazed by the depth of the hole; that ritual was worth every bit of Essence it drained from me! I finally found the source of the oil, a massive cavern over forty thousand feet below me! That's twelve kilometers! Seven and a half miles! Why am I converting between Dwarven and human standard measurements? Because I am in shock! I felt around the cavern, and as far as I could tell, it stretched for miles. The crude oil was also swirling in a massive whirlpool. I was confused for a moment until I looked for the source and found the disk of spinning Essence from the boring ritual.

Huh. It seems to have stopped digging after finding nothing solid for a while. It was a fail-safe I had built in, but I had not expected this scenario. I figured it would have stopped after finding a lake of lava. Magma. Whatever. This worked well for me right now, though. I could not make this cavern a part of my dungeon yet; there was too much distance between my main area and this huge space. The hole to get down here was now a part of me, but I would need to be *much* more powerful to hold the entire area as my own. For now, I relaxed and allowed the flow of oil to continue.

I settled back, thinking hard. I was feeling bad for being so excited without Dani here, but I needed to get stronger in order to get her back. Quite the conundrum. With the source of Essence and corruption I had just found, it was time to start putting my plan into action. It was time to start writing Runescript.

CHAPTER NINETEEN

"Can we go?" Dale elbowed Tom in the hip. This most recent meeting was dragging on, as various groups were trying to leverage for better deals.

"I wish to adjourn as well, but the treacherous Amazonians are speaking currently," Tom 'whispered' in reply, his voice loud enough to garner nasty glances from the supremely muscular women.

"We are *not* treacherous! Who let this filthy brute in here anyway?" one of the Amazonians spoke loudly in response. "I think it is shedding."

Tom reddened. "My most sincere apologies. You were not meant to hear that–"

"Well, I did! I think that recompense is–" the Amazonian was cut off by Tom's next words.

Tom calmly finished his small speech, ignoring her interruption, "–because I was sure that you would try to find a way to twist my words like the filthy liars you are."

The Amazonian threw herself across the table, hands grasping for Tom's throat. "You are little better than *breeding* stock, you disgusting *man!*"

"You don't even make *my* top one hundred list for potential breeding companions!" Tom laughed in her face as Dark Elves appeared to hold back the furious Amazon.

"Tom, I think it is time to go," Dale firmly stated, standing and lifting Tom from his seat. Tom tried to resist, but much to the mirth of those around the table, Dale easily carried the huge barbarian away. Cultivation was everything.

The Amazonian laughed spitefully as she was led back to her seat. "Hah! And he is so *tiny*. Like a doll."

Dale set Tom down when they reached open air, assuming the blowing snow would at least cool the huge man down. "What the *abyss* was that about, Tom? That is a table representing one of the largest diplomatic deals in known history!"

Tom stood and brushed himself off unnecessarily. "You cannot trust them. Do you know what they did to get around a treaty they had made with the Kingdom of the Wolf?"

"Obviously not, Tom," Dale spoke in a hard tone.

"They killed their own Princess!" Tom roared, slamming his warhammer into the frozen earth. The ground shattered, throwing a huge amount of dirt and snow into the air. "She had been the one to sign the accords, and the Mana of the contract enforced all oaths! Her people moved without her knowledge, on the *Queen's* orders! Her *mother's* orders! As soon as they struck, the Princess withered! She died *screaming* as her body was ravaged by Mana! *That* is the honorless people you are making a deal with!"

"When was this?" Dale was shocked by the fury in Tom's voice. Wouldn't he have heard about this somehow?

"Four hundred years ago!" Tom spat to the side. "It has not even passed from living memory yet. It will not, so long as I, my brothers, or my father continue to survive."

"Four hundred years...?" Dale shook his head at the vast time scale. "Why is it so meaningful to you? You are not even close to being that old."

Tom tried to calm down, his hands shaking. "It was my *mother*. My father's first wife. No, not the woman who bore me, but *all* of my Father's wives are my mother. We are given the memories of all the male children my father has, to tie us together as siblings. You know the power of memory stones. The memories become your own."

"How many childhoods do you have in your head?" Dale was astonished by this revelation.

"Fifty," Tom stated bluntly. "It is needed. To help us train faster, to see the folly of weakness and lethargy. You want to know why we train so hard? One of us... the happiest of us... was allowed a pampered childhood, filled with love and lavished with toys and gifts. That is the first stone we are always given. We are then given memories of how that one died, how weak he was. Then we are trained as *true* Northmen. Failure is allowed, but weakness is not."

"That sounds terrible," Dale admitted softly. "I am sad to say I do not know my companions very well."

"You know me now." Tom shrugged his broad arms. "I would have held my words, but I needed you to know what you are getting into. Their ruler will *never* sign a contract herself, just in case she decides to break it. She will sacrifice anyone, obviously even her own *daughters*, to attain her twisted goals."

Dale was silent for a bit as they walked toward the tavern. "Thank you for telling me this, but I cannot restrict them entirely if I want this to work. I will keep a close eye on them, I swear to you. Why did they break their treaty?"

Tom huffed at the memory. "They killed off all of their men. By accident or design, I am uncertain. The treaty was a way for our people to be joined, slowly. Then they got sick of allowing men to have any rights whatsoever in their society, so they attacked us, trying to capture 'breeding stock'. The only reason they failed their cowardly assault was the onset of the Great War. The necromancers seemed to focus on their front. We have never learned why. I dislike the thought, but in truth, I am grateful for necromancers."

Hans walked out of the tavern just as they were walking up and caught the last bit of the conversation. "They have their uses. Tend to go insane though."

"I thought they were the worst thing ever?" Dale looked between the two.

"I'd say they get... led astray. No one starts as a bad person." A dark look crossed Hans' face. "If you ever have the misfortune to chat up a demon, you will understand. I'll try to get you free of them before you start killing *too* many people."

"...Thanks?" Dale had a lot to think about as they went to dinner.

Later, as night was falling, Dale sprinted away from his Essence control class taught by Craig, who was eying him oddly and greedily. No matter how Dale phrased his question, Craig wouldn't say why he was acting strangely. Not pressing the matter, Dale had decided to hurry away. He was fretting about the next round of tonight's training, as he had been told that his Moon Elf instructor had something 'special' for him. 'Nervous' could not fully explain the way Dale was feeling. Fortunately or unfortunately, he didn't have to wait long to find out what was awaiting him.

"Good! You are early. That should make this easier for you. Smart move." The Moon Elf appeared with his customary abruptness. "Tonight is special because we get to see if you have made any *actual* progress. Tonight, we test your ability to shape Essence under pressure as well as how devoted you are to surviving!"

Dale nodded, bracing himself for combat. "What do you want me to do?"

The Elf's eyes twinkled as he walked towards Dale. "Isn't it obvious? I just said it! Survive, brat." He grabbed Dale and threw him, *hard*. Dale twisted himself, preparing for the impact of landing. He was terrified as he turned and saw that he had passed the edge of the cliff face a dozen feet ago.

"What the *abyss*!" Dale screamed as he entered free-fall. He tried to 'swim' in the air, attempting to get closer to the sheer rock face he was falling past. As he got closer, he realized he was falling too fast to grab the passing rock without the potential of seriously injuring himself. He looked at the ground far below him, trying to ascertain a place he could land without dying. The chill winter was not as bad at the base of the mountain, which was moving toward him unpleasantly rapidly. This was good and bad. The milder temperature meant that ice wouldn't be as thickly set into the earth but bad as the snow would not have deep drifts to soften his landing.

He eyed the lake, which was frozen over. If he was going to smash into it, he needed to time the use of his Essence correctly. Or he would die. At least he knew better than to let the Moon Elf ever get near him again. Dale started trying to form his Essence into a pattern, but his new, strengthened aura kept blocking his attempts to send out a Chi thread. Dale began panicking. Was he about to die because his aura had gotten too *strong*? Because it was blocking him from using his own Essence?! In desperation, he reached into his bag and pulled out a Core. If he was too strong *externally*, he needed to boost his internal reserves to match it! He crushed the Core in his hand without looking at it.

The Core had been pulled from a Wither Cat and contained *far* more Essence than he had ever attempted to absorb through his gauntlet. His hand went numb as the Core shattered, and Dale was surrounded by a halo of Essence as it tried to simultaneously rush into him and escape into the environment. Dale's eyes blazed with blue light as he formed and completed the technique he was after. Harsh screams escaped his lips as he activated the technique that had not been intended for use with water. A tower of light visible to the naked eye shot from his hand, collecting the majority of Essence from the halo around him. The bolt shot down into the ice, passing through it and detonating a dozen feet underwater. The shattering technique forced each drop of water away from any other that was near it, creating a massive cavitation bubble that shot water in the only direction it was allowed to go. Up.

A massive geyser of water, shattered ice, and somehow... steam, shot toward Dale, slamming into him and arresting his descent. He resumed falling, but now it was with multiple thousands of gallons of water. The water fell ahead of him, and with a great crash, all of the liquid slapped back into the lake. Dale was in the midst of the water as it landed, his body horrendously bruised but unbroken. Luck and cultivation had saved him, and now, he was swimming madly for the surface. The water was oddly warm, most likely from all of it being agitated and forcefully moved. He burst through the surface, drawing in a lungful of life-giving air.

As he pulled himself on to land and sat, he began shaking first from reaction, then from the cold. A gust of wind reminded him that he was soaking and slowly drifting into a state of numbness. Staggering to his feet, he tried to ignore his body as it attempted to shut down from shock. Dale understood what tonight's test was about now. It was less about ability than willpower. Did he have what it took to survive?

Dale shook himself like a dog, trying to dry his clothes before they became too icy. With a start, he realized that there was a simple solution to this problem. He cycled his Essence aggressively, then made the same motions as when he had been bathing. The water around him sprayed away in loops, and within a moment, Dale was mostly dry. His teacher's favorite saying was 'adversity breeds innovation', which made sense to him for the first time.

"Nowhere to go but up," Dale muttered, looking at the imposing hike ahead of him. He was near the base of the mountain, far from any easy path. He knew this mountain very well though, having lived here all of his life. If he climbed the sheer face *there*, he could cut a few hours off his trip. The climb should bring him to a trail, and from there, it would just be walking. He started climbing; his enhanced body and tireless muscles allowing him to make good time. For an hour, he climbed almost vertically. Pulling himself over the edge, he stepped on to the path he had been aiming for. Dale grinned; it was good to be proven correct.

He took a few steps before a vicious roar tore the satisfied grin from his face. Dale flinched and dropped into a combat pose quickly. What was that? He saw a blurry shape beginning to rise from the snow and quietly began moving away from it. He stepped as softly as he could, making his way toward home. The form began snuffling at the air, groaning and grunting a bit. Its head whipped in his direction, and a pair of reflective eyes stared right at him. Dale grimaced, preparing to fight.

The beast stepped forward, coming into view. Dale swore softly at the size of what had to be a natural Beast. As in, a *minimum* C-rank creature with a stable Core that grew to that rank by killing others. It looked like a cross between a rhinoceros and a bear, a Bearocerous? A Rhinobear? Its paws were large and seemed designed to keep its bulk out of deep snow, and it was heavily furred. Tiny eyes peered at Dale's still form, and a large double horn on its snout rose above dangerously sharp teeth.

"What are you doing here?" Dale whispered to himself. The Beast pawed at the ground and bellowed, charging at him. Dale knew that he had no chance of beating this creature in a stand-up fight, so he did the thing anyone trying to survive would. He turned and ran. "Abyss, abyss, *abyss!*" he called over and over like a mantra as he poured on the speed. The Bearocerous was gaining ground, obviously better suited to the drifts of snow that were becoming larger and harder to traverse.

Just before the charging Beast could catch up, Dale remembered that he was not the same as he had been years ago. He was so used to relying on his physical form at this point that he had trouble adapting to situations that called for something *more.* He activated his earthen movement technique and suddenly shot forward on a wave of earth. The Beast behind him roared in frustration but slowed and turned around after ensuring the puny human was out of its territory. It chuffed and growled, but Dale was safe from this threat.

Dale rode his minor earth ability for a few minutes, covering ground as fast as a horse could sprint. A break was needed between uses of this ability; he was not used to using it in a continuous fashion. Riding along the wall of the cliffs, he was able to avoid a half-dozen Beasts that were wandering the mountain. Those creatures weren't native to this area; why were they here? An hour of pure running and hiding later, the newly rebuilt wall of his town appeared over the horizon, and his heart soared as he rushed to the gate. A few minutes after being admitted to the town, Dale approached his training ground and spotted the Moon Elf patiently waiting for him.

"So has tonight been a productive night?" the Moon Elf called with a smirk. Dale waited until he was close, then took a vicious swing at the pompous Elf. With easy grace, the Elf avoided the blow and frowned. "Well, it didn't make you smarter. Let's try again! Bye-bye." He grabbed Dale and threw him toward the edge of the cliff again.

This time, Dale was prepared. With a flare of Essence, he sent strands of Chi into the air around him. He gripped the air, not trying to form a technique but to simply interact with it. The result was akin to what a snowshoe did on snow; it evened out the force of his weight and movement. He came to a stop in midair and slowly dropped to the ground.

"Well, *that's* new." The Moon Elf's eyes were glistening as Dale stood firmly. "You got back early enough for us to continue, and it looks like we can finally *start* your training." He seemed to flicker, and Dale felt a fist smash into his stomach. It was going to be a long night, full of harsh, painful lessons.

CHAPTER TWENTY

<What would you say is the most difficult portion of cultivating, Bob?> I murmured to my Goblin as I played with a ritual that would almost certainly do a massive amount of damage if I got the components wrong.

"For my people, it has always been surviving long enough to get any substantial amount of it done," Bob answered calmly. "Now though, I would say the tedium of refining through meditation is what drives our people from taking advantage of it."

<Hmm. Good point. Why bother to cultivate when killing my enemies gives you a portion of their Essence?> I mused sardonically.

"Just so." He nodded, flinching as my Essence shattered a rock that was in the way. "Your power has grown substantially, Great Spirit. You must have bound yourself to a powerful law."

I chuckled. <I did, but it is a real jerk to talk to.>

Bob just looked confused.

<You'll know soon enough. We'll get you to be an *actual* Mage soon enough,> I promised as I carved another line into the floor. I stopped, inspecting my work. A small breeze kicked up, blowing the dust out of my carving. <For me, the issue of cultivation is not the *doing* of it but having access to enough space to drain the Essence. This ritual should—if I have thought it through correctly—take care of that problem for me.>

"Ah, to have such issues," Bob wistfully joked.

<Pah. You laugh, but breaking into the higher ranks is going to be *really* difficult for me. I'm going to need knowledge and a quantity of Essence that I cannot even fathom. My law is absolute and demands perfection from me.> When I said the last

word, Bob cried out, holding his head in pain. The ambient Essence around my Core was drained into me, and the liquid Essence I had been storing was forcefully 'donated' to my law, my 'word of power'. Internally, I felt a rush of Mana as a few more universal truths suddenly made sense to me.

Bob looked around, blood streaming from his ears. I quickly healed him, wincing mentally as I found his eardrums had been pulped. "What just happened?" he shouted, clapping his hands over his ears as sound came rushing back to him.

I felt my Core in astonishment. <I... I think I just ranked up? I'm B-rank one now?>

Bob shuddered. "Well. I'm glad I was this far from your Core then. I think perhaps you misjudged your needs for ranking higher?"

I thought about his words. <No, I think that I stumbled upon a bit of truth that I needed. I admitted to myself and aloud what I had to do to connect more fully to my law. It recognized that, and I was able to move slightly further into its embrace.>

My shaman nodded. "That is plausible, especially seeing now that you have already grown in strength. Maybe in the future though, you bounce ideas like that one off of adventurers? It may make a good trap. Killed by complaining."

<Funny.> I ignored him as he laughed, still wiping away blood from his face. I finished my carving. <I can't activate this yet, but we need to make sure that we didn't miss anything. Take a few days and a few Bobs, and really go over this. Tear it apart with critical thinking. It *literally* needs to be perfect for me to activate it.>

"Your will, my command." Bob bowed as the pressure of my presence exited the room.

I sighed. Everything I was doing was feeling like busy-work. Like I was just marking time until I...

"Cal?" a voice called out.

My attention whipped toward the intrusive noise. <Minya! Welcome back. How are things going?>

Her voice had preceded her into the dungeon via the portals, and when she stepped in, a look of horror crossed her face as she grabbed at her chest and collapsed to her knees. It took a second for me to realize what was happening. Our bond was being updated via my Mana, replacing the Essence that had connected us. After a moment, she shuddered and stood.

"Celestial..." she muttered, holding her hand to her head. "That was unexpected. You moved into the Mage ranks? You are a B-ranked dungeon now? Congratulations! The church of Cal will grow wonderfully when this news is spread!"

<Thank you! I have a church?> I was going to say more, but she started to barrage me with questions.

"You must have bound to a powerful law to have that kind of effect on me just after reaching this rank! What did you bind to? Or can't you tell me? Is it a jealous law? I know some can be overly secretive, so don't worry if you can't let me know, but what is it?" She finally stopped to take a breath.

I quickly cut her off and explained my ascension. She was a good audience and got really excited at all the right parts. When I explained about how the Silverwood tree had intervened, she actually squealed with delight.

"The question of Silverwood trees has bothered me my entire life! So *that* is how they help? They let you push into a higher tier you normally wouldn't be able to? Amazing!" Minya gushed happily. "This is going directly into the dungeon manual I am writing!"

<So, I've told you my story. You, uhm, have anything for me?> I tried to jog her memory.

She nodded, reaching into her bag and pulling out an assortment of goods. "Don't absorb these yet—let me explain them." Good thing she told me, I was ready to take a bite. She started pointing at the items in sequence. "These are Runes that are forbidden in the cultivation world outside of actual wartime emergencies. If I were to have been found giving these to you, I would be hunted down for treason. As the lowest charge."

<The black market was that good?> I would be dancing if I had feet. A few nearby Bashers were forced to do it for me. They were pretty good, too.

"You have no idea! I got the good stuff," she promised with a scary grin. "This is a Rune known as 'taunt'. Anything that sees it while it is active is drawn to it like a moth to a flame. It ignites hatred and fury, causing those afflicted to attack it and the one *using* it. There are a few conditions to use it properly though. It has to be moving, at least a little. Like bait. For example, you can't connect it to a wall and expect it to force people to pound on the stone."

<Okay. That seems doable. So set it on to helmets or something for my Goblins?> I offered examples for clarity sake. <Or I could just make the wall vibrate?>

"Use helmets only if you want people to bash them in the head over and over, sure. I'd suggest shields." Minya chuckled warmly. I would have blushed if I could; that was so obvious! "This one over here is known as a 'catapult defense' Rune. It has the ability to affect the weight of things that pass over it. The heavier the object, the more it affects it. In a siege, these are placed in strategic locations. When a rock or ballista bolt goes over them, they suddenly are much heavier for a second or two. This forces them to drop to the ground much faster than intended, which can be really beneficial."

<Sounds like a gravity altering Rune,> I muttered softly, looking it over. <Maybe a weak version of that crushing Rune formed from Dani's Mithril armor breaking?>

"What? You *broke* Mithril armor?" Minya was so surprised that she stopped explaining. "Is that a joke?"

<Don't worry about it, keep going,> I forced the conversation back on track.

"Uhm. Right. This is a wound-healing Rune. This was certainly, by far, the best find!" she told me excitedly.

<A healing Rune?> I scoffed a bit. <Minya, I was kind of looking for *dangerous* Runes.>

"Oh, this is dangerous." She nodded as if in deep thought. "Improperly used or used overmuch, it causes the target of the Rune to be in a state of extreme metabolism. Their body is trying to divert all resources to healing, but without a wound, it just stays in 'high alert' if you will. The stress damages the body, which is then healed, which causes more damage. They can't sleep, they make mistakes, they fall apart. This draws heavily upon all the resources of the body."

She looked at the Rune with a creepy grin. "Outside of actually healing, this Rune has a different name. It's called a 'starvation' Rune."

<Well, that's ominous.> I looked at these Runes in a new light. Sure, they might not seem overly useful, but in the right context... who knows?

Minya shook herself out of her reverie. "Sadly, those are the only Runes I found that were unknown to you. I have a few traps though. This one is similar to what was used to capture... Dani. It creates a net of Mana that constricts around a target and holds them. If they aren't Mages, they won't be able to free themselves. Even if they are Mages, it'll take a moment to break out of it. This version over here is similar, but instead of holding, it cuts. Think full-body bear trap. Next, we have a sleep trap, a 'slow' trap, and a 'speed' trap."

I interrupted her, <Whoa, whoa! Slow down! What do those do? The sleep one is self-explanatory, but...>

"The 'slow' trap is used to hinder movements. If you have a really fast animal you are after, and it goes through this, it will move like it is stuck in honey. Very slowly," Minya explained impatiently. "The speed trap is just the opposite. Say you have a large, powerful creature chasing you. If it goes through the trap, its momentum is increased drastically in whatever direction it is moving. Suddenly, the creature sprints headlong into a wall or off a cliff. Useful for that kind of thing."

<Fun! I'll need to see if I can replicate the effects for more interesting combinations.> I started to go off topic, but Minya pulled me back.

"One more thing!" Her teeth were showing in a wide grin. "I found a collector..."

<Of?> I asked with a dubious tone.

"Well, there is a group out there that studies animals, Beasts, and all manner of plants and minerals. A subset of them likes to prove their studies, or encounters, by taking samples. This started a group that collects samples of perfectly preserved blood. I bought his whole collection."

She opened a case filled with dozens of vials. Each vial was marked with a tag, and each tag had a small entry in a journal. All of these entries had a seal on them, guaranteeing authenticity. Reading over a few of the entries, I got as excited as Minya.

<Oh... my. Oh, yes. This will do *nicely*. You've done really well, Minya. Can I reward you somehow?> I was staring at the vials, practically drooling. If they were fresh blood samples, I could recreate the creature it came from easily.

"Just let me know how your research goes. Maybe let me bring some of it into polite society and present it as my own work?" she requested with a grin.

<Sure.> Then I grumbled a bit, sourly muttering, <If I ever *make* progress.>

Minya shook her head. "The way you use Essence and corruption is revolutionary. That alone would be more than enough to make a compendium that would be studied the world over. What is getting you down?"

<Corruption. Turns out, you were all wrong about the best items to use for directing Essence. Emerald to contain earth Essence or corruption? Please,> I scoffed.

She had a look on her face like I slapped her. "Those aren't the best? What makes you say that?"

<Opal,> I informed her. <The transfer rate of infernal Essence and corruption along opal is more powerful than any other type by a factor of *three*. I just highly doubt that there is no other material that would be a better conductor for the remaining types of Essence. What is the likelihood that *infernal* Essence is the lucky one?>

"Huh. Well, if you think that... why not just pass some Essence or corruption over a bunch of things at the same time?" Minya casually offered with a shrug.

I felt stricken. <Why didn't I think of that?>

"I'm unsure. Also, Cal..."

<Yes?>

"You seem... better. More awake." Minya squirmed as she talked, clearly uncomfortable.

<I'd guess that ascending to the B-ranks gave me better mental fortitude?> I was wondering what she was getting at.

She spoke in a conciliatory manner, "I know that something changed for you recently and getting to the B-ranks seems to have further slowed the degradation of your mind, but who knows how long that will last? To that end, I am going to start hiring entire mercenary companies to begin searching. I'm going to need a lot of gold. Platinum would be preferable, actually. I need to take care of you, and that would help a lot."

<I... don't have platinum,> I dazedly muttered. I felt numb, I hadn't realized she was actually this devoted to me. It was incredibly touching.

"I figured." She flipped a coin into the air which I snapped up like a dog being tossed a treat. "Take this, and let's get to work."

<Okay.> I steadied myself and began absorbing the vials of blood. <I will be opening a new floor in a few days, Minya. Anyone below the B-ranks will be walking into near-certain death. Don't tell anyone.>

"You got it, Boss." Minya left with a happy smile and a treasure trove of platinum coins.

CHAPTER TWENTY-ONE

"So we are going straight to the fourth floor today?" Tom boomed, flexing his muscles to generate heat in the sub-zero wind.

Dale nodded. "If that is alright with you all. I had a *really* rough night, and I'm not feeling up to a full dungeon dive. I'd like to cultivate for a while, clear the floor, make a bit of money, and then sleep for six hours."

"I'll let you do all of that except the sleep." Hans poked fun at the team leader. "You've been lazing around too much recently."

His joke fell flat. Dale was coated in bruises, had deep bags under his eyes, and was still painfully thin despite the large portions of food he forced himself to eat at each meal.

Dale tried to play along, but his voice came out a bit too close to sounding dead to be funny. "Well, you know me—a useless, lazy guy that can't get anything done. If I were in a storybook, I'd be a side character."

Tyler found them just then, braving the snow and wind. "Hello! I have a new toy, er, weapon for you all to try! Also, a request, if you don't mind."

"Good morning. We are only going to the fourth floor today. Will that be a problem?" Adam spoke for the group in his melodic voice.

"No, on the contrary! It is perfect!" Tyler rubbed his hands together. "You see, we think that we have found a way to make that floor's Boss's fur into more than *just* a stylish cloak. Sadly, the process is... well, not perfected?"

"You need several because it gets ruined a lot?" Adam supplied a translation.

Tyler nodded, unabashedly rubbing his hands together. "Precisely!"

"He used to be so timid and quiet..." Hans teared up, sighing like he had lost a longtime friend.

"We will do it if we can, but Snowball is getting a lot smarter these days. Fewer and fewer people are able to end him before he runs away," Adam told the merchant.

"Not a problem! Do your best! Also, this new dagger. Hans, you use blades like this, yes?" Tyler gingerly held out a blade.

Hans took it, testing its balance and bending it a bit to see how flexible it was. It had an oddly curved, serrated edge. "This is..."

"Yes?"

"Garbage." Hans shook his head and tried to give it back. "It is balanced like a lead warhammer and as flexible as a brick. I can't throw it, and I can't use it in a fight."

Tyler frantically backed away just as Hans tried to push the knife back to him. "Careful with that!" he yelped and tumbled to the frozen ground. "There is a reason it is so awkward. This is a blade made from the claws of a Flesh Cat. When it is swung with any force, it seems to project... *something*. About six inches from the blade. That *something* tears apart bodies. It ignores anything in the way. Try it out on something heavily armored? Ah... also, after it is swung hard, it tends to shatter."

Hans stared at him with dead eyes. "So it is a *single-use* garbage dagger? No thank you."

"Oh, just try it!" Tyler huffed as he wiped snow off his butt. "We want to start marketing it soon as a way to kill Raile without blunt weapons. Also, it is called a 'Rune Tooth'. So, when you want to buy more, now you know what to call it."

Hans looked at the dagger. "At least you seem confident in it. I don't see any Runes on it though..."

"Oh it works well." Tyler nodded at Hans' perception. "No Runes, you are correct. Actually, the original creator got to name it because he nearly bled to death trying it out."

"Hmm. Seems misleading." Hans tucked away the dagger and walked away without another word.

"I guess he is trying it?" Tyler muttered into the empty area. "Maybe?"

The group stepped through the portal into the fourth floor, quietly discussing their plans. Dale stepped out and dropped to the floor forthwith.

"Dale?" Rose prodded him with her bow. "Dale is unconscious. Guys?"

"What happened?" Adam tried to heal him.

"A new foe!" Tom looked about excitedly.

Dale spasmed, and his eyes popped open.

<I would have warned you if it had been possible to do so,> I whispered to him apologetically.

"*So you are up and about, then?*" Dale thought at me as he got to his feet.

<More powerful and sane than any dungeon out there!>

"*You're a B-ranked dungeon, then?*" accused my original dungeon born.

<I am, but don't tell anyone,> I playfully ordered. Dale started to glare, but then his eyes glazed over for a moment and he acquiesced, slowly nodding. This was new. Interesting.

"Dale, are you alright?" Adam asked the blank-faced Dale.

"Yeah. Sorry, something came up." Dale looked at his worried friends blankly.

Adam nodded. "I figured it was the dungeon. I felt its attention on us like a weight as soon as you collapsed." The weight of a watchful glare increased at these words as if to confirm their validity.

Dale heard muttering in his head, <Stupid corrupted human...>

They started discussing which direction they wanted to take. Standing at the entrance to the labyrinth, they were looking at the four doors that each opened into a different tunnel. Remembering from past experience that it didn't matter which path they strode, they started walking, going through the 'fire' door. Too bad for them; I had been making changes whenever I got bored. As the door shut behind them, fire corruption started to thicken the air. Now, the fourth floor was a time trial as well as a maze. Pass through quickly or suffer.

"Is it getting hot in here?" Rose was fanning herself. "Or is it just me?"

Hans waggled his eyebrows at her. "Oh, it is you. It is *also* getting a bit warm, though."

Cue the fire traps! A blast of flame spurted from the wall in front of them, splashing across the wall parallel to its point of egress.

"Wha!" Tom jumped back, swinging his hammer at the sudden light. Sorry, big boy. That won't hurt fire. The next flame sprayed out, and soon, a consistent pattern was followed by the flames. So numerous were the traps that the entire fire portion of the tunnel was lit up intermittently. The air began to rapidly heat, sucking away breathable air. Among the flames, Coiled Cats were sometimes revealed, flickering into and out of view.

"All of this overnight?" Adam looked at the light show with wide eyes.

<When you don't sleep, and your other projects are maturing... you find ways to entertain yourself,> I spoke, making a familiar look of annoyance cross Dale's face.

Hans—oddly—was the only one to notice the seriousness of the situation. He spoke in a tone full of urgency. "We need to get moving. The fire in the room is producing corruption, and wind Essence is rapidly depleting. We need to go, or the flames won't be what kills us. We will just stop being able to breathe."

After Hans spoke, the others paled. As much as the blistering heat would allow them to while their facial capillaries opened, at least. They tried to simply dash through to the end of the hall, but the intermittent flames forced them to stop and retreat several times as their hair started to burn. It took a few minutes, but Rose suddenly perked up.

"They are moving in a pattern!" she gasped out through a dehydrated mouth. The others looked at her in confusion until she pointed at the fire. "Three, two, one... fire!" As she said 'fire', roaring flame shot from the wall and floor. Rose kept talking. "Two, one..." and the way was clear. She kept staring as the flames appeared and vanished.

"Here we go. Move forward when I tell you to!" Rose moved, and the others stepped forward with her, careful not to move until she spoke. There were several repeated patterns, then she suddenly yelled, "Back!" They lunged backward just as a flare appeared and shot forward again just before they would have been incinerated. They made it to a clear platform at the end of the hallway and had to choose which way to go.

"Good job, Rose. You really saved us there!" Dale smiled at the slightly singed archer. He looked around, intending to speak again but instead frowned. "Where is Hans?"

There was a moment of panic as the others didn't see the eccentric assassin, but he suddenly strolled up to them, flames parting around him without issue. He looked at their stricken faces. "What? I'm a C-ranked fire cultivator. This level of heat can't hurt me. Actually kinda tickles, I guess."

"...Then why were you so worried?" Rose growled at him.

Hans smirked at her. "I can't do *everything* for you. If you couldn't work out a simple repeating pattern, how could you call yourselves assass– ...Err... adventurers?"

The others stared at him for a few moments. Rose made a rude gesture.

"Well, that's uncalled for," Hans grumbled, looking around for something to fight.

MINION OF THE MASTER

Two *very* unremarkable men stepped out of the portal into Mountaindale, eying everything—and everyone—around them cautiously. They casually strolled through the slowly growing city, taking note of any interesting landmarks. The roads were straight, which was beneficial to moving around but unfortunate for those with weak constitutions, as the wind at this altitude had nothing to slow it down. The men eventually gravitated toward the tavern after taking note of the looming steeples of the church and spitting.

After the normal grumblings about the door being open to the wind, the men slowly ingratiated themselves with the drinking people, buying drinks and hearing gossip. They were interested in all news of the place, from the start of the dungeon town to the new rumors circulating about trade agreements. When Amazons were mentioned, the two men paled and made eye contact. Eventually, they had wrung their conversations dry and left. Without a word, they made their way to the shimmering, humming portal run by the Portal Guild. They paid the fee and stepped through. Halfway across the continent, they hurried past other people and swiftly made their way to a safe house.

The men hustled along the winding tunnels under the house, eventually coming to a place that caressed them with insidious Essence. They smiled; the infernal dungeon had been expanding at a prodigious rate. They bypassed various undead as they delved deeper. Skeletons, rotting zombies, drifting wraiths, and towering abominations simply ignored the men. Traps were stepped around, and they soon found themselves kowtowing to The Master.

"Report," his sonorous voice rang out.

"Master, all is as we expected it to be. There have been recent developments, but as expected, the dungeon has been acting erratically. Various plans to help it recover have been brought to the council, but apparently, nothing is working to balance the *thing's* mind," the first lackey reported succinctly.

The second lackey began speaking as soon as the other stopped. "There is talk of trade dealings and alliances between multiple factions. Dwarves, High Elves, Dark Elves, Barbarians, and *Amazons* have been seen speaking together amicably."

The Master quietly digested all of this information. "I see." His silence after these words stretched for a long time. "Yes. I see. We will need to hurry along before they do something... foolish. I need three teams assembled. If the dungeon is imbalanced, it will not need too many of our resources. Are you *certain* of your report?"

Lackey number one nodded. "I am, Master."

"Good." The Master gestured, and a person appeared near him. "The first two teams will include a summoner each.

Their job will be to cause havoc and disrupt the town. While the forces are concentrated above, attempting to contain our threat, the third team will go after the dungeon's Core. A 'normal' five-man team. I want at most one lower-ranked Mage to accompany them. Any more will raise too much suspicion, and they may be found out before even entering the dungeon. Bringing the dungeon's Core here intact would please me, but destroying it is acceptable. Is this understood?"

"Yes, Master. To hear is to obey." The Mage The Master was speaking to flickered, soon vanishing from sight.

Dani—who was trapped on an altar just beyond the conversation—wept bitterly at this confirmation of Cal's mental state... and her impending loss.

CHAPTER TWENTY-TWO

I looked over my storage rooms, pleased with the results of the last few days. When a Core was too full of corruption to be able to absorb more, I put the dull stone in here, switching it out with a fresh one. Before my ascension to the B-ranks, the elemental Cores like earth and fire had by far outnumbered the more ethereal ones, such as infernal and celestial. Now, those two rare types were catching up! Oil is awesome!

I was focused on this area because I was about to start flooding a contained space with these corruptions then drop items into the fumes and see what stuck. I began, and soon, I had six small chambers filled with a thick, deadly-to-life miasma. For hours, I dropped various materials and minerals into these rooms. As I had expected, almost everything was a dud. A few things took in a bit of the taint, but nothing was even comparable to what I already had access to.

I was getting annoyed, so I started throwing in common, everyday usage minerals. Iron? Useless. Dirt? Nope. I threw in platinum and got a strange reaction. I focused in on the material and saw that a little bit of it had absorbed a huge amount of earth corruption, relative to its size. I tore the platinum apart, looking for what was different. This coin was an exact replica of what Minya had given me, and as I looked closer, I saw that it was an alloy, a mixture of metals. I pulled out the strange metal and analyzed it closely. I had seen this before, I realized, but only in conjunction with other things. Osmium. This was the most dense metal I had ever had the pleasure of finding, and it was sucking up enough corruption that I wanted to test a larger portion.

I stopped dropping other things, just so I wouldn't get distracted and made a large ingot of pure osmium. It took a surprisingly large amount of Essence due to its density, which was about *double* what lead was! I dropped the bar into the small chamber and was amazed by how quickly it took in corruption. It left a blank space in the air it passed through as it fell, taking the taint in fast enough that the corruption couldn't refill the area instantly. It hit the ground, and the swirling fumes were quickly pulled into it without my assistance. Soon, the room was clear!

<Yes!> I shouted in joy. <I have found it!>

"*Found what?*" Dale's voice interrupted my glee. "*What are you doing, you psychopath?*"

<Oh, be quiet, Dale. You have no part in this,> I shushed him nonchalantly.

"*You found something interesting?*" Minya's voice sounded in my head.

<Minya?> She wasn't in my dungeon, was she? I glanced around. Nope.

"*You found Minya?*" Dale seemed very confused. I ignored him, focusing *very* hard on bypassing him and only talking to Minya.

<Can you hear me?> I carefully called into the ether.

"*I can!*" Minya spoke excitedly. "*Let's test the range of this. We will start really far away, I'm on my way to the portal now.*"

<Great!> I was really lucky to have such a good person bonded to me. I shot a glare at Dale and directed a few more Cats toward his direction. I returned to my osmium and started playing with it. A beautiful metal, it had originally been a blue, shiny material. Now, it was dark green and gave off an earthy, brutal feel. I made a bit of it as rewards and rare finds for

miners, just to see their reactions to it. Was this something useful or known to others? I had to know!

On that note, I was struck by a sudden idea. <Minya, are there elemental weapons out there? Legendary materials, anything like that?>

"*I can still hear you! This is excellent! Could you hear me before you tried to talk to me? Can you hear me now?*" She seemed happy. Good. Happy meant safe.

<Not before, but I can now. Must be a thing I need to initiate...> I called back. I also could 'feel' her general location. She was far, far away to the east.

"*Legendary metals or weapons... hmm.*" She thought for a bit and got back to me, "*Well, different factions have something that they use in their own way. Humans discovered that opals could enhance infernal essence collection. Elves use some kind of glass that they refuse to share the recipe of, which does something they won't share.*"

<Useful,> I scoffed with great annoyance.

"*Right? Hmm, Dwarves use Mithril when they can get it but have something they use in their furnaces that makes them hotter than any other kind of furnace. Maybe that is worth looking into? Orcs have a weapon they revere that is green, like really shiny, old copper, and–*"

<Wait, green? Shiny?> That sounded familiar.

"*Yes, it is called 'Orichalcum'. We call it 'mountain copper' usually because we can only get it off their corpses, and they come from mountainous areas. It is pretty rare.*"

<I see. Go on!> I had made orichalcum, it seemed.

"*The church leaders all seem to wear some kind of golden artifact. I don't know if it is actually gold or not. I think it is just for show, but somehow, they are always stronger than others around them. I think there must be more, but I can't seem to think of any others right now,"* Minya finished her stray thoughts. I thanked her and moved on with my experiments.

I would keep on with my research, but as I was underground, it was important to get the osmium spread through the dungeon. There was a lot of earth corruption generated each day, and if I didn't collect it, the taint would get as dense as the Essence in the air. No one wanted that.

The tendrils of osmium flowed out from my Core room, slowly grinding through the rock. It took almost a full day, but at the end, I had veins of the material for the corruption to flow through. I opened the veins up to the air, and quickly, it was easier for everything in the dungeon to breathe. The lower levels were much more affected by the change, and I was getting a steady stream of the corruption delivered.

Feeling better about my life decisions, I decided that it was time to create the Boss of the fifth floor. The fourth floor was getting much more dangerous, but I wanted the fifth to be terrifying for even those that came prepared. To that end, I started making monsters. I had absorbed the vials of blood Minya had brought me and needed to create the creature they correlated to. Realistically, I was unsure what they would turn out to be. I knew their names and capabilities, but what about their personalities or habits?

Soon, I had a swarm of various creatures I had never seen before. I quickly eliminated all of the herbivores and non-predatory species and was soon left with only a few options to choose from. I had my Cats wipe them all out and started trying to create combinations. I looked, measured, and tested, often having to call in a few Mobs to destroy the failures. I *literally* could not let them live if they were imperfect in their pattern. My law was absolute about this, and it seemed to have a strong obsessive need to always be correct. At the end of my experiments, I had a single monster that was entirely unified in its purpose and design. It was beautiful.

All that was left was to design the arena it would use for battle. I already had a circular room, so I made it utterly flat. As a defensive advantage for my Boss, I added tunnels under the floor. They were long and curved, with one entrance per exit. I tried to think of anything else I could add in to help him out, but looking at his towering, imposing form made me shrug. He really didn't need a greater advantage. A bit of poison dripped to the floor from my Beast's mouth, pitting the rock as the acidic toxins came in contact with it. Yeah, this guy was ready. He was all *sorts* of set.

Since I was done with what *needed* to be done, I took the time to create some distractions and cosmetic changes on my new floor. There were levers in the room that would open windows in the ceiling, allowing daylight to pour in from above. Along the roof and halfway down to the ground, I made a mirrored surface that increased the brightness of the room a hundred fold—but only if the lever was pulled and the light was allowed to enter through the crystal windows above.

The extra light *could* be helpful, in theory, but it would hamper the people using it more than they would realize. The room was filled with fog, not steam, and the light would make it very difficult to see through. I still expected the lever to be pulled, simply as a natural response to, well, a lever existing. Most people will pull an unknown lever or push a random button, just to see what happens. Even if they knew what it did, there was a good chance of it being used. Humans prefer light, even if they had been in a dark dungeon all day and it would destroy their night vision.

They would likely also think it would help them destroy the Boss, and this could distract them from actually *fighting*. My new Beast was waiting hungrily for challengers, so after a few finishing touches, I created the stairway. The fifth floor was open for business.

MINION OF THE MASTER

Stepping into this frozen mountain air was disgusting to the bronze-skinned man from the southern isles. He looked around at the people cheerfully moving around and crossed his arms. Someone walked into him, causing him to stumble and glare at the boorish man who had done the unthinkable atrocity of touching him.

The filthy man that had run into him turned. "Get outta the way, ya stupid shit. Standing at the exit to the portal like a fishy! Never seen a portal before? Need a hand getting up? Do you have any raspberries? Look at that, it's a male. Wouldn't have guessed it with the hair and purty face!" The flow of words slowed as the man squinted at him through ragged, matted hair.

"Oh, a necromancer, eh? Well, good for you. Not too many people these days are willing to do things the hard way! I hope you aren't planning to do anything stupid. Though I suppose if you decided to cultivate in an 'illegal' manner, you wouldn't be as stupid and ridiculous as to go to a place swarming with cultivators. Have fun, youngster. Don't do anything I wouldn't!"

The bronze-skinned man watched in horror as the filthy—old?—man walked away from him, intermittently skipping and humming. How had he been able to see that he was a necromancer? Only his cultivation ranking should have been noticeable, but as an A-ranked summoner, he had long ago been able to hide his affinity. He began to worry that this was an ill-fated mission, but as the rest of his people started coming through the portal, his resolve solidified as he issued orders. The Master's commands *would* be followed.

A few minutes after the necromancers moved off into the town, the portal shimmered again, and an agitated, regal looking man stepped through. He looked around carefully, the twin swords on his back swaying gently in the wind, creating a slight chiming sound. Sighing, he turned toward the portal attendant.

"Pardon me, child. Have you perchance seen a greasy, old pervert come through here?" The unkind words didn't match up with his mellow voice.

The attendant didn't look up from his ledger. "My job is to monitor outgoing, not incoming. If you have a question or complaint, please feel free to contact the department of magical vergence located at the Portal Guild in the capital–"

"I get it, you aren't going to be useful." The man began to walk away gracefully, his every movement flowing and screaming that a master of the sword had appeared.

The attendant finally looked up from his book over a minute later. "Hey, there's no call to be rude." He blinked owlishly as he noticed no one was around. "Ugh."

CHAPTER TWENTY-THREE

"...and that is why it is so important for you to stabilize your cultivation after increasing in ranking. Your body can and *will* break down. Burnout is a real possibility." Craig was just finishing his most recent lecture of Essence usage. "One that you seem to be avoiding, but by the look of you, it will start tearing you apart pretty soon if you continue at this pace."

"But burnout is just the temporary damage of your meridians, is it not?" Dale questioned. "If you use too much or absorb too much, it just means you need to take it easy for a while afterward. Like catching a cold."

Craig looked thoughtful. Pondering the answer he should give his student, he stroked his chin. "Well, initially that may be true, but I believe you need to think of it in a slightly different way. For example, if you build a sturdy wall and a chunk of it is smashed out, you can repair it, correct?"

"Yes. Fairly easily, too, I assume." Dale nodded along as he re-read his most recent notes.

"Now, say that you keep putting holes in that wall and slowly patching it," Craig continued, knowing that he had Dale hooked with this parable. "Wherever you have many patches, the overall wall becomes weak. Now, say you have patches all over the place and you take a solid hit to the wall. What happens? The entire wall crumbles, no longer able to support itself. That is real burnout, the total collapse of your meridians. Burnout is something everyone under the Mage ranks is fighting against, and it is a race against time."

"Because reaching the Mage ranks fixes your meridians to their original perfection?" Dale inserted a question while furiously scribbling fresh notes.

"It does. Also, it is normally a very *slow* race, since it takes decades to enter the Mage ranks. When done by following the *standard* practices, anyway." His voice was getting quite pointed, which Dale didn't fail to notice as he wrote. Though he would prefer to have the lad looking at him while they talked, Craig was pleased to have such an attentive student. "The fewer 'patches' that Mana needs to fix, the higher your overall strength and control will be to start with. This is why people getting into the Mage ranks very young is cause for them to be celebrated as geniuses and massive talents. A very young Mage and a very old Mage are things to be afraid of."

"The young because he is very skilled, and the old because an elderly looking Mage is exceedingly powerful?" Dale was continuing to write rapidly as he asked this.

"Correct." Craig smiled warmly. "I think that is all for tonight. I'll see you tomorrow."

"I have more questions!" Dale protested anxiously, finally looking up from his paper.

Craig shook his head. "We have time. If you progress correctly, you are essentially immortal. Take your time. Really *learn* what you are taught. Maybe take a vacation, as well."

Dale sighed and stood up. He bowed, thanked Craig, and left the small room they had been occupying. His mind was in disarray as new ideas whirled around his brain. He wanted to find a quiet place to look at his meridians, which had been forcibly opened. How long did he have before he burned out like Craig was talking about? If he did, would the dungeon be able to fix him?

A splashing sound jarred him from his thoughts as he took a step. A puddle? No way, it was the middle of winter. Puddles didn't happen naturally this time of year. He grimaced and kicked his shoe, trying to stop his feet from getting soaked.

As he did so, a very familiar smell assaulted his nostrils. The coppery tang of blood. Instantly, Dale was on high alert. He wanted to shout a warning to the town, but he didn't know what kind of enemy they were facing. Dale looked around, seeing no one standing. He peeked around the corner and found the source of the blood. A trio of Dark Elves were unceremoniously piled together, chunks of flesh torn out of them.

"The dungeon must have let out a swarm!" Dale thought in fury. He started to shout but stopped at the last second. "Wait... Dark Elves are almost all at least at the Mage ranking... and if not, there will always be at least one Mage in their squads. It *can't* have been the dungeon." He quickly spun around, hurrying back to the room he had been studying in with Craig.

Craig was already gone, having found an egress in the opposite direction. Dale hurried down the hallway, frustrated at his uselessness. He was in the newest building in the city, a town hall that was built to host negotiations and delegations. There were rooms for meetings and for sleeping quarters. Right now there were only a few people living in the building, so it was mostly empty. Where was everyone? It was so quiet. *Too* quiet. His instincts suddenly screamed a warning, and he dove forward, rolling away.

He jumped to his feet and looked around. Nothing there. It was just his imagination. Dale took a few deep breaths and broke into a run, scurrying toward the front entryway. He threw open the door, revealing a scene straight from a nightmare. Screaming cultivators ran through the streets, either toward battle or away from it. The sky was clear tonight, and the moon cast a ghastly glow on the city. Fresh blood was flowing downhill as a horde of undead marched the streets.

A flash of fire ignited the walking corpses, burning them terribly. All this did was throw ash in the air and create charred, walking skeletons. The flames were not intense enough to incinerate the group of bodies completely, so only the weak, leading edge was affected. The shambling zombies that had their flesh removed in this manner were suddenly able to move much more nimbly, clattering along the road. Using their bones as their weapons, they stabbed at any available target. Groups of cultivators worked together, now trying to dismantle or pulverize the animated dead.

Any cultivator that fell didn't get a chance to rest peacefully, as they were soon inhabited and worn as a carapace for an infernal soul. The cultivators were losing and losing badly. The reason for this was abundantly clear; the entire battle was absolutely silent. Someone had obviously used a powerful technique or incantation to block sound from traveling. Because of this, there were far too few defenders showing up. They trickled into the fight one by one, and because of this, they were rolled over and assimilated into the attacking force.

Dale was furious. He ran as fast as he could toward the Guild area, noticing that there seemed to be a barricade of the dead preventing people from getting into the entrance, and the new wall around the Guildhall made other entry points nonexistent. If he had to guess, no one in the central Guild had been informed of—or noticed—what was going on in the rest of the town. Stupid shutters on windows! Why hadn't he just forced everyone to stay in tents?

He looked for any way that he could get into the area, and his eyes landed on the church. For the first time, he was happy that Father Richard had built such a grandiose building. Dale raced to the church, finding that there was a similar series of undead blocking the entrances. Luckily, they had not done more than cluster around the main door yet. He ran at the wall, hidden from the view of any undead, and focused on his

Essence. With a rapid series of movements, he released his Chi as an attack. With a soundless explosion, the wall in front of him shattered—well... a small hole appeared, just large enough for him to squeeze through in a very undignified manner.

A cleric ran up as Dale stood, dust covering him. "Are you out of your mind?" The cleric blustered at the dust-covered man. "Father Richard paid a fortune to have those walls made and reinforced! You are coming with me *right now* to get held accountable for your actions!"

"You want me to go with you to Father Richard?" Dale stopped his current plan to just start shouting and looked at the red-faced cleric. "Is he in here?"

"Of course he is! And yes, you are coming, whether you want to or not!" The cleric was literally hopping mad. "Follow!"

Dale started jogging, making the cleric sputter as he tried to match the pace and lead the way. "Hmph! Well! At least you are in a hurry to make amends!"

Dale wanted to grin, but the situation was grim. He held his tongue until the cleric began pounding on a door. Father Richard opened it almost instantly, though there was no way he had been standing near it. "Yes?" he asked the cleric respectfully, knowing that he wouldn't be interrupted without a good reason.

"Father Richard, this man–" the cleric began, instantly being cut off by Dale.

"Father! The city is under attack by the undead. We need to alert the Guild and launch a counter attack!" Dale shouted over the now-white-faced cleric.

"Are you joking...? Of course you aren't." Father Richard stepped into the hall. He looked at the cleric. "Good job getting him here quickly. Go alert the remaining chosen. It is time to fulfill our duty and protect our flock."

Dale and Richard ran toward the arena where the clerics would begin gathering. They ran to the top of the arena wall, jumping to the edge to look at the bloody scene. Father Richard looked grim. "I can destroy the majority of these easily, but there must be an A-ranked summoner here. Look." He pointed at the mountainous abominations. "Those are actually a swarm of bodies, a huge mound of fused flesh. Only High Summoners can control them—barely—and they are moving *easily*. This is someone powerful. I don't see any behemoths, but these abominations will be more than enough to wipe out this city if we don't act soon."

"What should I do?" Dale began warming up, preparing to fight his way to the Guild.

"Hide like a scared little Forest Elf?" Father Richard suggested offhandedly. "Dale, I am serious. You don't seem to understand the difference in power here. You've been defeating enemies you should not be able to and surviving situations you shouldn't have. That won't happen if you try to fight these things. You need to go find a defendable place, take others of similar ranking with you, and hope that the monsters outside don't look for you too hard."

"I can help!" Dale insisted, shocked that he had been told to flee like a coward.

Richard looked at him angrily. "Boy, I think you need another lesson. *I* am an A-ranked Mage. Let me show you what we are up against. What *you* are volunteering to go fight."

Father Richard looked out at the gathered undead and began to chant in a sonorous voice. The first syllable that fell from his lips made the air shake, "*And in Thy loving kindness, cut off mine enemies and destroy all those who afflict mine soul; for I am Thy servant.*" As he chanted, it seemed that dawn had come. The heavens lit up, and the stars dimmed to indiscernibility. "*For Thou doth connect all things, and all things are connected to Thee. By the power Thou hast imparted upon me, reduce all things unnatural to their unbound form, that they may be returned to the earth to be used in Thine works.*"

Dale had blood dripping from his eyes as he struggled to stay conscious. The air was *thrumming* with accumulated power, and what sounded like a great blast from a horn was heard throughout the city. All of the undead in sight were torn apart as celestial Mana ravaged them. They began falling into piles of meat or dust, depending on their original state. Whatever had been sealing sound was broken, and screaming was soon filling the night. Wounded were everywhere, and the celestial attack had not been perfectly targeted, damaging many that were not undead. Not just a few were bleeding from their ears, and survivors of the night caught in the vibrations would be urinating blood for at least a week.

"That seemed to work," Dale quipped when he was again able to speak. Richard shot him an uncharacteristic glare.

"Think so? Take another look." The priest gestured at the largest mounds of flesh as the abominations began shifting and reconfiguring into mobile forms. The piles of destroyed undead around the mounds flowed into them, and the formless masses rose higher and stronger than before. One of them grasped its arm, tearing it off and throwing it into an area where many dead people were strewn about. The arm landed and swiftly expanded, covering the bodies and forming into a small, new abomination.

"...So where would you like me to hide? Who should I bring with me?" Dale turned toward the now-smirking priest.

"I am sure that the necromancers are in the dungeon by this point. The open rooms and even the fortifications will be useless. I want you to get everyone into the fourth floor, find an out of the way tunnel, and bunker down. Your only hope is that they ignore you in favor of whatever they are after. Now that the Guild is alerted," indeed, the Guild was now moving like a kicked anthill, "we will soon have several Mages on their way. We have me, Frank, Chandra, and Amber for certain. We may have more in the way of Dark Elves, but it is unlikely that any of them could challenge an A-ranker."

"Can *Frank* challenge an A-ranker?" Dale was surprised. Frank was well-known to be in the B-ranks. His hopes for an easy victory were crushed.

"Doubtful. But if there are A-ranks, there are certainly subordinate B-rankers as well. All of our Mages will be needed tonight, I'm afraid," Richard finished heavily, jabbing a finger toward the door. "Now go!"

Dale rushed down to the gathered clerics and began to relay Richard's orders. Soon they were all moving to the fourth floor of the dungeon as Dale held the portal open for them.

CHAPTER TWENTY-FOUR

I knew they were Necromancers almost as soon as they walked in. Their auras stank of death and fear. Also, they soon began throwing around infernal Essence. It didn't help their case when they brought a Basher back to life, either. I glared at them as they walked along my tunnels, using the poor bunny to set off each trap in their way.

"Too bad we had to lay low. I'd love to be there when the ranks are 'bolstered'." One of the reeking men giggled at whatever twisted thoughts were niggling along his puny mind. "Gonna need a lot of 'em to finish off the Lion Kingdom."

"Not really. They are so weak from that mushroom plague that they are on the verge of collapse already," another commented, making me annoyed. I get it, I did something dumb. "I bet we could finish the Lion off with one solid attack."

The Mage in their group spoke suddenly, making the others flinch at the venom in his tone, "Rushing ahead is what got us into this mess! First the lost war and now a mere ten years after what happened with Kantor, where we found the key to victory, you want to rush *again*?"

What the abyss? Kantor? What did they do to Kantor? *How* did they do something to Kantor? I was sucked into the conversation, listening raptly, even while boosting the traps and outfitting the Goblins with better gear. Even my Cats were getting a bit of armor on them. The Bobs were frantically drawing Runes and preparing for a full-scale war against the five men. I started pulling out the weapon we designed after the terrifying greasy man threatened me.

"It isn't about *rushing*, per se," the first invader wheedled. "It's more... getting a nice place in society while young enough to enjoy it! We've been on the outskirts for so long, pushed down whenever we got *close* to respect. I think it is time we got ours! Got *our* chance to be on top!" The other C-rankers grinned and nodded along with the impromptu speech.

The Mage had a look of fury on his face. In a fit of anger, he swung his fist and reduced a Basher to a shower of gore. "You fools," he breathed softly. "What have you done to *earn* a place in society? You self-righteous, entitled little shits. Have you learned *nothing* from The Master? You think that we are here to *play* at being better than others, to lord our victory over them? That when we inevitably win, *we* are going to be the oppressors? Fools." He cursed loudly and marched past them.

"Well, then, what's the abyssal point?" the ornery speaker broke in. "Why bother with all of this?"

"Why indeed." The Mage looked over coldly. "Since you seem to have forgotten, I'll make sure The Master gives you a refresher course."

"Hey, hey. No need for any of that! I'm just making conversation!" The man had broken out in a sweat now. Apparently, this 'Master' was a scary fellow.

"Let's get the job done, and we will talk more about this later." The Mage groaned. "I hate people."

"You know you love us."

The Mage seemed to have a permanent scowl by this point. "I'd sell you to a demon for a copper."

"That's cold, boss-man."

"So is the abyss. Wanna visit?" The Mage had a bit of a smirk now.

"Hey, now. I've been at that lecture. The abyss isn't cold; it isn't anything. It just... is."

"I thought that was the void?"

"Oh dang. Yeah, you're right."

They eventually made it to the second floor, not stopping for treasure or going out of their way to look for other things of interest. This told me that they could only be here for one thing. Me. I wasn't sure why or what they were planning to do with me, but I needed to make sure they failed.

<Bob, abandon all other forts and make for the Boss area. We are going to be having a Goblin's last stand,> I ordered each of the Bobs. <Hurry. Make sure everyone gets going.>

They looked up in surprise. One of them asked the question they were all dying to know. "Are you going to let us use... *it?*"

<Oh, you know it, Bob-oh. I've been opening its box since these necromancers entered the dungeon.> They could hear the glee in my voice, even though it was a serious situation. I began preparations, and an entire section of the wall moved to the side, revealing a huge, pointed opal. <You know what to do. Get it ready.>

This was one of the 'last resort' weapons that had been suggested by the Goblins after some of the changes we had been able to make in the dungeon. An oversized opal on a pedestal didn't sound particularly frightening, but this was a weapon based off of Bob's staff. While it wasn't nearly as quickly accessible and couldn't be used in standard combat, if used correctly it would be worth the wait. It took quite a while to charge the Runes that would send Essence into the Opal, so I hoped that it would be ready in time. The necromantic Mage walked into the room containing Raile, sighing as the massive Mob rushed him. With a simple backhand, Raile was dead, brain splattered along the inside of his armor.

<We don't have much time. They aren't sprinting, but they *are* moving at a steady pace. Five minutes until they are at the base of the stairs,> I informed the oddly calm Bobs. <I'm

setting out a target for you to aim for. This way we can test the effectiveness of the taunt Runes as well. I can't guarantee they will be standing in the perfect spot, but by the abyss, I can try!>

"Target point acknowledged! Charging now, Great Spirit!" The first Bob to make it to the opal began pouring infernal Essence into the wooden frame holding the gemstone in place. The Runes in the wood began to activate, directing the Essence to create a single-use charge. The frame began vibrating as the flow ran unchecked and would explode eventually if it had to store the Essence for a long period of time. If all went according to my plan, they would be using the charge *well* before that point. More Bobs began arriving, and the flow of Essence into the Runes increased and stabilized. Some were activating the wind-based Essence receptacles, and the combined power began to fuse together in the opal.

<This is a serious threat, so I will help directly as long as I am able.> The Bobs were startled as an Assimilator floated up to them. Reaching out with a tendril of its overgrown jellyfish body, it began firing a focused stream of Essence into the Rune. With my direct help, the charging process became *much* faster.

The Necromancers stepped into the third floor, groaning when they saw the size of it. The Mage shushed them. "At least we don't need to wander around tunnels like a bunch of morons. It's an open room. The exit is in sight. Walk. Your legs aren't for show."

<Yoo-hoo!> I called, knowing they couldn't hear me. At the same time, a Rune on an armored Basher began to glow intensely. <Over here, boys! Take a gander at that pretty accumulation of everything you hate! What a pretty little taunt Rune!>

The 'taunt' Rune on the poor Basher utterly captivated the C-rankers, but the Mage only looked at it and frowned in consternation. The C-rankers sprinted forward in a brutal rage and began pummeling the rabbit into the ground with earth-shaking force. Only the inherent durability of the Rune kept the floor the Mob was now splattered across from breaking immediately, but it would not last long against this level of power.

I gave the order to the Bobs, <Targets in range! Specified point of aim is focused! They are being held in place. Commence attack.>

"Runes prepared! Essence levels critical! Clear the area!" Bob 'one' spoke.

"Back blast area clear!" Bob 'two' announced as Goblins dove away from the pedestal. "Go, go, go!"

The opal discharged. A ray of darkness raced in a straight line across the floor, spiraling as it did so. This bolt flew at the speed of darkness, and there should have been no possible way to dodge if you weren't already in the process of doing so. This Mage though... he was something else. He *plucked* at the empty air, and his motion somehow scattered the C-rankers like they had been hit in the chest. Only one of them was still in the path of the attack, and the hissing darkness passed through the unfortunate man without slowing.

The beam reached the opposite wall and silently vanished before the man even hit the ground. There was no mark on him, nothing to show how he had been killed. The others gathered around, looking at the dead man. I watched as well, fascinated by the effects of my previously untested weapon. The Mage inspected the carcass and shook his head. "A direct assault on the soul. It was... *ripped* out of him whole! Genius! We should look for the means behind this after we complete the job."

The others looked at him in horror. "He's *dead*, you bastard! You've known him for *years*. How can you be so cold?"

The Mage looked confused. "What are you talking about? Death is what we *do*." He made a motion, and a flow of Mana went into the corpse. An outpouring of Essence cascaded from the body, and it hopped lightly to its feet.

"Hmm." The undead man looked at his hands. "Very nice. Clean. No need to fight for the possession but somehow incredibly fresh. No rot at all." The body looked at the Mage with a smile, its eyes now completely black. "Thank you, Master, what a thoughtful gift."

"Yes, well. We have determined that this dungeon is using a new weapon that launches a direct soul-tearing attack. I needed another Mage-ranked creature here; these C-rankers are not cutting it." The Mage looked askance at the men on his team.

"Hey, hey, that is not fair, boss!" The surviving C-rankers were looking at the demon-inhabited man that was staring at them hungrily. "We are... useful."

"Let's find out who is *more* useful?" The demon had an unnaturally wide grin on its face. "If you are less useful than I am, at least promise to let us use your bodies when I tear you apart. I'm going to go kill everything on this floor, 'kay?" The C-rankers went white-faced as the demon sprinted off toward the clustered Goblins.

<Oof, looks like they were sent here as fodder for the Mage's spells. Yikes, that's harsh! Bobs, you all have incoming. Get the opal tucked away; there won't be another chance to use it. They are moving too fast now, and they are alerted,> I warned as the demon began approaching speedily.

"Runes are ready," Bob seemed nervous but was keeping it together nicely. Maybe I'd give him a raise. To the next ranking. They don't use money. The Bobs were chanting, and with a final push, a surprisingly large number of wraiths appeared. "Go, slay the invaders!" Bob ordered the pack of wraiths. They began drifting towards the demon.

The Goblins arranged themselves into formations, getting ready to defend themselves. <Bob, do we have any more of those hollow armor guys?> I wondered aloud.

"Sadly, no. They were all destroyed in the first few days, and I have been unable to lure more people into the needed ritual-trap," Bob answered with tension evident in his voice.

<I understand. I can't seem to make them, as they require an infernal soul. They don't really die, they just kinda go 'poof' and vanish into the abyss,> I lamented. <If they weren't so useful, I'd call them a waste of Essence.>

Bob looked around, a bit uncomfortable. "Is this the best time to be discussing this?"

<No, probably not. I'll join this fight, by the way. I'm pulling out the Goblin Amazon.> I really didn't want to, but desperate times...

"Oh, really?!" Bob seemed elated. "That will be excellent! Oh... I know that must be hard to do..."

<Just stop, Bob. I know I won't be as good at controlling it as Dani, but I need to work to save myself. I...> I fell silent. Dani was captured because she was in the Goblin Queen's body. She was amazing, being able to hop into a body and use it perfectly. Comparatively, I was only decent at controlling it. I had not bothered to create another since she was gone, leaving a gaping hole in my defenses. No floor Boss, no real struggle to get to the next floor. A coffin-like object rose from the floor, swinging open to show an immobile body. I poured celestial Essence into the aluminum armor it was wearing, transforming it into a powerful weapon against the infernal. A box appeared

from the floor next to the Amazon, holding my swords and a large amount of demon-banishing weapons.

These weapons were quickly handed out. Now, all we needed to do was land a single attack and the demon would be banished, using its own power to accomplish the task. I took direct control of the Amazon, opened my eyes, and stepped into the courtyard. There was golden light reflecting from my armor, and my swords shifted to a golden hue. I took a few exploratory swings, jumped in place, and did a few stretches.

"Alright, let's do this." My voice startled me; I was unused to my words causing vibrations in the air. I was also not used to the feminine vocal cords. "Words! Words. Speaking is fun. Words."

Bob seemed concerned. "Are... you okay?"

"Yes. Ye-es. Words are fun to say." Gah! I bit my tongue! The demon hopped over the wall at that point, a disconcerting smile on its face.

"Hellooo." He waved at the assembled Goblins. "If you would hold still, this will be much easier. No less painful though." The possessed body charged forward, weaving between a storm of arrows. Not a single one touched him as inhuman contortions allowed his body to move out of the way of each shot. I heard his bones snapping as he bent backward, his spine unable to take the abuse. He started laughing and continued to do so, irrespective of the normal human need for air.

The Goblin Berserkers charged forward as a wave and began shrieking in glee as their weapons began to find the mark. The demon was fast, but a dozen weapons swinging at it was near impossible to avoid at the speeds it could muster. The demon's face twisted into a scowl as its bones snapped from the pressure.

"I *just* got this body! If anyone is tearing it apart, it's me! Back off!" The demon punctuated his sentence by swinging at the Berserkers, bones elongating from its hands. The bones burst into a flame I knew well—hellfire. A few of my advanced Bashers had the same flame coating their horns. His claws sliced through the minimal armor the Berserkers had been convinced to wear, leaving long gashes that continued to burn. The flames quickly spread, ravaging their bodies as they continued to throw themselves at the demon. Bones shattered under their blows, and as the last Berserker fell, the demon dropped to the floor.

Legs twisted into highly damaged shapes, the demon sprinted forward on its hands. Like a sick jester, it wrenched and contorted its body. Bones that had been poking through the skin became weapons as the demon swung the mangled limbs into my Goblins. The possessed body began laughing as my Mobs fell, somehow killing them though its own form was being pulverized.

"Just *banish* it already!" I barked in exasperation. "Why are you using blunt weapons? Stab!" We had *just* talked about this!

A warrior Goblin jumped forward at my order, his new war pick catching the demon in the chest. The residual momentum slapped the body to the ground, pinning it in place as the Runes on the pick activated. A wash of fire spread from the point of impact, and the demon looked at me in fury, unable to move as its power was drained to fuel the Runes.

"No! *No!* You made a *big* mistake, dungeon," the demon furiously hissed, all pretense of humanity gone. "Before, I was only under orders to capture you. When I get back here, I will torture your soul for eternity."

"Shoo." I waved off the threat as the *thing* collapsed into itself, flakes of burnt skin were soon all that remained. I directed my aura to begin absorbing all of the bodies of my fallen Goblins, didn't want to leave anything here for the incoming necromancers to use, after all. Speaking of... "Here they come!"

The Goblins that had relaxed after seeing the demon fall became the first casualties. They were easy prey for the invaders and potential bodies to be possessed. Bob and the others quickly began a counter-attack but were greatly outmatched. The black bolts of Essence from the Bobs' staffs seemed to vanish as they approached the Mage, though not always perfectly. The bolts that *did* make it to the Mage seemed to do no damage, and he simply strolled through the other attacks. That 'near physical immunity' feature was beginning to piss me right off. The other Goblins were having better luck against the C-ranked invaders, but all of the wounds inflicted were superficial. We were completely outmatched in terms of raw power. Time for me to join the fight.

I pushed my new body to the absolute limits, screaming through the air at the Mage. There was a brilliant line of light along the edge of my weapon, and as I swung, I *pushed* a touch of Mana into my sword. Since I had waited to add Mana, the Mage had been ignoring my attack. His reaction time was insane and was also the only thing that saved him from being sheared in half. He created a shield of infernal Mana right where the sword was set to impact, but the power of my attack sent him flying across the room. The forced interaction of celestial and infernal created a dazzling light show of chaos, for a moment blinding and confusing anyone who saw it. He hit the wall hard enough to crack the reinforced stone and dropped to the floor coughing blood.

"Oh, *really?*" The Mage stood up, smirking. Great. That was always a good sign. He strode forward, then turned into a blur of speed. He kicked, and I managed to get my swords in the path of his attack, but it was a feint. His fist snapped out, crushing my C-ranked Goblin head. Just like that, I was simply a part of the dungeon again. A spectator. Drat.

I would need to form a body and forge it with Mana if I wanted to be able to directly interact on this level. I watched dispassionately as my Goblins were systematically butchered. I was unable to help them right now, though they would be back soon.

"Hey, boss-man. Look at *this*." One of the C-rankers held up Bob's staff. "Looks like a cylinder of opal surrounded by aspen! This thing is a relic! If we got a good Inscriber to work some Runes into it, our Incantations could be boosted to almost triple the power for half the cost!"

Yikes. If he was that excited about the staff, I was even happier that the infernal soul-ripper had been returned to its underground armory.

The Mage seemed passingly interested, but the other C-rankers were so excited that only a stern warning kept them from abandoning the mission they were on in favor of better equipment. They stepped into the stairwell and descended to the fourth floor.

CHAPTER TWENTY-FIVE

Dale stepped into the dungeon, allowing the portal to close behind him. The walls and floor this deep underground were tremoring slightly as the powers above began to throw around vast concentrations of Mana. Dale took a deep breath, looking at the four doors ahead of him. Which one would be the easiest to defend? To barricade themselves in? The 'fire' hall was no good; with over a dozen clerics, there was no way they would be able to move as a group to get past the torrents of flame. He didn't trust their judgment in a high-stress environment like that. *Someone* would panic, and Father Richard would blame him.

Making his choice, Dale took a deep breath and gave an order, "Come on, through this door." He stepped forward, crossing the threshold for the 'earth' tunnel. If he was going to be trying to protect someone, Dale wanted to do it in an area where he was most comfortable with the element at hand. The group walked behind him, nervous and jumpy. The majority of them were in the F or D-ranks with only one C-rank to act as a mentor to them. They should *not* be on this level, and at any other time, they would have likely been picked off very quickly.

My attention flicked on to them just long enough to see Dale. Then I focused my ire on the other invaders. Dale's group was lucky though. If the situation were any less dire for me, I would concentrate all my efforts on destroying such a large group. But... not now. The main focus for this evening was the necromancers, and I needed all of my creatures to be focused on ending *them*. That didn't mean my exceedingly deadly traps were just going to *let* the assorted people pass, of course.

"Stop!" Dale called suddenly. "That area is dangerous, go around it."

"What are you talking about?" The cleric mentor scoffed, making a sweeping at the tunnel. "There's nothing there."

Dale agreed with him. "Exactly. It is clean. Too clean. There are small marks all over the place from the Mobs down here, but there is a circle on the ground here without a single scuff or imperfection. It's screaming 'trap' to me."

The cleric looked at the space and sighed. "I really hope that there was a good reason for Father to put you in charge. I am not used to this... this... *dungeon diving*, so I am going to trust your and Father's judgment. Our lives are in your hands, Baron Dale." The cleric helped Dale to direct the others around the potential trap, and they moved deeper.

Right about that time, the necromancers reached the fourth floor. A dozen Goblins were stumbling along with them, their eyes vacant and lifeless. They looked around and chose a path at random. Want to make a guess as to which tunnel they followed? Looks like Dale might have company soon. The Goblins started marching forward, a few feet between each one. Ugh. They are planning on using them to set off the traps. Necromancers are so annoying.

Dale's group moved forward, skillfully avoiding traps and encountering almost no Mobs. They did have a few scares as assorted Cats sometimes ran past them, hissing at the group before moving on. The group reached a branching path and went to the left. Moving forward, the tunnel widened into a full room, and they all looked around in interest. There was a stone pedestal in the center of the room, but there seemed to be no exit. After the last person filed in, the entryway was quietly hidden by a sliding stone door.

Approaching the pedestal in a circuitous manner, Dale inspected it for traps. He was unsure how he felt being down here with all of these unknown people but was doubly responsible for them. One, because they came into the dungeon with him, and two, because they were residents of his town. He set his mind toward ensuring that they all survived the night. He got close enough to the pedestal to read the writing on it.

"You have entered the trials. Trial one: Carry your weight, and the rewards shall be great. Else; one for all." He read aloud, catching everyone's attention. He kept reading as a stone slab unfolded itself from the pedestal. "A challenger appears. Will this end in victory or tears?"

"What is that supposed to mean?" A young cleric started panicking. *Were my poems really that bad?*

"The roof! It's collapsing!"

CAL

I watched as the two groups closed in on each other. As expected, the necromancers were allowing their zombies to take the lead. I looked on as they started across the large trap that Dale had pointed out, laughing as a pillar of stone launched upward into the ceiling. I liked this trap. The pillar was about ten feet in diameter, and when a certain percentage of it was crossed, a reaction occurred underneath it, making a huge amount of pressure build. At the halfway point, the pressure was released, and the whole thing blasted upward. Eight Goblins were caught in the trap, and as it receded, a thick paste was all that remained of the once-three-dimensional Goblins. I winced at the sight; those were *my* Goblins. Though I was pleased with the effectiveness of the device, I still was upset about the desecration of their bodies. The necromancers would pay for this. Somehow.

With the trap disarmed, the group of men hurried along, silent and serious for the first time. That trap could have killed any of them except the Mage, and even he may have been slightly damaged. The zombies weren't allowed to shamble anymore, breaking into a light jog. Traps began to spring, all of them earth-themed to go with the path they chose. Spikes shot out of the walls, rocks fell, pits opened up, and acid sprayed! The last Goblin corpse collapsed, unable to sustain itself.

"Good thing we had those with us," one of the men sneered and kicked the melting body out of his way. "Would have been a pain to go slow enough to move around those." They walked up to where a fork in the path would have been, but the smooth wall in the left doorway forced them to the right. They walked into a room that was identical to the one Dale was in, sighing when they saw the pedestal.

"What do you think it will be?"

"Either the place will fill up with sand, the walls will close in, or the ceiling will slowly drop. Just like every other dungeon out there."

"Hey, another piece of the poem on this rock just uncovered. It says: A challenger appears. Will this end in victory or tears?"

"Yup, there it goes. The roof is dropping. Why does this trap show up in practically every dungeon?"

The Mage interjected, "I'll hold it up. Smash the wall where the exit should be." The C-rankers pulled hammers and picks from their interspatial storage bags, one of them finding the exit by pushing a burst of necrotic Essence through the walls and finding empty space. These people... as much as I needed them to fail and die, I was impressed by their professionalism and flexibility in dangerous situations.

The men started swinging their tools, doing almost no damage to the walls. The walls had been built with a combination of corruption and Runes; they would need to be *way* stronger if they wanted to break *my* work. I was gloating to myself, watching the ineffectual attacks. The Mage held up a hand, the ceiling coming to rest on his palm. Seemingly bored, he simply held it in place as I increased the weight. I kept adding layers of stone on the top. This trap was designed to match the strength of the people in the room almost exactly, so I had created a way to reach that point! I started noting signs of strain on the Mage as I reached the ten-ton point. Both his hands were now being used, and he had adjusted into a much more solid stance.

"Yah need to hurry up, boys!" the Mage grunted through gritted teeth. "Starting to get annoyed over here."

<Gonna do him in with a trap. Ironic and fitting.> I gave a self-satisfied sigh as I talked to Bob. <Bob? Oh, right, all of your iterations are dead...>

I glanced at the room Dale was in, silently applauding their tenacity. All of the clerics and Dale were working to hold up the ceiling, none of them diving for the little room off to the side that would deactivate the trap. I had created this trap to get rid of disloyal people, people who couldn't be trusted. After the fiasco with The Collective—when the leader had joined Dale's group and used them to get close enough to steal Dani—I had thought of this design. Anyone trying to save themselves and let their people die would instead end up saving them at the cost of their own life. To escape, all they needed to do was attempt to hold it up. Just long enough to *almost* collapse from exhaustion.

Of course, when two groups met and went into the rooms at roughly the same time, they would compete to have a winner. Losing team would be crushed. Of course, that was only if the game were fair. Right now... it wasn't looking good. The necromancers were infusing huge amounts of Essence into their weapons, and with each swing, they pushed infernal taint into the Runes holding the stone together. The Runes were weakening, the Essence causing interruptions and damage to their structural integrity. Feeling they were getting close, the invaders shifted tactics.

One pulled out a strange weapon. It was an awl connected to a pickaxe shaft. The others exchanged their picks for hammers. The awl-man swung, chipping into the stone and holding in place. The next swung a hammer, driving the awl in deeper. The hammer dropped just in time for the next hammer to land. Each strike released Essence and drove the awl in.

"Just a little more!" the awl-man cried out. The hammers flew, fast and furious. A final blow shattered the Rune in the stone, creating a chain reaction of force. Half the wall exploded, the Runes detonating and odd shapes forming. Before anything could be resolved from the shadows, the Mage released a wall of black flames, incinerating any life that had been trying to form from the twisted paths in the air.

"Out! Out!" the Mage screeched, directing Mana around himself. His shadow seemed to drift forward, raising itself from the floor as it did so. In a moment, there was a pitch-black version of himself safely outside of the room. His form flickered, and he and the shadow exchanged places. The stone *slammed* to the ground, and the men cheered as dust rose around them. I frowned, also releasing the pressure on Dale's group. Technically this team had lost, so Dale's people were free to go.

A blast of hellfire roasted Snowball as he leaped from the concealing steams, making me grunt in annoyance.

The Mage's team rushed onward, thinking their goal was in sight... and found a stairwell. "Those *lying* Guild bastards!" the

Mage roared as he found the empty room. "This was supposed to be the end!"

"What do we do, boss?"

"We hurry up!" They rushed down the stairwell as Dale began to speak.

"Cal, I don't know if you care, but there is an attack going on above us. Necromancers invaded and are killing people. I'm trying to protect these clerics, but I need to rescue more people. Will you help us?" Dale's words echoed hollowly like he was not expecting to receive anything but scorn.

He deserved scorn. Dale was weak; he was lying on the ground trembling from exertion. He couldn't fight these people, he couldn't inflict a bit of damage to them if he shattered his Core while hugging them! But. But, he wasn't giving up. It was something.

<Dale, dig into that chest. I didn't want to unveil this area because it isn't finished yet, but I think it will serve a purpose tonight. I need to go. Don't judge too harshly, or I won't let you back into it later.>

DALE

He was so shocked that the dungeon had answered. Especially that it had answered nicely! Dale looked around, wincing as his torn muscles twitched in pain. There was the chest! He stood up, cycling Essence through his body to speed the healing process. The clerics were still on the ground, but the strongest among them were beginning to heal themselves, then the others. Dale opened the chest, pulling out only a keygem. He looked at it, confused. It was a soft pink color and didn't match any of the others he had found to this point.

Dale felt a sudden relief, looking to the side to see a cleric working to fix his damaged body. The cleric suddenly grimaced and paled. "Ugh. You have a lot more damage than the last one. It goes so deep too... What have you been doing to yourself? This isn't all from just now, some of it is beginning to scar. Good God, man!" He almost puked as Essence flowed out of him. "That's all I can do for now. You need to get to the church after this is over. Have you been living on a diet of healing potions or something?"

"Thank you, either way," Dale stated abruptly, shaking the cleric's hand. "I feel better than I have in weeks! Let's get moving."

The entire group started walking, stepping into the heart of the maze. Dale looked around, expecting to see Snowball appearing from the steam. Noting a chunk of seared flesh and the acrid smell of burnt fur, Dale blanched. "They're in here too..."

Looking around, he noticed that something was different. The Silverwood tree was gone! That meant... "The dungeon grew again. A new level?" He walked to the stairwell, inspecting it for a moment before turning to the portal. Dale held up the keygem, and a soft pink light matching the keygem emanated from the portal. Stepping through, his eyes widened, and he grinned.

"Get in here!" Dale ordered the clerics. They piled through, looking around with great interest. "I'm going back to the surface. I'm going to start sending people through as I find them, so get ready to take care of the wounded!"

The clerics nodded to him. Dale switched his keygem, stepping through the portal into hell on earth. An entire wall of the church had been shattered, exposing the arena to the natural and unnatural forces at play on the mountain. Wind laced with snow howled through the gap in the stone barrier, pushing some less balanced undead off of their feet as a layer of ice rapidly formed. A small crowd of people had collected in the arena, trying their best to hold off the ravenous dead. Dale called out to them, getting their attention at once.

"Start evacuating into the portal! I need someone to get over here and be in charge of keeping it open or closing it if we start to get overrun!" Dale ordered as loudly as he could, his voice just barely being heard over the wind and screams. The non-combatants charged at him, nearly trampling others in their rush to escape. Dale had to scream at them in order to be paid attention to, and they still dove through the portal like maniacs.

"Good to see you, Dale! Having a good night?" Hans' cheeky voice cut through the hubbub. Dale turned to see him poking holes in the undead, his daggers punching through their spines and incapacitating the bodies. Then the remainder of Dale's team would smash the skull, and the body would stop moving as gray matter leaked out.

"Two points of repair if the necromancer tries to raise the bodies again," Hans explained as he caught Dale's disgusted look. "It'd be better to burn them, but we don't have that kind of time right now."

Dale had to take a deep breath. "I cannot tell you all how much I missed you."

The others rushed over and fell into formation. Hans snorted at Dale as he threw a dagger that seemed to ignore the wind. "No need to get all weepy! Are you going to break into song? Cry, perhaps?"

Dale studiously ignored him. "Has anyone else seen any survivors? Anyone at all that we can rescue?"

Tom spoke loudly, pretending not to be impacted by the cold, "There are pockets of resistance at the Guild, a few shops, and almost any building made of stone. That is, if they weren't destroyed in the start of the fight."

"We need to get to the shops first," Adam demanded insistently. "They will have fewer fighters and a greater chance of being overrun, and we need to go *now* if we are going to have a chance at saving them."

"Let's go, then!" Rose turned and ran for the demolished wall. The others behind her caught up just as there was a break in the storm.

The area was littered with shambling bodies, and tree-tall abominations were moving, shaking the earth with each ponderous step. The Mages from the area were counter-attacking, the energy moving through the air hot enough to vaporize the falling precipitation. Mist was beginning to settle across the ground, further hindering visibility. One of the abominations screamed. Not in pain but fury.

It was surrounded by a huge wall of thorns, each of which was barbed and oversized. The thorns drove into the diseased flesh, grasping and refusing to let go. The abomination thrashed, tearing itself free but leaving huge tracts of tissue behind. It tried to reabsorb the flesh, only to find that it was trapped again. The brambles got thicker and denser until movement was impossible. An opportunistic Mage used this chance to light the brambles on fire and burned the abomination with unmatched heat.

The Mages were fighting the undead, but this was palliative; they were the symptom, not the true cause of the night's horrors. While the most powerful members of the council were pausing the advance of the towering flesh, others were searching high and low for the necromancer acting as puppet master. Dale's group ran across the open area, drawing the attention of many lesser undead. Han's advice and tactics were followed exactingly when fighting the dead, and the party targeted the brain and the spine whenever the opportunity presented itself.

"Where are we going?" Tom shouted as he swung his warhammer in a half-moon arc. When he attacked something, there was no need to slow and finish the job. Usually, the upper half of what he hit would turn to a pulp, painting crimson whatever was behind his target.

Rose responded harshly, her voice damaged by the cold and yelling, "We're going to Tyler's store! It is doubly reinforced since they've been conducting experiments on things that explode!"

"They've *what?*" Dale yelled in shock, almost halting his attacks.

"Are you *really* surprised about that, Dale?" Adam laughed as Dale's face contorted.

Rose continued, "I'm betting they've gathered as many people as they can and then barricaded themselves inside. Oh..." Rose trailed off as the group skid to a halt. Five necrotic Mages stood in front of them, almost as astonished as Dale's group.

"What the...?" The dark Mage closest to them laughed. "Really? Volunteers! Excellent!"

A ripple of inky darkness sped toward Rose, who was standing in the front of the group. She yelped, twisting unsuccessfully to dodge out of the way. She squeezed her eyes shut... opening them in a moment when nothing began to hurt. Rose stared at the form before her. Golden white hair spilled down from the head, a body standing erect in a noble pose. What surprised her most were the twin sheaths hanging down the person's back. Rose took a step back to fully take in the view of the man who had saved her.

"Assaulting youngsters like this? Villains, your time has come. Justice has arrived!" The man raised his twin swords, their edges reflecting the necromancers' wide eyes.

CHAPTER TWENTY-SIX

"What kind of a cheesy line was that?" a dark Mage howled with laughter. "'Justice has arrived'! Ha ha ha!"

The golden-haired man blushed slightly. "Your taunts only highlight thine craven nature. Answer two questions for me and thou shalt perish swiftly."

"Sure, why not? We are only ransacking a *city*. We have time to visit." The Mages laughed again as weapons were raised.

"It is much appreciated," the man spoke peacefully. "Firstly, hast thou seen a disturbing, greasy, perverted old man?"

"We weren't being serious. Get out of the... you know what? Why not." The Mage seemed to deflate. "No, we haven't seen anyone like that."

"Secondly then, where is the person controlling yonder abominations? They must needs be held accountable for their despicable actions." The swords were beginning to shine, garnering everyone's undivided attention.

The Mages ignored his words, throwing themselves forward. Mana rose like a wave, crashing down upon the golden man. A beam of light slashed the wall of darkness, and the man stepped through the resulting mephitis calmly.

Adam grabbed Dale, his eyes wide. He was trembling. "Dale. We need to leave. We need to leave *now*."

"I agree, let's slip away, and–" Dale started scooting backward.

"No!" Adam shouted, shaking him harder than his thin form should allow. "Run! Run now, all of you! There is only one person who that could be! That's *Kere Nolsen*!"

Adam turned and started sprinting away, slipping once before scrambling to his feet. The others, bemused by his oddly changed personality but still trusting him implicitly, ran with him. Dale heard Kere speaking behind him. "Let the trial begin! I judge you as..."

Dale's group had only made it a few meters when the world turned white. Not in the same way as an explosion, but as though all pigment had been drained away. Only shades of black and white remained. Every sound seemed to echo strangely, and Dale, concerned, looked at his friends. A scream slipped out of his lips as he did so.

Each of them had also been drained of color, leaving them looking flat. Only one color returned then. Black. The darkness crawled across them, leaving tracks like mud. For some reason, the hue was terrifying. Dale turned to Hans and nearly fainted. Hans was *coated* in black, with only his central being still shining with a flat white. He tried to avert his eyes, and his gaze landed upon a man dancing on the roof of a building.

This must be the person the golden man had been looking for. Dale didn't know why or what it meant, but the man didn't have a speck of black on him. He was stripping erotically though, prompting Dale to look away from him in shock. Dale's eyes flashed back, trying to keep track of him, but the man was already gone.

"*Guilty!*" Kere announced, his words echoing across the desaturated space. "I can see the sins crawling up your back! Your soul craves redemption, but all I can offer... is justice!"

Dale looked over his shoulder as color seemed to return to the world. There was a small mushroom-shaped cloud of blood in the area behind them, where Kere had last been seen.

"Why did we run from that area?" Tom snarled as they approached Tyler's shop. "We could have helped."

Adam's hands were shaking, his eyes still wide. "That was Cardinal *Kere Nolsen*, the High Inquisitor of the Holy

Church, the man known as 'The Slayer of Shades'. The single most terrifying embodiment of pure justice known to mankind. When he accesses his power, he *needs* to mete out punishments for your sins. He makes them visible to all around him so that everyone can see that justice is being done. There are no people that are immune to his influence. If he decides to give you a 'trial', like he just did with those necromancers, and you are found guilty... he erases you from the face of the planet."

"Sounds like a really fun guy to have at a party," Hans quipped, attempting to lighten the mood.

"He is very highly respected," Adam tried to explain defensively. "He is the role model for a huge amount of clerics, myself included."

"And yet... you run from him in terror," Tom softly added his thoughts to the conversation.

Adam glanced at Hans. "Not all of us were as good in the past as we are now. If we have sin in our souls, it is visible during a 'trial'." Adam's words made Dale think about the man he had seen with no black on or in him. Did that mean the man was a total innocent?

They stopped their conversation as they approached a group of undead trying to break into Tyler's shop. Just as the heavy door cracked from the repeated blows falling upon it, the zombies at the rear were assaulted by the adventurers. Tom was using his ingot hammer, and each swing against an unprotected head allowed gray matter to slosh to the ground. Rose pulled out an arrow and aimed far beyond the zombies, activating the enchantment and allowing her first arrow to pierce through a half-dozen heads as it flew along its path. Dale and Hans' arms turned to blurs as they attacked furiously, one with glinting daggers and the other with metal-capped knuckles.

The low-ranked zombies stood no chance against this group, and as reinforcements came around the corner, Hans glanced at Tom and nodded. Tom half spun, planted his feet firmly, and blew air over his outstretched hand. As he did so, his technique took hold, and a gout of flame launched into the undead. The sustained flame made even the most robust amongst them fall to the ground, too charred to continue moving.

"Good form." Hans nodded as Tom dropped to a knee, exhausted from using so much Essence at once. "It was a little wasteful, but it is designed to be that way. Keep it up, make sure to refine your Essence more carefully, and I'll get you a better technique when you are ready for it."

"Purposely wasteful?" Adam looked at them oddly. "Why would you do that?"

"Well, he had too much corruption in him. He needed to reduce it. Ergo, he uses a wasteful ability so that he can shed some corruption." Hans chanced a glance at Adam. "Father Richard hasn't told you about this? With your abundance of corruption, I thought he would..."

"He offered to help, but I thought he meant in a more... direct way," Adam mused with interest. "I thought it would mean me swallowing a Core, and I decided that I'd be fine without. Hmm."

"Talk to people!" Hans admonished him sternly. "Just because you can do freaky stuff with your eyes doesn't mean you should stop taking advice." He knocked on the damaged door. "Tyler! Let's go! Your chaperone has arrived. No more hoarding all the beautiful women for yourself!"

"Hans!" a muffled voice came through the damaged wood. "You came back for us?"

"We did, yeah. Hurry up! There are Mages going *nuts* out here," Hans spoke in a conversational tone, ignoring the gravity of the situation completely.

"I have dozens of people!" Tyler spoke as he tried to pull open the battered door. Its hinges were twisted enough that Tom had to break it down fully. "Do you have a shelter we can all fit in?"

"I do," Dale said as people began streaming out. "We need to hurry. Is there anyone who can't run?"

"I'm a bit out of shape, but I think that in these circumstances I can be convinced." Tyler released a half-hearted chuckle. "These are all non-combatants. Non-cultivators. You okay with helping us out?"

"Yes, let's go," Dale ordered as they began jogging toward the church. "You sure you have everyone?"

"Absolutely certain," Tyler stated after a quick headcount. They made their way to safety, but the people near the rear began to scream as they saw the abominations moving their way. The shrill sounds, in turn, drew *more* undead to them, forcing Dale and his team to hold a defensive line while the people piled through the portal. The undead began massing, and larger versions came sprinting.

"I do not think we can defend against this," Tom announced firmly. "It has been an honor to fight with you all and stand by your sides."

"For God's sake man." Hans grabbed Tom and threw him toward the portal. "Stop being so dramatic and get in the portal!" As the dead closed in on them, the living retreated into the portal and closed it behind them.

"Is everyone alright?" Dale called, looking around at the people huddled or crying nearby.

"*Alright?* Are you sure this isn't heaven?" Tyler was looking around the area, mouth agape. He was hugging the alchemist that worked for him; both seemed incredibly happy, given the circumstances. "We *are* alive, right?"

Dale looked around, and he found that he could understand their joy. This was a long main hall with dozens of smaller rooms set into the walls. One of the largest portions of the open area was a workbench suitable for alchemy with tubes and vials filled and labeled. There was an area for every trade that the dungeon knew of. An apothecary lab, a smithy, leather tanning, weapons salles, archery ranges, Runecrafting areas, and what appeared to be an inn. Splashing water even signified a bathing area tucked away somewhere.

"I'm not sure what this is for, and I'm not sure why it exists," Dale informed Tyler. "I'm certain there is more to this place than meets the eye."

"Who cares?" Tyler was nearly crying with happiness. "Look at all of those ingredients!"

CHAPTER TWENTY-SEVEN

I had recreated Bob, who was keeping me company and trying to help me remain calm. He was still on the third floor, but I linked his sight to mine so that he could see the same things I did. The necromancers were at the bottom of the stairs to the fifth floor, following the only path. I had made it as a spiral, so if they went at a normal walking speed, they should be occupied for at least ten minutes. The reason for creating such a long walkway was embedded in the walls.

"It's not worth it! Go! Please!"

"Turn back! No! Run!"

"Run away!"

"I am so tired. I am so tired all of the time..."

Bob seemed confused at my laughter. "What is saying those things? Are those... rocks?"

<Yeah they are!> I continued to laugh maniacally. <I made rocks that scream like humans!>

Bob watched for a bit longer. "So... are they supposed to scare people off?"

<Yes. No. Well, it is a kind of mental torture, to make them extra unsettled for the fight,> I informed him as I waited for low morale to take effect on the intruders.

"They don't seem bothered." Bob had a point. The C-ranked necromancers were just plugging their ears. The Mage didn't even bother doing that.

<Huh. Well, it was still fun to do,> I grouched at Bob. I thought he would be smug about this, but I was wrong.

"Pff. Messed up some perfectly good rocks is what you did. Look at them! Have you ever seen rocks with anxiety before?" the Goblin demanded, eyelid twitching.

<Oh, be quiet, you spoilsport.> I watched as the men looked around cautiously, their vision inhibited by the mists and Essence swirling in the air. Bob's rant had made me miss the intruders entering the Boss Room! They stepped forward, and one of them tripped, a hole in the floor catching his foot. The Mage waved his hand, attempting to disperse the cloying moisture, but here in the seat of my power, I was able to counteract him with ease. He frowned, trying again. Another failure. I was only able to counter him because of the large area he was attempting to effect. He'd still be able to cast spells, but large area effects on small molecules was my forte.

"Did you feel that?"

"What?"

"Something... shifted."

"I feel heavy, what's happening?"

The Mage snapped at them, "Silence! This is something different, something new."

Screams broke the sudden silence as a sharp bone rammed through the back of a C-ranker, stabbing all the way through him to extend from his front. Blood and black ichor poured from the wound while purple lines traced their way across the man's body. The bone pulled from him with a wet *slurp* and vanished into a hole.

"Get up!"

"He's dead! What happened?"

"Move!" The Mage pushed the others out of the way, then formulated and cast a summoning on the dead body. It started to move again, standing violently.

"Hmm. Body is filled with an unknown poison. Hole in chest. Repairing for most efficient usage," the *thing* inhabiting the body stated. "Oh? Two summons in a day? Tisk-tisk. You've been a bad boy, Mr. Mage! Where is the other?"

"Banished," the Mage explained shortly. "We are under attack by an unknown entity. Find and kill it."

"Why not? Nice to meet you, too." The inhabited body started glowing, then coated itself in hellflame. The fire flashed across the entire room, burning away the mists and revealing my monster. The Dungeon Boss; my Manticore.

The Manticore had a head very similar to Snowball, fluffy and cat-like, though there were some obvious deviations from the norm. This creature had six eyes, three on each side of its face in a triangular pattern. It had teeth similar to a shark, jagged and multi-rowed. Wings extended from his back, heavy with scales and spikes. Runic patterns were traced on several of these scales, creating a disturbing hypnotic effect. A tail extended behind it and into the ground; on the end of it was a stinger laden with the most vicious poison I had been able to concoct from my acquisitions. His tail was uncannily flexible and could extend and contract faster than a snake could strike. I was still working on a name for him, but being a nameless Manticore wouldn't stop him from killing!

A hiss came from the massive Beast, drawing out and climbing to a full-throated roar. Stains spread down the leg of one of the remaining C-rankers, the aggressive Mage-rank aura causing him to revert to primal flight instincts. He turned to flee and was met by the sharp, hollow stinger of the Manticore. By the time he hit the floor, his soul had fled the mortal plane.

<Two down in the first thirty seconds!> I crowed, exulting in my upcoming victory.

The Mage and demon sprinted at the Manticore, and it retracted its tail from the corpse, arching the scaled limb above his head like a scorpion. It crouched momentarily before springing to meet them. His scorpion tail lashed out, but the armored arm of the demon deflected it. In response, the

Manticore swiped his paw—as large as the human body it was attacking—and tore off the demon's leg as it tried to vault over the meter-length claws. The demon's appendage turned black and rancid as poison began to rot away at it. Hopefully, the demon wouldn't be able to fix its body again before it was completely destroyed. The Mage stabbed forward with the large dagger that had been unnecessary before now but was blocked by an armored wing that stopped the blade like it wasn't even moving.

The scale that had been hit glowed and fired from the wing like an arrow. The Mage dodged, and the scale embedded in the stone wall just before exploding and reducing a cubic foot of granite to rubble. The demon—down one leg—used this distraction to find a different way to move around. He completed an astounding series of cartwheels, bouncing off of the floor and walls before latching on to a giant paw. It dug its claws into the tree-thick, scaly ankle and started releasing hellfire. A lance of flame went through the palm of the Boss and broiled all meat it passed through.

The Manticore roared in agony as it lifted its now-skeletal paw from the ground and limped on three feet. It kicked sharply, and the demon flew into the mist. With this respite, the Manticore grabbed a chunk of meat and jumped into the air, flapping its wings a few times before twisting around and gripping the ceiling. It hung there like a bat, lashing out with its tail whenever his attackers got too close. Chewing the stained flesh from a human body, the Boss's damaged paw began to quickly recover, cells dividing and growing to cover the enormous foot. When it was mostly healed, the Manticore dropped from the roof, swirling in a murderous blur of claws, tail, and wings.

The demon sprinted to the back wall, which was an amusing sight as it had to use its hands to 'walk'. It got to the stone barricade, turned to use its momentum, and jumped at the Manticore. The possessed corpse caught a wing as the great Beast dodged, causing the creature to stumble. The Mage took this opportunity to jump on to the Boss's face, plunging a hand deep into an eye socket and releasing a continuous stream of necrotic Mana. The Manticore screamed in pain as its brain was assaulted. It rolled and thrashed heavily, trying to dislodge and kill the Mage causing it so much pain. My beautiful Beast was unable to do so and fell almost sullenly to the ground, dying slowly. It hacked up a key, which clattered to the ground with a ring of finality.

The Mage stood, smiling, and turned to look at the demon. His smile fell from his face as his summoned creature was sucked away with a *pop*. I laughed silently; all of the spikes on the Manticore were designed to break off, and each of them had the demon banishing Rune etched on to them. The Mage started toward my Core room, taking only a few steps before gasping. He looked down, seeing the poison-dripping tip of a stinger protruding from his heart.

A low rumbling laugh came from the Manticore. Its lips moved, and a gravelly voice escaped, "Rage, fury, wrath, outrage, resentment, annoyance, vexation, displeasure... I'll... eat them... all..." The words trailed off as the Manticore expired. His first words were a little odd, but as his brain had somewhat dissolved, I'd let him try again when he was reborn. The Mage, already sweating as his body began to die, stumbled toward my Core room. He made it in, falling right before he got to the Silverwood tree and landing in a position that could be mistaken for worship.

<There we go!> I was pleased at the glorious outcome of the battle. <See, Bob? Want to go over improvements we could make? I know that Mage was a rank ahead of my Manticore, but–>

A hand plunged into the area under the tree, grasping the Core it found there and yanking it into the light. The last C-ranked member of the group smiled, looking first at the shining Core, then at the dead Mage. He couldn't seem to resist insulting his fallen leader. "You will make a perfect vessel for my next summon. Thank you for completing the mission and leaving all the glory to me!"

The necromancer laughed as he grabbed the Mage's body, opened the portal with a keygem, and stepped out of the dungeon. He sent a flare of light into the air and sprinted toward the exit from the mountain.

CHAPTER TWENTY-EIGHT

Frank was battered and bruised; his left eye was swollen shut, and he was leaking blood from many minor wounds. He shouted at a mountain of flesh that was rolling toward him and removed its kinetic energy, stopping it in place. Frank focused on blocking the motion of the abomination at a deeper level, and the flesh froze solid as the atoms were disallowed movement, the electrons freezing in place. His focus broke with a painful backlash; he could only maintain that state for a few seconds at a time against a creature summoned by an A-ranked being. Luckily, the abomination was only a B-ranked creature, and Frank's ability was enough to get the job done. The abomination toppled, shattering on the ground. The frozen flesh joined the other ice and snow on the ground, simply becoming sanguine scenery.

A shout rang out as a flare rose into the air, and the undead repositioned themselves. "They are blocking the way to the portal!" Acrimony filled High Magous Amber's words. "This filth thinks that they are going to mess with my portal settings? Stop them!"

Father Richard spearheaded the defender's formation, his blessings and rebukes to the undead opening a pathway to their goal. They surged forward but were now surrounded on all sides. As Frank turned to destroy a large zombie, a form tore its way out of an abomination and grabbed Father Richard by the neck.

"Stay where you are." The voice was decidedly calm. "We have completed our mission, and we are finished with this area. If you attempt to resist further, I will have this area destroyed."

Father Richard was choking, his ineffectual clawing at the hand holding him proving that this was the A-ranked summoner that had caused all of the destruction in the area. He must have been a few ranks higher than Father Richard to be able to hold the cleric so casually. The undead had all stopped moving, however, and the defenders were loath to restart combat while surrounded.

"Release him, and we can negotiate your surrender," Amber imperiously ordered, knowing that her words would be ignored.

The Mage surprised them all. "I will let him go. I only wanted your attention. Attack me and *they* die." He motioned, and a large cluster of people was revealed. It was the delegations from multiple nations, all of the people here to discuss terms of trade and alliances. There were three Mages surrounding them, and black arcs of energy shaped like chains moved between them and kept the hostages from running.

"We will leave, and if you don't attack me, I swear my people and I will never return to this city." The air shuddered as his oath was recognized by his Mana. He stepped away, and after a minute of slow backward walking, vanished through the portal. The towering abominations collapsed wetly to the earth, returning from undead to simply dead.

"He's gone, now free them!" Richard ordered the Mages, who gave a sly grin in return.

"Nah. That wasn't part of the *bargain*." The cocky Mage started to chant, only to be cut off as an object obliterated his brain. The other two Mages died in a mere moment as well, to the great shock of the onlookers. Someone had just silently killed three Mages in less than a second. This fact was as terrifying to the exhausted onlookers as the entire night had been.

"Boring, boring, *boring*!" a voice cackled into the still air. "Killing people sitting on the ground doing nothing would have made for terrible karma." The question of who the voice belonged to was resolved when a near-nude man stepped out from behind one of the few undamaged buildings.

"I show up to try out some legendary Dwarvish bathhouses, and children like that go interrupting my fun!" The greasy old man grouched—now not quite as dirty due to a relaxing bath—and walked over to the dead Mages to retrieve his belonging still embedded in a skull. The others leaned forward, trying to catch a glimpse of the artifact that could go through the skulls of three Mages without issue.

"Ew. Now there is brain on my toothbrush." The man sighed and tossed said item to the side. "Might as well get this next part over with. Come on out, Kere. At this point, you are just being embarrassing."

"I was hoping you would take this chance to repent." It felt like dawn had come as Kere Nolsen stepped closer to the man. Pulsating light seemed to collect around him, and everyone present felt at peace as his footsteps echoed amongst them. "Egil Nolsen. I stand before you in my role as High Inquisitor of the Holy Church. I shall now read a *much* abridged list of your sins. You have committed crimes against the church, Humanity, Elvenkind, Dwarvenkind, Goblins, Orcs, Beasts, and a variety of animals wild and domestic. You are accused of patricide, matricide, fratricide, and regicide, amongst a mountain of other crimes. Actually, you are also accused of attacking and somehow *killing* a mountain. As my post demands, I stand before you and am charged with granting you a fair trial and a swift death. How do you plead?"

"Would you believe me if I plead insanity?"

"Yes. Yes, I would. It will not lessen the sentence." Kere's eyes were hard as he stared upon the man who shared his name.

Egil grinned a mad grin, a myriad of chaotic lights shining in his eyes. "You may as well call me by my chosen name. No one else will understand what is going on otherwise... my dearest son."

Kere's mouth turned down into a frown. "After two decades of hunting you, Egil Nolsen—known to the world as 'Xenocide'—I stand before you to mete out... Justice!" A plethora of differing sounds were emitted. At the pronunciation of the name 'Xenocide', most people gasped, screamed, or tried to run from the area. Hue was leached from the world, as Kere spoke and the spectrum of color shifted to include only black and white. Everyone caught in the area had their sins exposed, no matter how minor they may have been. "I can see the sins crawling up your... huh?"

"You can see my *what* now?" Egil stood with a depraved smile on his face, beginning to dance in place.

Kere seemed a bit nonplussed, his face rigid as he looked at his father. Egil had not a single speck of black on him, seeming every bit as pure as new-fallen snow. The man in question strode forward, laying a hand on his son. "Aww. Two decades of hunting for no reason. No. Reason. At. All." He poked Kere on the nose as he said the last word, causing Kere to snap out of his shock.

"Im-impossible! I *witnessed* their murder!" Kere roared while drawing his sword and attempting to swing it. His arm didn't move an inch, his connection to Justice refusing to allow him to harm an 'innocent' person.

"Hmm. Am I innocent because I had to do it or because I feel no remorse?" Egil laughed as his son nearly frothed at the mouth. "Ah well. Either way, you should come over for dinner soon! I found a new recipe for roast puppy that I am just *dying* to try!"

"You're sick!" Kere bellowed, trying and failing to attack again.

"And you *limit* yourself!" Egil screamed in reply, his face twisting into something terrifying. His words caused the Inquisitor to flinch. "Following just one path, you *literally* see the world as black and white! *Everything* is shades of gray, boy! And it *abyss* well *should* be! Look at how weak you have become! Under your restrictive mindset, even breathing is a sin because you take air that another could use! Open your eyes, child!"

"You are insane! Your entire goal is to kill *everyone*!"

"I'm not going to argue! But as you can see, insanity has a few perks. Also, you are wrong about one thing... I don't have any *goals*. They are more like... things I want to do for giggles." Egil laughed in the face of the helpless inquisitor. He turned in a slow waltz, waved dramatically at the aghast crowd that had gathered, and danced through the portal.

Cal

When the Mage died, I had only been able to speak a few words before I was forced into my inner soul. His Mana flowed into me in a rush that took me by surprise. It was different than my own and sought to overpower my law. I freely admit, I panicked at first, but then I had a realization and needed to laugh. All other laws were inferior to mine and were only a small portion of my own, broken and splintered to fill a niche. The Mana continued flowing into me, but without me fighting it, the Mana was integrated into my own. The surge from the dead Mage allowed me to have a happy little boost to my own well of power.

It didn't propel me forward in ranking; the only thing that could do that at this point was forming a deeper connection and understanding with Acme. It did give me access to more Mana, but when it was used up, it was gone. I paused and chuckled. This had given me a few ideas. I had a dimensional bag *stuffed* with Mana! If I could use it as a power source, I could accelerate my plans to a huge degree!

I came back to myself, looking around in confusion. Hadn't there been a dead body in front of me? I looked around my body and realized my decoy Core was gone. <Bob, everything alright?>

"You are still here?" Bob half-screamed-half-asked. "Great Spirit! I am so sorry! I doubted you! Your silence was... disconcerting."

<Yeah, being alone must suck for you, sorry. I'll remake the other Goblins right away.> I smiled at him, and he felt the warmth of my joy.

"You got good news out of this somehow?" Bob questioned as his people began to take shape around him. He shivered. "Oh, this is so strange to see."

<Yes, the Manticore was a great success,> I informed him as he started pressing Cores to heads, allowing his people to function properly again. <I should really name the big guy. Also, Bob. All Bobs now, I guess. I have enough Mana to begin the ritual, finish inspecting it, and power it.>

"You do?" Bob was intrigued by my words. "*The* ritual?"

<I do.> I turned my attention to a part of the dungeon that was separate from the rest, connected only by a small portal

too small for anything but a Basher to fit through. <Dale! I think the danger has passed. You can leave now.>

"*I don't think they want to leave. What is this place?*" Dale seemed a bit grouchy tonight.

I looked closer, noting the alchemist and a few other craftsmen struggling to get at the workbenches only a few feet away from them. I chuckled, every time they tried to cross the Runes in the floor, gravity would increase by a massive amount, and they would be pressed to the ground. It was set up as a directional Rune, so when they gave up and attempted to back off, the weight would abate.

<Yeah, about that.> I decided to explain the function of this place to Dale. <This is an experiment of mine. I know that you have a shortage of craftsmen and thinkers, and I am as keen as you are to get access to their knowledge and production. So, this is the result.>

"*That doesn't actually tell me much,*" Dale thought at me. "*What is it? What do we do?*"

<It is an area they can pay to enter. There is space for dozens of crafters, and no monsters will spawn in here. People can come work in relative peace and security, and I will also benefit. If they bring me items I've never had before, they get a time token. Based on the rarity of their offering, they get more or less time to do things. I have a few options for everyone. They can pay with refined Essence or Mana and gain time that way. The other option is my personal favorite. They can copy their memories, and I will give them time in here that equals it. Ten years of your memories? Ten years of access. They may still need to pay for rare ingredients, but that will give them a *lot* of material.> I didn't tell him that I would take all of the memories either way. I was just going to credit them what they *thought*

they were giving. Easy to check when you had all of their memories.

"*No one would do that!*" Dale shouted in his head, very accusingly and—in my opinion—incorrectly.

<Really? They won't? For access to rare materials, equipment that fixes itself, free room and board for potentially *decades*? You overestimate people.> I snickered at his twisted expression of anger.

Dale stared at Tyler and decided to ask him directly. "Tyler, this room is a lab where you 'pay' to work. You can bring things in or donate power, and you'll get a token that lets you stay here with a room and food. Also, all the materials you want."

"What's the ratio?" Tyler whipped his head around so fast I thought it would break. "Where do I pay? There is crushed *opal* in there, Dale! I can *see* it! Is... is that powdered *aluminum*? I *need* to get in! I need to, Dale!"

<You didn't mention the memories!> I stated accusingly.

"*Bring it up to the Protectorate,*" Dale scoffed at me. "*No way in the abyss am I going to–*"

"Look! That sign says we can donate memories instead of things for an equal amount of time! Hot dang, I can stay here for years!" Tyler was nearly jumping for joy as he ran to a donation lectern. There was a memory stone embedded in it, and without hesitation, he pressed his head to it. A moment later, he looked up a bit dizzily. The stone dropped into the lectern, and a new one slid into place. A necklace with a pendant fell into a small drawer, and Tyler snatched it up and put it on as soon as he saw it. With a touch of Essence, it bound to him, and he ran to the edge of the Runescript. He took a deep breath and stepped over the line. Continuing forward to the workbench, he laughed as he started applying heat to a vial. Suddenly, the area around him grew too blurry to see clearly.

The others groaned as they saw the privacy filter snap into place; they had wanted to see what Tyler was doing! <Well, Dale. Once again, you are wrong.> I sighed in happiness as I made a copy of Tyler's stone, smashing it to gain his memories. Wow. A far more interesting life than I had expected him to have. I watched as he tried to leave with a bag of materials—having stuffed it with opal and aluminum—but was pressed to the floor. Heh. Anti-theft. Only finished products could leave and only after they had been given to me to copy. He seemed upset, but I knew he had read the rules.

<*He* seems happy with his purchase,> I told Dale haughtily. <Why do *you* fight me so hard?>

"*You are literally a monster.*" Dale sighed at me, then spoke softly, "I have no idea why other people refuse to see it."

<I think we're more alike than you will admit. By the way, you should let them know that all the tools in here are basic. The same tools will be offered as rewards in the deeper levels, and they will be Enchanted or Inscribed. This way, all of the crafters that come here will still have something to strive for.>

"I'm leaving," Dale announced to the mixed group of people. "I am going to go check on the surface. I think the danger has passed."

CHAPTER TWENTY-NINE

"Moron! Imbecile!" The Master threw the Core to the ground at his feet. It shattered, the Essence inside of it being sucked into the Core of the infernal dungeon.

"Master! I am so sorry! I had no idea that it would have a decoy! I will return immediately and–"

"You will do nothing of the sort!" The Master growled. "Your *leader* swore an oath that we would not go back if he wasn't attacked. We don't exactly have a plethora of A-ranked summoners, and going back would end him. We need to find a way to make them attack him, *then* we will go back. At least he kept the wording vague."

Behind them, Dani did all she could to keep from laughing aloud. Her mirth dwindled as she felt the attention of the infernal dungeon fall on her. It seemed to leer at her, reaching tendrils of Essence toward her as if it could *sneak* its way into a bond with her. "Shoo," she hissed at the looming presence.

<Oh, come now, little Wisp... I already approach the Mage ranks again. Even after finding a new body, I am bound to my law. I don't even need to ascend, just store enough Essence to pay tribute to my law and regain access to Mana. What can your old dungeon do for you... that I cannot?> the infernal dungeon whispered into her mind. It seemed to be licking imaginary lips.

"Show mercy? Have a good soul? Not allow extraplanar demons into our lives?" Dani brutally rebuffed the dark presence. "The real question is what could *you* offer that he can't? I can already tell that he is smarter than you."

The dungeon's presence seemed to twitch and slowly retreated. <You *will* be mine, one way... or another.>

CAL

<Whew!> I grunted as the Manticore stood, shaking itself like it had been soaked in water. <You are *really* difficult to resurrect, you know that?>

The Manticore really freaked me out when it responded in a deep, rumbling baritone, "I will do my best to ensure that you don't need to do so very often." It laughed, a rolling vibration that would terrify a normal being.

<Oh right, you can speak.> I laughed along with it for a moment. <Need anything? Food, a bed, company? I can make a plushy rug for you if you'd like.>

It answered, rolling it's Rs as it spoke, "I only desire prey. I will feast on them and find comfort in their demise. For the time being, they will be more than enough sustenance. I assure you that I am pleased."

<Well. Alrighty. Let me know if you need anything else!> I began talking to Bob next, <Bob, while the surface is mainly empty of people, I am going to extend the obelisks.> Obelisks were very simple structures, essentially just a tower of stone. They began to pierce the ground, growing like odd, petrified trees. There were six of them, arranged in a hexagonal array around the entirety of the town. Each of them was slightly differently sized, but each stopped moving upward at the same time, their points at the exact same elevation.

I had been working on this plan with Bob for some time. This was only the start of my machinations. Since I had used the obelisks to demarcate an 'enclosed' area, I was able to extend my influence upward. Cores inset into the top of the obelisks began to glow softly, releasing a tiny amount of Essence into the air. The Essence fed my influence, which grew into 'walls' around the town. To the trained eye, they were more like soap bubbles. A seventh, much larger obelisk grew in the exact center of the zoned-off space, which just so *happened* to be where the entrance to my dungeon lay. I smiled as the Core on its tip began to glow, and lines of Essence flowed between it and the six others. A bubble of influence began to form over the town, upon completion becoming a dome-like structure that could only be seen by cultivators.

It didn't do much right now, but over time, my influence would fill the area. It would take quite a while, as this was me *technically* adding another floor to the dungeon. I hoped that no one was stupid enough to destroy the stone, as this would help the town greatly. As a matter of fact, likely everyone would enjoy the benefits, and only Dale would complain about it. Already, I felt the beginnings of an influx of air Essence as the wind howled over the mountaintop. A trickle of influence began to seep across the ground, avoiding places where living people were standing. There seemed to be a conversation happening, and I noticed Dale was involved. Looking at all the blood, bodies, and damage, a flash of inspiration hit me, and I chuckled. Time to prove that the obelisks would be useful and that destroying them would be a terrible idea.

I actively began breaking down the bodies. They turned to goop, then nothingness as I finished decomposing them. I absorbed blood and other liquids, even tasting a new kind of snow for the first time. It had an odd yellow color, and I couldn't understand why people talked about catching this on their tongues... I found more snow, white this time, and cleared pathways between buildings, the snow simply vanishing. Rubble sunk into the ground, and I replaced it with usable bricks and various building materials. I wouldn't repair the buildings; they would get too lazy if they thought I'd just fix everything for them. I laughed to myself. When daylight came, I was sure there would be quite a bit of confusion.

"Great Spirit!" Bob called, pulling attention to my depths. "The ritual... after much study, we believe it is ready."

<Excellent, Bob.> I began collecting Mana in the air around him. What little hair was on his body began to stand on end. <I had checked it earlier, and I agree with you. I just needed a second opinion. Would you like to stay and watch or try to find somewhere you might be able to survive if this goes wrong?>

Bob, all of them, shared glances and nodded. "We will stay. This is not an occasion that we feel we should miss."

<I'm glad. Shall we find out if it works?> Without waiting for an answer, I began to pour Mana into the activation Rune. This was the first time I had used Mana for the purpose of using a Rune, and I was as excited to see it happening as the Bobs were. The perfection that was Acme began streaming into the Rune. Not too fast, not too slow, it went at the exact rate needed. There was no concern of a portion of the ritual activating before it should; this Mana was perfect for anything it was used for. I laughed as I watched the ritual complete and activate.

There was no flash. There was no sound, no waste of excess energy. The only way I was able to tell that the ritual was complete was the slow, constant drain of my Mana. <I... I think it worked.>

"Follow it!" Bob demanded shrilly, eyes alight with the thrill of discovery. "I need to know if it is doing what it should!"

I gave him a 'look' due to his tone, then looped my Mana through a Core. I poured the entirety of my excess Mana from the dead necromancer into the Core, allowing the ritual to sustain itself without my direct intervention. Then I followed Bob's order and dove into the earth. I sank down, down, following the hole that had been bored by my previous ritual. I got to the appropriate depth and looked around, daring to hope. I saw nothing. I looked closer, but still, no change was visible.

<Drat,> I complained softly. <This would have...> I saw it. I saw a change! Ha! I had simply gotten here too early! The ritual just hadn't reached this point yet! At a microscopic level no human eye could see, a Rune was being Inscribed into the rock. The rune finished, and another was drawn next to it. They slowly created a perfect, unbroken ring around the smooth surface of the hole. When that finished, I needed to extend a bit of Essence to see into the stone behind each of the runes. The Runes were so small that there were well over a hundred Runes in the initial ring. Behind each of them, another Rune was being created. That one finished and then another and another.

<Bob. It worked as expected!> I screeched in excitement. <A ring of Essence-releasing Runes, followed by interconnected lines of Essence-*gathering* Runes being created behind them!>

"That's great!" Bob yelled, all of them hugging or shaking each others' hands at the good news. "How are you going to activate the Runes?"

<Oh. Dammit.> I pondered this for a moment. <No, wait! They are small enough that any sufficiently Essence-rich area should activate at least *one* of them. That will, in turn, activate each in sequence along the chain until all of them are active. Also, the ritual is set to expand at any area that is sufficiently dense with Essence, so this will work in our favor.>

"Expand? How so?" Bob shrewdly questioned me. He hadn't been able to check the full effect of the ritual after all.

<The Runes will create a circle like the one below, off of the main line. Each line will then begin heading out along its own path. I got the idea from the tower of ascension, actually. You will see it for yourself eventually, but that is the gist of it.>

Bob nodded along sagely. "This could have interesting effects on the world at large if they last a long enough time. Essence will naturally be drawn to these lines, and where they cross and expand, there will be more Essence than is readily absorbable by the lines. I wonder if that will lead to people settling in locations that contain them? Will that help cities spring up? Make centers of learning? Currently, power in the world is chaotic, unevenly spread. I look forward to seeing what will happen..."

<Not our problem,> I cut him off happily. <Though I do have an idea of what I want the next floor of the dungeon to look like.>

Chapter Thirty

Dale walked out of the church into dead silence. He made a face at the impropriety of that thought. At least it *felt* inappropriate. After sharpening his ears with a thin thread of Essence, the ambient noise jumped into an audible range. Dale heard the crackle of fires, thankfully small due to the vast majority of buildings being made of stone. Screams in the distance, not of horror but just normal screams of pain. Dale grimaced when he realized that he thought screams of pain sounded normal. He perked up when he heard some tired voices; he recognized that tone!

Dale hurried over to a small group of people who were quietly talking but slowed when they drew weapons. Father Richard looked around and was the first to speak. "Dale! You survived!" He looked around at the weary faces around him. "Ah. Weapons away, we all know Dale."

There was a man in the group that took Dale a moment to place. He snapped his fingers after a short silence. "You are Kere Nolsen, then? Did we have that correct last night?"

The man seemed to be startled that he was recognized. "Yes, I am High Inquisitor Nolsen. I am also going to need to re-think my exploits if just anyone from such a remote village can recognize me."

Dale had a sly thought, remembering an old conversation with Hans. "Well, Sir, it is all because of the song! The 'Ballad of the Slayer of Shades' is quite popular around here. We have a bard from the capital that recently came to live here. Everyone can recognize you now!"

Kere looked mortified, his face draining of color. "Please... please tell me you are joking."

In response, Dale burst into song, "The man puts up a dome of white, purifies the evil with his holy might. The ladies swoon as Kere stares at the moon..." Kere seemed to deflate, his knees buckling.

"No... no!" The S-ranked man was pulling at his hair, almost collapsing to the ground.

Father Richard shot a look at Dale, a cross between amusement and annoyance. "Dale is joking. That song doesn't exist."

"It's true. I just needed to inject some humor into this situation." Dale chuckled as the man looked at him with hopeful eyes. "Is having a song made about you so terrible?"

Frank nodded gravely. "Well, lad, you made that song up on the fly, correct? Let me put it like this: that was better than the majority of songs minstrels actually put into circulation. For instance, you've heard the song 'Killer of Her Loneliness'?"

Dale nodded in the affirmative. It was a popular song in the tavern, as it had a catchy tune. Unfortunately, the lyrics were as bad as the title.

"Well," Frank smiled under his bushy mustache, "maybe you ask your old friend Hans how that song came around?"

"No!"

"Oh, yes." Frank grinned deviously.

"I should think that we have more *important* matters to discuss?" Madame Chandra interjected impatiently. "We have over two hundred people unaccounted for, at least a hundred dead, and dozens wounded. Also, the clerics are nowhere to be found, so the wounded are getting substandard treatment. Buildings are destroyed—bodies and trash are everywhere."

"I have the clerics in a safe location," Dale responded quickly. "Thanks to Inquisitor Kere, I was also able to complete a rescue mission. There was a large group settled into Tyler's shop, and we collected them and returned them to the dungeon."

"The dungeon? You brought non-combatants into the dungeon?" Frank glared at him. "How far in are they? After the second floor, the place becomes D-rank and above only!"

"This is a special place," Dale attempted to calm the Guild Leader. "There are no monsters and no traps that we have been able to find. It doesn't even seem to be a part of the main dungeon."

"Let's go collect them and get to cleaning this place up," Chandra loudly broke up the quiet huddle. "If we leave them to rot, we are opening the area to disease and–" Everyone snapped to an alert status as a whiff of Essence passed over them. "What in the...?"

Dale looked around, marveling at what he saw. All of the rubble, blood, and trash had been eradicated from the area. He looked at the few buildings that had a chimney with smoke coming from them and noticed that the smoke vanished mere inches after exiting. It had begun to snow, but the flakes weren't collecting or even reaching the ground before vanishing. The ever-present smells of a town diminished and were slowly being replaced with a faint hint of minty goodness. There were neatly stacked crates of building materials wherever a building had been damaged, and pathways were neat and clean.

"Who in the what now?" Dale managed to spit out a garbled question.

"It looks like a painting!" Chandra exclaimed with a clap of her hands. "What a beautiful change! Even the bodies are gone! Well, job's done. I am going to take a nap."

The group dispersed, walking around to look at the changes. Dale shook his head and walked off to collect the people in the dungeon. Seeing as he had the only key, it was his responsibility to let everyone–

The portal was open, and people were freely moving in and out of the crafting floor. Tyler was standing nearby it, holding his new pendant toward the portal to keep it open. "Danger is over, and it looks like the dungeon even cleaned up the town for us! Hop to it! Move, move, move! Who knows when my arm will get tired?"

Dale shrugged and was about to leave when an oddity occurred. High Magous Amber was waiting to enter the portal, but when she walked through, she bounced off the church wall. "Ow!" she cried out. She was obviously not in actual pain but simply quite surprised. Old habits die hard. "What? Why can't I go through the portal?" She tried again, but there was no change.

"That's odd..." Dale looked at the portal, looked around at the clean area and decided to try talking to the dungeon, "*Why can't Amber get into the crafting area?*"

As a confirmation that the dungeon now had access to the surface, he heard a voice in his head, <Well, Dale, the Runes in there aren't powerful enough to stop a Mage from just ignoring the instructions. They could walk through the portal, fill a bag with raw materials, and leave. Where would that leave me? Certainly no benefit in letting them come in and steal, you know?>

Dale tried to ask more questions, but silence was his only answer. "High Magous," Dale quickly had her undivided attention, "I think that the portal will not allow Mages through."

"What? No! There are so many things I want to make! I heard that there is a pile of aluminum in there!" Amber was getting dangerously worked up. "Do you know what I could do with a *Mithril* portal frame? I could *triple* the range of our portals! *Triple*, Dale! I could put a portal on the *moon* with that range!"

<Well that sounds fun...> Dale heard in his head.

"How about you find a talented Inscriber that isn't a Mage and have them build it?" Dale offered hurriedly, trying to stop her from giving ideas to the dungeon. "Why don't we focus on the plans for the academy? Then you will have your pick of talented trainees!"

Amber shook her head, groaning. "No one wants to be an Inscriber without being a Mage! The training can take over a decade, and the creation of each Rune can take years depending on the complexity! Have you ever seen the books spotters have? The complete listing of all known Runes? It's huge! Massive! Not possible for non-Mages to memorize!"

<*There's a book! Are you* kidding me *right now?*> Dale dropped to his knees from the force of the scream, prompting Amber to grab him in an attempt to steady him.

"Apparently," Dale responded through gritted teeth. He wiped away blood that was dripping from his nose.

<Get me that book and I will absolve you of any obligations you have to me except rescuing Dani, and I'll help you with town projects! I'll even make a copy of the book that you can keep! Two copies!>

Dale's first thought was to deny this request out of hand... but the offer was tempting. Dale frowned. Why was he always fighting the dungeon? It had never done anything to him beyond letting the Mobs attack and had made him rich and long-lived beyond his wildest dreams. He slowly nodded. "Deal."

Amber was looking at him like he had brain damage. Dale shrugged at her. Maybe he did.

CAL

<I can't believe that worked.> I chuckled to Bob, who had seen the whole exchange. <He didn't even notice my influence! He was totally convinced it was his own idea to work with me!>

"The power of a Mage versus a D-ranked human mind." Bob raised his glass of juice in salute to me.

<I didn't think it would be so easy is all.> I laughed as I watched Dale go about his day to day business. <I am so confused by their habits. Why do they–>

"My apologies, but I need to interrupt," Bob interrupted apologetically. "It seems that the grand ritual has... faltered."

<It ran out of power? Already?> I frowned discontentedly. <I don't have the Mana reserves to devote to getting it going again.>

"I was just bringing it to your attention, Great Spirit," Bob returned calmly. "I'm sorry to say I don't know how to fix it for you."

<Also, why did you call it a 'grand' ritual?> Much as I liked the term, I didn't want to use it incorrectly in a sentence.

"Ah. A 'grand' ritual is one that has the potential to affect the world as a whole," Bob answered me before turning to his own line of questioning, "Why do you not have enough Mana?"

<I am able to get Mana by exchanging Essence to my law. I don't really have a large surplus of Essence right now, especially if I want to continue my projects. Plus, I did just expand to the surface...> I trailed off. I didn't have unlimited Essence, I was just inordinately efficient with my usage of it. This allowed me to accomplish projects with much less Essence than

it would take from a less skilled individual. My hope had been that the 'grand' ritual would solve these issues for me. I wasn't too upset. After all, as the common saying went, you needed to spend Essence to make Essence.

"There is no way to speed your Essence accumulation with your currently available assets?" Bob intelligently pried, keeping his eyes on his glass. A drop of juice was licked off the rim just before it could fall.

I looked at him, meditating deeply on his words. <Bob... you seem more intelligent than you should be. Don't take this the wrong way, but my alterations shouldn't have been able to bring you to this level. What changed? Not too long ago you were hissing and scrabbling for the best cut of meat.>

He had the grace to look uncomfortable. "Ah... you remember how the Berserkers came to be?"

<Accumulating all memories of the various Goblins that started with the original template? That is, the first Goblin of the Berserker line?> I could see where this was going. <You *do* remember that he is now a screaming combat moron. He was reduced to mostly primal instincts? Ringing a bell?>

"Yes, well. We—the Bobs—felt that we should test the limits of our mind. Whichever of us is going to be Bob prime, the one that is our spokesperson, gets the memories of all the others. We have several of us reading at all times, studying, experimenting. When we combine the memories, we ensure that Bob prime doesn't lose his sanity. Then he becomes the baseline for the next iteration of Bob," Bob nervously explained to me.

<Brilliant.> I was seriously in awe of these Goblins. <Bob, that is amazing. You know that you don't need to hide things from me, right? I wouldn't ever tell you 'it is too dangerous'.>

"Yes, well. It has simply been a study on our mental capacity." Bob coughed nervously into his hand. "Back to my point, is there no other way for you to gain additional Essence or Mana?"

<No, I would need quite a bit of Essence or a Mage to die in here to collect their Mana, and–> I fell silent, prompting Bob to look around questioningly.

"Great Spirit?"

<Stupid, stupid, *stupid*!> I ranted, mentally banging my head against a wall. <The infected! A bunch of Mages died in here! I redirected their Mana to a dimensional bag! I'm a moron! I was thinking about that recently, too!> Rant complete, I sent Bob to the hidden storage room that held Cores filled with Essences and corruption, items that were in the process of being made for the first time, and one small bag that held six Mages worth of Mana.

<Alrighty, Bob-oh.> I cleared my nonexistent throat. <I could open this bag myself, but I'm not sure I could focus enough to close it again if the Mana started to overcome me. I want you to get next to my Core and open it up for only a few seconds.>

Bob followed my instructions, breaking into a nervous sweat as he passed the seven-meter-tall Manticore. It watched him hungrily but allowed him to pass after I asked nicely enough. Luckily, he was distracted by munching on an Elf that had been trying to get to my Core for guard duty.

"That thing is terrifying." Bob shuddered as he stood next to the soothing presence of the Silverwood tree. "What is it?"

<I call it a Manticore,> I jovially explained.

"Why is that?" Bob wondered.

<It is a 'mutated amalgamation of nascent terrifying existences' with a beastly Core!> I exclaimed proudly. I had been working to improve my naming schema.

Bob thought about that for a moment. "Wouldn't it be a Mant-e-core then?"

<Quiet, you,> I grumbled. <Manticore just sounds correct. How about you just open the bag?>

He shrugged and started to open the bag. <Bob!>

"Yes?" The Goblin tore his eyes away from the bag. He desperately wanted to learn its secrets.

<Don't point it at your face when you open it. It is filled with various types of Mana from infected Mages. *Might* be a bit dangerous.> I chuckled as his face paled. It made him look sickly as his dark green skin turned a pale lime color.

Opening the bag, carefully pointing it away from himself, the Goblin grunted as he struggled to retain his grip. There was a massive kickback from the bag as Mana blasted into the open air, finally granted a release from its imprisonment. Bob struggled to close the bag, and while he was eventually successful, it was a few seconds after he had been instructed to do so. There was a rumble as the air was charged with power. Various spacial distortions and mind-bending phenomena caused Bob to dive for cover. He glanced nervously at the area under the Silverwood tree where the naked power was swiftly draining.

Several minutes passed. Bob was almost ready to give up hope when my voice reached him, <That hurt like salt on a hellfire burn. That's if I were a snail who was *especially* susceptible to salt damage and fire.> All of this was stated in a calm tone.

Bob began kowtowing, "I'm so sorry! The bag got away from me, and I didn't close it fast enough!"

<Noted. Frick.> I groaned softly. <Well, the ritual has plenty of power now. I diverted into it almost seven times the amount it originally had. That should make it last for a few weeks at least. Honestly, I'd be surprised if it didn't last a couple of months. I even had to give Manny a boost, or else I would have likely self-destructed.>

"Manny?" Bob was caught off guard at the abrupt shift in conversation.

<Yeah, I just came up with it. New name for the Manticore.>

"Manny the Manticore? I thought you were trying to make better names for your creations, more... intelligent." Bob coughed to cover a grin as he finished his statement.

<Ouch. Well, his full name is 'Manny the man-eating Manticore',> I told him while trying to keep my tone serious. <It is all about puns. Intelligent naming comes secondary to that.>

"I... see," Bob unconvincingly replied.

<On a more serious note, I think I have decided how I am going to be going out to find Dani,> I told him, all mirth removed from my voice.

"Oh? How is that, Great One?" Bob was refocused on me, his eyes burning with a desire to help me regain my lost Wisp. "Are you creating a body? Riding along with one of your dungeon born?"

<No. That is too impersonal, too risky. What if they were to fail? I have to be more direct; I need to be there in person. You know that I have been researching flight, yes?> I demanded, fury and passion tinging my thoughts as I used him as a sounding board for my plans.

"Yes. What can I do to help?"

<Hold on, Bob. I *will* be flying, but not in the impersonal 'go with the wind' floating of my mentor, Kantor. No,

Bob. I will have full control of my flight path. I'm not sure how I will find a way to *control* the mechanism, but I have decided on the method.> I trailed off, thinking of the scale of this project.

"Well, what is it?" Bob stomped his foot. "You can't just say that and leave me wondering!"

I smiled, a deadly and dangerous thing. <It may have been a bit before your time, but I once created a weapon for Dale. It was a morningstar that used Runes to move the spiked ball portion away from the handle. When the handle turned, so did the ball. Distance didn't matter; objects crossing the path didn't interfere. We are going to recreate that system on a *much* larger scale.>

"Sounds challenging." Bob smiled as he realized that he was going to get to work with *very* dangerous items soon.

<It will be, but I've been working on making this idea a reality for quite some time. I've replaced the walls in the lower areas with much lighter stone. This should help reduce the cost in terms of Essence upkeep. I've sent out scouting bugs that no one has heard from since being released; they are either dead or closing in on their target by this point. Possibly most importantly, I am in the Mage ranks. I will hopefully be able to fight or outright destroy any obstacle in our way. Soon, we will just need to know where to go. Together, we can work out the mobility issues. We *will* be ready.> My voice was raw from emotion.

"That we will, Great Spirit." Bob ran off to inform himselves of the recent developments.

Chapter Thirty-one

"A place of peace and enlightenment enthralled by a murderous dungeon and beset upon by necromancers..." the Dwarven ambassador, Thaddius, commented wryly. "That is what you are proposing when you pursue your idea for an academy here. What an interesting life you must lead, Baron Dale."

Dale scowled, nodding his head. "I understand your hesitation, Thaddius." He looked around the table at the council and each delegation leader. "I understand everyone's hesitation in this matter. Recent events are disheartening, but we can–"

"*Disheartening*?" The High Elf ambassador stood sharply, chair falling to the ground behind him. "I lost a half dozen Elves! Do you even *understand* the loss that signifies? That is the birth rate for three entire *years* for my people! Am I to believe that the Dark Elves weren't behind this? That they just *happened* to let the necromancers through to my people? These are the 'trustworthy' beings you surround yourself with? Incompetent fools who–"

A dark wave of Mana washed through the room, coalescing into the Dark Elf princess Brianna occupying a chair near the head of the table. She looked stern and angry. "Do *not*," she growled at the suddenly silent High Elf, "try to push this on to my people. You *refused* to allow us to guard you, and you paid the price. If you want to blame someone, blame your fallen for being weak."

"That's *enough*!" Dale slammed his fist down on to the table which splintered, surprising the crowd into silence. "I am sick of this! We have a plan. We have worked out details. My people were attacked and took far greater casualties than any other group, and I am *still* here discussing how to better this area! You have all heard the terms; if you do not want to be here, then get the *abyss* out! If you are still here in ten minutes, I will assume you are agreeing to the most recent proposals, and we will have a contract drawn up! Until then, we are taking a break."

Silence reigned as Dale stood and stomped out of the room. Chandra walked over to him, and he glowered at her. "Dale, stop acting like a child. That cut to the heart of the matter but made you look like an unstable despot. Some of them may leave or withdraw their support because you cannot act according to your station."

Dale snorted and crossed his arms. "Support. Sure. At this point, if they are going to remain a pain in the ass to work with, I'd rather have them gone. We need to do a lot of work in the area, and instead, we keep getting caught in meetings with people that are only trying to get themselves a better deal."

"We were battered by a horrible sneak attack, Dale. There was nothing you could have done to prevent it." Chandra placed a hand on his arm.

"There is now." Dale's eyes glinted as he made his decision. "From now on, I am going to be working *with* the dungeon. We will get stronger as it does. We will have vetting systems for people that come here. We need to arm ourselves and find weapons we can use against these powerful enemies that we seem to have acquired for *no good reason*. If this is going to be a place of peace, we need to be ready for war."

Chandra watched him as he stalked back to the table. "It is always so painful to see a former innocent realize the truth of this world," she whispered sadly. Returning to the table, she took her spot as the meeting was called to order.

"Before any decisions are committed to," Dale began speaking before anyone else could, "there was another discovery this morning. The dungeon has created a place devoted to various crafts and training. There are alchemy tables, mining areas, forges, training rooms for various weapons, Inscription equipment, and so on. There is also every rare material the dungeon has ever produced, including Mithril, aluminum, and opal. All of this is accessible for a small fee and certain donations to the dungeon."

There was a confused roar as people tried to speak over each other. Dale hushed them and took their questions one at a time. Thaddius started the talks greedily. "There is Mithril and aluminum? Just there and ready to use?"

"Yes. As I understand it, the donations you make to the dungeon determine what resources you are allowed access to. The first person to go in offered his entire life as a memory gem, and was granted unlimited access to all materials with an endless amount of time to use them. Other people offered less and were given less to work with. But yes, there are entire chests filled with powdered aluminum, gold, gems, and books that detail various knowledge."

"Chests *filled* with Mithril? Ughh." The Dwarves at the table shivered slightly and flushed a bit. The ones that were standing moved objects they were holding–not-very-subtly–so they could cover the front of their pants.

The high Elf ambassador sneered at them. "Gross." He turned back to Dale. "What else can you tell us about this?"

Dale explained the limits and benefits of the area, which was shortly followed by everyone agreeing to the offers made in terms of trade, academic expertise, and political alliances. The meeting ended, and Dale hurried off to find his team when he heard some words that froze him in his tracks.

"Necromancers attacking, giant spider-bugs swarming into our city, and now a dungeon that plays at being a scholar!" There was a deep female laugh at these words. "Next, you'll see barbarians carrying us a fresh plate of cookies!"

Turning, Dale looked over to see the Amazonian delegation speaking to each other. He slowly walked toward them, as though he were in a dream. "Did you say... giant spider-bugs?"

He was eyed carefully, and the Amazonian almost didn't answer. Pursing her lips, she relented, "Yes. Dog-sized flying spiders swarmed our capital. They wove webs over every street, most of the larger buildings, and every sewer hole in the city. The city stank for days until we burned through enough webbing."

"I need to see. I need to go there," Dale announced in a shaken tone, then mumbled to himself. "Maybe I'm wrong?"

"As if you'd make it through the gate!" The Amazonian laughed in his face. "We learned our lesson hundreds of years ago; no man is allowed in our capital without a slave collar. Filthy animals like men need to live as animals, else you get 'ideas'. Like you, pretending to be Noble." She walked away, leaving a shocked Dale behind. He almost told her to leave, simply due to the fact that he had warned her that her brand of hateful speech was not allowed, but he simply had more important battles to fight right now. Plus, without even trying to, she had essentially just saved his life with the forewarning of what his trek to her city would result in.

Dale walked outside, coming to face a crowd that had been gathered. There were signs of exhaustion, trauma, fear, and anger. He quietly crushed a Core and shivered, now filled with confidence. Dale walked to a podium that was prepared for him, taking a deep breath. "People of Mountaindale. Above all else, I am horrified by the events of last night. We were attacked, harshly and without warning or provocation. Lives were lost. Friends, family, brothers-in-arms. I want to be the first to tell you that this assault will *not* be forgotten. We *will* find these cowards that attack in the dead of night and destroy them root and branch. We have made an agreement today, here in our humble town. The combined might of the Dwarves, High and Dark Elves, two of the Human kingdoms," Dale turned a stony glance upon the Amazons, "and the *Northmen* have all decided to devote resources and troops to eradicating this infestation. When we find them, we go to war."

Ragged cheers broke the stillness left by his words, and soon, people were clamoring to ask questions. Anger and fear had turned to righteous fury as people were given an outlet for their loss. All those gathered felt a surge of powerful emotion as they dedicated themselves to the destruction of their attackers.

"Today though, we mourn our dead." Dale motioned, large casks of ale and wine were tapped, and full mugs were passed around. "I ask that you not drink just yet but wait until everyone holds a stein." There were a few guilty faces as men tried to get the foam out of their moustaches. When everyone was holding a mug, Dale raised his own tankard. "A full cup is a sign of joy, happiness, and plenty. Today though, we are damaged. We do not have our entire populace, and within all of us, there is a place that is empty. Today, we mourn."

Taking a few deep breaths, Dale let the silence reign for a moment. "We all hold a full glass. In honor of those we have lost, who took a shard of us with them, let us pour out a portion of our drink and, hopefully, some of the sorrow we hold within ourselves." He tipped his mug, and the bubbling liquid slashed on the ground at his feet. Dale poured out more than the others around him, attempting to showcase his deep feelings of loss.

Around the area, his actions were mirrored. He tipped back the remainder, drinking as much as he could in a single gulp.

Looking around, all eyes were on him. Dale nodded respectfully at them. "We mourn, but we must go on. Food and drink are provided for anyone who would like to partake. Death is everywhere in the Phantom Mountains!"

"Death is everywhere!" the crowd chanted in reply. The mood remained somber that evening, but at midnight, Brakker the bard decided that it was time to leave the sadness behind and get on with life. He started playing merrily, and soon, people were laughing and sharing stories of the departed.

Brakker asked if there were any requests, and Dale chuckled evilly, snuck a look at Hans, and asked the bard to play "Killer of Her Loneliness". It was a popular drinking song, so people were soon singing and laughing along with the terrible lyrics.

"The killer of her heart; he had stolen her love like a thief in the darkest of nights!" Brakker drunkenly sang. People were clapping along and whistling. "His dangerousness forced them to part. His taste on her lips, she watched him go-o..."

As the song was coming to an end, everyone who knew the final refrain joined in, "*He was dangerlicious!*" Cheering broke out as people laughed and drank.

"Wow. That was unutterably terrible." Rose chuckled at the bard's antics. "Why oh why would you ask him to play that song, Dale?"

Dale looked at Hans, who was glowering at the bard and drinking heavily. "Oh, it just has deep, personal meaning to me." Hans choked on his ale and slowly lowered his cup. "I mean, how often are you found to be *dangerlicious?*"

Hans' eyes were locked on Dale, and if he had been a higher cultivation rank, his look may have killed the newly nobleman. "What do you think you know?" he whispered hoarsely.

Dale feigned innocence. "What do you mean, Hans?"

The ex-assassin narrowed his eyes. "You don't know... G'night all!" He got up and started hurriedly moving into the crowd.

Tom blocked his way seemingly unintentionally, then broke into a grin when he saw his mentor's face. "Hello! Heading out?"

"Ah. Yeah... tired or something," Hans mumbled as his eyes darted around.

"Sure you aren't off to steal love like a thief in the darkest of– oof!" Tom's sly grin vanished as he doubled over from a punch to the stomach.

Turning around with a jerky motion, Hans had a skull-like grin on his face. "So. You. Do. Know."

"Yeah, we do!" Rose released a deep belly laugh, shaking in her seat. "C'mere, killer, have a drink on me!" Hans rejoined the group and dealt with the good-natured ribbing, but no matter how they begged, he refused to tell the story associated with the horrible song.

Adam laughed breathily. "At least we know why Kere Nolsen was so adamantly against having his name immortalized in song."

Dawn was threatening as the revelry ended, and Dale took a deep breath, dreading the next thing that he needed to do. Saying his goodbyes and good nights, he wandered over to his room, sitting heavily on the bed. Almost hyperventilating, he called out to the dungeon, "Cal."

A few moments passed before he heard an incredulous response, <Dale? You called to *me*? Are you dying again or something? I saw your speech. Very uplifting.>

"No, Cal... I... I have some news." Dale swallowed, his throat drier than he believed possible.

<Well, spit it out then.>

"I need assurances from you first. I want to make a deal," Dale announced firmly.

<Oh? We're doing this again? Well, what are you offering, and what do you want?> The curiosity was pouring across their connection. The dungeon was getting a bit worked up, making Dale even more nervous.

"I want you to work with me. For the town. Help us build, grow, and learn. Help us look out for dangerous people, and give us warning when it looks like we might be under attack. Regulate the first couple levels of your dungeon so that we can train new people without the majority of them dying. You can charge for all of these services, but I want you to agree right now to do it and only charge a fair price." Dale almost coughed but didn't want to interrupt the seriousness of his words.

<I... see.> There was a pregnant pause. <In return?>

Dale nodded; he had expected this question. "In return, we will work to make you larger and stronger. A force to be reckoned with, with a city of protectors. If you need something, we will try to get it for you, for a fair cost."

<While that sounds fun–>

"In return," deciding it was time, Dale dropped the big news, "I also think that I have found where Dani is being held."

CAL

<*What?* Why didn't you *start* with that? Where is she? *Tell me!*> The reverberations in Dale's mind made his eyes roll into his head, and he fell to the ground. <Oh, for abyss sake.> At

this distance, my aura was too weak to either force itself into his mind or heal his body. His own aura interfered too much. I needed to be subtle to make changes. Like adding pleasing smells to the air around him when he was happy and using that to sway him to my side by making that scent when I wanted him to agree with me.

I waited a few minutes, and Dale started to stir. <Dale? Are you okay? I'm sorry about that, I was just–>

"Shut up," Dale ordered bluntly. "That proves it. I knew that you had been affecting me somehow. I can see that my mental defenses aren't strong enough to stop you anymore. My friends told me that I said things—and did things—in the dungeon that I don't remember doing. So we will add that to the deal. You will further agree not to insert thoughts or control me directly. Only *I* will control myself. I will *not* be a puppet."

The resolve in his eyes was as hard as my Core. "If you don't agree, I will not come into the dungeon anymore. I won't risk losing myself. I also will not tell you where Dani is and order people not to let you find out."

Well, he certainly had me over the coals. I thought about his deal, and really, it was more than fair. Mutual protection, mutual benefit, mutual gains. I sighed when I realized that I needed to agree. <Okay, Dale. If you accept my terms, I will swear that if you uphold your part of the deal, I will uphold mine to the best of my ability. This does not mean that I will give you anything you want. I reserve the right to refuse payment or exchange. If you break the deal, I am free of all constraints unless we make a new deal. Here is another point that you will have to deal with—if there is less danger, the rewards are going to drop sharply. If my Cats are corralled on the fourth floor and the monsters have a hard cap for what rank will be on each floor...

you are looking at coppers in chests across the entire floor. Not silver, *certainly* not gold. Agreed?>

"Agreed." A dollop of my Mana constricted around my Core, signifying the agreement and how I would die if I broke it. Looked like painfully. Fun times. Dale gave me the news I had been waiting for. "Dani is in the capital of the Amazon's Queendom. Your 'love-bugs' swarmed the place, covering streets, buildings, and the sewers in webs."

<Thank you for this information, Dale,> I sincerely stated. <How are you going to get her out? Do you have a plan yet? How can I help?>

He was shaking his head as I started asking questions. "I can't go there, Cal. The Queendom enslaves any man that attempts to enter the city. Not to mention that there are dozens of at *least* B-ranked necromancers that attacked us. There is sure to be more there."

I digested his words sourly. A flash of inspiration struck me. <Minya is a woman! And a Mage! I'll send her!> I focused on her, doing my best to interact with her at this distance. <Minya! Can you hear me?>

After a tenuous moment, her voice reached my mind. Her words were faint but understandable. "*Cal! I heard you were attacked! I'm on my way back now, but the Portal Guild is refusing to allow me to skip the queue! It could be days!*"

<Don't worry about it. I'm fine! I need you to go to the capital of the Amazon Queendom. My bugs swarmed it, so Dani must be there!> I shouted along our connection.

"*Got it! Do you have any specifics as to where she might be? Since that city is built from the slave labor of an entire nation's men, it is truly massive,*" Minya informed me regretfully.

She was going to go! Yes! I thought about the information I had and came to the most logical conclusion.

<They are holding her somewhere in the sewers! I am almost sure of it!>

There was silence from her end. I almost spoke again, when her wry words tickled me, "*You always send me to the best places. The black market, the sewers, what next? Undercover at a brothel?*"

<A what? Will that help you find Dani?> Minya was confusing. Did Dale have a brothel? Did he need one? Was it some kind of soup?

"*...Just try talking to me again in a few days. I'm going.*" Her voice abruptly stopped coming to me.

<Well, Dale, hopefully that is taken care of now,> I joyfully informed my now-somewhat-willing minion.

Dale had fallen asleep, but he cracked an eye open when I spoke at him. "Lovely. Now get out of my room," he muttered tiredly.

I left, quietly fuming. Dale had been able to blackmail me into making promises to him. For Dani, I would do anything, and he *used* me! He would have withheld information about *Dani*. The next time he stepped in my dungeon, he was going to have a rough day. For now, it was time to prepare weapons. <I'm coming for you, Dani,> I swore aloud. A band of Mana wrapped itself around me as my law acknowledged my oath. Good.

CHAPTER THIRTY-TWO

It had been two weeks since Dale told me about Dani, and I had been throwing myself at my various projects. I was almost ready, but I needed more power than I currently had if I wanted to be able to retrieve Dani by force. I was also beginning to become worried about Minya, as she hadn't reported in when she was supposed to. My attempts to contact her were met exclusively with silence.

"Arsenopyrite," Bob's words blared into the air, startling me from my current brooding.

<What? Um. Bless you?> I awkwardly tried to figure out what he was saying.

"Arsenopyrite. Chalcanthite. Cinnabar. Torbernite. Heliodor... Opal." Bob's grin stretched as did the silence.

I looked at him, waiting to have the joke explained when the last word he had spoken allowed me to make the connection. <You found them!> I gasped in shock and wonder.

"All of them." With a flourish, he produced a sample of each of the minerals he had just named. "At least we know why no one has found that these are the strongest conductors of their Essence type. These are unbelievably toxic. To my point, I am very dizzy and think I am dying." He swayed, collapsing to the ground.

The stones clattered away from him, and I ate them all by reflex. While Bob was unconscious, I looked at the damage in him and winced. I was amazed he had lasted this long. While I fixed him, I made sure to catalog the effects each stone created. Arsenopyrite, or iron arsenic sulfide. Air Essence and corruption absorbing. How strange. I have no idea how it damaged his lungs so badly.

Chalcanthite, or water-copper as it is known. It was in his blood and killing everything–blood cells, bacteria, nutrients. Left behind was pure water suffused with the mineral. I had seen this material before, but it had never had this effect!

Cinnabar, an amalgam of sulfur and mercury. Fire corruption and chunks of stone were coating Bob's hands, and rapidly burning through the muscle. I absorbed it and cringed at the damage that had been done to my Goblin from a simple touch.

Torbernite. Torbernite? This was all over the place in small amounts! Well, to be fair, it was only in the granite portion of my surroundings, but there *was* a lot of it around. With earth Essence swirling within it, the mineral released a soft green glow. The light that touched Bob was making his skin decompose, so I quickly removed him from contact with the stone.

I looked for any damage that had been done by the Heliodor, but as far as I could tell, it was just yellow beryl. No damaging effects that I knew of. Having fixed everything I could find, I gently woke Bob up.

"Huh? Whazzat?" Bob blinked sleepily as he stretched. "Oh! Right! I need to get these stones to... the stones are gone!" He burped upon saying the final word, robbing his statement of any tension.

<No, you got them to me. Don't worry about that. What happened though? Did you take that much damage from these rocks just because there was corruption in them?> I allowed him to become more fully awake and could practically see his memory of the situation coming back.

"Ah yes!" He stood, then leaned on his staff. "It seems that these will absorb corruption for a time, but once they are too full of the taint, they begin amplifying the dangerous and harmful effects they contain."

<You did good work today, Bob.> I was already growing a woven rope of these minerals toward the surface. Thanks to my experiments with opal, threading this rope would only take a short amount of time before it was fully set up. <If these do what they are supposed to, we will see an eighty percent increase in Essence purity within the dungeon.>

"Excellent news!" Bob happily chattered, waiting for instructions.

<Speaking of news, how goes the preparations for the flying rituals?> I was watching him carefully, but even if I hadn't been, it would have been hard to miss the flinch.

Bob squirmed, then sighed. "They aren't ready for you. We have been working tirelessly, and the extra dozen Bob's you made have helped, but... they aren't ready."

<What is the issue?>

"Too many Runes and effects." Bob rubbed his head as if he had a headache. Impossible, since he was at peak health right now. "We keep dying. Even the small-scale effects are so draining that we cannot fully activate them. Keeping them active would be too much even for you."

<I see. We need to make them more efficient, in that case. We need to find a Rune that encompasses multiple effects that we are after and find a way to have the Essence that is being wasted get transferred into areas that need it. I'll spend a day with you soon, and we will work that out.> My voice trailed off a bit as my mind was already deeply engrossed in the issue.

"Realistically, I don't even know how you are able to keep your ley-line ritual going. Every second, every day, it is growing and carving Runes farther and farther away from you," Bob scoffed at the sheer amount of resources that were being invested into the ritual.

<Hmm. You know, that's a good point. It'd have to be due to its function. Unlike the rituals we're working on now, that one does just one thing at a time and at such a small level that the individual cost is nominal. The total amount of work done is quite large though. Sadly, that isn't applicable to the current issues we are having.> Returning to my task of replacing all the stone in the dungeon with pumice, I continued speaking. <No, what we need is to find catalysts and reagents that will trim down the cost of activation and sustainment for us. We are really busy, so let's delegate a bit. Offer a reward in the workroom. Whoever can find what we need will get some kind of reward. You choose what it is. I am barely paying attention to what people are after right now.>

Bob nodded and walked toward the hidden room behind the workshop walls. There were always a few Bobs in there recording information, taking notes on projects, and trying to replicate the effects themselves. I could duplicate a completed potion, weapon, or Rune, but right now, there was nothing I could do to experiment. It wasn't like I could mix up a potion, or... wait a minute... I *could* make potions and experiment! All that was needed was the ability to stir and add ingredients over heat! I was intrigued by this idea but quickly frustrated as I remembered how little time I already had to devote to my current goals. I'm bad at delegating; I always feel that other people work too slowly. I can work for weeks straight, but there is only one of me.

I had tried to make another of me—a second Core with my memories—but when I tried to copy my thoughts to another Core, either it did nothing or tried to pull everything out and leave nothing behind. I would most likely ask Bob to become a dungeon Core eventually, but I was leery about sharing my territory. I was pushed from my thoughts as a rainbow lit up my room. What was going on? I almost lashed out, but luckily, I realized it was condensed Essence and corruption. I watched in awe as the taint remaining in the dungeon disappeared faster than a chubby knight falling into a pitfall trap.

Everything in the dungeon took on a crisp look, coming into better focus. With every breath, my Mobs became stronger. A few half-forgotten advanced Bashers—who had been flooded with Essence when I shouted at Minya a few weeks ago—started evolving! An Oppressor and an Impaler, the wind and infernal type Bashers respectively, grew larger. The Impaler grew claws on its feet, which became sharper and even sturdier after a few minutes. Its horn also grew and curved, gaining a decidedly sword-like quality. The Oppressor now had wind swirling around it constantly, albeit gently, and every move it made was enhanced. I watched it run around, no longer needing to jump off of walls in order to turn sharp corners.

Both were quite large at this point. They could look a young child in the eye while on all fours and would be able to look a tall man in the eye if they stood on their hind legs. There was an interesting side effect of a second evolution; they were *hungry*. No longer were they prey animals as they hunted and ate meat. They left their fellow bunny-type Mobs alone, but everything else seemed to be fair game. I pointed them at an adventuring party and watched as they charged in.

"Look out! Extra-large dinner incoming!" One of the invaders made his last joke, and the others chortled as they prepared for an easy fight. Normally, they would have been correct to assume this, but today was not their lucky day.

The... Oppressor—I'll need to rename them to keep them separate in my mind—accelerated to triple its previous speed. He was behind the adventurers even before the stupid grins were off their faces. The bunny jumped an impressive height into the air before contorting and releasing a howling gale. While this didn't have the same cutting power as its previous form, it had a much wider area of effect. The compressed air knocked three people off their feet and staggered the other two. The Impaler charged at the downed men, using its horn-sword to great effect. To be blunt, with a quick flick, the men's heads were parted from their bodies. Three strikes, three kills. It then jumped on to one of the standing men, raking him with his claws before slashing him with his horn.

<What the abyss,> I stated flatly. <You aren't allowed on this level. Heck no. I'd have to offer gold again. What are you...? C-rank? Yeah, no.> I thought about where they would fit in and struck upon an idea. Raile had turned into a joke with his easy to read attacks and ponderous movement. I would place them in with him and let them be a group. That would make the challenge much greater.

<What to name you... > Thinking about the battle that had just happened, I smiled and nodded to myself. <You shall be Raile and... the Hopsecutioners!>

DALE

Dale smiled as the roof of the final building slid into place. Dwarves had an unbelievable connection with—and understanding of—the earth. The sheer size of the academy would put a palace to shame yet had been completed in just over two weeks! Now he knew why everything they built was so intricate; doing things on a *large* scale was easy for them. As a nation, they could likely hollow out a mountain range in a few years! The intricate work though, that took time and dedication.

Dale looked around his city, smiling at the result of his bargaining. There were six large buildings, each of them dedicated to one of the affinities. There had been a bit of pressure not to include infernal in the school, but the angry voices eventually acquiesced. Opposite the infernal hall was the church. Dale hadn't even had to ask—Father Richard came to *him* and asked to be an official part of the academy. The buildings were evenly spaced from each other with the walls connecting them forming a huge hexagon. There were inner walls surrounding the dungeon entrance as well.

Between each building was a courtyard spectacularly designed for the affinity type a student would be training and had specialized materials donated from multiple nations to help with focus and cultivation. The professors would all have a place to stay in the buildings, but there were large student housing buildings being added outside the walls. News of the academy had flown across the sentient nations, and offers for teaching and requests for admittance were flooding in.

Dale's political power was soaring as well, to his great satisfaction. He had made a deal with the dungeon, and he was darn well going to honor it. Political power was going to be his contribution to the expedition, as he had already had his fill of being around Mages and the higher beings they had been fighting. He shivered as he remembered the lumbering mounds of flesh, the nigh-unstoppable abominations. No, thank you. Convincing people to fight for him, sure.

Dale's treasury was filling nicely as well. He was entirely out of personal debt and was finally saving most of the money that he earned. The city treasury was also doing well but was draining quickly as more and more buildings were added to the public domain.

"Excuse me, your Nobleness, we have a question for ya." The Dwarven foreman strolled up to him with his customary disregard for rank. Dale liked him quite a bit.

"What can I do for you?" Dale politely smiled at the enthusiastic Dwarf.

"I was wondering if you wanted more space to expand. You have a fairly large area, but the rest of the mountain over there means that you can only expand down or up. It would take a week or three, but we could knock the top of this mountain off. Make this the summit, and give ya a much larger flat area. Now, that sort of thing is expensive and not in the current contract but could be worth it. No worries about rockslides, lots of space..." The foreman trailed off, already knowing the answer he'd get.

"I'm going to give you a tentative yes, but this is something I need to discuss with the council before approving. I'm sure the city planner will lose his mind over... how much extra space would that give us?" Dale paused to hear the answer.

"It'd easily quadruple the space you have." The Dwarf looked a bit pained for a moment. "Errr... that means it'll–"

"Have four times as much space. Got it." Dale's face twitched as he saw the confusion on the Dwarves face. "Ah, right. I was able to get a memory stone with the Dwarven mathematical system in it."

"Ah. Well. Let me know, and we can start as soon as these buildings are done. We still need to finish a bit of Runework on them." The Dwarf started to leave.

"Wait!" Dale called. "You are putting Runes on them? What will they do?"

The Dwarf shrugged. "Standard stuff. Connect all the stone with itself, so that if you try to break it, you need to put in enough force to destroy the entire building at once."

"You do that on all buildings?" Dale's eyes were bulging. He was *so* glad this building was being donated by the Dwarven nation.

"We have a reputation to uphold! Can't let the Elves be the only ones that use Runes on their buildings!" The Dwarf chuckled at the thought.

"Elves use Runes on their buildings?" Dale yelped. "What do they do?" Now that he thought of it, he *did* remember... something.

"Forgetfulness. They use chaos-powered Runes to make people forget about their buildings and the locations they are in. Really useful to make people forget about them unless they *really* need something." The Dwarf picked up the pace, obviously trying not to get sucked into conversation again.

Dale's face turned red. "The Elves owe me technique memory stones!" He started to storm off but changed his path toward a certain redhead walking toward him. "Tom! I'm going to see the Elves! When I come back, ask me if they gave me the stones I am due!"

"Uh..." Tom tried to answer, but Dale was already running toward the Elven embassy. About twenty minutes passed, and Dale was walking by with a happy expression. "Ah! There you are! Did you get the stones you were after?"

Dale looked confused, then angry, and finally resigned. "I'll bring it up to her at the next council meeting. This is ridiculous." Dale dropped to the ground as a knife soared above his head. "Speaking of ridiculous..."

"Oh? My training is ridiculous? It must be ridiculously *easy* then, as you have barely been paying attention to my attacks. Good to know." A column of fire exploded upward, fully immolating Dale. He screamed, diving out of the fire, only to be met by a blast of wind. Dale slammed to the ground, bounced once, and screamed again as a stone spike slammed through his leg, pinning him against the road.

"You graduated from basic attacks to novice attacks. Feel pleased. Hopefully, you won't get *too* bored with this." The Dark Elf went silent and vanished, leaving only a shocked group of onlookers and a moaning Dale.

"You did kind of ask for that," Tom admonished as he pulled the stone from Dale, needing to put in a bit of force to allow it to come free of the ground under him. "You are acting arrogant again."

Dale glared at his friend as he was pulled to his feet. Tom started dragging him towards the clerics. "I know you think that you have it rough, but my training as a Noble was similar. This is what all Nobles go through. A variation of it at least. The difference is that this version of my training started when I was eight years of age. You are at least an adult, but you are far behind another Noble of your own age group. This is good for you. Your chances of survival are increasing. Slowly."

"Sure doesn't feel like it," Dale stated through charred lips. They walked into the church, and the cleric assigned to him winced when he saw the severe burns.

"Can't regenerate carbonized cells. Gonna need to heal a new layer of skin to the surface," the cleric apathetically stated. "Hope you haven't been trying to get a tan."

Dale painfully shook his head. "Nah, I don't bother. All I do is burn." His comment was met with total silence.

"...Is he in shock, or was that his actual sense of humor?" the cleric asked Tom. The barbarian shook his head in sad acknowledgment.

"I am in a lot of pain right now."

"Right! Sorry..."

It took about a quarter hour for the last patch of skin to flake off of Dale, revealing healthy skin beneath. As they left the building, Dale looked at his silent friend. "Tom, what is the trick to this? How do I find him and avoid his attacks? How do I not take damage from his elemental attacks?" He wasn't expecting an answer, but Tom gave him a huge smile.

"Finally! We aren't allowed to offer assistance; you have to ask for it! Now that you have though, we can begin by speaking to your instructor!" Tom threw a punch into the air, then patted Dale on the arm.

"You can help? Hey! Your hand is back!" Dale gripped Tom's hand and gave it a firm squeeze. "Excellent!"

"Personally, I greatly enjoy having my body back together. The answer to your issue, my friend, is personal shielding. You have been adding Essence to your aura; you need to alter your aura so that it contains a bit of your elements. While it won't protect you fully, it would have given you time to escape that column of fire without damage." Tom rambled on longer than Dale had ever heard from him at one time.

"You really know a lot about this, huh?" Dale was grinning at the thought of not succumbing to fire again. "I'm impressed!"

Tom was silent for a moment. "As you know... Nobles go through this training. At my age, I should be in the C-ranks in order to have my family acknowledge me. I was. When I was exiled, I was stripped of my cultivation base and forced to forget my family's techniques. All that remained was my years of combat instruction, but now, thanks to Hans, I once again have a chance to redeem myself."

CHAPTER THIRTY-THREE

The academy was about to open for business! While it had only taken a month of construction work, there had been more than enough time for the available instructor positions to fill up. Students were pouring into the area, most of them followed by retainers and house guards. You didn't need to be a Noble to attend, but the tuition was not cheap. Dale ensured that there were scholarships for naturally talented poor people, but those were distributed quickly even though the testing was rigorous. On the plus side, the entirety of the student body was held to a high standard. With the dangers of cultivating and the easy access to the dungeon, there would likely be plenty of room for new students throughout the year.

Several of the sentient races were represented, and guards' rotations were increased so they could ensure that there were no 'accidents' among them. This area was intended to be free of politics, but no one really believed it was possible. Looking down from the balcony of his new room, Dale marveled at what he saw. This area was now a fortress! The original site used by the camp was a walled city, and the academy had its own reinforced walls as well. With great fanfare and a festive atmosphere, the Dwarves had pushed the summit of the mountain off the northern face just days ago. The thunderous rumbling of stone tumbling into the valley below had echoed for hours as rock continued to fall. Now there was room for a *true* city to be created!

Dale sharpened his gaze as he saw a protuberance that shouldn't have existed. What would otherwise have been a perfectly flat plain had odd shapes jutting out of it! It took a few moments to register, but he growled when he made the connection. The dungeon had lifted more of those blasted obelisks! At least they were in a predictable, set pattern. In fact, if he looked at it from this angle, it was almost as if they were forming a–

"Dale! It's time to make a speech!" Rose called up to him. Dale was unceremoniously pulled from his thoughts. He blinked and looked down. Sure enough, hundreds of people were in the courtyard chattering. Right. It was time to *officially* allow entrance to everyone and open the school!

Clearing his throat, Dale started talking into the hoop on a rod he had been given. Wind Essence lifted his voice, carrying it across the city. "Hello, people of Mountaindale! Many of you know me, but most of you don't. I am Duke Dale Phantom, Lord of this wonderful city. It is my great honor—and pleasure— to announce the opening of the Phantom Academy! As you all know, this is the only center of learning that can boast the cooperation of many of the great races as well as grant access to a neutral affinity dungeon. We expect nothing but excellence from all of you! Know that when you graduate from here, you will have resources, connections, and combat potential higher than any of you had ever dared dream!"

Cheers greeted the start of his speech, and Dale smiled as he felt a rush of emotions. "There *is* cause for concern! This is *not* a safe place! To become stronger, to have greater personal power, you will be risking much! Our teachers will be harsh because that is what you will need in order to survive! The rules will be strict, but know that they are there for your protection! You are taking your life into your own hands here, and in return, you will be treated like adults, no matter your age." This caused a few dark mutters as well as a few of the younger faces to light up.

"The last thing you need to know!" Dale boomed, face now dark and serious. "This is *not* a tame dungeon! It *will* attempt to kill you! Don't let it! Learn your limits, learn your strengths! That is what we are here for, as an academy. If you need help, ask! But expect that you will be called on to help others in turn. Welcome... to the Phantom Academy!" Cheers burst out of the assembled people, the odd speech not putting them off, but instead, getting their blood pumping! Excited to begin training and in some cases learning to access their Essence, they quickly broke into groups and filed away to their various halls of affinity.

<Wow, Dale, that was really impressive! You didn't stutter once!> Dale groaned as his mind was invaded. <Hey, buddy, you haven't been coming deeper into the dungeon lately. Aren't you excited by the newest challenges and Mobs?>

Flopping on to a nearby chair, Dale responded aloud to the intrusive voice, "I've heard all about your new Boss Monster. No one who goes down there survives, so I'm certainly not going to try *my* luck."

<If no one survives when they go down there, how do you know 'all about it'?>

Ignoring the question, Dale kept speaking, "I *am* glad that you are honoring our deal though. No Cats have been seen on the first through third floors, though your Hopsecutioners have been doing a number on unprepared groups."

<Not my fault they are unprepared to fight in an area they were warned is trying to eat them. I won't feel bad for other people's greed and thoughtlessness. About the Cats, I wanted to let you know that the labyrinth has now doubled in size and complexity. I needed to add large, jungle-type areas to keep the Cats happy. They were getting cooped up and even *more* aggressive. Also, since we are being nice to each other, I am

giving you warning that Snowball has gotten bored being alone and is now wandering around that floor. So. Yeah.>

"Thank you for the information, Cal." Dale pulled a box out of a chest sitting next to him. Opening the box, he pulled out a book. "This is for you. It is *borrowed* from the remaining Spotters, and I only get to study it for a day."

<I-is that what I think it is?> Dale had never heard the dungeon sound so awestruck. <*All* Runes known to the Spotters guild?>

"This is it," Dale confirmed his words by setting the book down gently and stepping away.

<Wow. I am amazed Dale. Because of that, I'm going to give you first a warning, followed by a hint about something. You might want to turn around.> Dale looked confused but turned around. All that was behind him was the balcony and the chest. What was–

A screaming Goblin shot out of the chest, knife leading. Dale yelped and collapsed, rolling backward as the blade swished through the air. Coming to his feet, he launched forward and threw a massively powerful punch. Hitting the Goblin in the chest, blood tore out of the creature's back, and it collapsed to the ground, dead.

Before Dale could say a word, he felt a mental shrug. <Not *my* fault you put a chest in your room. About that hint, the Dungeon Boss you know 'all about' is no longer on the lowest floor.>

"That monstrosity is *roaming*?" Dale blanched and turned to run out of the room. People had to know!

<No, no. No need to get all personal. There is a new floor I built under it, and this floor has secrets that a few of the races have killed to *keep* secret. Soon, especially with these Runes I now have, a few of my floors will be impossible for

ninety-nine percent of your population. I'd say at least ninety-five percent of groups would die to the Dungeon Boss, but at least there is only *one* of him.> Dale really had no idea what to make of this information. He resolved to pass it on to the council. <Also, I have a gift for your city!>

Instantly wary, Dale was able to spit out the needed question. "And what might that be?"

<Since there is a Mana storm about to begin, you finally get to see what I have been slaving over for the last month and what those obelisks are *really* used for! I've been wanting to do this since I learned how to create Runes!>

"Cal, what are you doing?" Dale formed a fist, struggling to keep the nerves out of his voice.

<Oh, stop whining, and go back out on the balcony.>

"*Mana storm*!" an amplified voice rang through the city. Alarms shattered the peaceful mountain air, and Dale rushed to stand outside. Hans threw open the door to Dale's room, making sure his team leader wasn't doing anything foolish. But, of course he was.

"Dale! Get in here! There is a Mana storm starting!" Hans bellowed as he saw that Dale was standing unprotected on his balcony.

"Hans, come here. Something's about to happen." Dale sounded resigned enough that Hans did a double take to ensure Dale was not a body double.

Trusting his team leader but still wary, Hans slowly walked toward the balcony but stopped while he was still inside. "You can see pretty good from in here, you know. Like any other normal person can."

Dale was looking at the multicolored thunderclouds appearing above the city. "Looks like a big one," he commented calmly. It started to rain, or... at least, it looked like rain at first.

Grain seeds were pouring out of the clouds, pinging off the stone like hail.

"Come on inside, Dale," Hans cajoled his friend. "If you stand in the grain, you are going to get all wheat."

The horrible joke snapped Dale out of his apparent stupor. He turned and glared at the snorting assassin. "*Why* Hans? If Rose were here, she might have shot you for that."

"Dale. Dale. Look..." Hans had stopped laughing and was now pointing a shaking finger out at the storm. The clouds were doing something... different. Something that had never been seen in the previous storms. They were twisting, forming a funnel cloud. The twisting Mana and Essence released lightning bolts and raw chaos, but oddly, none of it seemed to strike anything. The funnel descended, finally making contact with the tallest obelisk. The obelisk lit up, and the clouds started to boil.

CAL

<Funnel cloud has touched down!> I shouted to the gathered Bobs. <Obelisk Alpha has reacted. Various Mana is streaming to the Core room! Avoid leaks. This is deadly! I repeat, do not touch any leaking Mana! It'll destroy your meridians so badly that even *I* won't be able to fix them!> The obelisk directed the Mana toward me, but small leaks were expected in our trial run. There was chaos in these streams after all. The Mana touched me and began to be assimilated by my personal law. Unlike my Goblins, I was protected from the effect of absorbing the 'wrong' type of Mana. As far as I knew, only my Mana could take in any other type of Mana and use it fully. No doubt a benefit of my law being what all other laws descended from.

The process wasn't perfectly smooth, but my Mana reserves were starting to become huge and dense. <Keeping the stream incoming! Now activating Runic formations on all other obelisks!>

"Understood! All Bobs are watching for anomalies; feel confident in us and focus your efforts on Mana redirection!" Bob retorted quickly.

I was glad for his words and followed his advice, focusing on directing the Mana as he had suggested. One by one, the obelisks the people on the surface could see began to light up. The clouds were still descending, twisting with fury and pseudo-sentience as it tried to escape my pull. Not a chance! I had my hooks in now, and months of work would not go to waste! I *needed* this Mana; there was no telling when I would be able to gain such a huge windfall again! Now, the obelisks *below* the surface began to light up, and Mana began to flow along the channels I had cut in the rock with thousands of painstaking hours of work.

The clouds were half gone, and the first layer of Runes activated! So much Essence rushed towards the mountain that the sky lit up as if a rainbow dawn had graced us. I had etched my cultivation pattern into the stone and lined it with tens of thousands of Essence absorption Runes. I had wanted one massive absorption Rune, but even this amount of Mana I had gained would likely have not been enough to initially power it. I kept the Mana flowing, forcing it—and not Essence—to power the Runes. The second layer was smaller with nearly half of the amount of Runes. When it fully activated, the Essence draw became even greater. The air was humming now. With the third layer, the ground started to tremble as the cultivation pathways filled with power.

After the fourth layer, Essence began to accumulate on the surface; no longer was it all able to be drawn into the ground or to me. Next, the fifth, sixth, all the way to the twenty-third layer of cultivation cut into the stone where the Essence became liquid and began to pour into my Core room like a gentle rain. It had passed through so many filters and taint accumulators that this Essence was entirely colorless. When looking through this pure Essence, only a distortion of the image behind it was visible, like peering through a heat wave.

An unexpected event almost made me lose control; the Silverwood tree began to grow! It shot up, basking in the thick rain of Essence. The tree grew over fifty feet high, stopping at the ceiling only because it couldn't easily cut through the stone. It began to widen instead, only growing to about four feet in diameter before stopping. The roots were now thicker, more numerous, and *those* began to push through the stone of the dungeon. They didn't grow over Runes or Essence pathways that I had made, but they did wind around them. The tree began to shine, but nothing else appeared to happen.

With great relief, I refocused on the Mana draining from the now-small clouds. The sun was again warming the surface, and I smiled as I poured everything I had left into the not-yet-activated Runescript Bob had been preparing for me. The Runescript was built into a marvelous toy I had blatantly stolen from a child. It had been designed by the reclusive Gnomish people, and I wasn't about to pass up an opportunity like that! They rarely made contact with the outside world, but when they did, their mechanical creativity was shown to be second to none.

I had built the Runescript on to a 'gyroscope'. The 'toy' had opened possibilities I would have never discovered otherwise. I felt confident the Runes would work, as I had prepared similar versions on one of the first weapons I had really set my mind to creating. Of course, we had tested this on a smaller scale, and it worked there, so I was almost positive nothing would go wrong... or the mountain would explode. The Runescript activated, and the last of the Mana poured into a specially prepared Core. This was what Dani had once dubbed a 'Mana accumulator'. The name was disingenuous, as it didn't accumulate Mana; it only stored what I gave it—efficiently, to be fair.

I finally relaxed, panting heavily as the storm faded and the cheering began. The Goblins were celebrating, and the new students of the academy on the surface were astounded at what they thought was a masterstroke by the city. The Essence density on the surface was now the same as a young dungeon, nearly triple the standard! At the academy where Essence was leaking out of the dungeon entrance, it was even higher. Suddenly, being enrolled at the academy was something that Kings would pay a Crown Prince's ransom to *visit!*

"Cal!" Dale called softly. "What is this? What just happened?"

<I made a way for both of us to benefit and a way for me to get to Dani. I heard from Minya, by the way. She confirmed that there is... if not a base of operations, then at least a swarm of necromancers in the sewers of the Tigress Queendom capital. Right after she made her report, she stopped responding to me. I don't know if she is captured or dead. We are going after her and Dani,> I told him, knowing his reaction would be fun to see.

"*We* are going? Who is we? *You* are somehow going?" Dale couldn't seem to focus on what he wanted to ask.

<Yes, Dale. We. Not just you and I... the whole city,> I finished smugly as the building he was in trembled a slight amount. I looked deep inside of myself and directed the

gyroscope to begin turning. It had to be moved very, *very* slowly. The same Runes—as well as a few new ones—that had been on Dale's old morningstar came to life. As the gyroscope changed position, the clay that surrounded the perimeter of my new territory broke apart as we ever so slowly lifted into the air. The area now lifting was—roughly—diamond shaped. The middle was a huge disk with the mountain proudly standing on top. I had also brought along plenty of room at the bottom to expand and protect the dungeon. Somehow, I had even managed to bring a portion of the forest and a lake! With these resources, I could easily be considered a flying island now! I looked at the amount of power the Runes were consuming to remain operational and winced. The Essence drain was huge, monumental, dare I say... mountainous?

"What are you doing, Cal? Why is my room... my building... the *city* trembling?" Dale seemed a bit underwhelmed even as he noticed that things were changing. I may be understating his anxiety a tad, but it was my prerogative.

<That is what you are concerned about? Dale. Come on, buddy. Look at the big picture here.> When he couldn't seem to make the connection, I sighed and gave him a hint. <Watch the horizon for a moment.>

"Is something coming? Are we coming under attack? Is... is the world sinking?" Dale finished his thought with dread as he finally noticed what was happening.

<Literally the opposite of that last one, actually. Dale! We're flying!> Dale seemed dazed at the news, and I am fairly certain that he looked resigned to his fate.

"I should have known it was too good to be true," he whispered to himself.

<What are you going on about?>

He looked up, shrugged, and laid down on the bed. "You are going to lift us up into the air and then crush us by dropping too fast aren't you? This is a mass execution. I knew things were going too well. You are insane after all."

<That's pretty dark.> I snorted at his attitude. <No, Dale, we are going after Dani. She is in the Amazon's city. You can't go there alone, or you become a slave. I can't go alone either, so I am bringing everyone!>

Dale was quiet for a moment. When he finally spoke again, it was not words of encouragement. "I think you are underestimating the odds you are up against, Cal. The Queen of the Amazons is S-ranked. She could destroy the entire mountain to the point of not allowing even *light* debris to land on her people. You are what? B-rank two?"

I checked and found he was correct about my ranking. My use of assimilated Mana had likely given me a better understanding of the components of my own law even if I didn't understand the nuances right now. <Yes. I know it is a long shot Dale, but it is something I need to do. I... I lost my mind for the first month after she was taken. I wasn't aware. I was a beast, a place of death. Then a greasy, old guy showed up and shouted at me, and I could suddenly think again. He only seemed like he wanted to fix me. I don't know what happened, but I'm afraid that if I wait too long, I will become an animal again.> I was feeling vulnerable and had really wanted Dale to be impressed that I was moving an island around. I may have said too much...

He closed his eyes. "Greasy guy? Looked like a hobo? You were going insane, and he only needed to visit you to fix... ugh. Cal, that man is known to the world as Xenocide. As far as we know, he is currently the highest-ranking cultivator on the planet. Legends are told about his brutality and lack of morals."

<You know him? Do you know how he was able to break me out of the haze I was in?> I was desperate for this information! If he could fix the issue, there was a chance I would be able to avoid it in the future!

"All I know about him is that he is a cultivator of insanity. Madness. Psychosis." Dale started to shiver as he recounted what little he knew. "He is the only cultivator for that particular concept, though others have tried going down that path. No one knows why."

<I know why. He kills anyone who tries. Now it makes sense. He told me to stop stealing 'his whispers'. When I agreed, he seemed surprised and left.> My words were filled with dread, perhaps a tiny bit of admiration as well.

"Don't think that he took your madness out of kindness, Cal. His name, Xenocide, was earned when he killed off an entire race. He liked the name so much that he has done it twice since then." Dale's reveries were cut off as members of his council burst into the room, the new door tearing from its hinges with a piteous squeal.

"Dale! The mountain is rising!" Madame Chandra started the conversation with a bang.

"The Mana storm has been... absorbed?" Father Richard seemed confused, making me laugh.

"Last but not least," Frank dryly input, "the Essence density of the area has at least tripled. What in the abyss is going on?"

"Isn't it obvious?" Dale rhetorically stated. "The dungeon learned how to fly."

CHAPTER THIRTY-FOUR

Overnight, the type of person delving into the dungeon had shifted radically. The first floor was positively *swarming* with F-ranked groups being led by a C-ranked 'assistant instructor'. I listened to their conversations and was able to bask in their awe for a while. Ahhh, being amazing is so rewarding.

"We are *flying*. Are we sure that this dungeon isn't Kantor reborn?"

"No, Kantor only floated. I hear we are going *against* the wind!"

"I don't know why we are going south though. There is only ocean that way." Oh dear. Seems that a course correction is in order. I checked in with Dale, stole a few maps from the Guild, and carefully rotated the direction-controlling gyroscope. There we go. North-east. Pretty sure. At this rate, we would be there in only a few weeks. I was still proud of the speed. For one, because I was able to move at all. For another, because I was now *fairly* certain we wouldn't fall out of the sky for lack of Energy to power the Runes.

The massive cultivation technique filled with Essence-gathering Runes was pulling in enough Essence per hour to raise an F-rank human to the C-rank in one giant leap. There were a few... caveats to this process. We needed to move continuously as the ambient Essence I was taking in depleted the area too fast for it to naturally refill and keep us afloat. Moving to new territory allowed us to gather at the highest rate possible. Keeping us moving while flying took ninety-seven percent of the Essence gathered, which allowed me to keep a bit for myself. Most of the excess went to large Cores for emergencies, but by my estimations, it would take a week of travel to store enough power for fifteen minutes of hovering. Moving was key. Moving was surviving.

Using small portals, I remained connected to my original area so that I had access to the massive pool of oil under where my mountain had stood. I had been nervous that my plan wouldn't work and my island would crash. So, I guess it *may* have been an escape route as well if the worst came to pass. I think I'll keep that tidbit from Dale. Bob started shouting, trying to capture my attention.

<Go ahead, Bob, I'm listening.>

"Great Spirit!" Bob was more anxious than anything I could see would explain. "We are flying into a thunderstorm. Not only that, but the area is extraordinarily dense with lightning Essence. I am almost positive that where we are passing over will hold either powerful cultivators or Beasts. Possibly both. I have an idea though, which may be profitable but will certainly be dangerous."

I told him to speak his mind. He thanked me and laid out his thoughts, "Since there is such a thick amount of Essence in the area naturally, I am almost certain that your ley line ritual will have extended its Runes to this area. If we can get close enough for you to activate them here, we won't have to wait for a build-up or accidental influx of Essence in order to make the entire series of Runescript activate."

<You think that it will take an *accident* to activate the whole thing? Why didn't you mention this sooner?>

"Well, it was never an option before! You just started to fly." Bob cringed as I stuck my 'tongue' out at him. Must have felt creepier in his mind than was intended.

<I could have made Dale or Minya go out and activate it!> Bob gained an 'oops' face at that moment. <Yeah, exactly. If

you thought it wouldn't work, why did you let me spend a huge amount of Essence on it for months?>

Bob seemed to have no answer for me. He kept trying and failing to speak, which I admit made me laugh and cheered me up a bit. <It's fine, Bob. What do I need to do?>

Visibly working to calm himself, Bob walked me through the steps I would need to take. "You need to descend to just above ground level and find where your Essence is creating the line of Runes. Yes, it will be deep underground, but since the ritual is powered by *your* Essence, you should be able to find it easily. Then all you have to do is activate one of the Runes. I wouldn't be surprised if this whole area is drained to power the Runes in a cascading activation effect, so we should leave as soon as possible when finished."

<Which is why you are concerned about Beasts or cultivators in the area, I assume. They will be looking for whoever took their source of easy Essence.> Bob nodded at my words, confirming my thoughts. <We should be able to do that. I'll start the descent now.>

Descending was never going to be a problem. Descending in a *controlled* manner, on the other hand, took quite a bit of doing. We couldn't go straight downward, as we would run out of ambient Essence to keep us afloat, so we inched down while continuing forward. I started to hear worried noises coming from the city above me, but I ignored them in favor of ensuring that we didn't crash into the ground or other terrain features. After about an hour, I started hearing screams coming from the entrance to the dungeon. Not human screams but screams of my Mobs dying. I chalked it up to a fresh group of too-powerful people entering at the first floor.

Working with Bob, I reached out and looked for my Essence signature. While it took almost an hour, I *was* able to eventually find a ley line. I inspected the line and found that it became a powerful node about a half-mile further ahead. Since a node was an intersection of multiple lines, I decided to wait to reach that point before spending the Essence to activate the Runes. We would get there soon enough, and activating the lines at a node would have a far greater efficiency than along a single line.

Deciding to investigate the screams of pain while I waited for us to arrive at our destination, I looked at my third floor just in time to see the Boss area half-hex get obliterated in a blaze of light. If I had a jaw, it would have dropped. When the light and rubble cleared, I was even more surprised. <What are you *doing*, Dale?>

Dale

"Anyone else feel that? My ears hurt!" A light buffet from the student's sparring partner drew the complainer back to the present.

"Try yawning, that seems to get rid of the pressure," someone called in response.

"That blow to the head probably already fixed it."

"I don't know many problems that can't be fixed by a blow to the head!" A few laughed at this.

"Flying dungeon. Island. Eats storms. Commoner, now a Noble. This is going to be amazing." The bard, Brakker, was writing about everything that he could see. His muttering was starting to get into people's heads, but he never even noticed. Noting the time with black-ringed eyes, he stumbled toward the Pleasure House for his daily performance. "Gotta warm up. Sixth sick sheikh's sixth sheep's sick. Sixth sick sheikh's sixth sheep's sick. Sixth sick sheikh's sixth sheep's sick..." When he was finally out of the area, people started to cheer brightly.

"Rose, does it look like we are dropping to you?" Tom was on the ground, looking at the sky when he asked this. Adam was working to pull arrows out of him, and Rose was looking a bit embarrassed. Her eyes held a spark of true annoyance, though.

"Tom, you can't just charge directly at a person shooting at you." She lightly kicked the incapacitated man. "Straight lines are great for me. You need to zig-zag. Change it up. At least *try* to make it harder for me."

"Noted. Again, I ask, are we falling?" Tom pointed at the swirling colors of the thunderstorm they were passing through without ill effect, then gestured to the side. "I feel like I'm falling. I feel light."

Rose frowned and looked up. "There is no way to tell; we are in a cloud." Her gaze sharpened as her perceptive eyes locked on shadows being cast with each peal of thunder. "What in the...? Someone find Dale!"

Three forms fell out of the clouds, impacting the ground hard enough to make the weakest in the area fall to the ground from the shockwave. Red cloak fluttering around him, a sharp pair of electric gold eyes looked out over the suddenly silent crowd. "Who dares bring a flying fortress into the lands of thunder? This is an obvious act of war!"

There was silence for a moment, then an awkward cough could be heard. A trembling F-ranked student spoke up. "Er... we had nothing to do with this. We're just students. Pretty sure that the city had nothing to do with this either. This is a flying dungeon, and it's not really under control."

"Cease your lies!" The man's thunderous voice echoed through the area. "Kantor was the only known flying dungeon!

He has been destroyed, which means that *you* are a flying invasion force!" The man stumbled suddenly, face paling. A heavy force fell on the area along with the existential feeling of dread only felt in a suddenly silent ancient forest.

Madame Chandra was walking up to the group, eyes shining a brilliant green. "If we are assumed to be an invasion force, why were simple *Mages* sent to deal with us? B-ranks one, two, and three." She pointed at the Mages in turn as she spoke. "Where are your elders? Where is the threat you are trying to deliver? You are yowling kittens. Where is the tiger?"

A slight crackle and a smell of ozone suffused the air, followed by a man appearing in front of the weighed-down Mages. He chuckled as he noticed who he was talking to, the bloodlust in his eyes vanishing. "Madame! How good it is to see you! These lads were just the scouts; please pardon their rudeness. You know how it goes, fifty years on guard duty and you get excited over every little flying island you see." He looked around, noting the silent people around him. "Is this a... school of some sort? Is this really a flying dungeon?"

"Indeed it is, Perun!" Chandra's demeanor seemed far warmer now, almost shy even. "It has been far too long! We should find somewhere to chat."

"I'd *love* to do that! Maybe you could take a few minutes to explain why this island is floating toward our city? Oh, and these lads will need a bit of exercise to calm down. Can we send them through the dungeon? What rank is it?" The man had an electric personality, and charisma seemed to ooze off of him.

"B-rank... two? I think that is correct at this point." Chandra looked over and noticed that Dale was running over, escorted by a few Dark Elf guards. "Ah, here comes the City

Lord. I'll have him get them into the dungeon ahead of the line, and we can go... catch up."

"B-rank two and already a flying island? It must have found an interesting solution to the Mana draw needed to take flight! Even Kantor was in the S-ranks when he lifted off the ground." The man seemed pleased by this fact. "How spectacular! I truly hope we will not need to blast you all out of the sky."

After a quick explanation of the situation, Dale was happy to escort the Mages to the opening of the dungeon. A few people booed them as they passed the line, but most were confused students planning on going into the dungeon for the first time. The Mages signed the standard non-Guild agreement, so Dale waved at them and turned to leave.

"Wait, child! My name is Jasper of the clan Azguardia. These are my brothers. Would you be willing to be our guide?" The Mage imperiously pointed his finger at Dale, beckoning him closer.

"I can certainly find you someone to act as a guide, but as City Lord, I have duties to–" Dale's smile started to become frosty as he was interrupted.

"Nonsense! A D-ranker like yourself should be thrilled to have tutelage from Mages! Do not fear, we will protect you from whatever dangers lie within!" Jasper joyfully wrapped his arm around Dale and walked into the cave. Arm acting as an irresistible force, Jasper dragged the Baron along while ignoring his complaints. Despite his protests, Dale was fairly pleased to have an excuse to avoid the meetings that had been planned for him today. Dancing lessons? No thank you. He would find a memory stone *somewhere* with that particular skillset instead.

The Mages laughed as Bashers threw themselves to their doom, screaming in fury as the humans took no damage whatsoever. The screams of the Mobs grew shriller as the Mages counterattacked. A simple flick of a finger turned anything hit into a red paste.

"What a young dungeon!" Jasper chuckled boisterously as they walked past the first floor Boss Squad. What remained of them, that is. "Are all the creatures this weak? How in the *world* did it find a way to fly?"

Attempting to convince the Mages that there were much, *much* more dangerous beings within only made them laugh. He explained that the dungeon 'didn't get more dangerous slowly, it was exponential danger growth' only gained him confused smirks. Explaining concepts by using math always had this reaction. Dale decided that they would have to experience the dungeon for themselves before they would bother to listen to him. He nervously absorbed a small Core, shuddering and relaxing a bit as the euphoria rushed through him.

After Raile was dealt with as easily as the standard Bashers, Dale started to have fun. One of the lightning Mages tried to keep the air-affinity Hopsecutioner as a pet but was ruthlessly shot down by the others. The mage shrugged and broke its neck, pulling out its Core and tossing it to Dale. He was *very* happy he came along now; they gave him all the Cores as they were 'useless to B-ranked cultivators'. As a fringe benefit, if the Cores were absorbed in the dungeon, they weren't subject to taxes! Dale revised his original opinion of these Mages as they kept lavishing gifts on him. He thought about what was coming next and tried to form a plan of attack. The Goblins should pose no problem, so he could breathe easy. At least until floor four. From there it may be more touch and go.

There was a terrifying moment when the B-rank three Mage noticed the Goblins trying to build up a charge of infernal Essence. What sort of attack could that deliver? They seemed familiar with the weapon they were using. Had they used it in combat before? Jasper frowned and created a huge spell circle in the air. A quick burst of Mana entered the circle, and a tree-wide bolt of lightning lashed out and impacted the wall of the Boss area. The entire fortification was blown to smithereens, and anything that had been alive in there was cooked beyond recognition. Dale stepped out of the cloud of dust, coughing and heard an incredulous voice. <What are you *doing*, Dale?>

"Not me, I swear!" Dale waved his hand in a dismissive motion. "We have guests, Mages, who are wanting to challenge the dungeon."

<You have really bad timing, Dale. I'm *unholy* busy right now, and if I get too distracted, we could fall out of the sky.>

"Please, *please*, feel free to focus on anything but us." Dale hacked up a small ball of mucus and dust before rejoining the Mages. "A bit of overkill, wasn't that?"

"Overkill is the best kind of kill. No chance of retaliation," the Mage replied in a chilly tone. "How about you go bother Jasper? I think he sees you as a mascot."

"Don't mind him, boy!" Jasper slapped Dale on the back hard enough to bruise. "He is always shockingly rude."

Dale winced and not from the slap. "Got a lot of, ah, lightning jokes you are planning to use?"

"You should be *amped* to hear how many I *currently* have." Jasper had a strange gleam in his eyes. Dale shrugged at him; he didn't understand the joke. He had no knowledge of how electricity worked. "You don't understand any of these, do you? Re-*volt*ing."

The impromptu team walked down the stairs, entering the labyrinth below. Looking at the four paths they could choose from, they ignored Dale's suggestion of the earth tunnel, instead walking through the door marked with water. "I haven't been down this path before! I have no idea what to expect!" Dale tried to reason with the Mages, but they simply shrugged and let him know that, in that case, he was on equal terms with them.

The first dead-end they found annoyed one of the Mages so much that he tried to blast his way through the wall. A bolt of energy equivalent to the one that had destroyed the entire Boss fortification on the previous level left only a fist-sized depression of molten slag in the wall. The defenses here were decidedly more powerful, and the walls were lined with Runes.

<It tickles! Yum, yum, yum.>

Dale grumbled murderous thoughts as the Mages started trying to use Mana for every little issue they encountered. "Just making the dungeon stronger. You're making my life harder, you useless brain-fried battle maniacs." He was careful to keep the volume low, but he was still overheard and laughed at. Luckily for Dale, they got serious as watery traps became more prevalent.

"Does this mean we are going the right way?" one of the unnamed Mages asked Dale. There was a Cloud Cat on the ground in front of him, dead but still twitching from all the electricity passing through it. Dale was watching the Cat hungrily, hands almost shaking as he thought about grabbing its Core.

"What? Oh. Um. Usually." Dale stammered almost incoherently. "The usual theme in here is if there are more enemies, you are going the right way. If the path becomes more dangerous, you are going the right way. The easy path is almost always a trap."

Jasper nodded along at the explanation. "Makes sense! Just like in life! If everyone is happy with your decisions, it is because you have done nothing worthy of notice. If you are working toward a goal, someone, *somewhere*, will have something negative to say about it."

"Jasper, stop trying to be all sage and mysterious. When people are sick of *you,* it is usually because you are making an electricity joke for the thousandth time!" The Mage's comment made Dale chuckle softly. He didn't want to be too loud and draw disaster down upon them.

The splashing of water around the next bend was enough to make Dale set himself into a combat pose. Cautiously peeking around the bend, he almost fell over as the boisterous Mages causally walked right past him. "Oh, this looks fun! I wonder... anyone want to just bypass this?"

The Mages shrugged, then vanished, reappearing on a platform over a hundred feet away. Since that was where the tunnel curved, it was assumed that they had to get to that point to continue. Upon landing on the platform, they were hit with several tons of pressurized water which sent them spiraling at high speed into the wall where Dale was still taking cover.

The Mages stood up, ugly expressions on their faces and seemed ready to try again. Their clothes were torn, but they seemed entirely unhurt otherwise. Dale quickly coughed and got their attention. "Remember how I am guiding you? If you keep trying to skip challenges, the dungeon will only throw harder ones in your path. While you might not be hurt, you could get trapped here pretty easily."

"Well, then. Guide us, oh wise 'City Lord'."

Dale's face colored a bit. "I've been trying. Now, this seems fairly straightforward, which means there is almost surely a hidden layer to it. What *should* be needed is to redirect those streams of water into the corresponding holes in the wall. That would be a pretty normal dungeon challenge and is a good place to start. We will likely see the *actual* challenge if we begin there."

Jasper walked over to one of the streams coming from the ceiling and put his hand in it. Dale's eye twitched as the Mage put his *hand* into a stream of water that was *cutting into* the rock it touched. "Huh, a bit of water pressure. You should probably not touch these, Dale."

"I wouldn't have," Dale ground out through his tightly clenched jaw. "Thank you for finally using my name. I'm betting that there will be a... a lever, a button, or a pressure plate around here. That should let you tilt the stream."

After a few moments of searching, Jasper lit up. Pointing at a button located between multiple high-pressure streams, he slammed his hand on to it and shouted, "Found one!"

"Don't press it–" Dale shouted back. Too late. The streams of water around the Mages started rotating but didn't stop after only a few degrees. Water washed over the offending Mage, and if he didn't have near immunity to physical damage, he would have been sliced into bleeding chunks. His clothes were utterly obliterated, becoming useless tatters in an instant.

"My robe!" Jasper looked mournfully at his now scantily clad body. The volume of his shouting almost made Dale miss a distinctive ticking noise.

"Quiet!" The ticking was more noticeable in the silence but stopped after a few seconds. At the same time, the streams of water returned to their original positions. "That's it! It's a timed sequence!"

When all Dale got in reply were blank looks, he cracked his neck and started walking around the area. "There will likely be clues that help us know which buttons to press first, and if we do it in the timeframe allowed, we should be able to move on." Going over the room carefully, three more buttons were found, as well as illegible words written at odd angles on the wall and ceiling.

"Are those Runes?"

"No, I think they are words. They aren't any language I've seen before, though."

While the others were inspecting the markings, Jasper got bored and started playing with sparks. Tiny lightning bolts raced between his fingers, and his eyes dilated as he played with them.

"Jasper! Are you listening?" These sharp words from his brother made Jasper lose concentration, and a bit of electricity hit the water. Dale's muscles seized up, and he flopped, twitching, into the water.

"Gah! Grab him before he drowns!" Jasper raced over to the fallen man. "You alright there, Dale? There's a good lad. Oh..."

"F-fine. I'm fine. Is someone making toast?" Dale's teeth chattered as he tried to control his randomly shaking limbs.

"I think I found the solution, by the way." Jasper spoke into the silence. He pointed at Dale, who only looked back in confusion. "Not you. Actually, move. You're in the way. There! You see!"

The group looked at the water, seeing the reflection of the scrawled text. Read in the water, it was perfectly legible instructions. Sure it waved around a bit, but they were able to understand what it said. Pressing the buttons in the correct order made the ticking sound start again, but the streams of water went into the holes they were supposed to. A loud *thunk* was heard, and they hurried to get around the bend before time ran out. Rushing forward, Dale noticed that the air was getting steamy.

"There might be a Boss ahead," Dale told the others. Much to his displeasure, they didn't take him seriously.

"Don't care. Under B-rank, it will just die like everything else in here," Jasper sneered at the weak creatures they had been fighting.

They walked into the steamy room that typically contained Snowball but faced no attack. This was both a relief and a frustration to Dale, as he had no chance to impress upon the Mages that the threats were getting dangerous to their health. They continued on, but Dale slowed as he looked at the stairwell leading down.

"What's the matter, boy?" The snarky Mage leered at him. "You look like you're about to piss yer pants. You obviously don't understand how happy you should be right now."

Rolling his eyes, Dale cautiously stepped forward. "The next floor houses a Dungeon Boss. We have no information about it. Each team that comes down here to fight fails to come back."

"Then how do you know it has a big bad Boss in it?"

Dale literally growled at the man. "I *hate* that question. There is something down there that affects the minds of whoever enters. A Mage scout took a look and was able to give us general information but no details. The generally accepted idea is that after you fight it and win, you will be able to remember information about the creature. There is a monster at least five meters tall and undoubtedly in the B-ranks. The room is filled with fog, and the air is dense enough with a mixture of Essence and Mana that trying to view the Boss with anything but standard vision is useless."

"Let's go take a look then!"

"Works for me—sounds fun."

"Did you not hear what I just said?" Dale barked at the Mages.

"They did." Jasper chuckled at Dale's livid expression. "Try to see our point of view though! We just walked through a dungeon without any challenge whatsoever! The water traps notwithstanding. We need to feel the blood race through our bodies! We need to fight!"

CHAPTER THIRTY-FIVE

"Turn back!"

"What was that?" Dale was shaking with fear as they continued along the *very* long tunnel connecting the fourth and fifth floors.

"No idea! Something we haven't fought before, boys!" Jasper grunted as he tripped over a loose stone. "How fun!"

"Five more minutes!" The rocks whimpered as they passed. "I'm so tired."

"I just can't deal with this today! Ugh! I just can't even!"

"No-o-o! More people are going to die today!"

"Run away! Run *away*!"

The voices became louder and more numerous as they progressed, the echoes blending with the new shouts. A door came into view, ornate and dangerous looking with a skull embedded in the wall above it. The eyes of the skull were filled with Cores which lit up as they came closer. A beam of light came from the jeweled sockets, creating a flat panel that had words scrawled across it.

"That is new. My understanding was that it was an open tunnel that merged into the Boss Room. The door must have been added recently." Since the others stayed silent, Dale stepped forward and read the words projected in the air. "Total challenges: fourteen groups, seventy people. Additionally, one *scout*. Total Boss losses: one. Total survivors after fighting: one. Total escapees: one necromancer, rank C-seven. One *scout*, rank unknown."

"Can written words sound annoyed?" Jasper laughed as he looked at the panel with wonder. "It seems quite peeved that a scout poked his head in but didn't fight! Shall we do our part and make that Boss loss count move to two?" The other Mages seemed to think this was a splendid idea, and the vitriol and curses that Dale spit at them as he was dragged along seemed to have no effect on their good humor.

"Insane Mages, let me go!" Dale shrieked in far too high of a pitch to be taken seriously. "I can't survive in there!"

Jasper pushed on the ornate door, and it swung open silently. Fog billowed out into the tunnel, hiding their feet, then their knees within moments. When the last person was inside—willing or not—the door swung closed behind them. It sunk into the floor, leaving behind only a smooth, blank wall. "Huh! Looks like the only way backward is forward! No need to keep attempting to escape, Dale. You are in this with us!"

The air trembled as a growl began filling the room. It had such a low pitch that Dale could only feel it in his bones and wasn't even aware of it for a moment. The sub vocalizations rose into the human range of hearing, but this did less to comfort Dale than the Mages seemed to think it should. For a moment, the fog seemed to clear, and Dale looked into a pair of eyes that had never existed to this point in history. Pupils were dilated, the irises were hexagonal, and the sclera was blacker than the darkness of the room.

Dale's view was interrupted as an incredibly sharp stinger stopped in front of his nose with a discharge of electricity. There was a *boom* as what turned out to be the Boss's tail was repulsed by a barrier of energy that had sprung up around the terrified human.

"Nice job on that barrier, brother!" Jasper slapped his comrade. "That could have been dangerous, Dale! You need to learn how to dodge! Good place to learn!"

"Y-you have a barrier around me? Since when?" Dale sputtered, staring at where the black eyes had loomed out of the mists.

"Since we entered the dungeon, of course! You think we are going to let a child run around with us without protection?" Jasper chuckled at the thought. He whipped around faster than Dale could see, swinging his hammer into the stinger that had been darting at him. "Now we are talking! This fluffy little creature might be able to put out some actual damage!"

"Fluffy? It's scaled! I saw scales! Where was the fluffy? They're insane! I'm locked in a room with lightning-driven insane people." Dale's words were hushed, as he did all he could not to draw attention.

The hammer strike had broken the very tip of the stinger. Not only did this anger the Beast, it also left a trail of acidic poison on the ground. The humans were forced to watch their step even as the stinger was whipping at them at a furious pace.

"Anyone have eyes on the main body of this thing?" Jasper's stress was beginning to surface; he struggled to speak calmly.

"I got it. Over here," the deadpan voice could have been describing his morning tea for all the enthusiasm it exuded. The Mage jumped at the fog-coated body, swinging his electrified hammer. Just before his blow landed, the Manticore's wings snapped open, throwing the Mage across the rooms and blowing the fog away momentarily. The Manticore was revealed in all of its terrifying glory, and its aura was suddenly powerful enough to lock all of Dale's muscles in place. He found himself unable to move.

The lightning Mages charged the great Beast, and it roared at them in challenge, "Come to me, snacks! I hunger for the flesh of the living!"

"It can speak," Dale whimpered as fog began to cover the battle. As the condensation rolled in, the aura of terror was diffused, the ambient Essence and Mana refracting the otherwise overwhelming power of the Manticore. Dale took a few steps, attempting to walk toward the exit. A particularly powerful hammer blow created a shockwave that revealed the battle, and Dale was again frozen in place. He took the time he couldn't move to observe the fight, moving each time he was physically able to do so.

The Mages were swinging their hammers, each individual blow having no apparent effect. The huge, room-shaking strokes made the fog disperse each time they landed, but the Manticore only chuckled and counterattacked twice as hard. Huge claws wove through the air, and when they landed, the affected Mage would be sent spiraling into the wall at bone-shattering speed. They would hop back up and rejoin the fight, but their clothes and armor were being melted away. Thus far, they had been able to avoid the sharp portions of the claws and had not been injected with any poison. It was only a matter of time until they were affected unless something changed drastically.

Dale kept sprinting and freezing as if he were in a child's game that he was forced to play. He reached the wall and heard another discharge as the barrier around him deflected a thrust meant to end his life. He looked back in time to see the Mages each land a simultaneous blow, then slide back a few feet. They raised their hands and lightning arched between them, making an equidistant triangle around the Manticore. It roared in outrage as the Mana in the air transformed to be dominated by an electric affinity. The power surrounding the Boss flashed into the exact spot his opponents had landed their recent blows. The Beast was cooked over the course of a few seconds as lightning continuously flowed into, out of, and around him as the Mages directed their ultimate attack.

Resolving not to go out without inflicting casualties, the Manticore stabbed his broken stinger forward, giving one last scream of rage before falling down, lifeless. The suffocating combined auras of Beast and Mage faded out of existence, and Dale was able to gulp down some fresh air. Fresh being a relative term, as the air was rank with the smell of ozone and overcooked meat. Jasper stepped forward and collected a key that had fallen to the floor, then proceeded to hack away at the Manticore's skull until it was broken open. Carefully not getting any blood on himself, he extracted the Core and washed it, finally placing it in his bag.

"You want any of this?" Jasper motioned toward the giant Beast. "I'm satisfied with just the Core." His eye was bleeding, it seemed the stinger had been able to penetrate his defenses while he was focused on the spellwork he and his brothers were using.

Dale was stunned at the offer, "Are you certain? That will be worth a fortune!"

"Sure thing, kid. After all, the city basically sacrificed you to the dungeon, you should sell this off and go find a safe place to cultivate for the rest of your life." Jasper gave Dale a look full of pity and misguided understanding.

"I keep telling you, I'm the City Lord!" Dale huffed as his dimensional bag sucked the giant creature into its depths. "Thank you for this. It will be a great tool for research."

"Of course you are." Jasper smiled again, using far too many teeth. "Next level then?"

"Are you insane?" Dale looked at the very serious face of the others. "You *are* insane. I just... I... let's at least open the chest." Inside were ingot tokens with a silvery sheen, coin tokens, a small bottle, and a keygem that would open a portal to this floor. It was black with white speckles, looking like a galaxy contained in a gem.

Not understanding the transactional system the dungeon had put in place and uninterested in the keygem after Dale explained its function, the Mages allowed Dale to walk away with a potential cornucopia of tokens. They closed the door leading to the next floor behind them and a spiral stairway leading deeper into the depths was revealed. An exit portal also shimmered invitingly, and Dale looked at it with unabashed desire. The Mages cheerfully frog-marched him down the stairs, loudly proclaiming his luck.

Jasper stumbled suddenly, falling to his knees and clutching his face. He howled in pain as the poison in his eye finally found a foothold, beginning to rot away at the tissue as it sought an outlet to his bloodstream. "My eye! My eye!" he screamed as he thrashed in pain.

The others grabbed him, holding him still as they inspected the wound. With a flash of inspiration, Dale produced the small bottle found in the Boss room and inspected it. The words 'sting-ex' were written on the bottle in a tiny script. "I have the antidote! I think..."

"You aren't sure?"

"*Just give it to me!*" Jasper screamed in pain. He grabbed the bottle and dumped the contents directly into his eye. There was a hissing sound as the antivenom counteracted the poison, and Jasper's eye bubbled as the tiny war was waged in the cells of his eyes. He began breathing easier and looked up. His eye was gone, having been destroyed, but he seemed cheerful either way. "Looks like I'm going to be visiting a flesh Mage in the near future. Bleh, I just paid off my last bill. I guess that's how they get you though."

"I told you not to get that cosmetic... *enhancement*," one of the other Mages muttered wryly.

"Huggin, you need to just let me live out my dreams. If I want to have horse-like aspects, I am allowed to do so! It's my money!" Jasper groused, then he looked at his other brother. "Muninn, don't you say a word."

They stepped on to the next floor and stopped speaking. Words failed them as they looked around. Having an open floor plan, the sixth floor was a massive hexagon. The hexagon was divided by various paths leading toward the center of the room, which the Mages were able to recognize as being similar to the paths in the tower of ascension. There were six entrances into the hexagon around the perimeter of the room. Each path led to a platform, and each platform apparently represented one of the basic affinities. Moving deeper from the basic platforms, there were paths that branched and led to slightly smaller platforms. Whichever affinities connected to this platform created the landscape and was an unspecified mix of the basic types of Essence.

Fire and celestial led to a platform brimming with holy fire, blue and three times as hot as the previous 'basic' fire platform. Water and earth led to a mud-filled area. This pattern continued around the room until you were able to reach the largest platform. There were five total rings, meaning that you had to cross five platforms at a minimum in order to reach the large, center platform. The Silverwood tree grew in the center of the room, now as massive as a hundred-year-old oak. Under the tree sat a figure petting a Basher, but the details of the figure were hidden by the haze of energy collected in this room.

"It's beautiful," Huggin whispered in awe. "This is the most beautiful thing I've ever seen."

"More than that," Muninn stated, already mapping out the paths. "Look at the platforms. The floor plan is a guide to ascending!"

There was shocked silence, but Dale had no idea what was going on. "What in the world are you talking about?"

"The paths!" Muninn turned blazing eyes on Dale. "There! The earth, water, and celestial intersection! What do you see?"

"Trees?" Dale smiled nervously as Muninn started to get worked up.

"No! Yes, but, look!" Muninn seemed enrapt over the paths. "The path to get to that platform—the path of wood—is exactly equal for earth and water, but only half as long for celestial!"

Dale was silent for a moment. "Again, I'm sorry, but I don't understand."

Making a frustrated noise, Jasper turned and looked at Dale. "This room is showing what affinities are needed to cultivate in order to acquire a certain type of Mana. Having equal parts earth and water and half that of celestial when you break into the B-ranks will give you the best chance of becoming a wood Mage. Look there! The paths of infernal, fire, and metal—metal being a second rank platform—lead to a cursed weapon platform! The ratio of that is two to one to three!"

"Is this information that is difficult to get?" Dale was greatly confused at their overwhelming reactions.

"Like you wouldn't *believe*," Jasper grimly affirmed. "The clans and kingdoms of this world only help those who are beholden to them and stamp out any outsiders who learn their secrets. This map goes all the way to the fifth tier! Unbelievable!"

Seeing Dale's nonplussed face, Huggin spoke in his normal monotone, "Dale. A lightning Mage like us is only a second tier Mage. A cursed weapon Mage would be third-tier. A portal Mage is fourth tier. Look at those paths. They show the *exact* ratio needed to have the best chance of getting the type of Mana you are after. This place is going to be popular enough that wars would be fought if that was what it took to gain access. People will want to measure those paths, and there are *hundreds* of varied combinations. Sadly, the portal is at the center of all of those, so let's get moving. We need to see what the requirements of the room are."

Dale resolved to get more details later since he had a cohort of Mages that he could question in the city. They stepped on to the path leading to the celestial platform and jumped back as portals opened, and all the ground *not* part of the path vanished. They looked into the holes that remained, shocked to see the ground far below them. The warning was clear, stay on the path or be dropped off of the flying island. Dale gulped. A barrier wouldn't save him from a multi-mile fall.

As they stepped on to the first platform, a statue rose out of the ground. Golden and shining with accumulated power, Dale was almost unsurprised when it began moving. The entire statue was made from some kind of yellow gem, and at its center was a Core directing its motions. Jasper ran at it, swinging his hammer. His weapon *clanged* against a wall of golden light that had sprung into existence. The statue stepped forward, and the wall of golden energy moved with it. With each step, the wall of light reduced the amount of room on the platform, pushing the humans toward the open air at the edge of the platform.

"I can't believe we are fighting an honest-to-God *golem!*" Muninn squealed like a teenage girl talking about her first crush. "I've only fought puppeted versions or Gnomish constructs!"

"Be happy *after* you kill it!" Huggin roared back at him in consternation. The wall of solidified Mana shattered from the triple blow as the Mages struck at the same moment, forcing the golem to its knees as a huge amount of its energy was depleted. Its hands were against its head, and it released a silent scream. Dale watched in awe as Jasper dealt the final blow, the golem crumbling to shards as he collected the Core.

"What is this?" Jasper muttered into the air, looking over the gem that the golem's body had consisted of. "It seems to be a conduit for... celestial essence? Take some of this up to the church when you leave here, Dale. I'm sure they'll be excited. Next path?"

After resting a short while, the group pushed on. After a minor debate about the best way to go, they walked across the path connecting celestial and water together. Up to their ankles in water, they watched as a golem pushed out of the ground, displacing the fluid around itself. Dale wanted to know what type of Mana this golem was likely to use, and the others shrugged.

"Could be any number of things. Unless we get the exact measurements of the path, we won't be able to know for sure." Jasper informed him with a casual wave. A torrent of water washed over him at that moment, nearly throwing him over the edge of the platform. His weapon dulled noticeably as lightning stopped travelling through it, and his clothes—which had been held together by a thread—were washed away. Jasper looked at his hammer in annoyance before setting it down.

"Ugh. 'Cleansing waters'." Huggin spat in disgust as he avoided looking at his near-naked brother.

"Yeah, looks that way." Jasper almost threw a tantrum but decided to take out his anger against the Golem. He sprinted forward, thrusting a hand into the water surrounding the construct. He gripped the statue hard, pulling it into a bear hug. "Someone else has to sacrifice their hammer too! Hit it, now!"

Muninn ran forward, slamming the pick end of his hammer into the golem. On the second strike, the golem's chest shattered, as did the hammer. Grabbing the Core, Muninn tossed the hilt of his weapon to the side in disgust. Dale was watching in fascination. "What just happened?"

"A very rare and *very* annoying type of Mana," Jasper grumped, adding chunks of the mineral the golem was composed of to his bag after ensuring they were dry. "This is called 'cleansing waters'. The combination to create it has been lost in time because all it does is disenchant. It renders Runes inert, gets rid of the special effects of potions and herbs, and makes everything boring and useless. It is also self-propagating, using the water type Essence and Mana it absorbs to create more of itself."

"If that's the case, why do we even have normal water?" Dale wondered, looking at his battle gauntlets and debating on using the water to get rid of them. They tightened on his hands as if they could understand the way his thoughts were moving.

"Exceedingly short-lived effect," Huggin spoke blandly. "Drop some in the ocean, and it will spread across the entire sea within hours, removing any enchantments or effects it finds. The next day, the water will be normal and creating water affinity Essence again. No use storing it—doesn't work. Preserving enchantments fail. Good for killing Mages or cultivators, but it needs to be fresh."

Dale nodded along. "I can see why it would be lost to time."

"Yeah, it's a pain in the ass for everyone. Cultivating it is *stupid* hard too, I hear." Muninn spat into the water. "Any training aids you use get disenchanted."

"Should we press on?" Jasper was obviously slowing down, the fighting using unfamiliar tactics. Plus he was now weaponless.

"The real question is *can* we press on?" Huggin questioned, looking at the next platforms. "There are three branches that take us closer, but this path joins with wood, that one with mud, and the final with some combination of air and celestial. I think we would die on the path of wood, since the combination of disenchantment and growth would likely allow for Mana-ignoring weapons. The mud may be possible, but I just don't know that we can go against the third tier of this area without more knowledge."

"Turn back?" Jasper sadly inquired.

"Turn back," the others conceded.

"Thank God." Dale breathed out a sigh of relief. "It's over."

CHAPTER THIRTY-SIX

<Well that was an impressive first run. What do you think, Bob? Three Mages could only get to the second tier without severe danger.> I allowed a chest to bubble out of the floor, rewards for defeating two golem guardians. I smiled as Dale excitedly pocketed the tokens and the keygem for this floor. It looked similar to the previous one, but instead of being black with white formations inside I had inverted the colors, and it was now white with black pathways and galaxies. When Dale got to the point where the keys were useful to him, he would finally be a force to be reckoned with.

"I think the golems did well. I am also surprised that those Mages seemed to grasp your intent with the floor plan instantly. I thought it would take years before they realized the significance of walking the paths." Bob's decidedly intellectual reply made me grin. "You should also change the layout once every few weeks to use a different portion of the tower; the changes will just keep them wanting more!"

<I love that Goblins are actually smart. Yeah, there was no way to put all the paths in here without making a truly massive floor. Maybe when I make another floor, it will be tier six through ten. I'd like to see anyone get through *that* easily.> I returned to my search for the ley lines below me. I was hovering over a small city, which apparently contained a single clan of lightning cultivators—basically one city's worth of family members. If my information was correct, the clouds in this area were *perpetually* in a state of storming. If overheard conversations were correct, the storm raged two hundred and seventy days out of the year. That was a *lot* of lightning Essence.

I was hopeful that they wouldn't even notice me siphoning off some for my personal use.

"Of course we are smart, we *are* part Gnome. Also, remember that I am essentially the sixtieth generation of Bob since entering the dungeon. If that many generations had gone by without improving my mind, I would have been greatly upset." Bob looked a bit nostalgic for his original body but also seemed pleased at his current immortality. I decided to leave that conversation alone for now.

<So what exactly am I trying to... never mind, I think I found it. Wow.> The ritual had created an intricate spiral of Runes at this Node. The small Essence accumulation Runes had layered, forming a circle of joined Runescript. If the ritual had been formed correctly, I could activate a single Rune at the center. As it gathered Essence, it would activate more and more of the Runes, culminating in the ritual activating and expanding the reach of the ley lines! All the extra Essence would flow back along the ley line to the original ritual, which I was still connected to via portal. Eventually, this could be the entire world's worth of Essence. I loved the *abyss* out of my portals.

With an outpouring of Essence, I activated the 'key' Rune. It wasn't shaped like a key, it was just the important Rune to activate. It took quite a bit of Essence to reach the Rune at this range, and it likely wouldn't have been possible if the Rune hadn't been carved with my power. As it was, it was more like connecting to yourself in an awkward manner, similar to a person scratching the top of their head while wearing an overly large helmet. Possible if you had flexible fingers but still frustrating. I watched the Rune glow with Essence and waited to disconnect until it had gathered enough Essence to activate the next in the sequence.

With that side task complete I twisted the gyroscope, and we started moving up, up, and away. Bob went over the results of this mission with me, discussing what we could do to streamline the process if a similar situation came up in the future. "It would be best if we didn't need to enter population centers like that city if we don't need to." Bob looked with slight worry at the city that had prepared to attack us if we showed even the slightest hint of aggressiveness.

<I disagree, Bob. Think about it. This place had a naturally high accumulation of lightning Essence. That would be a huge draw for people that were cultivating that precious resource.> I focused for a moment on avoiding a mountain that seemed to rise from the middle of an otherwise flat area. <If the situation is the same in the future, it is likely that the area will be populated.>

Bob grunted in reply as I turned my attention to conversations happening on the surface. The lightning Mages seemed to be apologizing to Dale for some reason, so I listened in. Jasper was making strange faces. "Sorry, boy. That is, I apologize for not taking you seriously, Your Grace."

"No, I'm glad you took me along. It was an interesting... learning experience." Dale nodded at them before walking away. The Mages seemed excited to meet one of the Mages that was temporarily residing in the area. Apparently, Nez was something of a folk hero in their lightning cultivator community. They talked for a few hours before flying off toward the tavern. They would stay the night, then return to the city we had hovered over the next day.

When they were gone, Dale hurried back to the portal area with two Dark Elf guards. He stepped through, and to my great surprise, teleported to the sixth floor. <Why, hello there,

Dale. Come to try your luck against the golems? Gonna jump off the mountain in a secluded location?>

"I'm not suicidal. No thanks." He was walking with purpose though, and after looking around, I realized what was going on.

<Oh I see! You came back to use those tokens, huh? Decided to leave your zappy new friends out of the loop? Keeping all the rewards for yourself? I must say, Dale, you're growing up so fast!> I teased him as he approached the place the tokens could be put into the slot.

"What?" Dale was obviously directing this word at Hans, who had snuck into the portal after them and made his way to the slot area.

"Oh, uh, hey there, Dale." Hans was feverishly pushing tokens into the slot and opening the chest to see what he gained. "I'm just–jackpot!" Golden coins rained down into the chest as Hans whooped and jumped around.

"I have no idea why you are here Hans, but I need to use this thing."

"No, wait, just... do you have a few tokens I can borrow? I'm on a good streak here, and I'm betting I can–" Hans was staring at the slot with a feverish expression.

"I'm cutting you off," Dale bluntly told him, "and you called *me* an addict!"

"Dale, I'm fine, I just need some tokens! This is so fun. I keep winning!" Hans was now being restrained and dragged toward the exit portal. "Dale, nooo–" His cries were cut off as the portal closed. Dale rolled his eyes and returned to the slot, slipping in some of the tokens he had gained from the Manticore.

"I knew it," he breathed. I swear there was a physical manifestation of greed in his eyes. "These were tokens for..." He stopped speaking aloud, remembering that there were Dark Elves watching and listening to him.

<You can say it, Dale. Aluminum! Yup, ingots of the metal those Dwarves are all hot and heavy for. Good luck using it without drawing so much attention that you give up adventuring! I'll even give you an extra bar.> Another bar of soft metal clunked into the chest in front of him. He lifted the lid only far enough to slip his hand and bag in, scooping up the light metal and stuffing it into his bag.

Trying not to act in a suspicious manner and completely failing, Dale led the guards out of the dungeon. I performed my version of rolling my eyes, then opened the portals on the sixth floor. Wind rushed into the dungeon, fresh air flowing through the hallways and twisting pathways of the deep. The Goblins smiled as they felt the cool breeze, a few of them even shouting their thanks to me. I smiled; it was good to be appreciated.

I examined the ground below me, comparing it to what maps I had been able to acquire. We were getting close to the Amazon's territory. Soon, I would have Dani back. Thankfully, I had created a manual option for the flight controls, so I was able to leave steering to Bob for now. I started actively cultivating, working hard to glean even the slightest hint of enlightenment about my law. Who knew if a single extra rank would be the line between victory and defeat? I sighed as I remembered the simple days, the early part of my life where all I was doing was trying to survive. Now I was a flying island. Maybe someday I would even be able to *enjoy* my newfound freedom.

JASPER OF THE CLAN AZGUARDIA

"What a joyous day this has turned out to be!" Jasper shouted as he flew a loop in the air. "A dungeon, Cores, and we met 'Nez the Thundering'! He even gave me a spear as a keepsake! Truly, we will have tales to tell at our Father's table this night! I am also *infernally* grateful that flesh Mage joined our clan this year. My eye socket itches something fierce!"

"Almost back now." Muninn's monotone voice sounded almost happy. "I agree, we will have–"

The sky seemed to form cracks around them, and their forward momentum could not have been arrested faster if they had hit a wall. If they hadn't been in the B-ranks, they would have been pasted across the barrier in their path. Locked in their position in defiance of gravity, they could only watch in horror as the Essence and Mana filling the clouds condensed. The perpetual thunderstorm was swirling lower than the brothers had ever seen. A river of fluid streamed down from the shrinking thunder clouds, touching the center of the city.

Unbeknownst to the horrified Mages, a flaw had appeared in a ritual created under their fair city. The ritual was now trying to compensate for the damaged Rune in its pattern by drawing in and adding extra ambient Essence and Mana from the environment. Draining the sky of energy resulted in a massive pressure as the thick power trapped everything in range like flies in a web. The human who had been mining with a powerful pickaxe he bought from the Adventurers' Guild was the first to die as his body became a conductor for elemental lightning. Unfortunately for the people above, his death was only the first of far, far too many.

Unable to move, the trapped Mages watched as the energy swirling over and within the city collected to the point that it went out of control. The resulting detonation was similar to a volcano in that it threw thousands of tons of earth into the sky. Instead of flaming gases and lava from deep in the earth, lightning raged unchecked through the epicenter of this disaster. The earth and air mixed together, generating even *more* lightning Essence. Eventually turning to liquid as plasma raged through the area, the minerals and stone fell to the ground as a rain of liquid earth and metal. Under a city's worth of molten slag, the destroyed spell formations reformed layer by layer, powered by the ritual safely housed in a flying dungeon far away.

Now created and appearing without interference—as well as being steeped in ambient Essence—the brand-new ritual activated. The raging, uncontrollable Essence and Mana in the area gradually sank into the earth. Like water in a dehydrated riverbed, the power flowed away along the newly established ley lines. For a day after it started to drain, the energies swirled and thrashed in the sky. A point finally came where the power calmed enough to release Jasper and his brothers, and they fell from the sky, changed by the power that had suffused them.

Huggin was the first to awaken, but as he opened his eyes, all of the brothers did the same. Turning to them, Huggin tried to persuade them that they should look for whoever may have possibly survived the calamity, but all that left his mouth was a single sound. "Caw!"

Muninn turned in confusion. How had a crow survived that hurricane of force? Everything in the area should be dead! He tried to ask if they had seen what had happened, but all that was heard was a resounding... "Caw?"

Jasper opened his eye painfully, looking at his siblings in horror. "Brothers," his voice trembled with raw emotion, "is that you?"

"Caw!"

"Caw!"

Somehow, their words translated perfectly into Jasper's mind, and he nodded. "I don't know exactly, but I agree that we should save those we can before hunting whoever did this. From this point forward, we seek knowledge, we hunt the destroyer of our people, and we give ourselves to rage. Until such a time as this debt is repaid, I cast aside my name and assume the mantle of responsibility for this hunt. From now until eternity if needs must, until this quest has been completed, I shall bear the name of Odin."

Odin grasped his spear and looked into the sky, watching as Essence and Mana continued to stream into the ground. "Let's go." He took a step forward and collapsed on to the still cooling ground, unconscious. Two exasperated *caws* accompanied his fall.

CHAPTER THIRTY-SEVEN

Watching Tyler's team strip the enormous Manticore's corpse of every material was a wonder to behold. Especially because they never got close to it, not trusting their ability to avoid every drop of its dangerous blood. With practiced motions, the skin and scales were flayed off by directed Mana. The meat followed, with the blood being collected in large vats. All of the organs were separated out, and the bones were greedily stacked for later usage. Tyler looked back at Dale, still unable to believe his outstanding luck. "You are *sure* I can have everything that remains just by making armor for your team?"

"Yes. Well, first let me know what those Runes on the spikes do. I may need to take them. I want anything that will help us in the coming days." Dale watched as the hide and scales were put to good use, floating in the air while being forcefully tanned. "You are sure it will make decent armor, yes?"

"Of course I am!" Tyler laughed uneasily. "While not as potent as it was when connected to the Beast properly, the leather and scales are still infused with Mana. They will be tougher than almost any other armor you could find and far more flexible than anything else. I suppose dragonhide would be better, but I wouldn't be able to form it into anything. Too stiff."

"How do you have all of our sizes again?" Dale mumbled his thoughts as the leather was shaped into fashionable armor.

Tyler coughed abruptly and had the grace to look embarrassed. He had never had them here to be measured. "Let's just let the men work, shall we?"

They moved to the front of the shop, discussing changes in the dungeon and the usefulness of the items created by Tyler's shop of oddities. Dale made sure to swear him to secrecy for the time being and told him about the secrets contained on the sixth floor. Tyler was quite pleased to have this information and made a deal with Dale to map out the paths... eventually.

Carrying large sets of leather armor, a few of Tyler's employees walked into the room. Bypassing Dale, they handed the garments to another employee, who directed Dale to the next sectioned-off area. Tyler began to follow, but Dale shook his head. The merchant had to stay behind for this part; it was too sensitive to allow a third person to know the secret he was about to reveal. A Dwarf was waiting for them, and he almost snarled when he was handed unfinished leather armor. "Is this some kind of sick joke? Who bothers to wear animal hide into battle?"

"Not *my* team." Dale tried to appease him. "Not after you finish these, anyway. I need you to swear not to reveal the details of the job I am offering you. *If* you can complete it, you will be greatly rewarded."

The Dwarf looked at Dale coldly. "If I am swearing a binding oath, it *abyss* well better be lucrative. I reserve the right to cancel the oath if I am not paid enough for the job. You still fine with that?"

"...Yes?" Dale gulped at the murderous stare. "As long as you let me offer more if I fail to meet your requirement to the point you are satisfied?"

The Dwarf grunted and made his oath. Dale reached into his bag. "I need you to create threads out of this metal and create a fine mesh throughout the entirety of this armor."

"That's it?" The Dwarf snorted in fury. "Chainmail armor would be lighter and cheaper. There is no reason to do this job! You made me swear an oath... Mithril!" The last word was gasped through clenched teeth, the shift from anger to incredulousness creating an odd tone. "But why? How? If you have enough Mithril to fill all of this armor, why not just wear it proudly?"

"Just aluminum—it's not Mithril yet. Listen, my team is still too low ranked, and we could never hold on to the armor if it were public knowledge that we had it." Dale slowly piled the bars of aluminum higher, watching the reactions playing across the normally stoic face of the Dwarf. "Will you take the job?"

"And..." the Dwarf swallowed the saliva building in his mouth, "the pay?"

"How much of this metal is required to complete the job?" Dale fired back a question.

The Dwarf wanted to lie, Dale could tell. Because of this, he had gotten an approximation of doing it with copper wire. It shouldn't take *too* much more aluminum to do the same job. To his credit, the truth fell from the Dwarf's lips. "At least... seven ingots. Possibly part of an eighth bar; I am uncertain what the joints will need."

Dale nodded, smiling at the staring Dwarf. "Then I want you to use a full eight ingots on this project. Reinforce areas that need extra protection and create a masterpiece that we can reveal to the world when we are powerful enough to protect it." He placed ten ingots on the counter. "Keep the change. That work for you?"

Dropping to a knee, the Dwarf intoned, "I swear that I shall create the best armor I possibly can and will use these materials to the best of my abilities on your behalf. I will never tell another soul about your armor until you choose to reveal it." The earth around him shuddered, showing that his oath was accepted.

Dale helped him stand, laughing. "I appreciate the sentiment, but that was a little overdramatic for me. So long as I get the armor in a timely manner, I'm happy."

"Give me but a day," the Dwarf made his joyful promise, pocketing two bars of the rare material right away. "I will make you impervious to your enemies."

CAL

<Hey, we are starting to get some Essence trickling in from the ley lines! It must have taken forever to fully activate the ritual in that city. Maybe there wasn't as much ambient Essence as I thought there was.> I sighed contentedly as the much-needed Essence flowed into the Cores keeping the island flying. I siphoned a bit of the power into the ritual creating the ley lines; it had drawn a lot of power the last few days, but happily, it now seemed to be self-sustaining. My thoughts returned to the main tactical issue on my mind. How was I going to attack a city full of warriors when I got there? I had tried various methods for creating Mobs and armies, but nothing seemed to work as I needed it to. I had even gone the other way with my bug swarms, miniaturizing them to the point that they were hard to see.

I snorted as I looked at the never-before-seen bug I had created. Sadly, it had almost zero combat potential. I had intended for it to eat people, but I had messed up somewhere. It flew slowly and was very loud. It *did* drink blood, but... I was going to have to label them a failure. I couldn't bear to kill them all off myself, so I opened a small portal and dropped all of this type of bug into the world below. They had decent survivability, but against the much more dangerous creatures in the wild, I didn't expect my Mosquitos to last long at all.

My golems were very powerful within their own territory, and powering them during combat was fine, but they took too much Mana to maintain for any real length of time. Plus, it took over a day for them to be rebuilt if they were destroyed! I had to hope that diplomacy would win out in the end, and the Amazons would help us wipe the necromantic threat from this world. The threat was growing in their own home! I was already getting furious, certain that they would deny us the help we desperately needed.

A surprising amount of auras were beginning to appear upon my surface, and I felt the need for a break, so my mind drifted upward to lazily listen in on the hurried conversations. "Get Frank! We need to talk to him at once!" Oh? At least this sounded interesting.

Dozens of people were pouring through the portal that connected cities. They seemed haggard, and many of them were bleeding. A scream alerted me to something else that had come through the portal on the heels of the latest... refugee?

A huge, clawed hand grabbed the entire torso of the bleeding man. He was saved as the portal was redirected to another location, severing the arm. Frank—who had sprinted into the area—caught the man, shock evident on his face. "Prince Henry?"

"I... I think it is King Henry now, for what little the title is worth," King Henry bitterly stated. Bleary eyes looked up at the assembled masses, hardly seeing them through tear-filled eyes. "The Kingdom of the Lion has fallen."

"As has the Phoenix," another heart-wrenching moment played out as a female voice broke the horrified silence.

Henry looked over at her, and any composure he had been able to maintain was eradicated. "Princess Marie!" He ran to her, catching her in a desperate embrace.

"My title has changed... it is now *Queen* Marie for me as well." She began to sob, as did Henry. The loss of their families had been sudden, terrifying. For so many people that could theoretically live forever to die in a single day heralded terror on the horizon. My full attention was on these people at this point, and the drama involved made me wish for a snack as I watched. Dozens more people charged through the portal, some with *things* chasing them. Soon, far too soon, the tide of refugees stopped entirely.

On the plus side, the bodies didn't stick around to further traumatize the poor, fleeing people. *Bur-r-p!* Whew, pardon me. I guess my wish for a snack was granted. I watched as Amber—the High Magous of the Portal Guild—ran over and recalibrated the portal manually. I was fairly impressed. The power and control needed to do something like that on the fly showed how exceptional she was. She muttered something about 'removing fallen cities from the network'.

The new King and Queen were ushered into a meeting with the council, and even a slightly charred Dale was found and dragged in. Henry began speaking, his voice full of sorrow, "They came out of nowhere! Undead suddenly started pouring into the streets, into the castle. They were *everywhere*. A man in a black robe walked into the throne room and spoke to my parents. He *walked* in midway through a session where the entire *court* was gathered! At least twenty Mages were present, and the man killed *all* of them! He had weapons and access to power that I have never heard even *hinted* at! I am only alive due to my guards hastily removing me before he started the killing."

Marie picked up the conversation, "A similar man, possibly the same man, came to our throne and made impossible demands. When he was denied and asked for proof of his power, he produced," she looked at Henry with great pity, "he produced a pile of heads."

There was affronted murmuring around the table. "He told us that he was going to every seat of power in the world and 'unifying' all of us. The heads were from leaders that refused him. My... my father's head joined the pile soon after. The dark power... it was completely overwhelming. Unstoppable."

Silence reigned supreme for a long minute, eventually broken by Frank, "Well, abyss. The rulers of countries are considered some of the strongest cultivators in their respective countries. The last line of defense against the destruction of their people. For this person to kill *multiple* rulers in a single day... we aren't even talking about S-rank anymore. He must be at or approaching double S-rank. Possibly triple S."

"Do we have any clue, any *hint* of his identity?" Amber looked around the defeated faces in the room.

"He called himself 'The Master'," Henry spat out the title like a curse.

Chandra's face blanched, and her eyes gazed at nothing. "No... it can't be. The Master is dead. I know this for a *fact!* It was my responsibility to... this *must* be a copycat."

"If you have information about who this man is or who he is pretending to be, you need to tell us right now," Father Richard intoned impatiently.

"We need to warn the others." Chandra stood up hurriedly, her chair flying into the wall behind her and being reduced to kindling. "The Amazons especially! The Elves! Oh, God!" She flickered, running from the room at speeds too great for the non-Mages to follow.

<Dale. You need to see something.> We were floating toward the capital city, and from our position far above the world, my goal was in sight. A flicker of Essence trickled into my senses, and I nearly lost all coherent thought as Dani's thoughts tickled my senses for the first time in months. I lost the connection just as fast though. She was in the city! She was *here*!

"Cal, I am *really* busy right now." Dale was commiserating with the Royals, but his habit had been to speak aloud for his team's benefit.

<I'm *aware*.> My frustration nearly knocked him off of his feet. <Get outside; get to a point you can look at the city. Bring the others with you. Go! Hurry, this is important!>

Dale had little trouble convincing everyone to join him. Direct intervention from me was rare, and he urged them quite intensely. They hurried to get to a point where they could see over the edge, and as they stood high on the walls, my fear became theirs.

The Amazons came running, having been directed by Chandra to get to the meeting at all costs. "What is so important that you are interrupting our baths?" The leader of the Amazonian delegation screeched up at them. Her hair was still wet, and she huffed as she was waved up. She stomped up the stairs, angry and demanding answers. All she got in reply was a pointed finger. Turning, she looked over at the capital city of the Amazon people-what little remained of it.

A huge plume of black, oily smoke rose as a column from the city. What they could see of the place with their enhanced vision showed that the city had been reduced to rubble. The outer wall was demolished, and though there seemed to be massive amounts of movement going on, no one could tell if the crowds were comprised of invaders or refugees. Looking at the area with sight enhanced by Essence or Mana showed a huge accumulation of infernal Essence gathering over the city. This meant that either an unimaginably massive amount of death had been visited upon the land or there was such a high amount of powerful infernal auras in the area that everything else was hidden from view. The worst possibility... was that both scenarios were true.

"What do we do?" Marie whispered as she clutched the arm of her oldest friend, Henry.

"What *can* we do?" Henry replied despondently as he watched the smoke continue to rise. "Our Kingdoms have fallen. Our leaders slaughtered like animals. Our allies... gone."

Tyler turned to the side and puked, making a few of the Mages wince away in disgust. Dale raised his hands helplessly.

<We destroy them,> I coldly demanded. Dale froze in place as he realized what I was saying.

"You can't be saying... Cal, you can't go to that city!" Dale's words exploded out of him, making the others look at him cautiously.

<Dani is in there, Dale. I'm going. If you all stay on me like parasites, you are coming too. Make your peace with this fact because it *is* a fact.> The island tilted forward almost imperceptibly, gaining speed and losing altitude.

"Infuriating dungeon!" Dale shouted into the empty air. "You're going to get us all killed!"

"Or..." Marie spoke up, eyes alight with calculating intensity, "or this dungeon could be exactly what we needed. Dungeon! I want to make a deal!"

<I'm listening.>

"You can't be serious!" Dale shouted at her, catching himself after the first words and lowering his voice. "Marie, Your Majesty, you don't know what making a deal with the dungeon entails. There is no way for you to come out with a better end of the deal! *Demons* make better deals!"

"If I am stronger, if I am able to take revenge and save my people," Marie gulped, "then I don't care."

<I like those terms.> My nonchalant tone seemed to throw Dale into a state of apoplexy.

"Dungeon! I may not be as powerful as you would wish for, but if I reclaim my Kingdom, you will have my eternal gratitude. I will work my entire life to repay your help. If you give me the power I need, the troops, the weapons... I will serve you faithfully—second only to my people—for as long as I am able!" Her hand shot to her chest as she was knocked from her feet from the creation of such a powerful oath. The air around her hummed with power, the heavens accepting her words and preparing to enforce them. Mana restricted her soul, and just like that... I had a new dungeon born. This one had *true* influence as well.

<Can you hear me?> I tested our connection along the brand new pathway of Mana engraved in her soul. Her face turned into a mix of wonder and fear.

"I... I can. What have I done?" she whispered softly, eyes trembling. The whites around her irises were entirely visible. Obviously, she had made this oath in the heat of the moment and was already regretting it. Time to calm her down; I needed a powerful asset like her.

<You made the smart decision. You did the right thing. Allow me to show you the benefits. Step away from the group; make sure you have about five meters between you and the nearest person.> I directed her to the side, not anticipating her next question.

"What's a meter?"

<Just... go over here.> A small platform of stone was created, and I had her stand on it. Everyone else seemed to be in shock at her actions and was watching the proceedings with concern. As she stepped on the platform and waited, I chuckled loudly. <This next part is going to be fun.> The stone under her vanished, and she slid into my depths with a scream. The stone reappeared as the onlookers charged at the opening. They didn't make it in time.

CHAPTER THIRTY-EIGHT

<Now that you are comfy, let's discuss your capabilities. I'll adjust you and your gear to the best possible configuration for your goals after our little talk,> I told the trembling Queen. She stood shakily at the foot of the Silverwood tree, fearfully looking at the golem protecting me.

"What... what is that? Isn't she an Elf?" She raised a hand and pointed a trembling finger at the golem.

<Her? Oh, that's just a golem. I mean, she does have a fully aware mind, but she's happy to be where she is.> I looked at the golem petting a Basher, laughing as I remembered her original body. Leporiday Lagomorpha had charged into my dungeon, trying to convince everyone that the place was safe if you were nice, and the people killing bunnies were terrible examples of human refuse. She was correct about them being terrible people, but the rest... heh. As soon as Bashers had surrounded her, she started screaming in delight and hugging the furry Mobs. She had a brain aneurysm at that moment and would have been erased from the world forever if I hadn't collected her mind into a memory stone.

Now, *finally*, I had a use for her. She was now my guardian, and in return, I provided her with fluffy animals to play with. Her weak constitution in life had made cultivation impossible for her, so she had died while in the F-ranks. Now filled with *my* Mana, she was the epitome of the cultivation paths. Her body was composed of a perfectly balanced amount of minerals, allowing any type of ambient Essence to be used. She was also the only self-sustaining golem here. Since her mind was intact, she was able to cultivate like a living person. I had provided her with my cultivation technique and passed Mana to her when she donated an appropriate amount of Essence to me.

<We are talking about *you* though, Marie. What do you want? What weapon do you use? How do you want to be seen on the battlefield? Shall we begin?>

We started talking, and she told me about her training, her strengths and weaknesses. She told me of her family, and I commiserated with her over her loss. By the end, she was fully committed to me and overjoyed that she had chosen to align her goals with mine. It seemed I had gained a new priestess for the cult of Cal. We began working on modifications, and while she was unconscious, I created a few... contingencies. Just in case she ever tried to sacrifice herself for the 'greater good' and get rid of me. It was unlikely; obviously, everyone loves me, but... just in case.

An hour later, the portal opened in the church with a faint zapping noise. The council had been debating on their course of action the entire time, while Henry had been desperate to get into the dungeon and find Marie. Dale had been able to convince him that Marie was alive, but the fear in the man's eyes showed how deep his devotion to Marie truly was. The Queen stepped through the curtain of shimmering energy, and the people around the room almost drew their weapons at the sight of her. Her body had been altered subtly, forcing the best portions of her bloodline to surface. Elves would be jealous of her beauty and enemies would fear her. Her features were sharp, designed to draw attention and inspire loyalty. She was a foot taller, and her body was coated with sleek, powerful muscles.

Marie's form-fitting armor moved with her, a second skin of gleaming Mithril interspersed with the most potent combination of materials for her affinities. There was a Core on each of her shoulders, which were absorbing the ambient

Essence in the air as she moved. Upon her brow was a tiara mounted upon a helmet, which allowed any who looked upon her to know exactly who she was. Another Core rested in the helmet like a jewel, pretending to be decoration.

<Well, Dale! Allow me to present the newly improved Queen: Battle Tyrant Marie!>

DALE

"Battle Tyrant Marie?" Dale repeated aloud, making a few people glare at him. "Are you coated in... Mithril?"

"It's the most beautiful thing I've ever seen in my life!" Thaddius and his people had gathered, and after determining that their people hadn't been attacked, he joined the emergency war council. The other Dwarves nodded, a few unsubtly adjusting their pants or wiping tears from their eyes.

"Thank you," Marie's voice echoed through the room. The Dwarves got closer, looking for seams in her armor, but it wasn't designed in a way they recognized. This armor didn't come off without my direct help. Good thing Mages didn't need to use the bathroom... "I didn't know you would be so worried."

"Huh?" Thaddius looked up at her blankly. "Oh, yeah, glad you're safe. Can I look at the inlay on your greaves? Kota! Come look at this."

A new Dwarf sprinted over and almost drooled on the shiny material.

"Are you sure this is Mithril?" the Dwarf asked as he wiped his mouth.

"Duh, Kota! Look at it!" Thaddius smacked him, and they devolved into a conversation about the benefits and detriments of form-fitting Mithril.

Henry shot a glare at the Dwarves, his bloodshot eyes making the glance far scarier than it should have been. "Marie, we thought you were dead. I thought I lost the last person that I..."

"I told you she was alive." Dale fell silent when he noticed he was being ignored.

Marie looked sadly at the man before her. "We have a war on our hands, Henry. You know that I love you, but this comes first. As we have always told each other, our people need to be protected, raised out of their troubles. No matter what. I have a chance to do that now, and I hope you'll join me."

"You want me to make a pledge to the dungeon?" Henry was aghast at the suggestion.

"Yes. I do," Marie firmly confirmed. "I'll tell you right now, it's worth it." After a few long seconds, Henry nodded in response. He repeated the oath she had stated earlier and stepped into the awaiting portal. A few moments passed as the changes to Marie were noted, but then the conversations picked up. The council had heard Henry's thoughts, though he had been heavily distracted. Marie was able to calmly discuss her ideas, and a rough battle plan was drawn up. Shock and awe would be the order of the day.

An hour after he had stepped through, Henry emerged from the light. Now calm, collected, and in control of himself, he nodded to the others and joined in the planning. His armor was similar to Marie's, a coat of Mithril interspersed with Cores and minerals. His eyes were focused and sharp, and he had a large shield on one arm and a sword for the other that was nearly humming with power.

Around the room, the other people waited to see the downside to the oath that had been made by the Royals. The King and Queen, now towering above the others by nearly a foot, started to look uncomfortable as the quiet lengthened. I decided that it was time to get things moving, so I thought I would help out my Tyrants at the same time. <So, can I send out the troops?>

"Yes!" Marie barked with relief evident in her voice, startling herself and the onlookers. "I mean... yes, please, send out the troops you are going to loan us."

<Will do. First, can you please close off the entrance to the dungeon? I'm stopping production of all Mobs, all treasure, everything not needed for the upcoming battle. I don't want anyone to walk around in here killing off all my defenses while I'm busy helping all of *you*.> Dale nodded at these words, sending a runner to close the gates. It would take a few hours for everyone currently in the dungeon to get out, but by that time, battle would be joined.

"We are ready, Cal. Send out the troops," Henry ordered sternly.

<Watch your tone.> Henry paled and started to apologize, earning a chuckle from me. <Just kidding. I've just wanted to see what someone who took me seriously would do when I said that. Dale just makes rude hand gestures.>

The portal began to shimmer once again, and the first Goblin, a Berserker, stepped through. They weren't equipped with Mithril armor or weapons, but the equipment they were wearing was high quality. I praised the details of the changes in them as well as their usefulness in combat. I needed to enunciate my usefulness and make these people well and truly indebted to me.

<This is a Goblin Berserker. This is going to be the most common type of Goblin in the army. They have no fear and will attack anything they are ordered to. They will all be using an Enchanted weapon. Force enhancement is the only ability that is

granted to them via the Runes, as they can't seem to grasp the concept of using Inscriptions. They are strong, but fairly... thick-headed.>

There was a pause, and the Goblin pointed at a thorn that jutted out of its armor. <As a last resort—or as needed—the Berserkers will slam this thorn into themselves. As they tend to do massive damage to themselves when they fight, I created this in hopes that they will be able to fight for a longer time before dying. It is a Rune designed for healing. Also known as a starvation Rune, this will heal them incredibly quickly but also will make them die soon after if the Rune remains in them and they aren't fed.>

The Berserker stepped out of the way, allowing a shield-bearing Goblin to step through the portal. <A basic defender, this type of Goblin has Runes on its shield that—when activated—will enrage whatever sees them. A secondary enchantment allows the shield to absorb a huge amount of force. There is a downside to this Rune, in that when it has taken all the damage it can, the shield will explode. The detonation *should* be directed toward the enemies it is facing, but the defense of a shield is gone, and the Goblin will likely follow.>

Next out was an archer, and since they were self-explanatory, the conversation moved forward quickly. A standard fighter was next, followed by a Goblin that made the humans recoil in fear. Bob stepped out of the portal, easily as tall as King Henry. His staff tapped imperiously on the floor as he walked, the only noise in the echoing room.

<As you can all see, Bob here is a Goblin Shaman. Well, actually, Bob is a full-fledged death Mage now!> Bob had lost all pigment in his skin, turning albino. His teeth were needles, and his eyes were completely black. Beyond these changes, he looked almost human. Hair covered his head, hiding his pointed

ears. An aura of power surrounded him, his connection to a law evident to those who knew what they were looking for.

"T-this... you can make warriors like *this*?" Tyler sputtered incredulously after the descriptions of the Goblins were repeated to those not bound to the dungeon. "Why haven't you been using them against us?"

<Did you want me to?> This reply was met with a quickly shaking head. <I made a deal with Dale not to make the early floors too dangerous for people to move through. Bob was raised to the B-ranks just this morning after we found that he had achieved a deep enough understanding of death. These others are my *elites* and have been training ever since the Wailing War. The Essence and Mana cost of recreating them for frequent use is also too high. The only reason I am doing it *now* is that I am shutting everything else off and have to honor my deal with the Royals.>

"How many of these troops can we expect?" Frank's direct question was met with trepidation; how many troops could the dungeon *really* bring to bear in a short time?

<There will be seventeen Berserkers, thirteen standard warriors, eleven archers, seven defenders, and one Bob per unit,> there was some relief, as well as some disgruntlement at the low numbers, <with a total of fifty units. All of them will follow the commands passed down by the Battle Tyrants but are also used to working together under the guidance of Bob.>

There were shouts of disbelief. Father Richard spoke up, "Does this dungeon think we will believe that he can create... uh, *that* many troops in this short amount of time?"

"Two thousand four hundred fifty Goblins," Tyler stated quietly. His words made the gathered people shudder. Overdramatic worrywarts.

<No, I don't expect you to believe that because I can't.> Dale sat down and stopped interpreting for me, throwing his hands up. He seemed to be 'done', to use a term I heard frequently. Luckily, Marie took up the slack. <I've been making and training these units for *weeks*. This is *not* a spur of the moment creation. Now think on this—multiple cities were wiped out today! Kingdoms have fallen, and I am the only one that has a standing army at this point! Be happy that at least *one* of our groups was prepared for this, and remember that it shouldn't have *had* to be me!>

The final comment sobered up the group, reminding them of what they would soon be facing. "Is there anything else you can do for us?" Amber nearly begged the empty air. Imagine that. A crisis hits, and the people who scorned you and called for your death are now begging for help.

<I'm done talking now, Marie. Tell her that when we are in range, I am going to send packs of Cloud Cats over the edge of the mountain. They will drift down and begin killing, hopefully softening the defenders for our arrival. Also, I am going to eventually land in the ruins, and hopefully, that squishes anything below us.>

There was a bit more discussed, but the general consensus was that everyone was as ready as they could be. "I can't believe we are doing this." Dale laughed a bit manically as Goblins began to march in formation out of the dungeon's portal.

Chapter Thirty-Nine

The smoke from the city was getting into Dale's lungs. He coughed dryly in a vain attempt to clear his airway. Why wasn't the dungeon absorbing the ash? There were only two positive aspects of the smoke. The first was that it was obscuring their location from the people below. Second... it was blocking the view of the carnage. There were areas where so many people had been killed that the ground looked like it was covered in a chunky salsa, and it would have been visible and stomach churning, even from this height. Through the smoke, Dale was still able to see the buildings and walls that they were passing over and *had* been passing over for over an hour. They were on a flying *mountain*, and they still didn't match even a quarter of the size of the city below them. He couldn't believe that so many people lived in one area—*had* lived in one area. Dale shook his head and wiped away a tear, deeply saddened by the purposeless loss of life.

A Mage had flown down to scout quite a while ago, looking for survivors or defenders. She had just returned, bringing news that someone else had apparently already collected anyone living and hauled them to a holding area on the outskirts of the capital. From the look of the rotting guards, their stay wouldn't end up being a pleasant one. Or a long one, for that matter. Dale flinched as a huge pack of Cloud Cats sprinted past him, jumping off the wall and gliding toward the city a mile below. While they couldn't survive outside of the dungeon for any real length of time, if they made it back within a day, there wouldn't be *too* many detrimental effects. Especially if they were well fed, and the sad truth was that there was plenty of meat below.

Tom strolled up to Dale, golden armor gleaming in the weak sunlight that diffused through the choking smoke. The unit's armor had arrived, the rush order being completed in record time by a very happy Dwarf. After being processed, the scales from the Manticore had taken a golden shine, and the leather was a soft golden brown. Dale was happy to see Tom using both hands to carry his oversized warhammer, and he waved at the barbarian as he walked up.

"Looks to be a good day for battle, Baron Dale." Tom was very somber today, his green eyes looking down at the burned husk of a city that used to contain his least favorite people.

"It does, indeed. Outside of the smoke, it's a beautiful day." Dale tore his eyes away from the minor explosions and waves of darkness erupting on the distant ground. Rarely the screaming roar of the cloud Cats would drift up to them and cause him to shiver. "Are you going to be okay doing this, Tom? We are trying to rescue *Amazons*."

Tom leaned on the wall, body posture relaxed in a way Dale couldn't match when he was this tense. "We are saving their people, their man-slaves. If I understand correctly, the first action that would have been taken is to kill the leadership of the nation. If so, this means that my family has been avenged. Now, there is no place in my soul that holds anger toward the desperate people below. I will fight to the best of my abilities."

"That's good, Tom. I'm glad to hear it." Dale reached over and grabbed his new helmet, slowly pulling it on. A perfect fit, as expected of Dwarven work. "Let's get to it." They walked over to their team, and Hans struck a heroic pose at them. Now that they were in matching armor, they really *looked* like a team. Of course, Adam was still wearing his brilliantly white robe. Instead of detracting from the uniform, the robe instead highlighted the armor he now wore underneath. Dale looked at each of them and felt that he had done all he could to protect them. He rolled his arms to relax his stress-clenched muscles and took a deep breath.

"Are we ready for this?" Rose looked at the pale faces surrounding her, receiving shakes of their head 'no' from all of them. "Oh, good. I thought it was just me." She looked out over the sea of people waiting to attack, but her attention was caught and held by the portal Mages. They were doing... *something* together, and their voices were rising and falling in an intricate chant. Mana was intertwining and accumulating above them, forming a rift in the air above the city.

"Are we certain the city is populated only with the dead or necromancers?" Frank called to the scouts. They nodded, eyes wide and staring. They had seen horrors today. "Bring it out, then." A ball of tungsten was rolled in front of the waiting army, pushed by four straining Mages. The ball was set into an indentation on the stone floor, waiting to be used. At first glance, it was just a lump of metal, but Dale could feel the dungeon's work at play and decided to look closer. As tall as a man—roughly six feet—the ball was so heavy that it left a furrow in the ground it rolled over. What made Dale catch the breath in his throat were the Runes engraved on the ball—extra weight, force, and demon banishing. What was happening?

Tyler was glaring at the ball. "Six feet in diameter, nineteen point three grams per cubic centimeter... that is two hundred four *thousand* six hundred eighty-five pounds of Inscribed tungsten we are throwing away."

"We aren't *throwing* it away, Tyler." Chandra stepped toward them as she decided to take a moment to explain what was happening. "I'm not sure you will understand the significance, but there is a *Tomb Lord* down there."

Tyler shrugged at her. "You're right, I don't understand."

"There is a hierarchy of undead summons. There are basic versions like zombie and wraiths, a mid-tier like abominations and minor demons, and a higher tier that contains beings like standard demons. These are all things you have seen before and are the usual *things* summoned by Mage-rank necromancers. Then there are beings summoned exclusively by A-ranks and higher. The weakest of these is a Behemoth, which is twice the size of an abomination and armored."

Chandra took a deep breath and continued, "One of the strongest in the A-ranks is the Tomb Lord. This is a *heavily* armored being that commands armies of the undead. They are puppets of demon lords in that they are inhabited and controlled by them. This means that they not only have all the power of the dead but the infernal powers of the abyss as well. Fast, intelligent, powerful. Nearly impossible to kill with conventional weaponry. Thus, we have *that.*" She pointed at the ball the Portal Mages were surrounding.

The second in command of the portal Mages, James, started a secondary chant that created a harmony to the first. Next to the ball, a portal slowly opened on the ground. Ten feet above it, another portal opened simultaneously. As it widened, James's face became more and more strained. "Now!" He gasped as his strength began to wane.

The attending Mages shoved the ball, and it ponderously began to move. *Ever* so slowly, it tipped over the edge of the portal and fell. And fell. And fell. The wind began to shimmer as the ball dropped from the air above, only to drop into the waiting portal and appear in the air again. The friction in the air was causing the ball to heat up, and in seconds, it was glowing a bright cherry-red. Now falling so fast that the air began to catch on fire around it, the ball was now almost impossible for people to look at directly. A huge amount of Essence began to be generated as wind Essence was torn apart and created fire and lightning Essence. James tried to let the ball 'fall' for as long as he could maintain the portal; just as he was about to collapse, Amber hijacked the portal on the ground and connected it with a different hole in the world.

Impossibly fast, the ball of tungsten entered the portal on the ground and exited the portal high in the air, aimed at the city below. Specifically, it was aimed at an armored form that towered over the highest of the buildings still standing. With meteoric speed, the ball impacted the form that was standing in the center of the largest wave of undead, causing a shockwave that forced the floating dungeon higher on a blast of air. The ground collapsed in all directions, and the earth of the dead city rose into the air as debris. The dust reached the edge of the dungeon's influence and was absorbed, protecting the people waiting to attack whatever survived. Optimistically looking at the power of the artillery, they all hoped there would be nothing left to fight at this point.

It took a few minutes for the air to clear enough to see the ground below, and the view confused many. The Tomb Lord was still standing, though everything else had been annihilated by the shockwave. It looked at its hand and seemed to laugh as it tried to toss away the ball it had caught. It seemed confused that the ball wouldn't leave its hand. It violently shook its appendage, and a furious screech left its mouth. The ball glowed brighter for a long moment, then it and the Tomb Lord vanished with a faint *pop*.

"Banished. Thank goodness." James collapsed, lying on his back and breathing deeply.

"Good God!" Tyler whispered as he looked at Chandra with wide eyes. "You would have had to *fight* that thing?"

She nodded. "It would have been *very* difficult. It had the power of the Mage who summoned it as well as the demon's strength. It was essentially two A-ranked Mages working together in perfect harmony. If it hadn't tried to show off by catching the ball, we would have needed to retreat."

While their conversation continued, the scouts were making reports on the city below. There had been quite a bit of damage, but the city center remained completely intact. The Amazons cleared up the confusion generated by this revelation. "The Queen's circle. There were powerful protections in place, powerful enough to slow S-ranked attacks. Though this was a potent blow against weak creatures, that ball was not infused with Mana. It was just moving quickly. Obviously, the protections designed by Amazonians were enough to stop that mediocre damage from spreading."

<Looks like we know where we are attacking. If I am correct and the dungeon is hidden down there, I am sure it will be using those protections to the best of its abilities.> The island began to descend. <Good luck, everyone. When I am on the ground, all the Mana and Essence I've been devoting to flying will be directed toward creating more troops. Expect reinforcements... soonish!>

While it took over thirty minutes to land, the time seemed to pass in the blink of an eye. After the first tremor of touching down shook the mountain, the gathered people began walking out of a portal maintained by the dungeon. There was a short drop at the exit, but the real shock came from the change in environment. With a single movement, they stepped from a virtual paradise into the ashen ruins of what had once been a great city. Ash and foul stenches clogged the air while thick infernal Essence cloyed against their meridians. The people rushed to get into formation; weaker undead were already charging across the flat expanse of the tungsten meteor's killing zone. Stronger undead were taking their time, and intelligent demons were holding back to direct the assault of their puppets.

Mages from Mountaindale—specifically scouts and Spotters—were searching for any hint of where the necromancers in charge of the creatures were hiding. If the people controlling the undead and demons were killed, all of their puppets would return to the piles of rotten meat that they were supposed to be. Until then, the army needed to defend themselves, and barriers began appearing around the shield walls. The advantage of earth Mages in an army cannot be understated. Walls of stone rose, blocking a charge that could have shattered the defensive lines of the living.

The Goblins howled in response to a rousing speech given by Bob, and they slammed their weapons either on the ground, their shields, or else stamped their feet. Their enthusiasm for the upcoming fight was intoxicating, and the adventurers were not to be outdone! Battle cries and bloodlust-filled shouts rose into the toxic air. The Goblins cheered as Bob directed the placement of a totem. This was a mobile version of my obelisks and used earth Essence to activate. When the totem was inserted into the ground, a Core in it lit up and connected to obelisks in the city. The people smiled, feeling fresh air as my influence was spread to the area and began changing the battleground in their favor. Smoke lessened, ash stopped raining on them, undead began to melt away, and in the small area my influence occupied, everyone could see and hear each other clearly.

"How many of those pillar things do the Goblins have?" Frank yelled over the din of battle coming from the outskirts of their formation.

"No idea! Who cares?" Dale screamed back with a chilling grin on his face. He was looking forward to this fight. He didn't think he'd need to wait long; the pounding steps of the dead were drawing nearer.

<They have as many as they need. Most importantly, they need to get one into the evil dungeon under the city so that I can directly counter its influence, or you will all be screwed. All of the totems need to be in range of each other, so make sure they stay undamaged, or you'll need to go back!> Dale heard in his mind. For once, he had no qualms about listening to advice given by the voice in his head.

A thought struck him, and he smiled grimly. "Frank! There is a dungeon in the sewers; find an undamaged tunnel into it! I'd bet my last gold that the necromancers controlling all of this are taking defensive positions below us!"

There was a brief discussion between the leadership of the army, but Marie and Henry seemed to agree with Dale's calculated assessment. The administration pulled an Amazon over to them and told her to direct them to a sewer entrance. After she looked at them like they were insane, she tried her best to find a landmark that she could use to locate a sewer entrance. The process was difficult as this entire area had recently been reduced to rubble at best and, at worst, the terrain had completely flipped over.

While the Amazon worked to find a tunnel opening, the army was doing their best to survive, beset upon on all sides by the ravenous dead. Luckily, the necromancers were in seclusion, else there would have been ranged Mana-based attacks to work against from more than just the demons. Arrows flew from

Goblin, Elf, and human alike while large ballista bolts flew from Dwarven war machines placed on the mountain. It turned out that swords and other close range weapons were more effective against the undead, as the bodies had to be quite damaged before they would stop moving. Arrows and ranged weapons, though they didn't destroy many of the undead outright, were useful in pinning bodies in place so the warriors could destroy them easier. On the other hand, the ballista bolts could tear several bodies apart before losing momentum. The speed at which the Dwarves had been able to create these siege weapons gave the other races pause. When all of this was over, the delegations planned to make alliances immediately. All of the people represented in the army were *very* pleased they had not made enemies of the Dwarves.

Another great asset in the battle was that Tyler's shop of oddities had harvested the spikes on the Manticore then distributed the anti-demon weapons amongst the army. This forced the demons to make a choice—fight and possibly be banished or observe and make tactical strikes. While there *were* dedicated demon fighters such as Father Richard amongst the clerics, the weapons that allowed you to banish the foul creatures were rare, expensive, and single use. Unfortunately, the demons seemed to have decided that with such weapons in use, they should stay on the sidelines to control the movements of their minions. The 'taskmaster' type of demon, though not front line fighters themselves, could control the undead with a master's touch. Thanks to their subtle influence, attacks that should have been absorbed by shields or parries were instead landing against living flesh and armor. The people wouldn't last too long against the waves of enemies if this continued.

The dead were working as a unit, making the battle far more difficult for the living. A wall crumbled as an abomination made its presence known, walking through the mundane fortification like it wasn't even there. Rose noticed a dark miasma of Essence on the outskirts of the platoon of walking dead that had just arrived and recognized the signs that showed that a demon was present. Her sharp eyes pierced the swirling particles in the air, and she lined up an arrow for what should have been an impossible shot. She pulled back *hard* on the bowstring and released with an inaudible exhale of breath. Her arrow screamed as it flew in a straight line across four hundred meters, causing a tiny sonic boom as it broke the sound barrier. The arrow shattered as it entered the demon, but the Rune on the arrow's tip stayed intact! That was all that mattered.

Screaming as it felt all of the Essence that sustained it upon this plane vanishing, the demon furiously gave one last order to charge. It vanished with an echoing *pop* as the Rune came to life. After stopping in place for a moment as their withered brains processed the order, three abominations charged directly forward from where they were standing. Luckily, two of the mounds of flesh were facing away from the living army and trampled various minor undead as they sprinted off into the distance. Only one of them charged into an area that contained Goblins, but this was still devastating as the massive undead ignored all defenses and attacks. Defenders were tossed aside or trampled, and with each death, the abomination grew larger and stronger. It sucked the blood, bones, and flesh out of anything dead as it passed, nearly doubling in size before the Mages were able to counter its movement.

Incantations began to reach completion as the Mages directed their Mana and laws to destroy these unholy beings. Elements, particles, energy, and abstract thought ran rampant around the area, causing the earth to tremble, the particles in the air to be charged with Mana, and the undead to become *just* dead as they fell to pieces. Madame Chandra tossed seeds into the air, and they scattered on the wind. When they landed, they remained inert if they fell on living things, contrarily burrowing into flesh if they landed on dead beings. Splashes of color other than sanguine or various hues of dirt began appearing as flowers started to bloom with beautiful pigments.

The flowers released an invigorating scent, covering the odor of decay and death that otherwise permeated the area. Morale improving, the army roared a challenge to the dead and screamed their hatred toward the cowardly necromancers fighting from afar! Attacks redoubled in strength and speed, potions were chugged, and war was waged!

The Goblin Berserkers began decimating the minor undead, their blunt weapons and powerful blows perfect for the situation they found themselves in. As time wore on, the effects of the flowers began to wane, and the Goblins become fatigued, yet still, they threw everything they had into battle. The assault gained ground, and they pushed deeper toward the city center. Another totem was raised, and the Goblins cheered as they felt their connection to the dungeon reappear. The Berserkers—now approaching exhaustion—slammed a closed fist into their chest and pressed the Runes of healing into their bodies. In moments, they were feeling relief as lactic acid buildup was removed, wounds began to close, and exhaustion faded. They returned to combat, the undead in their paths being destroyed brutally and mercilessly. An hour into the battle, a voice rang out, clearly heard by those in charge of the army. "Here! There is a path into the sewers over here!"

Frank directed an earth Mage to test the sewer, but unfortunately, it had collapsed. The army—though disappointed—returned to taking ground slowly and painfully. A surprise attack wiped out over half of the Goblin Berserkers as demons and undead that had buried themselves in the dirt sprang to their feet. Like a knife through butter, the Goblins were torn to shreds only to be pulled into a waiting abomination's body. Now over eight meters tall, the abomination howled and ran into the army. It slew over a hundred Goblins before Father Richard was forced to incinerate the horror in its entirety by dousing it with holy light.

People were tiring quickly, but fortunately, an intact sewer entrance was found. A pained cheer rang out, and people began filing into the minor protection the area provided, hurrying to get everyone inside. Father Richard was nearly overwhelmed as he felt a massive concentration of demons and necromancers within the sewer. The real battle was about to begin.

CHAPTER FORTY

I really couldn't do much to help with this fight. I watched the battles rage and focused on creating reinforcements and aides to send with them. Each Goblin left the area with a small bag full of potions which they were instructed to distribute to the people who needed them. Elites took far too long to outfit so they left their spawning point with standard equipment. They had their memories though, which included all of their training, so my hope was that at least *some* of them would survive and succeed.

Having landed the mountain and deactivated the Runes and rituals needed for flying, Essence was pouring into my domain like a river. Ley lines were collecting Essence and Mana, and I was absorbing everything I could hold. I was lucky that I had access to this extra power because every time a totem was placed by my Goblins, a rush of power left me and created a new area under my influence. As the army slowly moved further and further from me, more power was needed for me to take control of the space pinned by the totems. Without all of my various systems for power collection, I would have spread myself far too thin and been rendered totally useless.

The war was continuing apace, and Essence was moving into and out of me as huge sheets of power. Totally exhausting! For a human, it would be like sprinting a mile at maximum exertion, puking, then suddenly being full of vigor and forced to run at top speed again. When the battle turned subterranean, I lost sight of the conflict for several minutes. When they finally reached a good spot, the Goblins sank a totem into the ground and activated it. I knew something was different as soon as my influence began to spread. Instead of sweeping into the area and expanding like gas in a container, *something* tried to attack and absorb my aura.

<I don't *think* so, you raggedy, little demon-hole!> I shouted at the pathetic dungeon trying to eat *me*. <You want to fight? Let's *fight!*>

Essence exploded outward from the totem as I forced more and more into the area. All of it converted to influence, powering up my aura. The dungeon in my way... blinked? It didn't seem to have a very good handle on its own aura and struggled to shape itself into a defensive formation. I stopped using Essence and instead began sinking Mana into my aura. Screaming in pain as the exceedingly powerful Mana impacted it, the dungeon I was invading fractured and lost a chunk of territory. I quickly filled the room and began drinking down the excessive infernal Essence in the area.

<Bob, I broke its hold in this area. If anyone is fighting you right now, they are doing it under their own power. There will be no help from the dungeon, so press forward! You need to get those totems in place in each room; it will help me stabilize myself. As you get closer to the dungeon's seat of power, I may need you to place more than one so that I have a greater foothold.> A new totem began to form, painfully slowly. <I'm going to make you some extras right now so that I don't need to do it while fighting. Try to keep people away from this area for a moment so their auras don't get in the way!>

The Goblins rapidly formed a perimeter, blocking all the non-initiated from entering the area. I quickly created every extra totem they should need; 'quickly' being relative in this case. The necromancers in the area sent wave after wave of undead against the room our front line was holding, obviously trying to reclaim it for the infernal dungeon. The dead seemed a little strange, a little too smooth featured and... *not* rotten... to have been real people. I nodded in understanding as I realized that they were made by the dungeon. An interesting idea—create creatures and let them be controlled by other people. That would let you get around their need for sustenance via Essence... Maybe I could convince Dale to be a bunny summoner? Later, later.

Totems complete, the war band rolled forward once again. As the leading edge turned the corner, a burst of dark hellfire roared down the tunnel. Anyone caught in the flames was reduced to a charred husk, and we lost *easily* a dozen Goblins. I hated that the Goblins were considered more expendable than the humans they were traveling with, but it did make sense tactically. I could re-create the Goblins, but the humans and assorted sentients would need to be bound to me *and* have granted me a full mapping of their memories if they were to be resurrected. That was a rare combination.

I 'caught' the hellfire when it entered my influence, draining the Essence away and making the flames sputter to nothingness. Yum. I felt bad that there was so little I could help with, but it was up to the army to set those totems up so I could take part in the fight. Looking over the allied forces, I did a double take when I saw a Goblin collapse after taking no noticeable damage. What the...? He looked perfectly healthy! Oh... *perfectly* healthy. I pointed him out to another Goblin, who went over to him and pulled on the 'thorn' that was stuck into his body. The fallen Goblin's eyes fluttered open after a moment, only to see a large steak dangling in front of his nose. He grabbed it and started devouring it like, well... like a starving Goblin. Messy. Before moving forward again, any Goblin with a healing Rune was checked and fed.

Allowing the army to pause so long may have been a mistake. A posse of demons sprinted into the room followed by what *must* have been an A-rank necromancer. The oppressive aura he exuded forced anyone under the Mage ranks to freeze in place, trembling uncontrollably as the demons began a wholesale slaughter. Fifty people in the crowd were dead before the Mages in our army counterattacked. A sparkle of light announced that Nez was fighting, and a demon fell in half as the sword-wielding speedster moved past him. Now, this didn't kill or banish the demon, but it did slow him down enough that he was easy prey for a crossbow that fired demon-banishing bolts.

A ripple of celestial energy moved through the room, freeing the people caught in the oppressive aura. My people rallied, emboldened by the morale boost that followed while the demons faltered and hissed as the diametrically opposed power washed over them. Father Richard stepped forward, joy etched on his face as celestial Mana moved through him. "Demons, your time tainting this plane has come to an end. If it were possible, I would end your suffering. Sadly, all I can do is return you to the plain of despair, the abyss, as you await judgment for your crimes. I know this human waste called a necromancer is not your master, as Sonder tells me that your bond is held by another."

The power in his voice held the entire battlefield enraptured. "*Your master has broken a sacred taboo and will pay for his crimes against the world by joining you upon the plains of despair,*" he began to chant, "*but it is not this way among you. Whoever wishes to become great among you shall be your servant. Whoever calls upon the darkness to destroy another shall be returned to the darkness. The mighty shall be pulled to captivity, and those that do his bidding shall descend with him!*"

A lance of golden Mana moved through the room too fast to avoid, piercing the four remaining demons. The Mana then moved past them, racing through stone and dirt to find the man who had summoned these foul creatures. Four golden beams impacted the man, and a shimmering pentagram formed, linking all of the beings. Between one breath and the next, all five vanished into the abyss. A terrified wail floated down the tunnels to the army.

The A-rank necromancer was trembling in rage, looking at the shining priest. "You will *pay* for that! You sent a man to the *abyss!*"

"He paid his own price. As will you," Richard stated coldly. The shaken necromancer began attacking, and dark rings began swirling around him. Anyone unfortunate enough to be caught by a ring started to rot away at a terrifying pace. If they died before their body was gone, they rose again as undead and started attacking the gathered people.

Now, one Mage against an army sounds like a swift death for the Mage, right? This would be true in most cases, but an A-rank Mage is the equal of at least ten B-rank Mages. In the confining sewer, this Mage could easily block the entire force indefinitely. At the A-ranks, there was no need for food or sleep. The only way to stop him was to match him, and besides Father Richard, there were only two A-rank Mages in the army of the living: Madame Chandra and High Magous Amber. Amber had stayed on the mountain to recover her strength; the portal she created to destroy the main forces of the dead had cost her much of her Mana reserves. Chandra made her way to the fight as Richard and the other Mages worked desperately to fend off the advancing necromancer.

Walking forward, Chandra seemed to change. Those who didn't know her looked on in confusion; those who truly *did* know her looked on in fear. Plants were writhing around her, and they grew with every step she took. Vines completely wrapped her like an elegant uniform, and large, leafy plants hung behind her like wings. She started jogging faster. A tree grew from her wrist, transforming first into a thorn and then into a beautiful, massive sword. A stump grew in a circle on her other arm, elongating and becoming a polished wooden shield. The leaves on her back stretched, and she lifted into the air, moving at high speeds.

A blur slammed into the necromancer, who was now coated in darkness and hovering a foot off the floor. The dark rings around him attempted to constrict around the flying rainforest but failed as she moved out of their range. Chandra shouted at the necromancer, "It doesn't need to be like this! We don't *need* to be at war! Tell him that we can make peace! Tell him his revenge has been taken! What more can he want?"

A voice responded from the blot of inky blackness, echoing like it came from a deep well, "What more? *What more?* What *don't* we want? So *his* revenge is realized! So *his* plans are nearing completion! What about the *rest of us?* Unlike you, he cares for us and will ensure our place in the world! We will go from the lowest class of person, hiding, scurrying like *rats*, to the Kings! Dukes! Princes! The world is *ours*, Dark Valkyrie!" His laughter was loud and manic, then wet as roots exploded through his skin. In moments, he was fertilizer for the plants that had been embedded in him during the first attack.

Chandra landed softly on the ground, shaking her head. "I need to hear it from *him*. If only he would have ignored the 'screens' telling him what to do. He could have done great things for his people."

"What are you talking about?" Father Richard limped over to Chandra, blessing the bodies that he passed.

"When he was young, I knew 'The Master'," Chandra spit the title. "He was normal, intelligent. He opened my eyes to the plight of men in the city. All my life, I was told that men were only useful for a few things, and otherwise, they were barely tolerated. Like cattle. Then one day he told me about a 'screen' that appeared in his vision. Practically overnight, he was a powerful cultivator. He moved through the ranks faster even than Dale has. Of course, even though I didn't tell on him, he was found out. It didn't matter that he wasn't a necromancer; men were forbidden to cultivate. Long story short, he was the cause of the first necromantic war and the reason men in this land now wear slave collars."

"Long story short? That's a huge leap! That's like saying a child lost his sweets, one thing led to another, and a continent was plunged into war! Do you know why he did all of this?" Richard glanced at her sharply as he finished consecrating the bodies piled knee high around him.

"I don't." She groaned as she looked at the devastation. "I will stop him though. One way or another."

"He isn't here," Adam called to the Mages. When they looked at him curiously, he shrugged. "He wasn't here earlier, and the Portal Mages cut off and then *destroyed* the portal system in this area. Unless he has a different way of crossing the continent, he isn't here."

The army started moving again, not encountering much resistance for nearly a mile of twisting tunnels. Rooms were cleared, totems were set, and the army was refreshed. They turned one final corner and entered the heart of the dungeon. This was a massive room where all waste had once flowed to since it would be washed away by a river that cut through the space. On the other side of the river, an altar was safeguarded by the necromantic army. Thousands of undead swarmed the room, controlled by demons and necromancers alike. A huge ritual was underway, and if Amber had been present, she would have been able to tell the group that the necromancers were preparing a one-way portal.

There was shock on the faces of the living people, and my Goblins were preparing themselves for death. Outnumbered by a huge margin, they could only pray for a miracle.

CHAPTER FORTY-ONE

<Set up the totems, Bob.> My words caused Bob to jump. He grabbed four totem poles and slammed them into the rock. His strength was so great, and the floor was so brittle that the totems were easily planted. My influence in the area began to grow, but this was the seat of the infernal dungeon's power. It was crushing my attempts to expand, protecting its defenders and creations. I stubbornly set myself against it. <More totems, Bob.>

Weapons were drawn, and the dead started charging at our meager defensive line. More of our people were arriving, but the tunnels were fairly narrow. Bob kept slamming the totems into the ground, and they connected their power together as he did so. Soon, I was able to gain a foothold. I *slammed* Mana into the room, and the infernal dungeon's hold on the entryway shattered like glass. We owned the land up to the river now. Unfortunately, the dungeon must have already been in the Mage ranks, or else I'd have shattered its Core with that blow. My Mana began to suffuse the area, and I made it available to Bob as a weapon.

Tyler's oddities were coming into play in interesting ways. The arrows he created flew into the mass of dead and exploded with holy fire, seemingly blessed by clerics and infused with celestial Essence. The Dwarves were assembling the siege weapons they had brought with them, and the Amazons were standing on the front lines with my Berserkers. The first wave of the dead reached us and drove directly through the people in the way. Completely overwhelming us, it looked like they would push to the mouth of the tunnel when Chandra strode into the room like an avenging angel.

Her sword grew and became as flexible as a whip. With every swing, scores of bodies were dismembered, and chunks were falling to the ground. Seeds flew from her, planting themselves in bodies and growing at astounding rates. Whatever she attacked soon had plants growing in it, the voracious plants eating all the flesh touched. This denied the abominations food, and they had to begin eating the dead that hadn't been damaged in order to grow stronger.

More Mages began to pile into the room, supporting Chandra. All fighters under the B-ranks were assigned to holding off the lesser undead, eliminating the distractions as the Mages began fighting abominations, demons, and necromantic Mages. The air was thick with power, but the Necromancers began draining it of usable Mana and feeding it into the portal that was growing near the altar.

"Soon, The Master shall arrive, and all of your pathetic death throes shall have been for naught!" a Necromancer helpfully screamed at the army. He yelped as the ground beneath him exploded, tossing him backward and into a plant. The plant began feasting on him as he screamed. Being infused with Mana, the potency of Chandra's plants was not to be trifled with.

Dale gasped happily as he stood back. His earth shattering technique had been more effective than he had been able to manage in the past. Reaching into his pocket, a burst of Essence flowed into him. His breathing evened out, and he began punching the undead with renewed vigor. Every blow was followed with either a wave of fluid as Dale's battle gauntlet activated or a slight drain of the Essence keeping the undead moving. He didn't know it, but by draining the undead, he was draining the necromancer connected to the walking carcass. After yet another corpse fell, drained of all Essence, an entire segment of the dead fell. The necromancer controlling them had fallen unconscious from Essence loss! Must have been in the low C-ranks...

This was going too easily for us. I looked over the remaining necromancers, studying them quickly. What the abyss? *This* was the great force protecting a necromantic dungeon? Most of the living people were in the low to mid C-ranks with a few B-ranks and a single remaining A-ranked Mage. Suddenly, the purpose of the portal was clear. The main troops weren't here! They were off subjugating the world or some other nonsense. An attack upon a defeated city, which should have been their foothold, was entirely unexpected!

I laughed wholeheartedly as I poured Mana into a spell formation Bob was creating, allowing it to pull ambient Mana from the room. The Mages working the portal stumbled as they suddenly had to double the resources they were devoting to the tear in the world. Bob's spell landed in the midst of a group of C-ranked necromancers, and the undead they were controlling fell to the ground. The Mages in our army rushed forward into the gap, reaching the necromancers and engaging in direct combat with them. They fell in droves, weaker in close combat than expected. Too much time devoted to summoning things to fight instead of training themselves, I suppose.

The last A-ranked Mage in the area stepped away from the portal, leaving its creation up to the remaining necromancers. He charged into the fray, and his first blow slapped Chandra away, leaving her buried in the stone of the wall across the room. She struggled to escape as Frank stepped forward to engage the threat.

"Come on, ya pissant little body-snatcher!" Frank growled at the unamused Mage. "Let's see ya get in a hit!"

Frank bounded forward, greatsword flashing forward faster than an arrow. The A-ranker tried to swing at him, only to have Frank bark 'Redirect!' at him. The force behind the necromancer's blow transferred to enhance Frank's swing, and the dark Mage got to experience what being buried in the wall felt like.

The Mage made the wall around him crumble and sprinted forward. Frank planned his strike and roared, 'Stop!'. The Mage was too powerful for Frank's law to fully affect him, but he did stumble at an opportune moment. The greatsword came down, and the Mage had his head buried in the stone below him.

The red-faced necromancer pushed himself up and pointed at Frank. "Blight!" An orb of darkness appeared in his open hand, and the Mage slammed it into Frank's chest. Blood shot out of Frank's mouth, and he dropped to his knees. The people behind him could see directly through Frank's chest. A hole the approximate size and shape of the necromancer's hand had appeared, and darkness was spreading over the remainder of his body.

"Frank!" Dale screamed across the room. "No!"

"Frank, yes." The Mage locked eyes with Dale as he mocked him. He stepped past the corpse at his feet and strode toward the encroaching army. "Time to deal with the rest of the rats." He raised his hands, and his head fell to the ground, a look of glee still etched on his face.

Brianna appeared next to the body, punting the head away. "That's why we get paid the big coins for assassinations."

Dale ran over to Frank, but his body was already crumbling away. Brianna caught Dale, keeping him from touching the blighted chunks remaining. "Careful! That might spread to you!"

"Frank...!" Dale cried out.

"Is already gone," Brianna firmly stated. "Don't let his sacrifice be in vain!"

<Dani!> The remaining necromancers had completed the portal and grabbed the dungeon Core. A Mana leash attached to a limp Dani pulled the Wisp along as the Mages attempted to flee.

DALE

Dale heard the dungeon cry out in anguish and leaped into motion without thinking through the full ramifications of his actions. He charged at the Mages that were entering the portal, grabbing an overly potent Core from his pocket as he did so. This Core was from the celestial type golem and was full of celestial-attuned Mana. Having no knowledge of celestial techniques, Dale simply tried to activate the earth shattering technique while running celestial Essence through it.

As the string of celestial Essence left his hand—pointed at the Mages—he shattered the Core and infused all of the Mana into the attack. The Mana arched to the portal and impacted it, but the celestial power failed to cancel out the infernal type powering the portal as Dale had intended. Instead, the portal hummed and shifted colors. The light in it grew brighter, and it seemed to stabilize. The remaining power returned to Dale and was absorbed.

"Ha hah!" There were only one Mage and four C-ranked necromancers remaining in front of the portal. "Thank you for stabilizing this. I thought we were going to be stuck here!"

They jumped through the portal, and the dead dropped to the ground, no longer animated by another's will. The vast chamber was quiet except for the wails of the wounded. Of all the possible outcomes, no one had thought the enemy would *run*! The veterans of many battles groaned; this would mean potentially *decades* of hunting down pockets of necromantic filth. Then they remembered that the main forces they were against hadn't even *been* here and whined louder.

<Dani! No! I was *so* close!> Dale's heart ached for the dungeon. He grimaced. His heart *really* ached for the dungeon. He coughed, and blood splattered on the ground.

"What... what's happening?" He coughed again, then vomited as blood shot from his mouth.

"Dale!" Brianna gripped him, trying to steady the sick man. "What's the matter? Why are you bleeding? Did you get wounded?"

Trying to understand the issue, Dale closed his eyes and attempted to look inside himself. He failed at his attempt. He tried to move Essence to his hands and again failed. Hands shaking, he looked up at Brianna. "Why can't I feel my Essence?"

Brianna's eyes glowed, and horror crossed her face. "Dale! Your affinity channels... they're collapsing! You used Mana somehow, didn't you? Your body is shutting down; some Mana got into your system, and your center can't handle it. Your... Core? You have a Core? Never mind, it's breaking!"

"So I'm dead no matter what I do?" Dale looked at Brianna with fear-filled eyes.

"No! We can get you to a cleric, we can–" Brianna lied as fast as she could open her mouth.

"I see." Dale stood up, nodded at her, and shoved her backward. Only because she was stunned by his actions did it affect her at all. The dungeon couldn't help him, and Dale knew it *wouldn't* help him if he lost his Wisp again. There was only one option. He turned and dove through the humming portal.

"After him!" Hans screamed in panic from across the room. Dale's team and Madame Chandra ran, jumping through the portal after their leader. Brianna stood looking at the portal for a long moment.

"Oh, you fools," she whispered in a heartbroken tone.

CHAPTER FORTY-TWO

Dale landed on the soft ground, grass tickling the sensitive skin on his face. He painfully forced himself to his feet, looking around. Blinking at the bright moonlight, Dale tried to discern where the necromancers could have gotten off to. The only sound was wind, but his glances revealed that he was on a mountain overlooking a shadowy forest. Had they escaped down past the tree line already?

Looking at where he had come from, a portal still hung empty in the air. Good. He could escape if he returned. Dale looked at the ground and finally got a hint as to where the others had gone. There were footprints in the dirt, and the grass had been bent in a specific manner that only happens when someone barges through it without knowing how to cover their tracks. Dale laughed even as blood dribbled down his chin. His training to be a Baron was all pointless now. All the math in the world couldn't help him; his knowledge of state dinners and dancing was pointless. His years as a sheepherder though, the tracking skills he had used to find lost lambs and avoid dangers, those would let him pursue his quarry.

He started trotting along the trail, confused at the signs he was finding. The trail was fairly obvious but looked at least a couple hours old. Dale worried that he may be following the wrong group, but what else could he do? He sped up, trying to think of how he would take Dani back from a freaking *Mage* as he was *dying*. As the predawn light began to brighten, Dale looked around and shivered. It was *way* too beautiful of a day for this. He felt like it should be raining, possibly snowing. That would have fit the mood much better.

Dale slowed as voices echoed down to him. "It's been hours! If they were going to come after us, they would have long ago!"

It seemed the necromancers were fighting amongst themselves. Perfect. Dale sunk to his knees and crawled as quietly as he could through the long grass. He left the path behind, trying to come upon the group at an angle they weren't expecting.

"At least let me try to contact The Master!" Dale could see a dark form silhouetted against the sky. "He may be able to open another portal to us or at least give us instructions!"

"No!" This command had hints of Mana in it and made Dale shiver in fear. "We... hee-hee, we have our orders!" The Mage seemed to be in a good mood and was maliciously grinning. "If we escape to somewhere safe, we re-plant the dungeon and take care of it!"

"It's basically powerless at this point, though! It had to sacrifice all of its power when we removed it from the dungeon! It'll be back in the D-rankings, at best!"

"So we get more *offerings* to power it up!" Spittle flew from the Mage's mouth, making the man arguing with him wipe his face. "We have a dungeon, which *we* now control! Let's make the best of it!"

While they obviously didn't fully agree, the others slowly moved to comply with the powerful person. Dale waited patiently as they gathered large, flat stones. After making an altar similar to what had been in the sewers—if a bit rough—they placed the dungeon Core on the rocks and poured a bit of their blood on it. Dale saw Dani attempt to avoid the rough men, flying in painfully slow circles to try and stay out of their way.

"Poor thing," Dale thought sadly, watching the Wisp. Dale started feeling even weaker, like his Core was leaking

Essence. If he didn't move soon, he wouldn't be able to. The Mage was the biggest threat, but if they would just be distracted for a *moment*, he would be able to do something. Dale's eyes bulged. He tried to cover his mouth, but he couldn't stop the chest-wracking cough as blood sprayed from his lips.

A rough hand grabbed Dale, lifting him into the air. "And *what* do we have here?"

"What is it?" the frantic Mage called nervously. "Did they find us?"

"Looks like we have a visitor!" The rank breath of his captor made Dale gag. He tried to swat at the man, but he was barely able to move his arms fast enough to hit the man. Obviously, the attack was ineffectual. "Ha, looks like we caught a fishy!"

"Perfect!" the Mage shrieked, coming toward them with long strides. "Bring him to the altar! He will help us wake the dungeon up!"

Struggling as hard as he could was ineffective; Dale may as well have been a child. The Mage was soon looming above him, smiling happily. "You won't understand this, but you are about to help us save the world!"

Dale screamed as the knife the man was holding came down, aimed for his heart. The knife impacted his chest, and Dale felt several ribs break from the force of the stab. The Mage's grin faltered. "Why aren't you dead?" The knife came again. Dale screamed again as more bones broke. "How odd! What tough skin you have!"

"Is his armor stopping the knife?" A C-ranked necromancer looked at the Mage askance.

"Of course it is! Don't question my strength or you will be able to gauge it firsthand!" The Mage looked malevolently at Dale. "I don't know who you are or how you got armor capable of stopping a blow from a Mage, but it doesn't matter! Strip him!" The cultivators grabbed Dale, roughly pulling off all of his armor. No matter how they tried though, they could not figure out how to remove his battle gauntlets.

"Forget it! We will take them off his carcass!" The Mage shoved aside one of the men and stabbed Dale in the leg. This time, the blade went through easily. Dale could barely manage a scream; the pain was too mind breaking. "There we go! That's more like it! Lay him on the altar!"

Dale was pressed down on the stone, looking right up at the glowing form of Dani. He smiled at her and whispered, "Dani. Run away *fast*, Dani. Tell Cal I kept my promise." Dani stilled, looking down tiredly at the man below her. She didn't understand what she was seeing as the knife rose into the air.

"...Dale?" the Wisp managed to ask.

As the knife came down to sacrifice him, Dale gripped the infernal Core by his side. No longer able to use Dale as a power source, the gauntlet wrapped itself around the gifted Core and *squeezed*. *Bamph!* The Core shattered with a soundless scream of agony, and the Essence that managed to escape the wrapped folds burned through Dale's skin.

The knife stopped falling, and the Mage listened to the shards of the broken Core *ping* off the stone altar. "No! No, no, *no*!" he shrieked at Dale's almost-still form. Realizing his mistake, he swiftly looked around for the Wisp, only to see it flying away at unmatchable speeds, refreshed by an influx of Essence. "*No*!"

He stabbed Dale, over and over again. "No! You filthy thief! You've killed us all! You... you *thief*!" He was screaming now and continuing to stab the dying body on the altar. Seeing Dale dying too swiftly, he cursed and infused him with infernal Mana. Now Dale was temporarily trapped in his body and aware of his surroundings. The Mage kept stabbing, until instead of a *squish*, he heard a *clink*. The sound was enough to break him out of his impotent rage, and he swiftly cut Dale's chest open.

"A Core? A Core! You had a Core in you? And it is already attuned to you?" The Mage began laughing as he looked at the gem in his hand. "Looks a bit damaged, but I can fix that..." He muttered a few words, and the Core, which was about to fall apart, was coated by a thin layer of Mana. The Essence that had been escaping instead returned, infused into the Core, and made minor repairs to the interior. Now there were no cracks on the outside, though the inside was still heavily damaged.

"Good, good," the Mage muttered. He looked at Dale's body which was beginning to cool as Dale's soul struggled to flee. The dark Mage laughed breathlessly as he saw the pain the soul was in.

"Oh no you don't!" The nasal, phlegmy voice of the necromancer shattered the silence. He loomed over the broken, tortured body Dale was fleeing. "Dying won't let you off the hook! Hee hee hee! Stealing from me was the worst decision you ever made! Now you will *serve* me, *beg me*," he screamed, spittle flying; his mood shifted abruptly, as madmen's are prone to do, "to free you because of your own stupidity! Ha ha ha!" A smile was back on his face, though his eyes were manic and unfocused.

With his declaration and an arcane gesture, pain shattered Dale's confused senses—pain more traumatizing than his recent death by repeated stabbing. "Welcome to your eternity, thief," the malicious voice spit at the Core in his hand. Then he coughed at the Core, spitting again. Wait... spit isn't red?

Tom

Tom landed flat on his face and had the wind knocked out of him by the others landing on his back. They all got up at various speeds until, finally, Tom was able to wheeze in a breath. "Dale! Where are you?" Tom bellowed, only to get whacked on the head by Chandra.

"Stop that!" she ordered demandingly. "There is a clear trail. Let's hurry."

The group began running up the trail, Chandra staying with them though she could have gone much faster. They were expecting to fall into the lair of The Master and so were looking for traps at every interval. A light suddenly appeared, bright even in the pre-dawn light. They prepared for a spell, but instead, it stopped a few feet from them.

"Hurry!" a tiny voice yelled at them tiredly. "They have Dale! They're *killing* him!"

"Lead us to him!" Hans stepped forward and nearly begged the Wisp.

"I... I can't. I'm so weak, starved, tortured." The Wisp began floating toward the portal. "Must get to Cal..."

"Abyss take it!" Adam swore vehemently as he started running up the slope. "Hurry!"

They raced up the incline but certainly arrived too late. Chandra grabbed a few of Rose's arrows, infused Mana into them, and threw them at the group of distracted necromancers. The arrows flew true and sprouted hungry roots as soon as they were in the bodies. The roots were meant to stop the bleeding so the target would experience every sensation until death, and the pain made them all spasm for long moments before dying. Tom saw a glimmer as something was flung from the twisted hand of their leader.

"Filthy necromancers!" Tom roared an earth-shattering cry, his voice almost unrecognizable in his grief. Distaste was evident in every motion he made, and he kicked a body and yelled at the others, "Make sure to burn their rotten corpses and everything they have with them. It is sure to be tainted by the infernal!" He glanced toward where Dale's body lay broken and covered with blood and filth.

"Poor bastard. I'm sorry we weren't fast enough... to save you," he managed to say brokenly, keeping his voice low in an attempt to preserve morale in his team. Mixed emotions skittered across his face before finally settling on anger. He then turned and began barking orders, "Take his body. We'll give him a proper burial. His armor too. The Mithril in there can be used for any number of purposes. Let's... let's get back."

CAL

I struggled to direct enough Mana into the room for me to reach the portal. I was *very* glad I did, as I was barely able to prop it open. It had almost collapsed and was now taking a huge amount of power to keep open. A bit of my influence crept through the tear in space, and I almost was sick from the vertigo I was experiencing. I struggled to understand why it was affecting me so badly when my soul connected to something in the distance, and I forgot everything else. To my surprise, it wasn't Dani that held my attention. I knew this place. I knew it intimately. This... this was a portal through time! I was connecting to... myself?

A part of my soul, a part I hadn't even realized was missing, integrated into my aura. I was suddenly in Dale's mind as he was dying. I watched as Dale was tortured for me and would have cried if it were possible when he told Dani that he kept his promise. As Dale's mind and soul was sucked into his Core—the same Core I had originally resided within—I realized that *this* was my origin. Dale was turning into *me*. As I watched Dale... myself... die, I realized that I had a monumental choice to make. I could keep the portion of my soul I had lost so long ago, or I could leave it with Dale and allow him to grow with all of his memories intact. I could allow my youngest self to be a complete being.

But... I hesitated. How different would I be today if I had kept my memories, my human morals, or my sense of self as a person? I likely wouldn't have survived to become what I now was as a dungeon. Reluctantly, I did what I must have done before, separating all of those memories from my soul of that time, pulling the soul-shard back, and absorbing it into myself. I felt like a terrible person. Time loops suck.

I now had all of Dale's... *my* memories. I knew everything he did, and I want to say it changed me. I really want to say it made me a more compassionate person... but it didn't. Having my unsegmented soul did make me more complete, but the memories I gained were like those I gained from a memory stone. Me... but also *not* me. I pulled away and watched as the Core that was *me* fall from the hand of the necromancer and disappear into the deep crevasse. I glanced around, nostalgic for this moment. The sun was pouring across the ground like a viscous liquid, the air temperature was perfect for comfort... Gorgeous. I had been correct back then. It truly was too beautiful a day to die.

CHAPTER FORTY-THREE

I kept holding the portal open and studied it as I waited for anyone to come back through. My insight into time and space jumped by leaps and bounds as I existed on both sides of time simultaneously. It was such an interesting portal and had only come into being through the power of chaos. The intermixing of infernal and celestial had created an interspatial flux. This was an uncontrollable portal, something that couldn't be replicated intentionally. Such is the power of chaos, I suppose.

I noticed a light in my influence and glanced over to see Dani, Hans, and the rest all come through the tear in space at almost the same time, though Dani had entered it over an hour before the others. Time seemed to have been running faster on the other side of the portal. They all fell, complaining savagely as the air was knocked out of them. They should be happy that they didn't all explode or mesh into a single being! Crazy people, jumping through random portals. Dale's body dropped to the floor, and if I hadn't had my new knowledge, I would have let them keep the body for a memorial service. Instead, I quickly absorbed my discarded husk.

Wait a second... *Dani came through the portal?* My mind screeched to a halt as my bond to her reconnected. Her light slowly started to shine brighter, and she began moving faster.

"Cal!" her tiny, perfect voice called out.

<*Dani!*> I screamed in joy, causing all beings connected to me to break into an uncontrollable smile. Point in fact, the Royals had gone to free captives and were now grinning at the necromancers that were living their last few moments. The

legend of the 'Smiling Battle Tyrants' grew exponentially during this fight for freedom.

"*Cal!*" she happily screamed, flying toward my mountain at great speed. She exited the sewers as a blur, only growing faster as she got closer to me. She kept emitting brighter light as more potent Essence entered her body. "You've gotten so strong!"

<I'm a Mage now!>

"*What!*" she exclaimed, moving even faster. "You're amazing! I need to hear all about it!"

<I need to hear all about *you*! What happened? Are you safe? Whole? I missed you so much!> Again, I would be crying if it were possible. She was above the mountain now and briefly stopped.

"You... you brought *the entire mountain*?" she admonished, half awed and half horrified.

<You really shouldn't leave me alone for long periods of time,> I sheepishly rebutted.

"I *love* you!" she bawled, flying down to the portal system. I approved. Going through the tunnels would be *far* too slow. She burst into my Core room, barely sparing a glance for the golems and paths. She reached the Silverwood tree as I registered her words.

<*I love you too!*> Unknowingly, she had entered my area of greatest influence. The Essence in her body glowed even brighter, and as I proclaimed my love for her, the Essence was replaced with Mana. A beam of light linked us like it did the day we met, and our souls were reintegrated and healed. The light connecting us passed through pollen that was falling from the Silverwood tree, subtly changing it into something greater. At that moment, we experienced the effect that Elves the world over were looking for, the greatest ability of Silverwood pollen. The

Essence that had been in her body was mingled with mine and condensed. A tiny, purple Wisp coalesced next to Dani, slowly floating around. It seemed confused. I was more confused. Dani seemed shaken.

<Um. Dani? What just happened?>

"I... I think we just had a child!" We watched the tiny Wisp explore her new home. Oh right, apparently, the Wisp was female. I have no idea how I knew this. The whole 'no external genitalia' thing was coming into play again here.

<What... uh... what do we do?> I was a bit shell shocked to suddenly have a child. This was rather unexpected.

"We teach her and love her, and... we should probably name her?" Dani ended the last as a question.

<She is moving so gracefully... She's beautiful. A true blessing...> I was more connected to Dani than ever before, and I knew that our bond of Mana would allow me to reach out to her no matter where she was in the world. Not that anyone would ever survive another attempt to steal her, so it didn't *really* matter.

"Perfect. Grace. I love the name!" Dani made her final decision and named our child before I was even able to register what had happened.

I watched the tiny copy of Dani moving around and had to nod. <I agree. It fits her well!>

DALE

Dale's eyes fluttered open, and the beautiful Silverwood tree was the first image he saw. "Mmm. Peaceful." He sighed contentedly. It was at that point that his memory started coming back to him.

More and more memories came to him—in fact, everything that he and the dungeon knew. He felt no fear anymore, no worry. He fully opened his mind, connecting to... himself.

"So *this* is why we couldn't stand each other?" Dale stated with a wry voice. "We were too similar?"

<Looks like. You were the baseline for my personality. You did everything for greed, you were only nice to a select few people, and you had an enormous capacity for Essence control.> Dale nodded as he heard this, knowing that he was not receiving an admonition but a compliment.

"How did you make me a distinct personality? You've never been able to copy your mind into another Core before." Dale was starting to get a slight headache from all the information he had to filter through. "Oh, wait... I know this, too."

<You should. We only started diverging into individuals again after you were created. I'll state it anyway, just in case some of the information doesn't make sense. You were a missing part of my soul, and because of that, I was unable to transfer a complete copy of my memories. With your death at my birth, I regained the missing fragments of my soul, and I had two choices. I could either make dungeons, clones of myself, or I could recreate you,> I explained carefully. This was a tricky subject to understand.

"And making clones of yourself would eventually devolve into competition with yourself," Dale took over the story while nodding. "So you shifted thought patterns and made me the dominant personality for this body."

<Well said, me.>

"Why, thank you, me!" The air was full of chuckles for a moment. "That explains why our humor has always been so perfect."

<Right? Listen, there are some drawbacks.>

"I know. I'm going to be stuck in your aura until I am able to generate Mana. No leaving the city for a few years." Dale shrugged expansively. "So what's different for me? I know what you know, so I'll be able to progress at a much faster rate. I finally have *my* cultivation technique back." He gave a mock glare at the floor.

<Ha! Took you long enough to get it. I have to say, I laughed at all your failed attempts to get the memory stones you were entitled to from the Dark Elves.>

"Oh, yeah, those Runes they have on their buildings are insidious. I'm going to need those stones though. I can't exactly use all the ambient Essence in your aura. I need to learn to use Essence and Mana as a human." Dale's brow furrowed. "Should be interesting. Compare notes every once in a while? I'd like to find ways to merge how we use our power. Perhaps we can find a way to keep you safer or make us more powerful by doing so."

<I like that. You know, you are going to be much stronger than a normal human of your ranking. Which, by the way, I was unable to boost. You have different requirements that I don't know how to work around, like boosting your aura. When you find what you need to do, talk to me, and I'll help you out. Also, try not to blow out your meridians in the future. That memory sucked. All in all, though, I think you and I will get along a *whole* lot better now.>

"I think you are correct."

<Want to meet our daughter?>

"Wait, what?"

EPILOGUE

"Well, what do *you* propose we do?" Father Richard glared at the assembled people. The council had gathered, but without Dale to force them to get along, they were becoming quite fractious. Since there was no clear leader for the city, many people were putting their hat in the ring.

"We need someone who can talk to the dungeon!" Minya spoke demandingly. She had been rescued by Prince Henry, having been taken captive and kept in Mana-sealing bindings by the necromancers. She was intended to be a sacrifice for the dungeon and would have been if the rescue had happened even a day later.

"He would have wanted someone who wasn't a *Mage* to run things!" Tyler shrewdly raised an eyebrow and quirked his lips. He was currently the favorite amongst the common people.

Amber snorted at him. "How would you propose to get the dungeon to move again? It has been two days, and here we sit in the middle of a ruined city."

"I can't believe this is happening *now*. He hasn't been gone a week!" Chandra chided the assemblage.

"We need a clear chain of command!" Richard thumped the table. For the city *and* the Guild! With Frank gone, we need another trustworthy Guild Leader to take his position!"

"*Ahem,*" a person clearing his throat tried to interrupt.

"The city needs to train these cultivators, and we need to sort out logistics to feed everyone," Richard continued speaking. "People are looking to us to *lead*, and we–"

"*Ahem!*"

"And someone *apparently* needs to go to a cleric to get a cough looked at!" Richard bellowed, turning toward the noisy individual. His next words died on his lips, as did all sound in the room.

Dale strode forward and took the empty seat at the table. "I think I can help a little with your leadership issues."

"Imposter!"

"Nope, it's really me." Dale smirked at the stunned faces. "What? Can't a guy die *again* and not be thought of as a fake?"

Amber gasped and pointed a shaking finger at him. "*Impossible!* He's real!"

This made many people stand and draw weapons. Dale waved his hands. "Whoa, whoa! What's the deal? Yes, I'm real, and yes, I'm Dale!"

"Prove it," the portal Mage, James, demanded with cold fury in his voice.

Dale looked at him, eyes sparkling with mischief. "Get off my mountain."

James forcefully turned and started jogging away. "Not again! I believe you! I believe you!"

"Come back!" Dale yelled as the people around him started laughing. The tension now broken and his legitimacy proven, it seemed Dale had a lot of explaining to do.

CAL

<It's official, Dani,> I stated smugly, happy to have my theories proven correct. <'Dale' is running around, completely separate from me. It is a little freaky to watch my body doing things without me. I am even more impressed with Bob now. I've never heard him complain about how strange this all is...>

"Just don't overextend yourself, Cal. I watched you working on your 'body' for the last couple days, and with *all* your memories, I think that Dale is going to be able to exploit a lot of things that other people would miss. I can imagine him needing a bit stronger armor and popping in and using a secret passage to get to a storage room." Dani was chasing after a speeding Grace, trying to keep her from running into walls as she laughed.

<I wouldn't cheat myself! There is no way that Dale would steal from... > I whined at her at first, then thought about it. <Maybe I shift all the tunnels a little.>

"Uh-huh," she commented dryly. It was good to have her back.

I took a deep breath, this time with actual lungs, and smiled grimly. The necromantic filth of this world had earned my anger and deserved retribution. They should run in terror, for I was coming for them. I looked at Dale as he went about his day. This 'Master' had gone way too far. He had stolen Dani and killed Dale. His servants had killed *me*. I was going to be the first person in history to take revenge for my own murder.

'The Master' was going to pay for his actions. Where Dale and the people seeking refuge on my mountain had earned my amity—a time of peace and my friendship—the only amity that would be granted to these necromancers... was a *Cala*mity.

Afterword

Thank you for reading! I hope you enjoyed Dungeon Calamity! Since reviews are the lifeblood of indie publishing, I'd love it if you could leave a positive review on Amazon! Please use this link to go to the Divine Dungeon: Dungeon Calamity Amazon product page to leave your review: geni.us/DungeonCalamity.

As always, thank you for your support! You are the reason I'm able to bring these stories to life.

The Divine Dungeon Universe

The Divine Dungeon

Dungeon Born (Book 1)

Dungeon Madness (Book 2)

Dungeon Calamity (Book 3)

Dungeon Desolation (Book 4)

Dungeon Eternium (Book 5)

The Completionist Chronicles

Ritualist (Book 1)

Regicide (Book 2)

Rexus (Book 2.5)

Raze (Book 3)

ABOUT DAKOTA KROUT

I live in a 'pretty much Canada' Minnesota city with my wife and daughter. I started writing The Divine Dungeon series because I enjoy reading and wanted to create a world all my own. To my surprise and great pleasure, I found like-minded people who enjoy the contents of my mind. Publishing my stories has been an incredible blessing thus far and I hope to keep you entertained for years to come!

Connect with Dakota:
Patreon.com/DakotaKrout
Facebook.com/TheDivineDungeon
Twitter.com/DakotaKrout

ABOUT MOUNTAINDALE PRESS

Dakota and Danielle Krout, a husband and wife team, strive to create as well as publish excellent fantasy and science fiction novels. Self-publishing *The Divine Dungeon: Dungeon Born* in 2016 transformed their careers from Dakota's military and programming background and Danielle's Ph.D. in pharmacology to President and CEO, respectively, of a small press. Their goal is to share their success with other authors and provide captivating fiction to readers with the purpose of solidifying Mountaindale Press as the place 'Where Fantasy Transforms Reality'.

Connect with Mountaindale Press:
MountaindalePress.com
Facebook.com/MountaindalePress
Twitter.com/_Mountaindale
Instagram.com/MountaindalePress
Krout@MountaindalePress.com

MOUNTAINDALE PRESS TITLES

GAMELIT AND LITRPG

The Completionist Chronicles Series
By: DAKOTA KROUT

A Touch of Power Series
By: JAY BOYCE

Red Mage: Advent
By: XANDER BOYCE

Ether Collapse: Equalize
By: RYAN DEBRUYN

Axe Druid Series
By: CHRISTOPHER JOHNS

Skeleton in Space: Histaff
By: ANDRIES LOUWS

Pixel Dust: Party Hard
By: DAVID PETRIE

APPENDIX

Adam – A mid-D-ranked cleric who joined Dale's group. He was corrupted by a massive influx of celestial Essence which may have given him powerful abilities.

Adventurers' Guild – A group from every non-hostile race that actively seeks treasure and cultivates to become stronger. They act as a mercenary group for Kingdoms that come under attack from monsters and other non-kingdom forces.

Affinity – A person's affinity denotes what element they need to cultivate Essence from. If they have multiple affinities, they need to cultivate all of those elements at the same time.

Affinity Channel – The pathway along the meridians that Essence flows through. Having multiple major affinities will open more pathways, allowing more Essence to flow into a person's center at one time.

Amber – The Mage in charge of the portal-making group near the dungeon. She is in the upper A rankings, which allows her to tap vast amounts of Mana.

Artificer – A person who devotes himself to creating powerful artifacts either by enchanting or inscribing them.

Assassin – A stealthy killer who tries to make kills without being detected by his victim.

Assimilator – A cross between a jellyfish and a Wisp, the Assimilator can float around and collect vast amounts of Essence. It releases this Essence as powerful elemental bursts. A pseudo-Mage, if you will.

Aura – The flows of Essence generated by living creatures which surround them and hold their pattern.

Bane – An F-ranked Boss Mob that is a giant mushroom. He can fire thorns and pull victims toward him with vines made of moss.

Basher – An evolved rabbit that attacks by head-butting enemies. Each has a small horn on its head that it can use to "bash" enemies.

Beast Core – A small gem that contains the Essence of Beasts.

>Flawed: An extremely weak crystallization of Essence that barely allows a Beast to cultivate, comparable to low F-rank.

>Weak: A weak crystallization of Essence that allows a Beast to cultivate, comparable to an upper F-rank.

>Standard: A crystallization of Essence that allows a Beast to cultivate well, comparable to the D-rankings.

>Strong: A crystallization of Essence that allows a Beast to cultivate very well, comparable to the lower C-rankings.

Beastly: A crystallization of Essence that allows a Beast to cultivate exceedingly well, comparable to the upper C-rankings.

Immaculate: An amalgamation of crystallized of Essence and Mana that allows a Beast to cultivate exceedingly well. Any Beast in the B-rankings or A-rankings will have this Core.

Luminous: A Core of pure spiritual Essence that is indestructible by normal means. A Beast with this core will be in at least the S-rankings, up to SSS-rank.

Radiant: A Core of Heavenly or Godly energies. A Beast with this Core is able to adjust reality on a whim.

Brianna – A Dark Elf princess that intends to build a city around the dungeon. She is a member of the council and knows that the dungeon is alive and sentient.

Cal – The heart of the Dungeon, Cal was a human murdered by Necromancers. After being forced into a soul gem, his identity was stripped as time passed. Now accompanied by Dani, he works to become stronger without attracting too much attention to himself. This may soon change.

Cats, Dungeon – There are several types:

Snowball: A Boss Mob, Snowball uses steam Essence to fuel his devastating attacks.

Cloud Cat: A Mob that glides along the air, attacking from positions of stealth.

Coiled Cat: A heavy Cat that uses metal Essence. It has a reinforced skeleton and can launch itself forward at high speeds.

Flesh Cat: This Cat uses flesh Essence to tear apart tissue from a short distance. The abilities of this Cat only work on flesh and veins and will not affect bone or harder materials.

Wither Cat: A Cat full of infernal Essence, the Wither Cat can induce a restriction of Essence flow with its attacks. Cutting off the flow of Essence or Mana will quickly leave the victim in a helpless state. The process is *quite* painful.

Catalyst – An item that allows an Inscription to be powered with less Essence.

Celestial – The Essence of Heaven, the embodiment of life and *considered* the ultimate good.

Center – The very center of a person's soul. This is the area Essence accumulates (in creatures that do not have a Core) before it binds to the lifeforce.

Chandra – Owner of an extremely well-appointed restaurant, this A-ranked Mage is the grandmother of Rose. She also spent a decade training the current Guild Master, Frank.

Chi spiral – A person's Chi spiral is a vast amount of intricately knotted Essence. The more complex and complete the pattern woven into it, the more Essence it can hold and the finer the Essence would be refined.

Cleric – A Cultivator of celestial Essence, a cleric tends to be support for a group, rarely fighting directly. Their main purpose in the lower rankings is to heal and comfort others.

Corruption – Corruption is the remnant of the matter that pure Essence was formed into. It taints Essence but allows beings to absorb it through open affinity channels. This taint has been argued about for centuries; is it the source of life or a nasty side effect?

Craig – A powerful C-ranked monk, Craig has dedicated his life to finding the secrets of Essence and passing on knowledge.

Currency values:
> Copper: one hundred copper coins are worth a silver coin
> Silver: one hundred silver coins are worth a gold coin
> Gold: one hundred gold coins were worth a platinum coin
> Platinum: the highest coin currency in the human kingdoms

Cultivate – Cultivating is the process of refining Essence by removing corruption then cycling the purified Essence into the center of the soul.

Cultivator – A cultivator is one who cultivates. See above. Seriously, it is the entry right before this one. I'm being all alphabetical here. Mostly.

Dale – Owner of the mountain the dungeon was found on, Dale is now a cultivator who attempts to not die on a regular basis. As a dungeon born person, he has a connection to the dungeon that he can never be rid of.

Dani – A *pink* Dungeon Wisp—Is that important?—Dani is the soul bound companion of Cal and acts as his moral compass and helper. She is also an integral portion of his psyche, and losing her would drive Cal into madness.

Dire – A prefix to a title that means "Way stronger than a normal version of this monster". Roughly. Kind of paraphrasing.

Distortion Cat – An upper C-ranked Beast that can bend light and create artificial darkness. In its home territory, it is attacked and bound by tentacle-like parasites that form a symbiotic relationship with it.

Dungeon Born – Being dungeon born means that the dungeon did not create the creature but gave it life. This gives the creature the ability to function autonomously without fear that the dungeon will be able to take direct control of its mind. The dungeon can "ride along" in a dungeon born creatures mind from any distance and may be able to influence the creature if it remains of a lower cultivation rank than the dungeon.

Dwarves – Stocky humanoids that like to work with stone, metal, and alcohol. Good miners.

Egil Nolsen – Known to the world as 'Xenocide', this man is of unknown ranking and fully insane.

Elves – A race of willowy humanoids with pointy ears. There are five main types:

> High Elves: The largest nation of Elvenkind, they spend most of their time as merchants, artists, or thinkers. Rich beyond any need to actually work, their King is an S-Ranked expert, and their cities shine with light and wealth. They like to think of themselves as 'above' other Elves, thus 'High' Elves.
>
> Wood Elves: Wood Elves live more simply than High-Elves, but have a greater connection to the earth and the elements. They are ruled by a council of S-ranked elders and rarely leave their woods. Though seen less often, they have great power. They grow and collect food and animal products for themselves and other Elven nations.
>
> Wild: Wild Elves are the outcasts of their societies. Basically feral, they scorn society, civilization, and the rules of others. They have the worst reputation of any of the races of Elves, practicing dark arts and infernal summoning. They have no homeland, living only where they can get away with their dark deeds.
>
> Dark: The Drow are known as Dark Elves. No one knows where they live, only where they can go to get in contact with them. Dark Elves also have a dark reputation as assassins and mercenaries for the other

races. The worst of their lot are 'Moon-Elves', the best-known assassins of any race. These are the Elves that Dale made a deal with for land and protection.

Sea: The Sea Elves live on boats their entire lives. They facilitate trade between all the races of Elves and man, trying not to take sides in conflicts. They work for themselves and are considered rather mysterious.

Enchantment – A *temporary* pattern made of Essence that creates an effect on the universe. Try not to get the pattern wrong as it could have... unintended consequences.

Essence – Essence is the fundamental energy of the universe, the pure power of heavens and earth that is used by the basic elements to become all forms of matter.

Father Richard – An A-ranked cleric that has made his living hunting demons and heretics. Tends to play fast and loose with rules and money.

Fighter – A generic archetype of a being that uses melee weapons to fight.

Frank – Guild Leader of the Adventurers' Guild. He has his Mana bound to the concept of kinetic energy and can stop the use of it, slowing or stopping others in place.

Glade – A Mini-Boss mushroom that uses tentacles and thorns to kill its prey.

Glitterflit – A Basher upgraded with celestial Essence, it has the ability to *mend* almost any non-fatal wound.

Hans – A cheeky assassin that has been with Dale since he began cultivating. He was a thief in his youth but changed lifestyles after his street guild was wiped out. He is deadly with a knife and is Dale's best friend.

Huggin – Brother of Jasper who sadly was transformed into a crow.

Impaler – A Basher upgraded with Infernal Essence, it has a sharpened horn on its head. At higher rankings, it gains the ability to coat that horn with hellfire.

Incantation – Essentially a spell, an incantation is created from words and gestures. It releases all of the power of an enchantment in a single burst.

Infected – A person or creature that has been infected with a rage-inducing mushroom growth. These people have no control of their bodies and attack any non-infected on sight.

Infernal – The Essence of death and demonic beings, *considered* to be always evil.

Inscription – A *permanent* pattern made of Essence that creates an effect on the universe. Try not to get the pattern wrong as it could have... unintended consequences. This is another name for an incomplete or unknown Rune.

Jasper – A lightning Mage who has taken on the name 'Odin' to seek revenge for the destruction of his people.

James – An uppity portal Mage who may have learned the error of his ways. We shall see.

Kere Nolsen – An S-ranked High Inquisitor.

Mages' Guild – A secretive sub-sect of the Adventurers' Guild only Mage level cultivators are allowed to join.

Mana – A higher stage of Essence only able to be cultivated by those who have broken into at least the B-rankings and found the true name of something in the universe.

Meridians – Meridians are energy channels that transport life energy (Chi/Essence) throughout the body.

Mob – A shortened version of "dungeon monster".

Muninn – Brother of Jasper who sadly was transformed into a crow.

Necromancer – An Infernal Essence cultivator who can raise and control the dead and demons.

Nick – Leader of 'The Collective', Nick is a C-ranked human that is only interested in gaining money at any cost.

Noble rankings:

King/Queen – Ruler of their country. (Addressed as 'Your Majesty')

Crown Prince/Princess – Next in line to the throne, has the same political power as a Grand Duke. (Addressed as 'Your Royal Highness')

Prince/Princess – Child of the King/Queen, has the same political power as a Duke. (Addressed as 'Your Highness')

Grand Duke – Ruler of a grand duchy and is senior to a Duke. (Addressed as "Your Grace")

Duke – Senior to a Marquis or Marquess. (Addressed as "Your Grace")

Marquis/Marquess – Senior to an Earl and has at least three Earls in their domain. (Addressed as 'Honorable')

Earl – Senior to a Baron. Each Earl has three barons under their power. (Addressed as 'My Lord/Lady')

Baron – Senior to knights, they control a minimum of ten knights and, therefore, their land. (Addressed as 'My Lord/Lady')

Knights – Sub rulers of plots of land and peasants. (Addressed as 'Sir')

Oppressor — A Basher upgraded with wind Essence, it has the ability to compress air and send it forward in an arc that slices unprotected flesh like a blade.

Pattern – A pattern is the intricate design that makes everything in the universe. An inanimate object has a far less complex pattern that a living being.

Raile – A massive, granite covered Boss Basher that attacks by ramming and attempting to squish its opponents.

Ranger – Typically an adventurer archetype that is able to attack from long range, usually with a bow.

Ranking System – The ranking system is a way to classify how powerful a creature has become through fighting and cultivation.

> G – At the lowest ranking is mostly non-organic matter such as rocks and ash. Mid-G contains small plants such as moss and mushrooms while the upper ranks form most of the other flora in the world.

> F – The F-ranks are where beings are becoming actually sentient, able to gather their own food and make short-term plans. The mid-F ranks are where most humans reach before adulthood without cultivating. This is known as the fishy or "failure" rank.

> E – The E-rank is known as the "echo" rank and is used to prepare a body for intense cultivation.

D – This is the rank where a cultivator starts to become actually dangerous. A D-ranked individual can usually fight off ten F-ranked beings without issue. They are characterized by a "fractal" in their Chi spiral.

C – The highest-ranked Essence cultivators, those in the C-rank usually have opened all of their meridians. A C-ranked cultivator can usually fight off ten D-ranked and one hundred F-ranked beings without being overwhelmed.

B – This is the first rank of Mana cultivators, known as Mages. They convert Essence into Mana through a nuanced refining process and release it through a true name of the universe.

A – Usually several hundred years are needed to attain this rank, known as High-Mage or High-Magous. They are the most powerful rank of Mages.

S – Very mysterious spiritual Essence cultivators. Not much is known about the requirements for this rank or those above it.

SS – Not much is known about the requirements for this rank or those above it.

SSS – Not much is known about the requirements for this rank or those above it.

Heavenly – Not much is known about the requirements for this rank or those above it.

Godly – Not much is known about the requirements for this rank or those above it.

Reagent – An item or potion that creates a specific effect when added to an inactive Inscription.

Rose – A Half Elf ranger that joined Dale's team. She has opposing affinities for Celestial and Infernal Essence, making her a chaos cultivator.

Rune – A *permanent* pattern made of Essence that creates an effect on the universe. Try not to get the pattern wrong as it could have... unintended consequences. This is another name for a completed Inscription.

Shroomish – A mushroom that has been evolved into a barely dangerous Mob. Really, only being completely unaware of them would pose danger to a person.

Silverwood tree – A mysterious tree that has silver wood and leaves. Some say that it helps cultivators move into the B-rankings.

Smasher – A Basher upgraded with earth Essence, it has no special abilities but is coated with thick armor made from stone. While the armor slows it, it also makes the Smasher a deadly battering ram.

Soul Stone – A *highly* refined Beast Core that is capable of containing a human soul.

Tank – An adventurer archetype that is built to defend his team from the worst of the attacks that come their way. Heavily armored and usually carrying a large shield, these powerful people are needed if a group plans on surviving more than one attack.

Tom – A huge red-haired barbarian prince from the northern wastes, he wields a powerful warhammer and has joined Dale's team. He is only half as handy to have around right now.